[Brackets]

A novel
By David Sloan

ISBN -13: 978-1479187904

Cover design by David Sloan

For Naomi,
With whom things have
been even better than predicted.

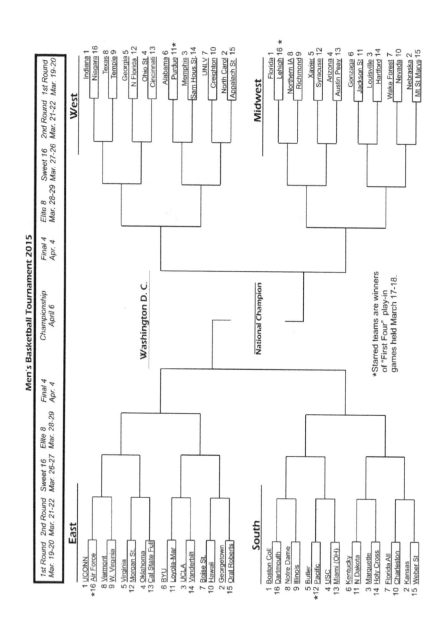

Men's Basketball Tournament 2015

East

West

Midwest

South

Washington D. C.

National Champion

*Starred teams are winners of "First Four" play-in games held March 17-18.

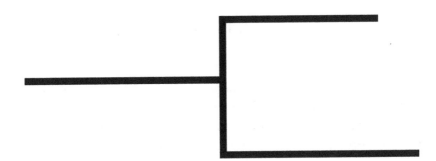

Selection Sunday

[Selection Sunday: March 15, 2015]

The office of Boston College's basketball coach was sparsely decorated. There were a few pictures of past glories, a framed jersey, but little else. After all, his job was really on the court. Offices were for short, to-the-point conversations. Like the one he was about to have.

There was a knock at the door. The coach barely looked up.

"Come in, Williams," he said.

The team's back-up shooting guard, one of two players with the last name of Williams, walked through the door. He moved with the distinctive glide of all talented basketball players, effortless and smooth despite his size. But he kept his eyes down as he slouched into the chair opposite the coach's desk, and when he eventually looked up, his face hardened. On the wall to his right, a projector beamed an enlarged still of some game film from the ACC finals that they had lost two days before. Williams recognized it instantly. It had been a highlight on all the sports shows, repeated over and over all day, mostly because of his error. He looked over at his coach in anticipation of what was coming next.

"How you doing?" asked the coach.

Williams shifted uncomfortably in his chair. "Fine."

The coach raised an eyebrow. "You're going to have to do better than just 'fine'. Your team is going to need you at your best this week. Are you up to it?"

"It don't matter," said the player, looking away. "I'm just the 'other' Williams anyways, right?"

"Hey," the coach half-rose, pointing his finger toward Williams' chest. "Don't you ever say that again. You are not a lesser part of this team unless you act like a lesser part of this team. You earned a place here, and no one—not the media, not the fans, not the bloggers—can take that away from you. It wouldn't matter if all of your teammates had the same last name, you are still an important part of this team. Got that?"

"Yes, coach," said Williams softly.

The coach paused for a long moment, examining his player. Then he turned to the wall with the projected image. "Okay, then," he said. "I want to talk about something on this video. I want you to watch it and tell me what you see."

He pressed a button on the remote and the play unfolded. North Carolina had the ball. Williams was on defense at the top of the key, knees bent, arms wide, face just a few feet from his opponent, who was dribbling in place. The others were scrambling around under the basket and on the wings, trying to make something happen. Second half, the Tar Heels up by three, one minute to go. With eight seconds left on the shot clock, the other North Carolina guard ran up to the man that Williams was guarding and took the ball. Williams immediately left his man and started to double team the other player. Shouts of a countdown came from the crowd as the North Carolina center ran up behind Williams to set a pick, and Williams' man took a stance outside the three-point line. The other guard passed the ball over Williams' head. Williams suddenly realized his mistake. Spinning around to reacquire his man, he slammed his shoulder into the North Carolina center and reached out desperately. His attempted block missed and the shot went up, but Williams' hand had tapped the shooter's forearm. The basket was good, the foul was called, and the coach signaled for a time-out. In just a few seconds, North Carolina had gone up by six. And it was Williams' fault.

"Now," said the coach at his desk, "what do you think I want to talk with you about?"

Williams shrugged. It seemed obvious. "I shouldn't have left my man. I shouldn't have doubled."

"You're right, that's true," said the coach. "But that isn't what most concerns me." He rewound to the moment just after the time-out was called. The camera angle had shifted so that there was a good shot of Williams' face as he made his way off the court. The coach froze the image.

"How would you describe your facial expression there?" he asked the player. Williams studied the face for a moment and half-heartedly relived it.

"I'm mad," he said.

"Maybe," said the coach. "But I remember distinctly what you looked like right then. I've seen that look before. It isn't anger, it isn't embarrassment. People look that way when they lose control in a big moment. That right there is *panic*."

The player looked at the still image of his face again. The eyes were wide, the corners of his open mouth drawn down. It was the agonizing expression of someone who couldn't breathe in a room full of air.

"Williams," said the coach, leaning forward and drawing the player's gaze from the video. "We are about to enter the most competitive, intense, and insane tournament experience in the nation. We will be watched not just by our school or our conference, but by the country. You haven't gone through this yet, but I have. The pressure all the way up to the championship is going to be intense, more so because we're a one-seed. There is no room for mental meltdowns like the one you had there. Do you understand what I'm telling you?"

The player shifted uncomfortably in the chair. The coach felt that he wasn't getting his point across and was about to explain further when Williams spoke up.

"Control is the goal, but roll with the whole, right?"

The coach mulled over the unexpected bit of wit. It took him a second to realize which spelling of "whole" had been used.

"That's interesting. Who said that?"

"It's something my uncle used to say to me in high school because I would get into trouble, get mad at other kids, stuff like that. He said that I had to try and keep my head in things, that when things got crazy I should just try to stay calm and go with it without worrying if I couldn't control it. It would work out."

"Good advice," said the coach. "I didn't know you had an uncle."

Williams shrugged. "He ain't really my uncle. We just called him that 'cause he would stop in sometimes and take care of us. He knew my dad. I didn't exactly listen to him much."

"Why not?"

"Because," said Williams, uncomfortable with this sudden discussion about his personal life, "the guy who was friends with your drug dealer dad isn't the guy you should be trusting."

The coach shook his head and tried to get back to his point. "But he was *right*. And I want you to take that advice, starting now. The ACC tournament is over, and you can't change what happened.

Roll with it. But now we have a new opportunity. Focus, maintain, stay in the game, just like I always tell you, right? So when it gets crazy again—and they don't call it March Madness for nothing—I expect to see a different look on your face."

"Yes, coach," Williams nodded.

The coach stood up and walked his player out of the office.

"You go out now and be with your teammates. You're a part of a number one-seeded team in the Big Dance. That's something to be proud of. Go out, enjoy the moment, call to brag to your mom and your uncle, then get some sleep. You have four days to figure out just what you can give this team during this tournament. We'll talk about it later, OK?"

"OK," said Williams. The coach patted his back as he left, then closed the door and walked back to his desk. On the way, he looked up at the frozen image of Williams walking to the bench. In the background, slightly blurry, the coach saw himself, standing with his arms folded, pacing away from the players. The memory of exactly what he felt during that moment came back to him, and he sat at his desk to think about listening to his own counsel.

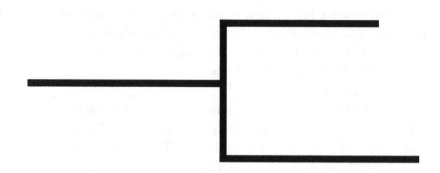

East Division

[**East Division**: Play-in Game]
[Tuesday, March 17]

      Late in the evening, in a cramped and cluttered apartment in Bridgeport, Connecticut, a massive man sat hunched in front of an outdated computer monitor. Methodically, he clicked through an online satellite map of a street of interest. He marveled at the divine providence that allowed him to observe locations from miles away. Not that he could be stopped if anyone found out what he was planning; he knew their limitations and he knew his strengths. But the freedom of the Web allowed him to operate in anonymity, provided that he was careful, and to do more without the distraction of weak, mortal reprisals. He could fulfill his purpose as intended. After taking a few hand-written notes, he shut down the computer and removed the ethernet cable, just in case.

      He put on a thick, dark coat with full pockets, locked the apartment, walked down the many flights of stairs to the street, and stepped into the bitter evening air. No one else was outside, which was good. It wasn't a safe neighborhood for most people. That suited him. The cold and the fear were his allies, allowing him to practice in privacy.

      He stepped into an empty lot near the back of the building. Aided only by lights from the street, he walked over to the faded gray brick wall that bordered the lot on one side. Snow drifts had accumulated on the plywood sheet that he had hidden. He brushed off the wet snow so that the red, round object nailed to the target's center was clean and visible, then leaned the wood against the wall so it was stable. Once satisfied with its position, he walked twenty paces back to a shallow mound of frozen, exposed dirt.

      He adjusted his glasses and looked toward the target. From his pocket, he took out the leather and hemp sling that he himself had woven together and a rough chunk of concrete the size of a chestnut that he had found near the wall. He gazed unblinking at the object nailed to the wood, accumulating enough internal hatred for the thing so that all of his energy would be channeled toward obliterating it. His great, bullish breaths quivered as he recited a tense prayer.

The Lord is my shepherd. I am the rock and the staff...

The tendons in his wrist contracted as he curled his fingers in succession.

I am the hot, cleansing fire, the purger of false prophecy from the green pastures...

He placed the cement in the pocket of the sling, began to whirl it, and raised his leg like a pitcher.

Though I walk in the valley of death, I cannot fear...

The full weight of his body thrust forward explosively as he released the sling.

...and I cannot be stopped.

The brittle projectile hit the poker chip in the dead center; it shattered into several tiny pieces against the target. The collision caused a thud, sharp but thick, followed by the sprinkled impacts of tiny clumps of debris echoing against the buildings in the otherwise quiet night. He adjusted his glasses and looked around to see if anyone heard, if anyone cared. No one came. Satisfied with his first attempt, he took out a larger chunk from his pocket, drew a deep breath, and aimed again.

His mind churned as he practiced. The next place was a good one, a sure target, but somehow it was unsatisfying. He knew that his targets were right. The wicked were becoming as stubble. His success proved the justice of his cause. But something was missing. There was a larger purpose that he had not yet found, a target toward which all of his previous work was building. He knew that if he remained vigilant, he would recognize it when he saw it, when he *felt* it. It would be unusual and glorious, logical and difficult, the manifest end to his inspired mission.

After ten more practice shots, all direct hits, he carefully wrapped up the sling, put it in his pocket, and headed back home. It was almost 11 o'clock, and he never missed the news.

[**East Division:** First Round]
[Thursday, March 19]

The icy Connecticut air was relentless, attacking every inch of skin exposed to the morning chill. For Cole Kaman, that meant he could no longer feel the tops of his ears. He made it to the front door of his office without slipping on the icy patch in the walkway, fumbled the keys with his thickly-gloved hands, and heaved inside with a shiver.

I can't believe it's like this in March, he thought.

The cubicled offices of the Cheney Real Estate Agency were empty. Cole was always the first one, and the unpleasant morning weather would ensure his solitude for at least another half-hour. He walked over to the switches on the wall and flipped them on one by one, illuminating in a fluorescent glaze the same array of desks, phones, computers, and chairs that he saw every morning. Eight and a half hours until he was off. Sixteen hours until the weekend. He ran his fingers through his floppy black hair and breathed in the smell of Thursday Morning.

Coming in early was not officially part of Cole's job description, but it had become part of a routine that the other office workers now expected. For him, the advantage was a leisurely start to the day, first dibs on the coffee he made, and a radio station of his choosing. There was a certain contentment in being king of the office for a few moments before succumbing to the title of office lackey. Within a half hour the coffee would be gone, replaced by a stack of to-do items all marked urgent, and the office music would be unceremoniously switched from classic rock to light hits. For reasons he sometimes acknowledged, there was more satisfaction to being alone in a place where privacy was a premium than in being alone in his apartment, where privacy was the default.

After nearly half an hour, Anne Marie Cheney, owner and manager of Cheney Real Estate, entered the building. She hustled in and shook off the snow that had fallen on her wool cap. Her high heels clicked on the tile as she stepped off the doormat.

"Hiya, Cole. How about this *weather*, huh?" she said brightly. He nodded. She had said almost the exact same thing every work day for the last three and a half months. The click-clack of her high heels followed her as she went into her office.

It was a nice enough job for him. He'd had so many in the last five years, most of them less comfortable, all of them equally unimpressive. For now, he was content where he was, and there was no pressure from within or without to search for something different. In his last job, as a cashier at a home improvement store, it was bad luck that had forced him into switching. The sharp clacking of Anne Marie's heels evoked the smallest shudder as he recalled being the victim of a disturbing collision between a box of hammers, a potted rhododendron, and a seeing-eye dog.

From the window, Cole watched as each coworker survived the ice and entered with the relief of coming from cold into warm. Tom, Linda, and Nera all arrived within five minutes of each other. Tom said hello to Cole with his eyebrows before slumping into his chair and rubbing his entire face several times. Linda promptly marched over to the radio and changed the station. Nera hung up her coat and brought some papers to Cole's desk.

"Hey Cole," she smiled, removing a scarf that clung to her hair.

"Hey. How about this weather, huh?" he replied, instantly loathing himself for not thinking of something else.

"Who cares about the weather?" she retorted. "It's Opening Day! The good times are going to roll."

Cole smiled involuntarily every time he talked to Nera, but now he could tell that he looked both goofy and clueless. "Opening Day?"

"For the tourney? March Madness?" She looked at him with surprise, then exasperation. "Tom didn't explain this to you on Monday?"

"Uhhhhh," Cole stalled. He did remember. Vaguely. But basketball had never been his thing, and neither had college. So when Tom had told him about the annual office ritual of filling out brackets for the big annual college basketball tournament, he had taken a blank bracket without questions and without enthusiasm and scrawled out his picks almost at random. If he remembered right, he had been eavesdropping on Nera talking about her weekend while he wrote. He had even given up ten dollars without thinking much about it. In fact, he would have preferred to keep that money.

Now Nera turned on Tom accusingly. "Tom, you didn't brief Cole about Opening Day?"

"I thought you did," Tom said. "We better do it now." Tom motioned Cole over to his desk. He sat forward, his receding hairline glowing under the lamps. Glancing covertly at Anne Marie's office, he began to speak in unnecessarily low tones.

"Every year, we all fill out our brackets on Monday. On Thursday, the first day of the games, today, we track what happens in the first few games, which start around noon. We used to listen to the games online and make a big deal of marking the brackets after each game ended. But a few years ago, Anne Marie heard a story about how much time people wasted following March Madness games at work. So, she thought of this 'clever' way to eliminate waste at work while still keeping up morale."

He checked his watch. "The games start at noon, and new games start about every two hours. That means there are two big blocks of games during the afternoon of the workday. So what's going to happen is that Anne Marie is going to call group meetings at 2:00 and 4:00. Everyone has to report on what they did during those two hours, and you need to show that you were productive. At 4:00, at the end of the second meeting, whoever is ahead in the bracket guesses gets to leave an hour early with pay, as long as that person worked through the afternoon. You understand?"

"What about the money?"

"Hey, shhhh." Tom's voice lowered even more. "That we keep to ourselves. We'll give it out at the end of the tournament."

"Oh," said Cole, thinking that this just wasn't as fun as Tom was making it out to be. But he wasn't the type to spoil a good mood.

Tom cleared off a medium-sized bulletin board on the wall near his desk. He put up, in very neat rows, each handwritten bracket from the office. With the passion of an artist, he explained to Cole that he preferred to have everything filled out and checked by hand instead of having everyone just make their picks online and seeing their wins and losses spewed out by a computer. "It needs to be tangible," he effused. "It needs to be organic." Cole's bracket, messy and hurried, was tacked right next to Nera's, which had been written carefully.

Nera walked by to inspect the picks. As she paused over his, Cole held his breath, looking sideways at her to take in the olive skin, the athletic build, and the certain knowledge that she could break his arm if he ever tried to make an unwelcomed move. *One of these days,* he let himself think. *And why not? I'm a good guy, there's no reason why we couldn't*... He was awakened by a sound that was part giggle, part scoff, part snort as Nera turned away from his bracket.

"Seriously Cole?" she asked, not even looking at him. "UCLA over Boston College? Sorry, but, wow." Cole went back to his desk with the enigmatic sensation of becoming defensive about something that, five minutes ago, he hadn't cared about at all.

As noon passed, Cole noticed that Tom began to slow down in his movements. He had headphones on. He seemed to be making notes on a legal pad, but he only used the pen in his hand occasionally. Every once in a while, he would adjust the volume or click on something, but otherwise he seemed to just sit tensely, eyes distant. When two o'clock approached, he began to whisper something that sounded like an urgent whimper. It looked like he wanted to jump out of his chair and was using all of his strength just to maintain the image of calm diligence. At one point, Cole distinctly heard Tom whisper, "Just shoot the ball!" Looking around the room, Cole noticed several others, including Nera, with headphones on and identically distracted looks.

At two o'clock sharp, Anne Marie popped out of her office and summoned everyone to the conference table, instructing them to bring what they had been working on for the afternoon. Cole printed off some documents and stretched his back as he left his desk, checking on Tom with a curious glance. Tom was standing, headphones still in, looking like there was just one more thing to listen to. When Anne Marie called over again, he ripped off the headphones in frustration, hastily reached into a drawer for a file, and huffed into the conference room. Cole followed.

Just as Tom described, Anne Marie very nicely asked to have short reports of their day's productivity. Cole was able to show that he had done exactly the same amount of work that he always did. Others gave similar reports.

When they got to Tom, he opened the folder and removed a set of documents, each filled out very neatly. His report was the longest, and the volume of work was superhuman.

"Tom, this is very impressive," Anne Marie glowed. "We should do this every day, huh? Am I right? OK, we'll see everyone again at 4:00." The praise drew annoyed, sarcastic glares from everyone else, but Tom perked up and bowed his head in fake modesty. Cole wondered how much time Tom spent to do an extra day's work in advance. He had to admire the foresight that he had never seen his coworker apply to any other workday.

During the next two hours, as his coworkers sank back into faux productivity, Cole felt a mild case of afternoon grogginess set in. He did the normal work, answering the normal phone calls and entering the normal data. He paid a few minutes of attention to the radio station's normal three o'clock news updates. The Thai ambassador was visiting somewhere, the inconclusive hunt for the Wall Street arsonist was ongoing, the American poultry industry was spooked by recent recalls. The reporter on the arsonist story was Anne Marie's sister, Deborah Cheney, whose local morning TV show occasionally featured Anne Marie as an industry expert in the housing market. When the radio began rattling off the scores of the first games of the tournament, Tom could apparently hear them through his headphones, and they made him growl. A client came in to ask for information on mortgage rates, and Cole took some pleasure in sending him to Tom right away.

As four o'clock neared, Tom, who had dispensed with the client very efficiently, ripped off his headphones in sudden disgust. He pounded his desk softly, grunted as if he'd been kicked from somewhere under his chair, and then composed himself as he turned toward the bulletin board full of brackets. He held two markers in his hand: a thin red one and a bright yellow hi-lighter. One by one, beginning with his own, he began to make marks. As a judge both exacting and merciless, he colored each bracket by crossing out or highlighting a team, leaving each sheet with a splash of golden approval and bloody punishment. When he finished Nera's, he made eye contact with her and chuckled maniacally, holding up three fingers. She nodded her capitulation. She already knew her score.

Then Tom arrived at Cole's bracket. Team by team, Tom

marked with the highlighter. After a pause, he dropped the red marker on his desk.

"Holy cow," he said to himself audibly.

Anne Marie came out and called everyone to the table. There wasn't much time, she prodded, and they needed to get this over with. Tom looked at Cole with a narrow-eyed expression that Cole couldn't interpret. Then he quickly reached into his desk, grabbed a second folder, and went to the conference table.

After they had issued their reports, Anne Marie drum-rolled on the table with her fingers. "So, Tom, who is today's lucky winner?"

Tom didn't answer for a moment. It looked like he was debating something internally and losing. "Cole, by a lot. Five for five," he finally said. There was weak applause around the table.

"Hey, Cole! On the first try! Congratulations!" Anne Marie cheered. "You can feel free to call it a day. For the rest of you, let's finish the day strong, OK!"

Tom fell in beside him as they went back to their seats. "I cannot *believe* how lucky you are," he grumbled. "You even had West Virginia over Boise. I had Boise in the Sweet Sixteen. I didn't even come close."

"Did you come in second?" Cole asked encouragingly. Tom drooped his head in shame.

"No. Linda did."

"Sorry, man," Cole apologized, but he wasn't really sorry. Going home early was going home early. Cole shut down his computer as Tom put his hands in his pockets in resigned disappointment. Grabbing his coat, Cole looked over at Nera, who was inspecting his bracket on the wall. She looked back at him, impressed, and gave him a smile.

To Cole, for whom every day was intensely, relentlessly normal, having a small change was nice. It was brief, it meant nothing, but it was nice. He took one more glance at Nera and walked nimbly out of the office. Too late, he realized that he had not yet put on his coat. An arctic blast punched him square in the face, and his thoughts about the day returned to the single-minded meditation of cold people whose only wish is to be warm.

[**East Division**: Second Round]
[Monday, March 25]

On Monday morning, Cole came in with a plan.

Part one of that plan involved the acquisition of tickets. The annual Hartford Indie Rock Fest (HAIR Fest to those in the know) was happening that weekend at the Dodge Center. The general seating tickets had been available for months, but there was a special promotion for tickets close to the stage, available only to a few lucky online buyers at exactly noon that day. Tickets would be gone by 12:02. The promotion included dream seats and backstage passes. His plan was to finish all lingering work by 11:50 and then focus his attention on logging in at just the right moment to ensure success. He had set his cell phone clock, his computer, and the office clock on the wall to the exact time shown on the countdown clock on the website. He had practiced logging on for a good hour the night before to get the timing right. He was *going* to get these tickets.

Part two of his plan was to catch Nera early that afternoon and casually mention that he had just lucked into two amazing tickets for a concert and one was available.

That morning, he completed his routine in good time. By 8:15, when his boss came through the door, he had already gotten a strong, productive jump on his chore list.

"Hi, Cole, getting nippy out there, right?" she jingled.

"It sure is," he chimed back automatically. Her feet tapped as his fingers typed.

His coworkers all entered in sequence, Linda changing the radio station, and began the week with their individual, distinctive Monday sighs.

All, except for Tom.

Tom rushed in, barely said hello, dumped his jacket in his chair, and stood directly in front of the bulletin board of brackets. He took out a red pen, which he hovered over one sheet of paper without ever touching it.

"Cole," he said after a momentous pause, "you are my hero forever."

To this unexpected promotion in Tom's eyes, Cole responded casually, "What's up?"

"What's up?!" Tom cried. He pulled the unblemished bracket from the board and slammed it down on Cole's desk. "What's up is that you are still perfect after the first two rounds. That means that out of 48 games that are friggin' impossible to predict, you got the winner right 48 out of 48 times. Nobody does that. *Ever*." Tom rubbed his forehead as he pondered it anew, then shoved Cole's bracket onto the keyboard in front of him. "How did you do it?"

Cole looked down at the paper, then back up at the comically exasperated face of Tom. "I dunno. Just lucky. Don't people get this right all the time? Maybe sometimes?"

"Lucky!" Tom scoffed in agony. "I've been filling out brackets since I was nine years old. I've never personally met anyone that got every game of the first two rounds right. I don't think that I've ever even *heard* of that. People get the Final Four right, but the first 48 games?! Do you know what the odds of that are?"

"No."

"Well, me neither, but it's almost impossible."

A lull in the conversation, as Tom waited in vain for signs of a budding two-way dialogue. When none came, Tom leaned in and spoke secretively.

"Can you just tell me if you saw any of this in a dream? Just between us."

Cole backed off a bit. "Dude, you were there when I filled it out. It took me like a minute and I wasn't even really paying attention. Listen Tom, I kind of need to get some things done before lunch, sooo..."

"OK, OK, go ahead. Good luck is wasted on people like you."

Tom went back to the bulletin board and rearranged all the brackets so that they fanned out in a circle around Cole's, as if paying homage. The attention of every incoming coworker was drawn to it, and each was granted a personal tour in which Tom explained the significance and impossibility of each perfect pick. Nera got the longest tour, and she paid the most attention.

Once she had inspected it for herself, she stepped over to

Cole. "I'm amazed. Truly amazed. How did you know Oral Roberts would beat Georgetown? 15-2 upsets are pretty rare."

Cole thought quickly… and arrived nowhere. "I don't know," he confessed. "I honestly have no explanation."

"I have to tell you, Cole," she said with mild but playful disapproval, "your lack of basketball knowledge is totally unacceptable. No one with a perfect bracket should know so little. So I'll tell you what I'm going to do, because I'm cool like this. I'll buy you lunch today, and I'll catch you up on the last hundred years. Sound good?"

Cole's smile almost vanished in complete shock. "Oh, yeah, sure. Absolutely. Totally. Awesome. Yes."

"OK then. Come get me when you're ready."

Now! Let's go right now! Cole thought as he watched her return to her desk. He realized that part two of the day's plan had just fallen into place. Now to come up with the exact words he would use to spontaneously bring up the topic of backstage passes.

The morning proceeded uneventfully until 11:15, when Anne Marie emerged from her office with a single sheet of paper. She clicked over to the center of the office and called everyone's attention.

"OK, everyone, please, I need to get a quick group consensus," she announced. She held up the piece of paper. "A contact of mine—do you all know Herb?—needs to offload some office property in New Haven. He has six good lots at bargain prices, but for a variety of reasons we can only get one. I know that this isn't our standard operating procedure, but I have to call him back by noon. So you're all analysts for now."

Everyone looked around at each other. They all knew that she wasn't asking whether or not they should do it at all, so no one demurred. Anne Marie read the list of square footages and locations for the six office buildings, re-read it, and asked for a vote by show of hands. Two promising candidates remained: a larger site in a business park, and a smaller site in downtown New Haven. To Cole, they sounded exactly equal, so he just picked the one that Nera picked. Not that anyone really cared what the receptionist thought anyway.

A second round of voting found the employees split in a tie.

The older ones, including Tom, chose the one closer to downtown, because it would be easier to fill. The younger people, including Nera, voted for the larger building because the profit would be potentially greater. Anne Marie sighed as the clock ticked to 11:32.

"OK people, we have to move on this now. How are we going to decide? Somebody make me a case." Linda, who very much valued her own opinion, spoke about the need to make rational judgments in the current economy and warned about acquiring properties that couldn't be unloaded quickly. It was a solid case, and Anne Marie seemed to agree.

"Anyone want to make the case for the business park office?" she asked. No one spoke up immediately. It was 11:38.

"We should ask Cole," Tom said. "He's the one on the hot streak."

Cole slunk down in his chair.

"What hot streak?"

We do not have to bring this up right now, thought Cole. *And seriously, who cares?*

"He has a perfect bracket through two rounds. 48 for 48. The man is a decision-making machine. Maybe we should be riding his luck."

All eyes remained on Cole. This was not good.

"Wow. So, what do you think, Cole?" Anne Marie asked expectantly.

He put his hands in his lap and thought. He had to argue for an opinion when he had no business having any opinions. If they listened to him and it was the wrong choice, Anne Marie might blame him. His only impulse was to stick with Nera somehow. He wished that he knew what she was thinking so he could think it too.

"Any day now, Cole," Anne Marie prodded.

He took a deep breath. "I just think, I'm, I think that long term, we want value, right? And this is a big offer, and you should seize the big offers because they don't always come around. Like, you want to be smart, I mean you don't want to do anything stupid or anything. I think we have to look for what's in the best interest here. I mean, for everyone, right?"

He could hear his words echoing in the silent room, and they were as moronic as he felt.

"So… which one did you say?" Anne Marie was losing patience.

Another deep breath. "Office park. I say office park."

"Fine," said Anne Marie. "Another vote. All in favor of going with Linda for the downtown office?" Most of the staff raised their hands, including a reluctant Nera, who cast an apologetic glance at Cole.

"Office park?" asked Anne Marie. It was a mere formality, though. Only Cole raised his hand. After a second, Tom did, too.

"Downtown it is," she announced. "Thanks everyone. I think this is a good plan. I will personally have a Cheney Real Estate sign on the property by one o'clock today." With that, she clicked back to her office.

When she was gone, Cole leaned in and whispered harshly to Tom. "Thanks a lot."

"Hey," Tom chuckled, "I didn't know you were going to bomb like that. You get nervous in front of people, huh?"

"No, it's… forget it," he said, and he returned to his desk. Tom was right, he didn't like standing out in groups. It made him feel like his entire brain was blushing. But with a glance of the clock, he knew that he had to get over it quickly. There were a few extra things that he had to finish for Anne Marie. It was 11:46.

Just before 11:50, he turned around to check on Nera. In eleven minutes, he'd have the tickets and they'd be heading out to lunch. But she was bent over, talking softly on the phone, and she didn't look happy. Hanging up abruptly, she walked over to Anne Marie's office and shut the door. When she returned to her desk, she began wrapping her scarf around her neck.

Nera was halfway out the door when she turned back, looking regretful but distracted. It was 11:57. "Oh, Cole, I almost forgot. I can't do lunch today. Some other time, maybe?"

Cole felt his self-esteem crumbling to dust inside, but didn't show it. "Oh, yeah, that's fine. I understand. I actually have a lot I could do anyway, so. Yeah, maybe later."

"Thanks. It's just that I have this family thing. I thought it could wait until I went up to their house this weekend, but it looks like they need me this afternoon, too." She turned back to the door.

No! he thought, and grasped for just one more thing to say.

"Hey Nera?"

"Yeah?" she stopped.

"I'm sorry that I wasn't more helpful on the office park thing…"

"Oh, no," she brushed his comment off. "It doesn't matter. They were right about the downtown space, it'll be better. Forget it. I have to go." And she was gone.

When Cole scored the tickets at 12:01, he did so joylessly.

The day moved on. Anne Marie left at lunch to personally take over the New Haven property. Nera didn't come back. Easy listening from the 1990's put Cole in a near comatose state.

When the three o'clock newscast began, nobody paid much attention until Linda jumped up and told everyone to be quiet. The announcer was reporting a building on fire. It was in New Haven, and the location sounded very familiar.

Tom logged on to the live video feed of the broadcast, and several people gathered around his desk. There was Deborah Cheney, the spitting image of her sister, speaking urgently across the street from a fire truck while people were being evacuated behind her. Tom turned up the volume.

"…just one hour ago," Deborah Cheney was saying, "smoke began pouring out of the first-floor windows of this small downtown New Haven brokerage firm. A few office workers received medical attention for smoke inhalation, but I'm told there were no casualties. However, the building has sustained massive damage. While fire fighters now have the blaze under control, it may be too late to save any of the interior. One witness reports that the fire started in a back room soon after a large rock was thrown through one of the windows. If confirmed, these facts may point to the Wall Street bomber as the culprit. We'll have more details as this story unfolds."

As the camera panned the front of the smoldering building, the attention of the office was focused on the empty brick building next door. A Cheney Real Estate sign was in the window, and a layer of smoke and debris now covered one side.

"Look at that," said Tom. "That building is going to be impossible to sell for at least a year." Others nodded solemnly. "Looks like we should have listened to Cole." Even Linda, whose face had gone ashen, had to nod in agreement. Cole could only watch as he wondered exactly what kind of luck he was having.

[East Division: Sweet Sixteen]
[Friday, March 27]

Cole came to work on Friday as early as usual. But this time, he found the door unlocked and the lights on. Strange. When he walked in, he found himself staring directly into the large black eye of a television camera lens, highlighted by a small red "on" light and crowned from behind with the scraggly hair of a cameraman. Cole wondered if he should say something.

Standing nearby to help was a reporter that he recognized immediately as Deborah Cheney. She shook his hand, introduced herself, and asked politely if he had a few minutes for an interview. He nodded.

Deborah began to explain what to do: try to smile, don't look at the camera, just stay loose. As she talked, he scanned the room and noticed Anne Marie, looking very pleased and wearing the smile that she usually reserved exclusively for clients and important people. Behind her was Nera, watching him with amusement. Tom was lurking in the background, shamelessly removing donuts from a box near the coffee machine.

Deborah moved in close, cleared her throat, and checked her jacket for anything unsightly. Cole tried to give himself a quick look too, since he hadn't spent more than five seconds on either hair or clothes that morning. But it was too late; the camera was on him again, and the interview began with a classic Deborah Cheney monologue.

"It's the dream of every March Madness fan: a perfect bracket. And for this young administrative assistant, that dream might come true. I'm here at the Cheney Real Estate Agency in South Windsor with Cole Kaman, a man who has successfully predicted each game of the tournament so far. Cole, how does it feel to have a perfect bracket going into the Sweet Sixteen?"

She lifted the microphone to Cole and he answered, forgetting whether he was supposed to look at her or the camera.

"Uh, it's pretty amazing. Definitely a new experience for me."

"I'll bet. What was your method for picking the winners?"

"Oh, uh, I don't know. Just whatever felt right when I looked at it, you know." Cole was having a hard time remembering to blink.

"I see." Deborah saw that she was going to have to inject the necessary energy into the conversation. "Looking at your bracket here, I see that you have UCLA winning it all in the final game, is that right?"

Cole blanked. He glanced over at Nera, who nodded her head.

"Yeah, that's right."

"I'll bet you have some friends and neighbors here who are wondering why you didn't pick UCONN to go all the way. Was it hard to pick against the local favorite?"

He hadn't thought about that at all, actually.

"Oh, no, I mean, it wasn't anything personal. Actually, though, they did turn me down when I applied there, but I didn't think of that when I was filling it out." He kept looking at the camera.

"I'll bet they wish they'd let you in now! It might have been the luck they needed against Vanderbilt last night."

"Yeah, I don't know. Maybe. That would have been good."

Cole saw the reporter thinking about searching for more of a story, then giving up as she turned back to speak directly into the camera. "We'll be keeping a watch on Cole and his amazing bracket as the tournament continues. For now, UCLA might want to send this young man a brochure. More news coming up."

The camera light went off, and Deborah Cheney turned to shake his hand again. "Good job. Let us know if you make it out of the next round."

Anne Marie walked up behind her. "That was great, Cole. He was very good, wasn't he?" The sisters exchanged a glance and walked back into Anne Marie's office. As they left, Nera approached, smiling. It felt good to see her. She had been out of the office for most of the week.

"So, that was weird," Cole said quietly. "What's going on?"

"Anne Marie was pretty bummed by the whole burning building thing, so when she remembered your perfect bracket, she had this idea about using it as a publicity stunt to promote the agency. She had Tom keep her posted about how you did on the

Sweet Sixteen yesterday. When you got all the picks right, she called her sister to have her do the interview. You'll be on local news state-wide in," she checked the clock, "they said in about five minutes."

"Wow," he responded. "Wait, does Anne Marie really think people are going to start buying houses from us just because the receptionist made a lot of lucky picks?"

"You never know." Nera raised her eyebrows. "People are weird about things. Remember that octopus that chose World Cup matches? They might think of you as a good luck charm. You're good karma. Like, did you notice how Deborah Cheney kept saying 'I'll bet'?"

"I did notice that."

"I kept wondering if she was trying to send you a message, like what she was really saying was, 'Hey, I will bet. Money. Right now'." Cole laughed along with Nera, then laughed again at the thought that she was actually talking to him.

"It's probably a good thing she didn't. I seriously couldn't remember who I put down as the winner, and I didn't even know that UCONN played last night. I probably would have told her to bet on a school that wasn't even playing."

"I'll bet," said Nera, with a sly smile. "By the way, I owe you lunch. Sorry I've been so busy this week. Would today work? 11:45?"

Before Cole could answer with an absolute, enthusiastic yes, Tom came up behind them, a clump of jelly donut still bulging from the corner of his lip.

"Cole Kaman, the man doing the impossible!" He slapped Cole on the back. "I've taken all the other brackets off the wall. They don't matter anymore. From now on, we're all on Team Cole."

Cole grinned. "Good to know. Just curious, how much is Linda beating you by?"

"I just said that doesn't matter anymore," Tom retorted. "I was going to give you your cash pool winnings now, but…" He took out an envelope and waved it at Cole. "Nah, I guess you can have it."

Cole accepted the envelope and looked at the wad of cash inside. "I already won?"

"No one else can beat you. Not a person in the office has an intact Final Four. I feel kind of bad for you, actually. If we had done this online, you could have been entered to win like a million dollars for a perfect bracket. Instead you just get ten bucks a piece from us. It's too bad."

Cole considered that bit of information as he sat down to his minimum-wage secretarial job. Most of his coworkers came in time to watch his interview broadcast and have some fun at his expense. When they returned to their desks, easy listening wafted overhead, and Cole was left alone with a stack of items marked 'Urgent' and time to think about a million dollars, fifteen seconds of fame, and the fact that very little had actually changed for him.

Half an hour after the segment aired, the phone rang.

"Cheney Real Estate," Cole said, with just the hint of a sigh as he put on his headset.

The voice on the other end sounded old and gravelly. "Ah, yes, this is Cheney Real Estate?"

"Yes, sir, how can I help you today?"

"Uh, yes, are you the young guy I saw on TV with the perfect basketball picks?"

"Um, yes sir," Cole answered cautiously.

The man's voice suddenly became much louder. "What do you mean not picking UCONN to win the championship? You should be ashamed. What's the matter with you?"

Cole looked around to see if he was being pranked. No one was even looking at him.

"Sir," Cole responded with professional courtesy, "I'm sorry that they lost. I just made a lucky guess, that's all. I didn't mean for them to lose."

"You have no right to influence games in this state! I am writing a complaint to the NCAA and drawing attention to your infractions. Shame on you, son!"

"Sir, are you interested in investing in some real estate or not?"

"Ha!" exclaimed the voice. "I wouldn't buy anything from you if you were the last real estate agency in the state. Are you even from Connecticut? You're from Massachusetts, aren't you? I'll bet that you work for the same crew that stole the Patriots from us, you..."

"Sir, would you be interested in some real estate if I weren't working here?"

"Well," he stuttered, "no, but you should be *ashamed…*"

"Thank you, have a nice day," said Cole, and he removed the headset.

"What was that about?" asked Tom, eating from a small bag of potato chips.

"Craziest old dude ever. He was yelling at me for making UCONN lose last night. I can't believe they let people like that have phones. There should be some kind of senile telephone law…"

He stopped as he heard a faint, digital hum that sounded like a voice. Tom pointed to Cole's desk.

"I think you forgot to hang up," he noted.

"Oh, no," Cole groaned, hitting the 'end' button on his phone. Then he leaned back and laughed. "He is not going to be happy."

"I bet he comes down and tears you a new one," Tom joked. Within a minute, the phone rang again. Cole didn't want to answer it, but he had to. It was his job.

For the rest of the morning, Tom got very little work done. He spent his time pretending to be busy, but his ears and attention were focused on Cole, who received bizarre call after bizarre call. Tom heard phrases that he never thought he would hear in a workplace:

"No, sir, I can't endorse your book if I haven't read it. And honestly, I'm just not that into mini-golf, so…."

Click.

"No, I can't get you tickets to the Final Four, but I can get you a free quote on a nice property we have in…hello?"

Click.

"I promise you that I'm not out to destroy your business. I have nothing against bookies. Wait, you're offering me a job?"

Click.

"Dude, seriously, I have no idea if it will work out between you two. Maybe if you had 63 other women fight it out I could tell you something."

Click.

Nera walked up behind Tom's desk as Cole was wrapping up a conversation with a woman who would only buy a house through them if he could promise that the house would last through the apocalypse.

"He's having a hard morning, isn't he?" she said gently.

"This is the best day I've had all year. I recorded the last three for my blog. My hit count is going to quadruple," replied Tom.

Cole's phone rang again. The poor receptionist sighed very hard, ran his fingers through his entire head of hair, and answered.

"How long do you think this can go on?" asked Nera.

"Until all the loony morning news viewers get distracted by the evening news. So…all day." Tom said.

*   *   *   *

The stress from his unusual morning was washed away when Nera came over to get him for lunch.

Down the street from the office was a small Chinese restaurant. It was the kind of place that seemed to stay open forever even though no one ever seemed to go in. Nera revealed to Cole that she was one of the mysterious individuals keeping it alive with regular visits. The host recognized her and showed them to a table in the corner. Without a glance at the menu, she ordered for both of them.

"Oh, wait, are you allergic to anything?" she asked as the waiter walked away. He wasn't.

"You're going to love this. I still don't know what they do to the chicken, but it's amazing."

Cole smiled and nodded without saying anything. He had always imagined that he would be on his game—affable, poised, maybe even funny—if he ever got the chance to be out with Nera. But now that they were there, all semblance of conversation escaped him.

Nera interpreted his silence differently. "Cole, you shouldn't let the calls this morning make you mad. They'll end soon."

"I know. I just really don't want to talk about it during lunch," he said, meaning it.

"OK," said Nera. "I'm just saying, it seems like you let them wind you up."

"I'm not wound up."

"You're not?"

"No," said Cole. "I know I can't take these things personally. I barely even thought about the stupid thing. It's not my fault that I didn't have UCONN winning."

"It wasn't? Whose fault was it?"

A good point, though he still felt that the events of the day were happening to him, not because of him.

"I blame Tom," he said, and Nera wholeheartedly agreed.

Lunch arrived. In a few cardboard containers placed before each of them was more food than Cole had ever been served at one time. What added to his embarrassment was that Nera was breaking out chopsticks as he reached for the fork.

"It's OK," she said sweetly. "You can use the fork on your Chinese food. I won't necessarily think you're any less of a man." Cole briefly considered whether trying to eat fried rice with two sticks would help prove his manhood. The fork it was.

They ate in silence for a while, mostly because the rice was very good, partly because Cole was very nervous. Cole began to realize that, although they had worked together for nearly a year, he actually didn't know that much about her. He knew that she was cool, that she played all the sports that she liked, that she was probably a little smarter than her job, and that she could wolf down a container of lo mein in half the time it took anybody else on the planet. But when he thought further, he began to draw blanks. Nera was the one to break the silence.

"How's your back doing?"

"Huh?"

"Didn't you hurt your back a few months ago trying to move that desk for Anne Marie?"

"Oh," Cole said, "that wasn't anything. I've had a bad back for a while."

"How did you hurt it the first time?"

"Skateboarding. Kind of a freak accident with this loose railing in a parking garage. I was in a body cast for a while after my senior year."

"I didn't know you were a skater."

"I haven't skated since the accident. I got into other stuff, like local bands and stuff." He took a drink of water, trying to swallow the nervousness. "You like music?"

She finished chewing her mouthful. "I like a little of everything. Pop, hip-hop, some latin, that kind of thing. You're into rock, right? I know they're always making you change your radio station."

"Yeah, I'm not really into dentist office music, but it's not a battle I can really win with Linda around, you know?"

She laughed and swallowed another bite of rice, almost without chewing. "I know. My mom was always listening to stuff from the seventies. Big Chicago fan. I still can't hear them without..." She stopped talking without any intention of continuing. Her chewing became much more slow and deliberate. After a long moment, she shrugged off whatever thought was in her head.

"Anyway. Any good local bands? I don't know much about who's hot in South Windsor."

Cole looked at her and debated whether he was brave enough to go back a step in their conversation. He decided not. "Molotov Entrails. It sounds gross, but their drummer is really good."

She smiled. "You go to any concerts?"

He nodded and took a deep breath. "Actually, I'm going up to a concert tonight at the Dodge Center."

"You mean HAIR?" she asked enthusiastically.

"Yeah, you know it?"

"Of course I do. I was going to go if I didn't have to be out of town. I'm so jealous! I mean, I probably wouldn't have known many of the bands like you would, but it sounded like fun."

Cole thought about his second ticket and felt a little sick. "So, your plans for the weekend must be really set in stone for you to miss out like that," he suggested, looking for a ray of hope.

Nera nodded soberly, disappointment among the emotions in her voice. "They are. I don't come back until Sunday afternoon. But get some good stories to tell me on Monday, OK?"

"Sure," he said, putting aside his fork. Suddenly he wasn't hungry anymore. "Now, what can you tell me about basketball?"

"Everything," she replied as she swallowed her last egg roll and began to attempt just that.

*   *   *   *

When they arrived back at the office, they were laughing. Cole had never felt better. He thanked Nera for the third time in ten minutes, and she squeezed his arm and returned to her desk. Hopping into his chair with a half-whistle, he caught Tom's eye. *So is something happening?* Tom asked with his eyebrows. Cole just grinned and called into his voicemail. He hadn't even heard the first irate UCONN fan when Anne Marie poked her head out of her door.

"Cole," she called, "can I see you a second?"

He entered the office; she closed the door.

"Cole, while you were out, I noticed that your phone was ringing pretty constantly. Tom told me that you had been getting unusual calls all morning, but I didn't want to miss any calls from clients, so I answered your phone."

She paused, as if she didn't quite know how to go on. "There was a man on the other end who was most definitely not a client. He didn't say anything at first. I kept saying 'hello,' and almost hung up. But then he asked for you by name. I said that you were at lunch and asked if I could leave a message. He said, 'Tell him that I know who he is now.' Then he hung up."

Cole took this in but didn't have anything to say about it. "So?"

"So, it was disturbing, Cole. This man sounded…cold. His voice was really just awful." She shuddered at the recollection. "Have all your calls been like that?"

"No," Cole assured. "Most of them were pretty harmless. Crazy, but not, you know."

"Well," said Anne Marie, still concerned, "I want you to let me know if you get any more calls that could be threatening. If we need to call the police, we can certainly do that."

Cole stood up. He was ready for his boss to stop giving him her undivided attention. "Thanks, Anne Marie, but I'm sure this will all be over by Monday."

Anne Marie looked up like she had failed to get her point across. "Fine, just be careful. The criminally insane have already cost our office once this week."

"Right," he said, starting to leave.

"Oh, and Cole?" Cole looked back. "Feel free to hang up on

anyone you want today."

*   *   *   *

That night, the festival was packed and the amps were loud. He had given his extra ticket to the only high school friend he still talked to. Within an hour, that friend had found a girl and Cole never saw him again. He stayed a while longer, but although the music was as good as he'd anticipated, he found his interest waning. The experience just wasn't what it could have been. He felt tired and left early.

The drive home was quick. Not much traffic, very few stop lights. Cole watched the houses go by, with snow-covered lawns and gleams of ice on the sidewalks. His usual practice was to drive while soaking in a healthy wash of electric guitar from his custom stereo. That night, he just turned it off.

The entrance to his apartment complex was a left turn up an incline, past a stretch of lawn and hedges. In the yellow lights of the street, he couldn't see that one of the sprinkler heads had burst earlier in the day, spewing a flow of now-frozen water across the driveway.

Making his left turn quickly, Cole zipped up the incline. The front wheel hit the ice patch and skidded, bucking the car sideways so that the left wheel knocked into the curb. He spun the wheel left, then right, trying to get the car under control before reaching the parking lot. When the car finally stopped, he was at an angle in the lot, with the front bumper six inches from the back end of an expensive-looking coup.

He sat for a minute, hands clenching the steering wheel, replaying the event. *What just happened?*

After checking himself once over for good measure, he eased carefully into a parking spot near his door and got out gingerly. No back pain, no spinal twinges. Safe.

"Excuse me?" a voice said behind him. Cole turned around and saw a figure, about twenty feet away from the stairs, standing rigid in a hooded sweatshirt. The man was massive and heavy, like a weightlifter. He had glasses that reflected the yellow lights over the parking lot, but most of his face was obscured by shadow under the hood. The figure was perfectly still, both hands deep in his pockets. Cole began digging for his keys uncomfortably.

"Yeah?" he asked back.

"Do you live here? I was looking around at apartments and was wondering if this would be a great place to live." The words were spoken slowly, as if there were no rush to get his meaning across.

"Sure, it's fine, for what it is." Cole found his key and used it.

"I see," the figure stated, still unmoving. Cole turned again as he waited for more. It came, after an irrational silence.

"And the inside?"

Um, weird. "It's fine. I'm going to…"

"It looks nice. Like a nice place to set up. To plan for the future. Is it nice?"

Cole opened the screen door. "Yeah, real nice. Look, it's really cold outside. I'm going in now. Good luck with the apartment hunt."

"Yes, yes it is cold," said the figure. "But you never know. It could get warm real soon."

Cole took one more look back. "Sure," he said, and quickly closed and locked the door behind him. By the time he'd unzipped his jacket and peeked through the front blinds, the figure was gone.

*   *   *   *

The next morning, when he left his apartment, something fell to the ground. It was a piece of paper with a typed message on it. A poem.

As the stone rolls forth
From David's arm,
The giant's reach will
Cease from harm,
And bracket's glory
Will lose its charm
For one man's blood is
Earth's alarm.

-Ichabod will come-

[**East Division**: Elite Eight]
[Sunday, March 29]

Cole took three phone calls from his bed on Sunday morning. The first was from Deborah Cheney, who couldn't help but notice that his bracket was still perfect halfway through the Elite Eight. To congratulate him, and as a human interest element to their Annual Spring Fundraiser that night, he was invited to meet the entire station as a guest of honor at the Player Pier in Hartford. He really, really didn't want to go. But he didn't think guests of honor could turn down invitations, so he said yes.

The second call was from Nera, who was very excited to hear about Cole's invitation. With a surge of hope, Cole suggested that he could really use some familiar company to help him avoid March Madness faux pas. Nera laughed and said it was too late for that, but she'd be there anyway.

The third call was a wrong number.

In none of those conversations did a large man in a hooded sweatshirt come up.

*   *   *   *

The Player Pier, said to be the best sports bar in a city without any professional sports, stood expansively on manicured grounds overlooking the Connecticut River. The river, along with everything else, was half-frozen that night. The lights from the small group of skyscrapers to the east were reflected darkly in the water. It was a stark contrast to the vibrant, audibly throbbing, neon mayhem inside the Pier.

Cole stood in the parking lot outside, looking at the building and watching people hurry to get out of the cold. He preferred freezing to going inside just yet. It was one thing to go into a concert, where he could lose himself in the anonymity of big noise and flashing lights. It was another to be a sideshow in celebration of a sport that he didn't really understand. There was no way that he was going in alone.

He recognized the blue Jetta as soon as it pulled into the lot, and he walked over to meet the car where it stopped. Nera stepped out and gave him an unexpected hug.

"Hi!" she squeezed. "I'm so excited! This is the weirdest thing. My parents don't even understand what's going on. Who would have guessed that you'd be a celebrity?"

"It's not a big deal." Cole downplayed. "I'm actually hoping I'll lose a game tonight, then we can steal as many wings as we can and life can get back to normal."

"Cole, you're the only man I know who would consider this a bad thing," she said.

They walked up to the building together. The curved facade of the Player Pier was a gaudy tribute to every sport imaginable. It was built to look like a stadium, with embedded pieces of green turf, leather, netting, and other sports paraphernalia surrounding the belt of stadium lights that marched around the entire building. But the outside was understated compared to the interior. Huge, cinema-sized screens filled the walls surrounding a phalanx of sofas, tables, and high seats. A small stage and microphone had been set up directly in front of one of the screens. What appeared to be the entire staff of WHAR, their family members, and half the city of Hartford were watching the game between Oklahoma and West Virginia. West Virginia was up by seven at ten minutes into the first half. Cole tried to remember if he had WVU winning. Nera would know.

They stopped by the bar, then found the least noisy corner of the upper level and sat down close to each other, Nera facing the big screens.

"So, Cole, I have to ask you," Nera started. "Why are you not thrilled about your bracket? This really is a big deal! I heard this story a few years back about an MIT physicist who thought that he'd found some algorithm for predicting March Madness winners, and his system only got like 60% of them right. He said the stock market was easier to predict than this. I know you're not into sports, but what you're doing is seriously cool!"

Cole stirred his drink and fidgeted under Nera's unblinking gaze.

"I guess…it's because it shouldn't really be me, you know? Smart people who know a lot about sports—people like you—you should be the ones making the perfect picks. I just feel like people are going to find out I'm a fake any minute."

Nera laughed and shook her head as she took a drink. "Cole, you aren't a fake. You can't fake luck. I mean, there you are, a secretary at a tiny real estate agency, typing all day…"

"I know," Cole interrupted, hiding a smile, "it's amazing that someone so, um…"

"Oh I didn't mean—I don't think you have a loser job or anything."

"No, I'm just messing with you. Seriously. And actually, it is kind of a loser job, but less of a loser job than I've had in the past."

"OK, then," she smiled. "So what were the worse jobs?"

"Oh, night clerk, janitor for dentist offices, data entry, cashier. My favorite was cleaning the ball pit at Chuck-E-Cheese right after I got out of my body cast. I've actually been at this job for longer than anything else. It has its perks." Cole couldn't keep himself from looking up at Nera as he finished. "But what about you? I know you can do more than just drive rich people around to big houses."

"Ha! No, Anne Marie keeps the rich ones to herself. You're right though—I actually got a master's in sports psychology at UCONN, did you know that? I was doing an internship with the women's basketball team and things were looking really good, but…"

Nera's voice faded, and she seemed overly interested in the Oklahoma coach calling a time-out. Cole just waited.

"So my mom has cancer. Pancreatic, so things aren't looking good. Only Anne Marie knows about it at the office, I don't really want Tom blogging about it. Anyway, Anne Marie knew my mom from way back, so she suggested that I get my real estate license and stay close to home. Anne Marie's been good to me, even if she is, you know, Anne Marie. And getting someone to buy a house isn't that different from getting a player to get back on the court."

Nera went back to watching the Oklahoma coach bawling out one of his players. "That guy needs to keep his cool," she said. Cole waited a little more, then reached over and put his hand over Nera's. They passed the rest of the game that way. With just five minutes left in the second half, they felt, then saw, the presence of a camera coming around to their side. And where there was a camera, there was Deborah Cheney.

"Hi, you two. Having fun?" she asked, putting her hands on their shoulders like a diplomat.

"Yeah," they said at the same time.

"Well, it's about to get even better. We'll be seeing more of you at the end of this game." She walked away with a sly grin to interview others in the crowd.

"What happens at the end of the game?" Cole asked Nera.

"I don't know. Maybe they'll give you something for winning."

"What if I don't win?"

"You will. Oklahoma is falling to pieces, and I think the last game will be more lopsided than people think. Besides, you're riding the luckiest wave I've ever seen. It would be almost unnatural for you to not win."

"Every streak has to end."

"Says who?"

"I don't know. Statistics guys. Me. It's like …so when I was in high school, my senior year, I was dating this girl, my skateboarding was going awesome—I was going to compete in an X games qualifier the week before I graduated. Everything was good, and then my accident happened. I was laid up for eight weeks, and then it took me another two months just to get right again. I missed the games, my girlfriend dumped me because she got bored, I missed my prom and my graduation. My point is, luck changes, fast, like that." He snapped his fingers.

"Was that your point?" Nera raised her eyebrows. "I thought your point was that if a streak of bad luck can last four months, a streak of good luck could at least last one."

Cole was about to retort when the final game buzzer blared and the sound to the television feed was shut off.

"My friends and co-workers!" Deborah Cheney began, now on the stage behind the microphone. "Are you having a good time tonight?" The crowd cheered that they were. "We'd like to thank Player Pier for hosting this party," applause, "and our wonderful executives and staff for putting this together for us." She joined in with more applause.

"We have five minutes before the final game of the evening begins, and I want to make a very special announcement." Cole noticed one of the cameras turning toward him. "As you know, I've been paying close attention to a certain South Windsor resident in my broadcasts this past week. This young man had a perfect bracket going into the Elite Eight. I can now tell you that if UCLA wins this next game, he will have a perfect bracket going into the Final Four. Cole Kaman, stand up and let us see you!"

Cole stood and gave a tight-mouthed wave. He stayed up long enough for everyone in the bar to turn around and notice him, and then he made a move to sink back in his previously anonymous seat.

"Wait, wait, Cole, stay standing a moment, because I have an extra special announcement. It turns out that Cole is not the only one to make it this far with a perfect record. Our colleagues at ESPN are telling us that there are three more people on their website who have also registered perfect brackets. And wait, wait, here's the amazing part. Cole, each of these contestants has the exact same Final Four teams that you do." She paused, knowing that she had everyone's rapt attention now. "But, each has a different team winning the tournament! Four people. Four brackets. Only one possible winner. Ladies and gentleman, the intriguing and improbable race for bracket perfection is on! Put that bracket up on the big screen!"

A dynamically animated version of Cole's picks went up, with each of the correct choices lighting up in exploding bright green. The crowd reacted in direct proportion to their individual drunkenness before Deborah put up her hands again.

"I know, I know, it's amazing. But now I have an even *more* special announcement." Cole wondered how many special announcements there could be in a row before they weren't special anymore. "ESPN awards a cash prize of one million dollars to whomever wins that year's bracket challenge, which Cole did not sign up for. But…" she continued, "the CBS higher-ups have agreed to officially sponsor Cole and award him the same cash prize should he be the final winner! *And*," she added, talking over the tide of voices and applause, "all four bracket holders will be flown out to Washington DC with a guest of their choosing to watch the Final Four in person!"

The camera found Cole's face again; it found his eyes opened very wide.

"Now, I don't care if you're a Hawaii fan or not. Let's cheer for this UCLA team, and let's send Cole Kaman to the Final Four!" Deborah applauded with everyone else in Cole's direction, then signaled for the screen to go back to the game. It meant just a little bit more to everyone there to see that UCLA had already gone up by six.

Nera watched as a few inebriated station members began making their way back toward their table. "C'mon," she said, grabbing his arm. "You need some air."

The Player Pier boasted a large deck overlooking one of the walking trails that paralleled the river. Crusts of snow capped the railings; the cold would give Cole and Nera some much-needed seclusion for as long as they could endure it. They leaned against the railing, looking out over the river to the sparkling constellation of streetlamps and windows that disappeared into the clusters of barren trees.

"So, wow!" said Nera. "I didn't see that coming."

"Yeah."

"You know, if you make it to the championship game, they play it on a Monday night. Anne Marie will probably give you paid leave as long as you wear a Cheney t-shirt."

Cole chuckled. They looked around in silence, watching their breath evaporate in white wisps.

"So how do you really feel about all this?" she asked sincerely.

Cole shook his head and laughed to himself. "Like I'm on a game show, one of those where they have some crazy thing that they have to do, but they keep adding things to make it harder, like, 'OK, you have to run from here to there carrying this egg in your mouth, but you'll have to cross this pit of cockroaches barefoot! And you'll be blindfolded! With a boa constrictor!'"

"Is that a real show?"

"I don't know. I'm saying that it feels like stuff keeps piling up for no reason. And the weirdest part of it all is, I don't have to do anything, and this will still go on. I could lock myself in my apartment, I could leave the country, and people will still get excited about this piece of paper that I filled out. And now there are three others with the same luck as me, and our pieces of paper are competing with each other for a million dollars. How did that happen?" Cole raised and dropped his shoulders with a deep breath. "But maybe it's just tonight. Maybe in a week people will calm down and they'll see all this for what it really is, and life will start being normal again."

"Maybe," Nera said thoughtfully. "But people like to believe that special things can happen. Like, not everybody can play college basketball, but everyone can fill out a bracket and maybe get it perfect one year. To see someone actually do it is fun; it gives people hope and excitement. The fact that there are four of you and four teams—that just adds mystery. It's good for people to see that improbable things can happen."

"Is it?" Cole asked, looking over at her.

"It's good for me," she conceded. "It's good for my mom. Why shouldn't it be good for you, too?" Cole shrugged his shoulders again and stared out at the river. A nice thought occurred to him.

"She did say that I could go with a guest, right?"

What could have been a truly romantic moment was ruined by Deborah Cheney.

"There you are, you two!" she called as she walked over. "We've been looking everywhere. There is *so* much to plan before next Saturday. We'd like to do another interview, one-on-one, for the Monday opening, and I think it might be nice to bring a crew over to your apartment for some human interest. I've already talked to Anne Marie about doing another on-site at the office, maybe interviewing some co-workers who've been in on it from the beginning. She mentioned there was a man with a blog?"

Nera glanced over to see Cole stiffening up.

"Uh, Deborah, would it be possible…"

"Oh *yes*, and you're the girlfriend, right? This is just perfect. So, I imagine that you'll be going to DC…"

Out of nowhere, a quick whooshing shot past Cole's left ear. Immediately, Deborah Cheney yelped in pain, reaching for her right shoulder as she fell back. Something shiny and hard had hit her square in the collar bone.

Cole grabbed Nera, almost pushing her against the rail, and they both hit the ground. Another object struck just above them, then ricocheted back over the steep ledge. Cole looked under the bottom of the rail as he lay flat, hand draped protectively over his head. Was that a man on the river trail below? Cole saw the flash of eye glasses reflecting the yellow light, the swooping motion of an arm. Then *crr-aaack!* A window broke above them and the figure ran off down the trail.

"Hey! Help!" Cole yelled.

"What was that?" The cameraman, who had been filming them from across the deck, came out running.

"Ms. Cheney!" Others came out when they heard the yelling. Deborah was rubbing her collarbone and using some language not fit for network broadcasting. Cole and Nera got tentatively up and stepped far away from the railing.

"Is this what hit you?" a man asked, bringing something over to Cole. It was a polished stone ball like a giant marble, the size of a chestnut. It had been crudely painted orange with black lines. The pattern of a basketball. On one side, in permanent marker, was the name '*Cole*'. On the opposite side was the outline of a flame overwritten with the name '*Ichabod*'.

"Who's Ichabod?" asked Nera.

A deafening *bang* rocked the deck and threw them again to the ground. Something had exploded from underneath. Smoke began to roll out from the windows beneath the patio ledge, along with screams of "Fire! Fire!" A mob swarmed out onto the patio, some running straight to the ledge to try and jump off, most running to the stairs along the side of the building. Nera had the sense to grab Cole in the confusion and nearly drag him to the other end of the patio, avoiding the crushing flow of the mob. They huddled for a moment before joining the outgoing, panicked mass. In that moment, over the cacophony of the alarms and the crowd, Cole could somehow hear an energized voice announcing a basket for UCLA. They made it off of the patio and joined others who were standing around, gazing horror-struck at the tongues of flame that flickered out from the thick smoke surrounding the windows.

The sound of speeding fire engines approached them from the city. Almost everyone around him had taken out their phones and were taking pictures and contacting people. Words like 'bombs', 'terrorists', and 'arson' emerged from the chatter. It was when he heard the word 'arson' that the identity of his attacker, the man who had been on his doorstep just a few nights before, finally clicked in Cole's mind. The revelations hit him hard and fast. The facts were so obvious that a sense of his own blind foolishness, mixed with the adrenaline, nauseated him.

It was cold. Before Cole could suggest that they go to one of their cars to get warm, he realized with a start that Nera was gripping his arm hard. She pulled him away from the crowd and spoke softly but intensely.

"What was that, Cole? Tell me what's going on." Cole had never seen Nera angry before, and he felt timid against the ire directed at him, and against the facts that infuriated her.

Someone had just tried to kill him. It was *his* name written on the rock. Someone who threw rocks into windows and set fire to buildings had singled *him* out as the target of an attack that would be all over the news before morning. That was even now burning one of Hartford's hippest venues. That had injured a few and spooked everyone else. That very easily could have…

"Cole!" Nera was almost yelling at him. "Cole, who is Ichabod? Do you know him?"

Like he had so many times over the past nine months, Cole found himself looking at Nera with no idea of what to say. Guilt clouded over his vocabulary.

"Nera, I—I'm so sorry, I didn't see any of this coming, I had no idea that this guy was trying to—you could have been—"

"*You* could have been," corrected Nera, looking at him fiercely. "He was trying to kill *you*, Cole. I would have just been collateral damage. Oh man, it's going to take my mom about five seconds to hear about this on the news. She's going to freak out." She left his side and began craning her neck to find her Jetta in the shifting melee of first responders and on-lookers. "You know what? I don't want to know what's going on. I have to get home right now before my mom has a heart attack." She began to laugh inappropriately and dug erratically for her keys.

Cole shook himself from his stupor and tried to clasp her arm.

"Nera, no, don't go—I can tell you who this guy is, I think I know what's going on."

"No," Nera snapped, lifting a finger to his face, "No, Cole. I can't…" She turned away. She paused. "I'm sorry, I didn't mean to… You have to stay and tell the police everything. Get safe. Whatever is going on, you have to just…" She jangled her keys and walked to her car without looking back at him. "I have to go. We'll talk soon, okay?"

[**East Division**: Final Four]
[Saturday, April 4]

But they didn't talk. From Sunday night through early Monday morning, Cole retold what he knew until his head ached. The police had many questions. He arrived at work after lunch on Monday, groggy, and told the story again. Nera never came. On Tuesday, he tried to prevent Tom from renaming his blog *Inside the OraCole*. Again, Nera never showed. On Wednesday, Anne Marie announced in staff meeting that Nera was out on personal leave for the week. He spent the entire afternoon writing her an e-mail explaining everything. On Thursday, he got a text message back: *I need to not be involved in all this right now. Take care.* On Friday, he felt miserable.

That night, he had a dream.

He was at the skate park in Manchester that he used to visit as a kid, but it was bigger, more expansive. It was nighttime, with bright white lights beaming down from somewhere overhead. He stood on his old skateboard, looking down over a ledge onto a deep ramp. It was too steep, and he hesitated in fear. But before he realized what was happening, he felt himself going forward, over, and down. With exhilarating speed, he flew down the ramp as it curved up into a bowl. *This isn't so bad*, he thought, and he looked for another ramp where he could launch for a trick.

Just as he approached the ramp, he realized that the entire floor was covered with ice. *Who put ice there?* He slid out of control and fell. Instinctively, he checked his lower back to see if it was hurt again. To his horror, he saw that it was bleeding dark red, and he was immobilized by the pain. *If only I hadn't tried to move that desk,* he reasoned, *I wouldn't have been so weak.*

His eyes were drawn to the top of the ramp. There was a figure, hooded and faceless except for a protruding pair of spectacles. He was just standing there, watching from a distance. Cole knew who it was and said his name: Ichabod. The figure threw something into the center of the bowl, a few feet in front of Cole. A grenade? It exploded. Suddenly, the whole sky was blackened with smoke. It was on fire. Ichabod had set the park on fire. Smoke was pouring into the bowl like storm clouds. He had to get out, but he couldn't feel his legs anymore. It was too cold on the ice. He saw Anne Marie pop up over the ramp and say, "This weather is *madness*, huh?"

Ichabod called down to him and demanded that he predict something. Cole could think of nothing. "Four," he shouted. It was the wrong answer.

The figure of Ichabod stretched to its full measure. Ichabod screamed like a warrior as he jumped over the ramp and slid down the icy wall on his feet, landing not far from where Cole lay. He charged Cole like a bull at full speed, full of rage, power, and cold blood, the reflection of orange flames on his glasses growing ever bigger in Cole's view. Cole heard the fire alarms go off as Ichabod leapt up above him...

Cole opened his eyes to the sound of his alarm clock. It was Saturday morning, six o'clock, the day of the Final Four. He looked out the window, feeling silly, just to make sure that Ichabod wasn't waiting for him. He saw only the police car that was assigned to his apartment that night. No pyromaniac stalkers in sight.

That was a bad omen, he thought groggily, the nightmare still fresh and vivid in his mind as he shuffled to the bathroom. But he had to be at the airport by 8:30, and he couldn't let a bad dream slow him down.

As he made his way north to the airport, burying himself in a blaring mix of drums and bass, he considered calling Nera. She wouldn't answer, he knew, and not just because it was too early. He settled on sending a text message just before boarding his flight. *Hope your mom is okay. Go Bruins!* Maybe she'd be impressed that he now knew the team's mascot.

*   *   *   *

The conference room at the Omni Hotel in downtown Washington D.C held an audience of press members waiting with cameras, recorders, and intense interest. All turned to look as four men, each very different from the others, walked onto the staged area and sat down in front of a bold ESPN banner. Lights flashed as the four responded in their own ways to the flock of lenses pointed at them.

The third of the four was Cole, dressed in a UCLA jersey with a white t-shirt underneath. His black hair had been combed back, but there was no way to smooth away his self-consciousness. It helped to sit behind the table and have something to lean on. Trying to calm himself down, he accidentally leaned too far forward and breathed hard into the microphone, eliciting muffled laughter from the crowd. He was tired from the quick flight and the jolting taxi ride and the rush to get settled before the press conference. He felt like his eyes were blinking at an unusually high rate.

Cole glanced around at the three other men sharing the spotlight. Each one was wearing the jersey of the team they had picked to win the championship. The one closest to the podium was balding and professional and seemed to know what he was doing. Cole had heard he was a business manager or something, and he now sat composed and assured. Next to him was a stocky, middle-aged man who was even more uncomfortable than Cole; he was sweating and could barely smile. To Cole's left was a college kid, about Cole's age, tall, black, and loving the moment. He was fist-pumping at the cameras and grinning like he was going to play in the games. Cole felt very alone. He looked out at the crowd and recognized only Deborah Cheney, sitting among the press with a conspicuous brace supporting her injured collar bone. She waved to Cole like a proud mom.

The moderator of the panel was a former WNBA player in a business suit. She took her place behind a separate podium that had been elevated just for her.

"Good morning, everyone, and welcome to a press conference that is truly unique in the history of this tournament. My name is Carol Clemente. Today, I represent ESPN and the 2015 Men's College Basketball Tourney Challenge. As you know, this year we have had the very unusual occurrence of four exceptional individuals correctly predicting each of the winners leading into the Final Four. It is a guarantee that one—and only one—of these contestants will emerge with a completely perfect bracket and the one-million-dollar prize. They are invited guests of ESPN at these games and will be sitting together as the tournament unfolds." Ms. Clemente turned herself toward the seated men.

"Now, for introductions." She pointed to each of them,

starting with the one closest to her podium. "We have here Dr. Neeson Faulkner of Miami, Florida. Next to him," she motioned to the heavy-set man, who was scratching at his cheek, "Mr. Perry Lynwood of Seattle, Washington. Next to him, Mr. Cole Kaman of South Windsor, Connecticut." Cole gave a little wave. "Finally, Mr. Tucker Barnes, a junior at the University of Nebraska. Truly, a group that is as diverse and representative of the nation as the teams playing in this year's tournament. We wish all of them luck, and they will now take questions. I ask that you please restrict the subjects of your questions to the games and their brackets." Cole was relieved at the last part; it might keep them from asking about Ichabod.

An older reporter raised her hand. "Did any of you have a system for choosing your teams?"

All four shook their heads, but Neeson Faulkner spoke. "As you may know, some of the greatest minds in mathematics and statistics have attempted to create a fool-proof prediction system, but none were ever able to overcome the realities of probability. It has never worked. So, the four of us up here would stand to make a lot of money if any of us had some sort of system that could accurately predict outcomes in March Madness, let alone other, more complicated scenarios. I don't doubt that someone will create one eventually, but I think I speak for all of us when I say that we are extremely lucky." The other three kind of nodded, though they weren't sure if he really spoke for all of them.

Next question. "Is the team that you chose to win your favorite team, or did you have a particular reason to like them?"

Tucker Barnes jumped on that one. "I don't know about these guys, but Nebraska is going to dominate the next two rounds. I knew it from day one. Like my man at the other end there said, we're really lucky and fortunate to be here, but my team is here because they're the best, and I feel like I'm just running with them today." Cole noticed some grins as reporters typed notes and looked up for more. The two older men were inspecting their hands, so Cole felt the burden of answering next fall to him.

"Yeah, uh, I think UCLA is a great team, which is why, you know, I picked them. I know some people were mad that I didn't go with UCONN, but, like, and I'm not saying they aren't a good team, but..." *Shut up right now*, he thought. "I'm just saying that I chose

UCLA this year." He finished, trailing off into a silent room. No one really knew what to write. Someone in the room cleared a throat. *Please don't let Nera be watching this*, Cole prayed as he, too, inspected his hands.

Next. "Who among you four is the most confident that you're going to win?" Tucker's hand shot up immediately, but Neeson also volunteered. Cole shrugged and Perry remained very quiet. "Mr. Lynwood, you don't think that you're going to win? Is that because you don't have much faith in your bracket, or is that a vote of no confidence for Georgia?"

Perry mumbled low and had to be told to speak into the microphone. "No, they're a great team and school and I have… but I just think that it's kind of weird for me to get all the ones right that I did so I don't see how I can really feel like I can just keep on winning forever." It was a depressing enough answer that they just moved on.

The next question was directed at Cole. It was Deborah Cheney, and she violated the disclaimer. "Mr. Kaman, local station WHAR in Connecticut has been tracking the fallout from the bombing of the Player Pier in Hartford, which was apparently a targeted attack at you by the Wall Street bomber, now known as Ichabod. Would you care to comment about what that incident means to you now? Are you concerned for your safety?" The other three men turned to listen, as curious as the reporters. It had been on the news that whole week.

You were there, you give a comment, Cole thought, trying not to glare at Deborah. "No, I mean, nothing happened after that. There was this crazy guy, he just threw a metal ball at us and started a fire. We haven't seen him since then, and nothing really weird happened all this week. The cops are still looking into it. I'm fine, I don't have much more to say than that."

Deborah followed up. "And your girlfriend?" Cole went red. *Thanks for that, you…*

"Uh, I'd rather not comment on that." Carol quickly moved to someone else, for which Cole was grateful.

It hadn't escaped one reporter's notice that, even though they were offered tickets for a guest, none of them had brought one. None of the four had a reason that they wanted to share, so the issue was dropped.

A few more questions were raised. Yes, all of them would accept the money and had big plans for it. Of the three, Tucker was the only one who actually played basketball, although Neeson had been following the game for a while. They were all aware of the nicknames being given to them by the media but had not decided among themselves which one they liked most, though Neeson was partial to the "Fourseers" and Tucker liked the "Four Bracketeers". Finally, they confirmed that none of them had a stake in the games outside of the prize money from the contest. It was all luck, and all in good fun.

"Well, if there are no more questions," said Carol Clemente, "I think we'll wrap things up. We'd like to thank these four men for being willing to come today, and again, we wish them luck. Next at this table, in fifteen minutes, will be some of the coaching staff for Boston College. Thank you." Carol dismissed the four, who exited to the left and found themselves in the hallway.

All around them, the chaos of media coverage at the Final Four closed in. An intern from ESPN was trying to give them instructions. They had a photo shoot in ten minutes, followed by filming of individual interviews to be used as potential fillers during the long time-outs. They had to hurry; there wasn't much time. Tip off was in just four hours.

*   *   *   *

When it was almost game time, Cole, Neeson, Perry, and Tucker were escorted up a long escalator to the second level of the newly renovated Verizon Center. Long banners were stretched over the escalators in both directions, and anxious crowds surrounded them on all sides. It was a festival atmosphere. On the way up, they saw the entrance to the brand-new private luxury suites that had been added during recent renovations, and Neeson wondered aloud why they didn't get one of those. The intern just shrugged.

They walked along the curved concourse, then through a short cement tunnel into the arena itself.

It was the first time Cole had ever been in an arena to watch a game. A giant jumbotron greeted them with frenetic basketball highlights and advertisements. The two teams of the first game, Georgia and Nebraska, were out on the floor running their shoot-around. Media workers were pacing the sideline and checking wires. Music blared out over the aggregated hum of the crowd. Cole was almost convinced that this was supposed to be fun.

Their seats were on the second row of the upper tier, facing the long end of the court behind the players' benches. They were so high that Cole couldn't make out the faces of people on the floor very well. He'd overheard an earlier discussion about the media wanting them to sit on the lower level so it would be easier to do quick cuts to them during time-outs, but they couldn't get it done. Still, the four men had an impressive view of the court and the crowd, and the television cameras on the floor could zoom in when needed.

Their escort wanted Perry, who had Georgia going all the way, to sit next to Tucker so that they could be more easily isolated in close camera shots. Tucker took the aisle seat on the right and Neeson grabbed the seat on Cole's left, so Cole and Perry were obligated to sit next to each other in the middle. As soon as they had been seated and the escort had departed, both Neeson and Tucker immediately retrieved their phones from their pockets and left. Cole felt awkwardly compelled to converse with the glum man next to him.

"So, Perry, right? You like living in Seattle? A lot of great bands up there," he half-heartedly attempted.

"Yeah, it's fine." Perry kept his arms folded and looked around nervously, a disconcerting stance that he had maintained since they had first met at the hotel.

"So, can I ask, you really feel like you're going to lose, huh? You have some kind of intuition about it?"

Perry snorted, but didn't answer right away. Cole shrugged and began to dig around for his own phone.

"Listen," Perry said, speaking as quietly as possible for no apparent reason. "Let me ask *you* something. What kind of luck have you been having since you filled out the bracket?"

"Kind of a mixed bag, I guess," Cole said evasively.

But Perry was unsatisfied. "Aren't you the guy who almost got blown up last week by a serial arsonist stalker?"

"Well, yeah, but…"

"And from what I remember in the press conference, you

have a girlfriend that you don't want to talk about. Things aren't going well?"

Cole frowned. "That's personal."

"What about work. You like your work? Things going well there?"

"What's your point?"

Perry shuffled his feet. "All of your bad luck really started with the bracket, didn't it?"

Cole thought a moment. "Maybe, but isn't having this bracket thing also really lucky?"

Perry pointed his finger. "That's my point. Don't you see how wrong it is that we're here? Do you know what the odds are of making it this far? For just one, it's like one in nine million trillion, or something. It's the odds of flipping a coin sixty times and having it come up heads each time. *Four* of us did it. And I didn't even look at the teams I was choosing. Did you?"

Cole thought about that morning that now seemed forever ago. He remembered thinking about Nera, but not much else. "Um, no."

"You see!" he cried, then hushed. "Since I filled out this bracket, everything in my life has blown up. I'm convinced, I *know* that something else is going on here. There is some force at work here, some greater power that has drawn us in. It's bigger than just the bracket. It's... it's..." Perry died down as he struggled to define what it really was. Cole just looked at him with raised eyebrows.

"Sooo... what's going to happen?"

Perry nodded opaquely. "I have a hunch."

"Is it a good hunch?"

Perry shook his head slowly. Then he asked, as if suddenly hopeful, "Have you ever been to Kaah Mukul?"

"No. Never tried it."

Perry sighed. "That's too bad. That would have helped us know."

Cole was about to ask what a game in a virtual city had to do with a real-life basketball tournament, but Tucker came back just then, stepping over their knees with his eyes trained to the court below. Behind him was Neeson. The players had cleared the floor, and the music was queuing up for the pre-game introductions.

Tucker looked down at the three men beside him.

"You guys ready for this?" he yelled, clapping his hands energetically. "It's game time!"

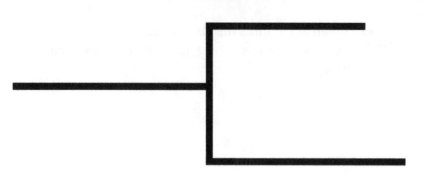

West Division

[**West Division**: Play-in Game]
[Wednesday, March 17]

The office of Myung-Ki Noh had been designed with the ostensible purpose of providing a private place to work. Though he would never admit it, most of his time was spent looking out of the window. The office walls, black, shining, and opaque from the outside, were completely clear from inside, allowing him the singular pleasure of pacing around the best vista in the entire city. This was his Olympus, his Cosmic Mountain, and he relished the opportunity to view the manifestation of his vision and the spectacle of his numerous subjects in panorama. The small desk in the center of the room, empty except for a video monitor, was rarely touched. There was no chair, no bathroom, no door, and no need for them. After all, he wasn't really there.

Much as he enjoyed it, Noh never allowed himself to come down unless he had a reason. This time, he had come to think. A meeting four days ago between himself and certain heads of state from China had provided an intriguing opportunity which he had accepted. With the help of some of his best programmers, he had developed a plan and set it in motion. Since that time, however, Noh had felt some doubts. He wondered if their plan was too simplistic, or not relevant enough. As he did whenever he needed to think, he descended to his office, stood before the window, and gazed.

It was night in Kaah Mukul. The moonlight was visible but diminished by the brilliant lights of the skyscrapers, the street lamps, and the occasional bursts of gunfire. To the north were the ruins of the old city, the complex of stone pyramids and rusty red plazas that was carefully preserved but scarred with history and war, surrounded on one side by the wall that had so miraculously held off the Conquistadors. To the east was the massive, sheer dome of the Montezuma Arena, the second-most dominant building in the city and the flagship arena for professional Ullamaball. Shifting clusters of green specks were the helmets of the Ahtzon, the Kaah Mukul police, patrolling the streets and getting into occasional fights. People flooded in and out of the arena, the plaza, the streets, all heading off to one adventure or another. He knew that many of them would die that night, some several times, but that was fine because everyone came with the understanding that the city was a place where failure had no meaning, where there were no lasting consequences. That was untrue, of course, but it was to his advantage not to let people know. Actions always have consequences.

The Chinese project was a welcome respite from the lesser, more mundane demands that were the curse and price of creative success. His real office was bombarded with stacks of requests from developers and advertisers, most of them uninspired. Some merely wanted access to ChangZhang technology, others some piece of the city itself. There was a Belgian company offering an absurd amount of money to rename a street after their product. An entomologist wanted to release virtual cockroaches into the city to observe their dispersal patterns. A company in the U.S. was asking for permission to install a new wind-powered technology onto the surface of one of the skyscrapers—that one was vaguely interesting. And, of course, there were the incessant requests for consultations from his own government. But these requests were from people who didn't really understand his company or his motivations. So he was thankful that the Chinese had come along. They understood the games of reality and the seriousness of fantasy.

Even as he stared, ideas began to come, as they invariably did. He looked through the glass, seeing past his dark, partial reflection, and set loose an untethered thought.

A game within a game within a game within...

A subtle ding from his desk brought him back to the video monitor. His assistant reminded him that he had a meeting with an American who wanted to integrate ChangZhang technology into a grand facility that was being built. Noh had nearly forgotten about it.

As he prepared to leave, he heard the muffled, anguished cries of someone getting his chest ripped open with an obsidian knife, and the dull thudding of a body being thrown down the stairs, right past his southern wall. He pushed a button on the controller in his hand. As his mind began to return to his own body in Seoul, where it was the middle of the day, he allowed one last gaze at his creation and smiled to himself. In a moment, it all vanished into blackness.

[**West Division**: First Round]
[Friday, March 20]

Perry Lynwood sat in his parked car, only forty feet from the strip mall's covered walkway. All he could see was a warped blur behind the steady flow of torrential raindrops on the windshield. The closest parking spot he'd been able to find was next to a large, well-polished black pick-up truck that had been parked just a little over the line. Perry's tiny Ford had barely squeezed in. He clutched his duffel bag and umbrella in his lap, preparing for a quick series of maneuvers. The plan was to open the door, open the umbrella, hop out, close the door, and jog a rapid forty feet to safety. He listened to the muted pattering of millions of engorged rain drops on the roof and counted:

3...2...1...

Door open, umbrella open, umbrella up, tight squeeze for Perry, tight squeeze for the duffel bag, a twist to close the door... and the sickening realization that the keys were still on the seat. Door open again, duffle bag over the shoulder, umbrella aloft with the other hand, squeeze back through the door, grab the keys, all set, plan executed. Suddenly, a powerful gust of wind yanked his umbrella and arm up and backwards, pulling his body into his car door, which slammed into the truck's polished side. Swearing through his teeth, Perry closed his door with his hip. He inspected the small dent in the truck as best he could through wet glasses. At last, he turned and walked across the lot to the walkway. When he was safe and sheltered, he looked back. It was too wet to leave a note, he reasoned, and too many stores to hunt the owner down. It was bad luck, but what could he do? A flash of lightning, slow and bright and closer than seemed normal, startled him into a quicker pace as he walked to the entrance of Seattle's largest KM Center.

"Brutal storm tonight, right?" commented the bored clerk, barely looking up from his phone as Perry dripped through the door, his sneakers squeaking conspicuously.

"Yeah." Perry shook his stubborn umbrella closed.

"Wasn't supposed to rain at all. I even brought my bike today. Ever feel like life is seriously just out to get you?" The clerk jawed some gum.

"Sometimes." Perry made his way to the large door in the back without a glance at the shelves of merchandise. He waved a magnetic membership pass over a sensor, and the door slid open. Taking a deep breath, he exhaled all thoughts of rain, expensive trucks, and Seattle, and walked underneath a sign that read: **"Ootzen. Welcome to Kaah Mukul."**

The door opened onto a wide platform that overlooked an amphitheater. On the stage below were four players, each wearing interface headsets around their eyes and ears and holding baton-like controllers strapped around their hands and feet. They ran and swerved in place, seeming to face each other blindly. The giant projection screen above them showed what the players were seeing: a wide, rectangular ball court covered with packed dirt and surrounded by vine-covered stone walls. The players danced and dodged as they each manipulated the movements of three virtual players with their bodies, trying desperately to get the ball into one of the two vertical hoops mounted over the court without getting kicked in the head. Ullamaball really was a beautiful game, Perry thought as he passed by the viewing platform. It was an elegant mix of soccer, basketball, and tae-kwon do, infused with the ancient Meso-American mystique that pervaded all of Kaah Mukul. But it wasn't for him.

Perry left the Ullamaball room behind and made his way down a hallway, past the large room full of consoles for those many Kaah Mukul patrons who hadn't spent as much time or money there as he had. His true domain was set apart for those who, like him, were truly serious about doing something significant in the virtual city.

The Tribal Room opened with a wave of Perry's ID card. His young fellow travelers were already inside, seated around a rectangular table that dominated the center of the room. Perry nodded hello to them as he made his way to his seat at the table's head. He looked down at the information already feeding into his personal monitor to see if there was anything new. A constant stream of statistics scrolled down, reloading every five seconds:

Warriors of Tsepes
Dominance Ranking.........32.70
Tribal membership...........27
Territory controlled (%)....16
Money accrued (K$)..........109,012
Total kills.......................146
Est. weapon strength...........

While he read, he removed a black and red bandana from the duffle bag and tied it around his right bicep. Then he plugged in his personal headset and controllers, put the bag behind his chair, and settled down in front of the nameplate which pronounced him General Studblood.

The table itself was striking. The wooden legs were thick as tree trunks and carved with ancient American motifs of pythons and jaguars. The tabletop was a computer interface. Each of the six chairs (only four of them occupied) commanded a small private interface, but the entire center of the table top displayed a vibrant, dynamic map of the city of Kaah Mukul. Lights representing the real-time movements of tribal members slid around the outlines of virtual streets and buildings. It was always beautiful, thought the General, always a work of genius.

He glanced around, contented, at the three individuals standing at the table, each staring into their interfaces. The officers of the Warriors of Tsepes were all wearing the tribal bandanas, all busy working, and all on time. The secrets of the city, the General repeatedly preached, were only revealed by diligence.

"OK, reports!" he barked. To the General's left was his first-in-command, a skinny twenty-something with a desperate, peach-fuzz moustache and a sharp chin. Killergremlin was always the first to report. The Tribe took pains to recognize rank. As he spoke, his wide, toothy smile seemed to stretch up on both sides to touch each of his unusually pointy ears.

"We broke the code," he announced.

"Put it up," the General ordered, pleased but not surprised. One of the many reasons he loved being in Kaah Mukul was the depth of the code-breaking necessary to progress as a tribe. The Tsepesians prided themselves on being able to decrypt anything they found at high speed, giving them a substantial edge over the other tribes. This particular code had been obtained just yesterday by one of his many underground contacts and was unusually difficult. That they had cracked it was a source of pride.

The translated text was full of garbled gaps, but embedded in the noise was a set of clear words:

Special opportunity: Sinan Cafe, Little Cuzco, 11:00 KMT, Saturday, contact Tula, codeword: Variolas. One representative only.

The General read over the string of words several times, then asked the group for an interpretation. A good leader always included everyone.

Their newest officer, a doughy high school graduate called Lazaro, spoke up. "Sounds like a commercial. They want us to show up so they can sell us something. Lame."

"Maybe," said Killergremlin, "but that was a pretty elaborate code for a commercial."

"But that's the game, right? Everything in code?" Lazaro argued.

The General cringed slightly at the word "game". Lazaro still didn't get it. Nevertheless, he could be right; the message did, in fact, have a certain commercial feel to it. But the contact that had passed it on to the General didn't usually handle junk mail. He wanted to take it seriously.

"I'll check it tomorrow," the General decided. "I'll take a back-up team. If it's some company making a pitch, you all can come help me shoot up the room."

"What's a Variolas?" asked Lazaro.

"Isn't it like a violin, but bigger?" Killergremlin answered.

"That's a viola," said Psychopedia, who was very smart for a tenth-grader. "I believe a Variolas is a kind of flower."

"It doesn't matter," said the General. "It's just the code word. It could be 'snotlicker' and it would do the same thing. Are there any other reports?"

There were none.

"Good. I'm going down to re-task some patrols. I think there's some Scarmada guys patrolling east of Tikal Street. We need to consolidate that sector before they get any more ground, so if I see them, I'll call you in." The General began to wrap the headset interface around his eyes, but he was interrupted.

"Soooo...." Lazaro interrupted, "you guys haven't forgotten my spring equinox party tomorrow, right?" The others looked around the table. It wasn't a group that was commonly invited to parties, much less ones that had to do with Lazaro's inventive form of paganism, so no one had forgotten. Nor had any of them accepted.

"I can't," said Psychopedia, sheepishly. "Bassoon recital."

"Wait, wasn't the equinox yesterday?" Killergremlin asked.

"No, tomorrow. Although, we are having our egg-swallowing ceremony at 11:45 tonight if you want to come to that, too."

The group looked over at the General, who avoided eye contact. He mumbled something that sounded like, "I think I can um maybe," and then cleared his throat as he tightened his headset. He couldn't leave reality fast enough. He secured the mask on his dark hair and sealed it around his ears and eyes, shutting off the world. When he was ready, he cracked his knuckles and pressed a button on his left ear to activate the interface, cutting him off from all of the sights and sounds of reality.

Grey, dark, whirling clouds spun past his face as he free-fell through the night sky, the whooshing air getting louder in his ears. Quickly, the clouds opened to a rich, sky-top view of the vast and glistening virtual city of Kaah Mukul in all its nighttime grandeur. He had little time to appreciate the view: the streets of the city were approaching very fast. With subtle and practiced movements on the control sticks, he maneuvered himself down like a skydiver, landing lightly near a highway overpass to the east of the Montezuma Arena. His body image materialized as an imposing, muscular soldier in black-and-red armored motif. As soon as he was fully in, he drew his gun and took in his surroundings.

All was normal. The streets had some nighttime pedestrians heading for the Arena, but they paid him little attention. The sounds of cars speeding, braking, and honking competed with the call of macaws—the Kaah Mukul pigeon—and the streetlights bleached out his view of the low, gray clouds above. His landing site was within close view of the most imposing edifice in the city. The Central Temple, just west of the Arena, reflected the city's brilliant lights from its sheer obsidian walls, its blood-stained sacrificial altar near the top bathed in crimson spotlights. The General waved up toward the temple, just in case. Rumor was that Myung-Ki Noh had a penthouse office up there, and the General always wondered if The Great Ahau of the city was watching. He soaked in the scene around him, and, for the thousandth time, felt at home.

But a good leader was always vigilant, so the General's contemplation was brief. Gun still drawn, he made his way to a highway overpass just on the east edge of downtown. Careful that no one was following him, he ducked behind the remnant of an oversized stone wall. Huddled there was a small group of eager Tsepesian rookies that had been recruited in the last few weeks. Their group leader, a capable warrior but notorious whiner named Ohmen, saw the General approach and rose to salute. The others joined.

"General Studblood sir," Ohmen greeted. "*Please* tell us that you need us to shoot somebody."

"Eventually. Any movement over here?" Ohmen brought him into view of a house on the opposite side of the overpass. Two guards were patrolling the front, each dressed in white armor with jagged red marks across their chests.

"No visitors since we've been here. Maybe they won't come down tonight."

"Maybe," said the General, thinking.

"Should we try and take out the guards?"

After a bit more observation, he said, "No, we don't want to blow our cover just to take care of a couple of guards. Save the surprise for the big fish." The General turned to face his troops. "This is an important mission. If we can take out the Scarmada here, we're in position to dominate the entire east side. Then things can get really fun." The group conceded unenthusiastically, and the General sensed the ebb in morale.

"I do have a side mission. I need a few of you to go to Little Cuzco, to a café on the north end called the 'Sinan'. I have a meet there on Saturday and I'd appreciate some recon." Some hands went up at that—Little Cuzco was always fun to visit. Ohmen still sulked in the general direction of the rival Scarmada guards.

"Good," the General said with vigor. "Anything else? I've got another patrol to check in on."

"Oh, wait," Ohmen called him back. "Typhoon has something for you."

The General turned to the rookie called Typhoon150. He had joined up just the past week—part of the usual late-winter surge in new recruits— and was an overzealous kiss-up.

"Have you seen it yet?" the rookie asked, his voice nasal and slightly digitized.

"Seen what?"

"Your bracket."

In his headset, the General rolled his eyes as he understood. The recruit was convinced that he'd found an encoded message from a confidential source in the Ahtzon through some sports thing outside of Kaah Mukul. The General had his serious doubts: why would the Ahtzon care about college basketball? But a good leader never quashed enthusiasm, so he had gone along with it. From what Typhoon had explained, the "bracket" was the General's message back to Typhoon's supposed source, and he'd insisted that it be posted directly onto the ESPN site using a non-Kaah Mukul e-mail account that retained the General's call sign. Anything more subtle would make him hard to find, the rookie said.

"What about it? Did your contact write back?"

"Not yet," Typhoon said, "I'm sure it's coming. But that's not the interesting thing."

"So what is?"

"The interesting thing is that all of the team choices we used to encode your message have won their games. You have a perfect bracket, General."

The General most definitely did *not* find this interesting, but before he could change the subject, they were startled from behind by a bright explosion. The Scarmada safe house was on fire. Sounds of gunfire blasted above the popping flames and panicked shouts. An approaching patrol of Ahtzon, dressed in green SWAT-like armor with bright stripes of paint on their helmets, was firing on the house. From behind the smoke, scattering Scarmada were haphazardly shooting back. Ohmen looked ecstatic.

"What do we do?" he asked, his weapon already raised. "Do we fight? Do we take them all?"

The General wasn't happy. It had taken them weeks to find this rival safe house, and now all the rumored munitions stockpiled inside were gone, thanks to a sloppy Ahtzon raid. His first instinct was to come from the rear of the Ahtzon and take them out for their stupidity. But, he remembered, a good leader couldn't let emotion get in the way. He had to do the logical thing.

"We let the Ahtzon do our work for us. We wait for them to clear out the Scarmada, then we set up an outpost in one of the nearby buildings. With them gone, we can take over the block."

"So we're just going to wait?" Ohmen complained incredulously.

"We have to wait."

"Why? How is that supposed to be fun?"

"Fun?" the General snarled. "Winning is fun. Winning means making smart decisions, like, not being insane and surprising an Ahtzon patrol that's already on alert. Once we control the whole east side, we can go out and kill whoever we want and they can't stop us. But right now, we're outnumbered, and that means they will make us die if we attack them. That's a loser move."

Ohmen just gripped his gun tighter and paced over to Typhoon150. The General ignored them, trying instead to make out what was going on in the smoke-obscured gunfight. There were some Scarmada members giving resistance, amazingly. The General could barely see one individual at the forefront. The man was big, with bright red hair and a thick beard. His uniform was mostly white but cut diagonally down the middle with a jagged green slash of paint. The Scarmada General. Studblood recognized him both by his looks and by the brazen display of his reputed fearlessness. Was there any way that his group could sneak around and take him down?

"Ohmen, what do you think about—"

But Studblood had barely spoken when Ohmen and Typhoon hurtled themselves toward the firefight, guns firing erratically toward the Ahtzon officers.

"Aaaaaaarh!" Ohmen screamed, plowing bullets into the nearest officer. The Ahtzon were surprised and turned away from the few remaining Scarmada to return fire. Typhoon, standing alone in the open, took shots to the chest and head, collapsing into a pile of virtual dead meat. Ohmen took cover behind a car as officers closed in on his position.

The General watched this all in disbelief. Ohmen had blatantly disregarded his orders. Not only that, but they had ruined any advantage they'd gained by watching things unfold in secret. Soldiers were approaching the besieged car from all sides as Ohmen called for help. But the General just stood, watching and calculating. The fire destroying the house in the background created a sudden flash so bright that he froze. Was it some heavy-duty explosives about to blow? Some Ahtzon distress signal calling for reinforcements? Just a glitch in the graphics display? One last squint at the scene confirmed that the house was beyond saving, as was Ohmen.

"Let's get out of here. Follow me," he ordered.

"What about Ohmen?" asked one of the other recruits.

"He made a choice, and it was bad," the General snapped back. "He disobeyed orders, and he's going to pay the consequences. Let's go."

There was little argument, and the diminished group turned away from Ohmen, still pleading for help over his intercom. The last thing the General heard was a final, angry curse directed at him, then nothing.

The General led the men away from the area and sent them on their way to Little Cuzco. He wanted to be alone.

Two men down from pure recklessness, he thought, making his way past the Central Temple to a park just south of the Montezuma. *Idiots.* And Typhoon had the makings of a decent code-breaker at that. He had to find a way to keep his people better disciplined. If and when Ohmen and Typhoon came back, which they eventually could, there would have to be some reckoning. There had to be order; his officers had to stick with the plan he chose or there would be serious consequences for the whole tribe. It was times like this that he lamented the youth and immaturity of so many of his tribe. He felt sometimes that he was a great man among great brats. He was sure that he wasn't the first general to feel that way.

As he stewed, he heard a thunderclap, then the ping of rain

on armor. Was it possible that the storm had followed him all the way in there from the parking lot outside? Of course not, he thought as he ventured out in the city. None of this was real.

[**West Division**: Second Round]
[Saturday, March 21]

Perry awoke the next morning with a headache. His vaguely Romanian facial features—remnants of his mother's genetic heritage—contorted in mild agony. He kept the lights dim because it was taking a long time for his eyes to grasp the concept of morning. With some coffee and Pop Tarts, he was out the door by eight AM, becoming part of that elite neighborhood club of Saturday early risers. The drive was familiar, taking him away from the small house he'd grown up in, left, moved back to, and eventually inherited from his mother, past the turnoff to the King County office where he was a data administrator for public records, and finally to the Yesler Way Plaza, where the Kaah Mukul Center had made the neighboring fast food joints more profitable almost overnight. For most people, the Center didn't open until nine o'clock, but his Tribal Wars key card allowed him access ahead of the masses, a privilege he was happy to maintain through a significant part of his monthly paycheck. Although, he acknowledged hungrily, it would be nice to be the top-ranked Tribe and have the monthly fees waived. He wondered what kind of money the Scarmada leader made outside of Kaah Mukul. Once inside the Tribal Room, Perry tied on his bandana out of habit and respect, then sat down for his Saturday morning ritual of cleaning out his e-mail accounts and scouring the Kaah Mukul community boards.

The morning's e-mail was mostly bland: some ads, some spam from the ESPN service where that code had been put up, and the usual chatter between the rank-and-file Tsepesian soldiers, many of them weekend warriors that he commanded from afar. Ohmen had written an angry rant using a limited and nasty vocabulary, but Perry deleted it before he read too much. Ohmen would be back once he cooled down, he reasoned.

An item of actual interest was a link to a video interview with Myung-Ki Noh and the sports editor of the *London Telegraph*. For a year, the Ullamaball Tier One league had been drawing such huge crowds of on-line spectators that it was now equaling live professional sports in popularity worldwide.

"To be clear, is it fair to say there is no way that Ullamaball, as it is played within Kaah Mukul, could become a real sport in real life?" the interviewer asked. Mr. Noh shrugged aloofly, a prickly bush of hair jutting out wildly from his youngish face. The interviewer continued:

"But Mr. Noh, don't you think it strange that a sport that isn't even humanly possible would draw more attention than a real-life athletic event?"

"No. In our collective history, things that were not humanly possible were the most interesting things for one to imagine. Now the time has come that what is not humanly possible is the most interesting thing one can achieve. I like to think in this way: there is a saying that art imitates life. Now we have Kaah Mukul, which is as much art as music or cinema, but far more enveloping and engaging. And we find now that life begins to imitate art. Those things that happen virtually begin to open our minds to possibilities that we would not consider when our lives were restricted to physical dimensions."

"Are you saying that what you create in your virtual city of Kaah Mukul will become possible in reality?"

"I'm saying that the distinction will eventually become irrelevant. What happens there will happen here, not because they are linked, but because they have become one."

Perry replayed the exchange a few times. The reality blending thing was an interesting idea, like all of Noh's ideas. He tucked it away in his mind for some future moment in which he would be more likely to ponder philosophy. He scanned the interview for updates on future developments in the city, found none, and continued his morning routine.

Killergremlin entered with his typically energetic flourish. "Did you see our D.R. went up a whole point over Scarmada last night? That raid hit them bad."

The General smiled. "I saw."

The Dominance Ranking was the most important metric in the tribal wars. It calculated the probability of any one Tribe taking over all other Tribes, based on numbers, weapons, resources, and leadership. The really good tribes, like the Warriors of Tsepes, were always within a few D.R. points of rivals, like the top-ranked Scarmada, but no tribe had ever established true city-wide dominance. It was the primary sign of progress for all Tribes, but the General knew that a good leader cared more about results than probability.

"Do you know if Ohmen or Typhoon tried to reconstitute back into the Tribe yet?"

"I haven't checked," said the General, busy with other things. "But I doubt Ohmen will be back for a while. He wrote me a pretty nasty message last night."

"Really? Can I read it?"

"I already deleted it."

Lazaro entered and waved as he scratched the pointy clump of beard that grew only on the tip of his chin. The beard had a drip of old egg in it. Perry said nothing; Lazaro would find out eventually.

"Everyone's coming tonight, right? Right!" Lazaro jovially answered for them. Perry kept his head down to avoid eye contact. Psychopedia came in with his backpack and bassoon case and stuffed them in a corner. Within a few moments, the high officers of the Warriors of Tsepes assembled, briefly discussed strategy, and descended again into the city.

The district of Little Cuzco was the only part of the city open to public internet connections. It was touristy, designed to hook new people to the city through mystical, creative visuals, harmless entertainment, and virtual shopping. The buildings evoked images of Machu Pichu, grey stone with step-like motifs that formed a serrated skyline, softened a little by mist and moss. The sidewalks were an open-air market with the latest KM fashions and toys for the throngs of avatars seeking to accessorize their virtual selves. But the General had seen it all before, so as he walked down the street, he only glanced momentarily at a small herd of llamas passing by dressed like Shakesperean actors ("drama llamas," he heard someone explain). Ahtzon guards patrolled the streets in small packs to keep the more violence-prone citizens from causing trouble that should be had elsewhere. But the Warriors of Tsepes caused no trouble…yet.

The Sinan Café was hidden away on the north end of the district in a side alley. The sign was so small that the General almost missed it. He dispersed his officers to look for any signs of an ambush, then went up the steps to the café door, pausing to look at the weathered image of a scorpion on the sign before entering.

The café was empty, which was unsurprising since virtual people don't drink. Places like this were typically used in the city for private meetings. Narrow tables and chairs were scattered around the main room, and there was a bar in one corner. Behind the bar was a woman, tall in her little black dress, with a face that reminded the General of a parrot.

"Are you Tula?" he asked. She nodded.

"Variolas," he spoke, and she nodded again. Stepping out from behind the bar, she opened a door that looked from the outside like a broom closet. As she motioned for him to go inside, the General wondered if she were attractive in real life. He doubted it.

The city was filled with ancient secret passages, but the General had never entered one through a restaurant, nor had he been invited to one as part of a sales pitch. He squeezed down a tight spiral staircase and into a dark corridor with rough-hewn stone walls. There was an orange light in the distance toward which he walked cautiously. As it became lighter, he heard air rushing through the corridor, like wind through an old castle, and the distinct sound of whispers.

The orange light emanated from a narrow opening between stone columns. The passage had opened into a large cavern formed like an amphitheater, and the first thing the General noted was a pool of dark water surrounded by a ring of rocks in front of the staging area. It was a remarkable room, even by KM standards, and he wondered about its origins. He didn't speculate long, however, because he noticed the red-headed bulk of the Scarmada General nearby. It was odd to have an enemy in such close range, and the General had to repress the urge to attack. Looking around, he recognized most of the other major Tribal Wars leaders. This would not be a good place to start a fight. The General sat down a safe distance from his Scarmada counterpart and cast another appraising look over the room. It was an impressive spectacle. Who could have organized this?

A voice came from nowhere. "Welcome to this very special presentation," it announced, filling the cavern. "You represent the select few that were able to break our code, which means that your tribe has the kind of ambition and expertise that will set you apart in the city. And that makes you our target audience."

A holographic image of the city materialized above the water, with ragged-edged sectors blocked out in different colors. The General recognized his 16%, a patchwork of the Tsepesian red and black on the east side, a territory that was above average in size but still puny compared to the General's ultimate goals. The voice continued: "We know the hardships you face as tribal leaders. You are constantly battling to maintain every inch of your territory and gain more. You must devote time to recruiting and forming tenuous alliances and spend precious resources just to keep ahead of the competition. We have invited you here to offer you a proposition that will allow you all of the satisfaction of fighting for your Tribe without the tedium of dealing with supplies, personnel, or funds. We are forming the first-ever Tribal Alliance."

There was some hushed talking in the audience. Alliances of more than four tribes were prohibited under the Tribal Wars bylaws and were enforced by the Ahtzon—ostensibly to protect newer, smaller tribes. But everyone always suspected that Kaah Mukul higher-ups just didn't want the Ahtzon challenged by mega-tribes. Legality aside, the General didn't like the sound of the proposition. The strategic nuances of tribal standing and dominance would be taken away by siding with their enemies. Others had the same opinion, and someone yelled out, "What's the point of being in the Tribal Wars if we're all on the same team?"

The voice replied, "But you are all on the same team already. The Ahtzon is your common enemy. While you are fighting each other, they hunt you down, constantly interfering and taking away your gains. You are lucky to kill off one or two at a time, and if you do, you are lucky to get away alive. But none of you has yet reached the point where you can take on a full Ahtzon patrol and win. We propose that you take your war to the next level."

The hologram of the city disappeared. In its place, something big began to rise from the pool. Water dripped off of a levitating table holding several kicking, struggling bodies, blindfolded and gagged. They were Ahtzon officers. The voice carried on calmly.

"We can provide you with weapons, funds, and recruits. The weapons we provide will only be functional for members of the alliance and will self-destruct in the hands of others. You can use our resources to deal with whomever you want. Only occasionally will we ask for something in return."

Tula walked up to the table and tapped one of the captive Ahtzon officers. The General watched closely. Either it was a vacant avatar, or there really was an officer in there, listening and sending information back to headquarters. If the body was empty, he would be unimpressed, but if it were a real officer—well, it would be like having a television camera in the room patched directly into Ahtzon headquarters. For Tula and her group not to be concerned about this was…unnerving. But the nature of the prisoner would be revealed soon enough. It was impossible, as far as he knew, to impersonate an Ahtzon officer. The uniforms were proprietary and impossible to steal. They were also weapons-resistant, making it very hard to kill an officer, much less capture one.

Tula pointed to the General. "You, General Studblood. Would you please come down and inspect these bodies for us?" He hesitated, wishing that she hadn't said his name out loud, but went down at her insistence. He stood behind their heads to stay out of their line of sight as best he could. Their armor certainly looked legitimate. Each of them had the official Ahtzon badge, which was impossible to duplicate. And they looked very much alive. "What do you think?" she asked.

"They look real," he announced.

At that, Tula began to hand out guns. The General had never seen a weapon like it before, and he had seen everything that had come to Kaah Mukul in the past two years. He hefted the gun in his hand, testing the feel of it. It was *nice.*

"Consider these a mere taste of what we can offer," the voice said when everyone had a gun in hand. "If any of you would like to give them a try, the Ahtzon are at your disposal."

No one moved immediately, and the General knew why. Conspiracy was one thing, but shooting an incapacitated officer would not be forgiven easily by the Ahtzon. If caught, the punishment for the shooter would be very heavy, including death and, much worse, a fine.

"Feel free to come up to the pool directly," the voice said again, almost tauntingly. A decisive clank of full battle armor, and the Scarmada general was on his feet, striding to the pool, holding the gun aloft. He stepped up to a helpless Ahtzon officer, smiled meanly beneath his full red beard, and pulled the trigger. The gun recoiled with a hefty blast, and the captured officer dissolved into a vapor of red. The cavern echoed with sudden talking and whooping, even some applause as half of the other tribal leaders jumped to their feet to take aim at the remaining officers. But the General sat immobilized. When the Scarmada leader had fired, a blinding flash of light had emanated from the pool, momentarily washing out the entire scene. The General had seen that light before when the Scarmada safe house went up in flames. It couldn't just be another graphics glitch; that would be too coincidental. Was the Scarmada already in on this weapons deal? Was their well-guarded safe house really the armory for this... The General realized that he didn't even know the name of this organization. But everything lined up. That's why the Ahtzon had moved in on the safe house; that's why the Scarmada General wasn't afraid to let the Ahtzon officer see him. He now had the fire power to kill with impunity, and the Ahtzon knew it. The General gripped his weapon and began looking through the smoke for the Scarmada leader. He had to take the red-bearded leader down before he got any more powerful.

The voice spoke again over the babble. "We will give you a week to consider our offer. If you wish to officially join our alliance and take advantage of our full package of resources, we will ask you to participate in a modest demonstration of our potential. It will be our introduction to the world of Kaah Mukul. You will be contacted soon with more details. Thank you, from all of us at Maascab."

The table receded under the water, replaced with a new holographic image: a rotating knife pointed down at an angle with the name *Maascab* written in block letters. Already the tribal leaders were descending the tiered seating, talking to each other or into their headsets, gesturing to the hologram and the blood-stained remains of Ahtzon uniforms. Studblood looked around the big room for the tall Scarmada leader and glimpsed him at the very back where Tula had opened a door and was silently nodding to the departing men. He held back a moment to whisper commands over the comm link.

"Hey, hey, all Tsepesian Warriors converge at the rear of the café now. Major haul coming up. Scarmada's General at the front, and we've got every other major player coming out behind him."

"We're here, we have the area surrounded. Which door are you coming out of?"

"There should be one to the…to the south. You should see a bunch of tribal generals coming out now." The General fell in at the very end of the line, taking his time and hoping that no one noticed. His men reported back; they couldn't see anyone. The General checked his own GPS, but it wasn't working inside.

"Hold on, I'm coming to you," he said as he looked out the door. He held the new gun close, expecting that the other tribal leaders had also recognized the ambush opportunity. But what met his eyes was completely surprising. He wasn't coming up from underground at all. In fact, he wasn't anywhere near the café. He found himself looking down from a small building that he recognized as across the street and much further to the east of where he thought he was. He was just below the mist, overlooking several boxed flower gardens and standing next to a stairway going down to the street level. His GPS came online and confirmed how far he had travelled.

"Everyone, I am *not* near the café. I didn't come out there. You need to move east…" But before he could finish calling his real position, a minor leader from some tribe he didn't know pushed back passed him and tried to enter the door that had been shut behind them. In a moment, the General saw why. A sizeable Ahtzon patrol was closing in from one side of the street. Several tribal leaders were retreating and trying to return fire, but the patrol was advancing inexorably. They would overtake his position soon.

"Ahtzon coming in heavy on the east side of the street. I need back-up!" he yelled into his headset as he also backed up the stairway. He quickly assessed his options. Going down the stairs would just put him in the middle of the firefight. The railing in front of him led nowhere.

"Killer, I'm a sitting duck, you need to get here—"

"You're too far away, Stud! There are all these freaking

tourists!"

Something whizzed past his head, and the General turned to see that he'd been noticed by the Ahtzon. The other leader fell off the stairway to the ground below. Another shot, and bullets struck the General in the right arm, knocking his gun over the railing and rendering his arm useless. He jumped over the railing and steadied himself on a window box. Another quick jump and he was on a roof, running at an angle and trying to find a way up and over the buildings. There was none. A narrow alleyway, partially hidden, branched off below. It seemed like his only chance. With a risky jump, he awkwardly maneuvered around stone and windows and ungracefully fell down into the corridor. But it was a mistake. The alleyway was a dead end. He turned around and noticed two Ahtzon guards closing in. There were no exits, no doors, no windows, not even any convenient tourists to use as human shields. He was cornered.

They had him. The warning light in his head-up display indicated that he couldn't jump out of the city—no one could leave without automatically dying once they were marked by the Ahtzon. He was General Studblood; if he was to die, he would die fighting. He turned low and away in a desperate attempt to duck, then he rolled forward and up to go out with a ferocious, possibly suicidal pounce.

Guns fired as the General landed, and then a voice. "Stud! Yo, Stud!" The General opened his eyes wide, stunned to see Lazaro in front of him with the two Ahtzon dead at his feet. "C'mon, Stud, there are more coming!" They snapped back into action, firing behind as they ran down the sidewalk and ducked around to safety behind a cluster of vendor stands.

"So," said Lazaro as the General looked back. "This will be fun to talk about at my party." The General sighed heavily and wondered if he should have just taken the bullets.

*   *   *   *

At one point during Perry's drive that night, he realized that he couldn't remember Lazaro's real name. He hoped that wouldn't be a problem.

There were lots of reasons for him not to go. For one, he was too old for this kind of stuff. He would certainly be older than any of

Lazaro's friends—not to mention more mature, not to mention more sane. He didn't like parties. He especially didn't like parties late at night when he could be doing other things, like sleeping or shooting something in Kaah Mukul or anything else in the world. He absolutely hated small talk. He couldn't even remember what people were supposed to wear to parties, and he'd settled, after a few minutes of half-hearted worry, on a Hawaiian shirt and some wrinkled khakis. But trumping all of these complaints was the knowledge that a good leader always supported his people, and a good leader always kept his word. It was about trust. He'd already said he would go, so he had to go. But he never said he wouldn't leave as soon as possible.

Both sides of the suburban street were lined with cars by the time Perry arrived. He took his time finding a parking spot, and then he took his time sitting in a silent car, mentally preparing to go in. Even from a full block away, he could hear the music. The neighbors could, too—he saw one man on his porch talking on the phone and gesturing down the street. *A good leader always keeps his word,* he repeated to himself like a mantra. Finally, he sighed heavily and counted:

3...2...1...

Time to go in.

The basement entrance to the party was around the back of the house, the way marked by a paper sign with an arrow that was utterly unnecessary, given the throbbing music and shifting slivers of strobe lights that spilled into the yard. The screen door opened to a staircase that descended into the thick of the fray. Perry took a deep breath of air that consisted of a dizzying blend of smoke, alcohol, and something vaguely like the smell of a public pool, and he descended. *Just ten minutes,* he decided.

Pausing at the bottom of the stairs, Perry found himself looking into a kitchen area, the counters covered with bottles and chip bags. A tall woman dressed in black was leaning against the counter, looking like she'd had too good a time already. She waved at Perry unsteadily and tossed him a bottle of beer, then gestured him on to the living room with a sick but evocative grin.

The living room was crammed with people lined shoulder-to-shoulder along three of the walls. It was hot, and the floor was pulsating with music so loud that screams and gestures were the only viable forms of communication. Everyone's attention was focused on a free-standing bathtub along the fourth wall that was filled with water and topped with bobbing pink and yellow marshmallow chicks floating on rafts made of plastic bowls. In the middle of the room, Lazaro was showing a girl how to operate a cannon made of PVC pipe and a compressed air cylinder. She closed her eyes, pulled the trigger, and squealed as the cannon popped. Perry squinted at a fantastic burst of light, then squinted again at the bath-tub which now had a new chocolate smear on it. A chick was floating sideways in the water in a mess of sugary carnage, and the girl was kissing Lazaro passionately.

This was too much for Perry, and he wanted to run back up and away from noise and lights and people and chaos. But he felt transfixed by the scene, as though he were pinned to his spot in the doorway and everything was taking place in slow-motion. He stood for a few minutes against his own will before ditching his unopened bottle on the floor and moving out of the room. When he reached the top of the stairs, he was relieved to see Killergremlin about to go down.

"You don't want to go in there," said Perry.

"It's bad?"

"Oh, yeah, it's bad."

Killergremlin grinned and ran downstairs to see for himself. In a few minutes he was back, holding two beers and looking shocked.

"That is bad," he said.

"Told you."

In one corner of the back patio was a table and a few tattered lawn chairs. They sat down together, listening to the sporadic sounds of merry insanity over beats. The streetlamps illuminated the night with a benign yellow glow.

"So, what are we going to do about this Mascaab thing?" asked Killergremlin.

"I have no idea," said Perry, turning toward him. "It definitely isn't legal, but having constant recruits, new weapons, constant funds? That's all stuff we could use. I don't know."

"How many other tribes do you think will join?"

"I don't know."

"Scarmada?"

Perry nodded as he drank. "I wouldn't be surprised if they're already in on it somehow. You should have seen their leader shoot that Ahtzon right in the head. He wants this for sure."

"So does that mean we need to be in it?" asked Killergremlin.

Perry resorted to his usual response. "Or we need to be against it. I don't know. I'll figure it out." A good leader exercised caution when making big decisions.

They heard more screaming than usual coming from downstairs, but they ignored it.

"You know what that thing is with the tub?" Perry asked.

"Yeah, I found out when I was down there. You have to hit two chicks, one yellow, one pink, with your girlfriend or significant other or whatever. If you get both, that's a good sign for your fertility that year."

"Um, it's a little creepy that he actually believes that."

"No," said Killergremlin. "What's creepy is that he's only doing it this way because he couldn't find live chicks."

A pair of laughing teens came up the stairs and disappeared around the side of the house. Perry noticed one of them wearing a pair of thick golden earrings. It was hard to see, but they looked like a trendy style invented in Kaah Mukul.

"Reality imitates art," he remarked to himself as he took a drink.

"Huh?"

"Nothing, I was, I was just thinking about something that Myung-Ki Noh said in this interview I saw this morning. He was saying that Kaah Mukul was becoming so real to people that stuff that happened in the city would start to happen in real life, that the line would blur. I think he was talking about, maybe, like, things that were invented in the city could be useful in real life. I don't know. It just popped into my head just now." He shifted in his chair.

Killergremlin shrugged and took a swig. "You think that happens?"

"What?"

"Stuff in the city becoming real."

"Maybe. I guess that's why so many people like Ullamaball, because it's like a real thing to them. Why?"

"Well…" thought Killergremlin. "Well, just say this, and I'm just speaking like, hypothetically. What if it got so real down there that events that happened down there actually started to happen out here?"

"How would that happen?"

"I'm just saying, hypothetically."

"It's a pretty stupid hypothetical."

"Listen, listen. You go into Kaah Mukul. You're the same person there that you are in reality, up here, so even though everything you do down there isn't like reality, you still think like you. It's like dreaming, where even though everything is weird, it's still you, and that's why sometimes things in life come out like your dreams. And vice versa."

Perry laughed. "If my real life were anything like my dreams, I wouldn't be on a lawn chair in Lazaro's backyard with you trying to avoid a party of lunatic Peeps worshipers."

"I'm serious!" said Killergremlin, who felt like he was on to something. "Take what you told me about today. You went to the café and you went down these stairs, right? And it was dark and weird, and, um, there was water there! And people shot guys in the water, right? And there was a woman dressed in black, Tula. And Lazaro was there with a gun. Now—I'm just thinking about this— now here you are, you're at a place and you go down these stairs to someplace dark and weird, and there's that hot woman in black down there, you saw her? And they're shooting stuff in the water…" His voice trailed off as he realized how it all sounded. "Never mind, that's ridiculous."

"Uh, yeah," Perry said with a smirk. "If life were actually like a mirror of Kaah Mukul, it would be terrible. I mean, don't get me wrong. I love KM. I think it's actually better than reality sometimes. But it could never be reality. This morning, in the story you're using as an example, I ended up getting shot in the arm and my safety depended on Lazaro having good aim. Can you imagine if that were our lives? Not only would we not survive very long, but it wouldn't be fun, either. No, what happens in the city should stay in the city, I don't care if it's art or not."

Killergremlin was well past his first bottle and began to argue for argument's sake. "Look, that's not what I meant to say. I'm not saying that everything that happens is the same. I'm saying that people act the same down there as they act up here, so things that happen down there *could* happen up here. It's retarded to think that the exact same things…" They heard the decisive click of a car door closing and looked up to see two police officers walking toward the house.

"Somebody called the cops?" asked Killergremlin.

"Could be a neighbor. I saw one that looked pretty mad about the music."

Killergremlin stood up. "Well, I don't think they're really going to like what they find in that party. Let's get out while we can." He made a move to hop over the fence to the next house. Perry hesitated. He wondered if someone should go down and warn them that the police had come. After all, Lazaro was part of his team, and a good leader left no man behind.

"Wait up, I'm going to yell down the stairs," Perry said to Killer's back, already struggling over the fence. Perry went down a few steps.

"Hey down there, the cops…"

The girl in black clomped very quickly up the stairs and pushed by him with her head down. She was whimpering. Perry stepped aside to let her pass, then looked back down the stairs. There was a burst, and a sharp pain on his right cheek that knocked him down. His shin hit an unforgiving cement step and he fell down onto the stairs, shoulder first. Catching himself, he looked down the stairs, eyes wide and furious. There was Lazaro, both his arms raised, the air gun on the floor. Everyone else was frozen, looking up the stairs at something behind Perry. The cops. He checked his cheek and noticed that it was covered with chocolate shards, some caramel filling, and a trace of blood. In a delirious, irrationally funny flash of thought, he wondered what all of this would do for his fertility that year.

*   *   *   *

The next day, the General showed up at his post a bit late. He had been up all night trying to explain to the police what had happened, and then his sleep had been restless and anxious. He was proud of himself for getting up and returning to the city when a lesser man would have taken a day off. A good leader leads by example, and for him that meant coming in to fight even when at considerable sacrifice. But that didn't mean that he was in a good mood, and he was intent on taking it out on some unsuspecting and soon-to-be-massacred tribe. Of course, he would have rather taken out his frustration on Lazaro. Instead, he had done the work to ensure that Lazaro had his KM Center clearance revoked. He considered it an unwritten rule that any tribe member who nearly kills another tribe member with a chocolate egg canon is, without argument, removed from the tribe.

Before he went down to the city, the General hastily checked his messages in several e-mail accounts. More spam from ESPN about a contest he could win, which he deleted without reading. But one message did catch his eye. It was an official dispatch from the Ahtzon Communications Division to all tribes.

> The tribes are reminded that all large-scale tribal alliances are strictly prohibited. Please be advised that the Ahtzon will be searching for members of any such alliances and exacting the prescribed punishment of ritual sacrifice and a one-month ban from the city. The Ahtzon have also issued a reward for information leading to the arrest of anyone involved in organizing such alliances. This reward will include exclusive, monitored access to Ahtzon files on select tribal leaders. As always, the Ahtzon are here to promote fairness and justice in the city.

The General reread the message several times before putting his head down on the table and sighing with mental exhaustion. The last thing he wanted to do at that moment was to make a decision. He needed to think. He needed to shoot something. On his way down, he wondered if there was still a drama llama out in the open.

[**West Division**: Sweet Sixteen]
[Thursday, March 26]

Very early on Thursday morning, the General walked down a narrow dirt path into one of the thick jungle regions north of the main city, where the Kaah Mukul Hunting Grounds were zoned off. He didn't have an entry pass to the region itself, nor did he want one. The Grounds were just for shooting and fighting, and he had long ago given up on such simplistic games. He had not gone down there to play; he had business. He made his way down the path to the gatehouse that guarded the entryway into the Grounds. He could hear snaps of gunfire coming from the thick green foliage behind the tall fences that enclosed the area, but his eyes were fixed on the Ahtzon officer posted outside, who waved briefly as the General approached.

"What's new, Studblood?" asked the officer, who had a distinct southern boondocks accent.

"Nothing. Anything going on with you, Halley?"

"Plenty," the officer replied. "Lots of people nervous about this Mascaab thing. You going in on that?"

"I don't know what you're talking about," the General said, just in case his exclusive secret source in the Ahtzon wasn't very exclusive. "Are you guys any closer to hunting them down?"

"Not that I've heard, but they're trying. From the looks of it, they aren't using the standard KM system. They patched in somehow. The higher-ups in the Ahtzon are waiting for the higher-ups at ChangZhang to come in and wipe them out, but the rumor is that Noh doesn't want to get involved. That dude loves to let things ride, know what I mean? Truth is, rules or not, I think anyone that gets in with the Mascaab could actually get away with it as far as ChangZhang is concerned. Of course, the Ahtzon will still be on 'em."

"Yeah," said the General, who always wondered if his source knew as much about Noh as he always bragged. "What about this reward? Are the Ahtzon files all that good?"

"Are they good?" Halley guffawed. "Yeah, they're good. They're good enough that most Ahtzon patrols don't get to see them because if they did, the tribes wouldn't stand any kind of chance. That stuff is controlled from the top. I don't know how much they would actually let you see, but that's good info right there. And that's your lifeblood as a tribe, ain't it? Info? Headquarters, recruit numbers, arms caches, code histories, maps... Rumor has it that Noh has his own personal notes on each general, too."

"So, have you seen the files?"

"A few times."

"Have you seen mine?"

"Now that there," said Halley with superiority, "is confidential information."

The General opened a pouch on his belt and handed some coins over. "Now. Anything on there that could compromise us?"

"I dunno," said Halley as he pocketed the money. "Haven't seen it."

"But you just said…"

"I said that whether I had or had not seen your file was confidential. Now you paid me, now you know."

"Oh, come on! Don't do that to me."

"Calm down there," Halley cautioned lazily. "I've got something else to tell you, and it's important." Halley's voice got lower as he looked around. "I've been asked to set up a meeting with you."

"With who?"

"I have a guess, but they didn't tell me for sure. All I know is that you have to be outside the Central Temple this evening, on the southeast side near the arena, at 7:30 KMT, that's 5:30 your time, right? And listen, trust me on this, you gotta go."

The General evaluated the helmeted face of the officer. "Fine," said the General. "See you around."

"See yah. Oh, wait!" Halley called. "I forgot to congratulate you on the bracket. That's pretty amazing what you done right there."

"Huh?"

"Your bracket. I've never seen anyone get them all right like that before."

"How did you know about that?"

"Your name is right at the top of the ESPN tournament list. You and two other guys, which, by the way, is pretty cool in itself. It's right there, anyone can see it. 'Studblood, 100%.' Course there's a while to go yet. We'll see where you are by the end of the day. And thanks for having Georgia go all the way. Them's my team."

The General was more troubled by this than he let on. He didn't like there to be information about himself that he didn't control, much less information that he didn't know about.

"Yeah," said the General. "Speaking of that, have you heard word about any Ahtzon passing codes using brackets on, um, bracket sites?"

"You mean, after you put 'em in online? How would you even do that? You can't change them once the tournament starts, it's just a one-time deal."

Perry stuttered. "I, I don't know, I heard about something like that."

Halley shook his head. "Sorry, man. No idea what you're talking about. I've never even heard of out-of-city codes. The game stays in Kaah Mukul, you know what I mean?"

"Yeah, I know," said the General. "You think my perfect bracket is in my Ahtzon file?"

"How would I know?" asked Halley, returning to his post.

The General walked back down the path to the city. Looking at his watch, he realized that he would have to move fast. He had to be at work in seven minutes, and he had already been late twice that week.

*   *   *   *

Killergremlin and Psychopedia usually had the Tribal room to themselves until Perry got off work at 5 pm, so when the door was flung open at 3:45 that afternoon, they looked up in surprise.

"Woah, what happened to you?" Killergremlin asked.

Perry's face was red and unsmiling. He threw down his equipment on the table with excessive force. "Nothing happened."

Killergremlin and Psychopedia glanced at each other. "Um, nothing happened?"

Perry tried to tie the bandana around his arm but was so flustered that he fumbled the knot several times.

"I just quit my job."

"Woah. Why?"

"Guys, I really don't want to talk about it. It's over, it happened, I'm here now. So, what do we got?"

The General stared at his fellow tribesmen in an uncomfortable silence. Finally, Psychopedia spoke up, his voice cracking.

"We got a message from the Mascaab."

Finally, thought the General. "Show me."

The message came up:

Ready to join the team? Come play at the Montezuma, Saturday, 2 PM KMT. Small entry fee of 2000 KM credits. You pay, you play. Bring the whole tribe. The view from the stands is worth the price of admission.

"Alright. So, in the stands at the Montezuma, Saturday at noon. What do you think?" asked the General, challenging his two officers with his stare. The outrageous price tag felt like yet another punch to the gut on an already painful day, but at the moment he only cared about getting to the heart of the Mascaab issue.

Killergremlin spoke slowly, analytically. "We still don't have any good intel on how secure these guys are. I've asked everyone, I've looked everywhere—as far as I can tell, Mascaab doesn't exist, which means they want to stay anonymous, which means they can disappear whenever they want and leave us with the consequences. I don't think we should trust them."

"Not to mention," added Psychopedia, "this message probably went out to everyone that was at that meeting last week. So if any of the tribes want to betray the group and get the reward from the Ahtzon, they have all the info they need to turn us in."

"That's a good point," the General said, thinking. "But the Mascaab must have thought of that. They aren't dumb. They either want the Ahtzon to be there because it's a diversion and they're really going to attack a different place, or they are going to be at the Montezuma because they plan to do something to the Ahtzon right there in the arena and they don't think they can be stopped."

Killergremlin and Psychopedia exchanged a glance, and then

Killer sighed and said, "It doesn't matter. We can't afford the fee anyway. Have you looked at our account recently? It's way too much for something so risky."

"I got it," the General said firmly.

Killergremlin gulped. "Uh… didn't you just lose your job? I mean quit?"

The General stared him down. "This is important. We have the chance to be part of something big here. It's worth some sacrifice. I can get another job, but this opportunity is right now."

"You really want to join the Mascaab then, huh?"

The General looked out at his counselors, the skinny, goblin-like twenty-something and the hypoallergenic teenager, and decided to be decisive. A good leader was decisive. Besides, he was tired of just letting things happen to him.

"Yes. I think it's our best shot at moving up in the world. The Ahtzon are only out for themselves, so we have no reason to let them control us just because we're scared of the alternative. Also, I have it on good authority that ChangZhang is letting this play out, so there isn't an immediate risk of getting kicked out. And I'm tired of spending so much time recruiting and getting money and supplies when we could be taking over some serious ground. This is what we need to do to get out in front in DR."

Killergremlin was still skeptical. "Do you know for sure that ChangZhang is staying out of it? They might be letting this play out as a test. What if they come out after this and say that everybody who sided with the Mascaab is banned for a year or something? And that's besides the fact that we still don't know anything about what the Mascaab will want from us after we join up."

"So you're questioning my decision?" said the General tersely.

Psychopedia almost said something, but didn't. Killergremlin just looked at him for a long moment. "No. You're the General," he finally said. "We'll do it if you think we should do it."

The General nodded. "Thank you. Now we have a lot of work to do. Killer, I want you to take a team inside the arena and scout it. Find all the ins and outs, try to think about what the Mascaab would be up to. And why Saturday at that particular time? Maybe we can outthink them."

Killergremlin nodded as he prepared his controllers. "Who should I take?" he asked.

"Try Ohmen's old patrol, they always want action."

"Can't," said Killergremlin. "They barely exist anymore."

That was news to the General. "What happened?"

"Well, Ohmen isn't back, obviously. The new leader was Tiburon, but he has carpal tunnel and can't use the controllers. Nutkraken just had a baby, and Typhoon150 never came back, either."

The General listened to the list with a frown. "I didn't know Nutkraken was married."

"Dude, Nutkraken is a woman."

"Oh," said the General. "Wait, Typhoon *still* hasn't come back?"

"Nope. I thought you knew that—you were the one that told me in the first place."

That was troubling for the General, and not just because they'd lost a potential codebreaker. Ever since Halley had debunked the brackets code, the General had wondered what Typhoon was up to, and he had intended on talking with Typhoon personally. But the worry would have to wait.

"Fine," he said, waving his hand. "Use whoever you want. But get in there and figure out how a trap would be set if it exists."

"What about me?" asked Psychopedia. "You want me to patrol the plaza outside?"

"Uh, no," the General said, looking at his watch. "I'll do that. I have a meet there tonight with a new contact anyway. You keep working our sources for any new details about the Mascaab. There has to be somebody that can give us something useful."

They were agreed, and each headed down to the city in his own direction.

The General landed directly in the middle of the plaza south of the Montezuma Arena. His coming was hardly noticed; the streets around the arena and the central temple were the busiest in the city. The General left the busy flow and walked around to a less trafficked area beneath a lamppost. He checked his watch. 7:15 pm KMT. There was enough time to unwind quietly before the meeting would take place. Although, the General never quite let himself be at ease in the city. There was always the possibility that some random tribal patrol would notice him and attack. He interrupted his fifteen minutes of calm by looking behind him often.

The arena was an impressive sight. The dark emerald glass that formed the oblong dome seemed to vibrate like the membrane of a tight drum, refracting the image of the surrounding colors like a prism. Crowds of people were streaming from the several entrances. Scoreboards and viewing screens were placed between doors to allow a view of the action inside. From where he stood, the General could see the long black tunnel of stone and cement that connected the arena to the Central Temple. The altar on top of the temple, bathed as always in red light, beckoned his mind momentarily into second guessing his decision.

His contemplation was interrupted by a voice from behind that was familiar in a surreal way.

"General Studblood. Thank you for coming."

The General whirled around and saw, to his astonishment, a slightly digitized version of a face that he had only ever seen in videos and pictures. The figure was shorter than him, young, Asian, with lightly bleached hair that flailed out in all directions. Around his neck he wore a round stone calendar medallion embedded with gold and emeralds, a symbolic accessory worn by only one person in Kaah Mukul. If it was the person Studblood suspected, he was the only one in the entire city who chose to resemble his real self.

"Are you Myung-Ki Noh?" the General asked in disbelief.

"Yes," replied the figure. The voice really did sound like him. But appearances were deceiving in the city.

"Prove it."

The figure that resembled Noh smiled briefly, then looked around and pointed to a tree that was planted next to the wide sidewalk leading up to the arena's entrance. The General heard a low rumbling sound. The tree began to wobble back and forth as the vibrations in the ground became violently localized around it. The top of the tree burst into a bright blaze of yellowish-orange light. It was transfixing, and then it was instantly over. The tree was exactly as it had been before, and all was quiet.

For a long moment the General stared, unmoving, then finally gushed, "Mr. Noh, it is so cool to meet you! It is such an honor. I've been the biggest Kaah Mukul fan since the beginning and I think you are a genius."

"Thank you, General. I am also an admirer of your recent work," Noh said gracefully.

"Really? I mean, I'm surprised that you know who I am," said the General, now very flattered as he remembered what Halley had told him about Noh's secret files. He thought of calling over the rest of the council, but that somehow felt impolite. He was there, in the moment, with the god of his favorite place standing there in the virtual flesh.

"How do you feel about your progress as a tribe?" asked Noh in his even tone. "Your ranking has been steadily increasing."

"We're doing awesome," the General blurted, eager to keep the conversation going. "We were actually going to do some recruiting this week but never got around to it, but we got some good fighters, and some rookies that, oh, and we have the best code breakers of all the Tribes, but you probably knew that. It is such an awesome pleasure. I mean, to meet you."

Polite enough not to note the General's fluster, Noh continued on with deliberate stride. "I'm glad you are doing well. I would expect nothing less from someone with your predictive abilities."

That was interesting. And confusing. "My predictive abilities?"

"Yes. Do not think that your bracket has gone unnoticed, even in the world of Kaah Mukul. You are on a very impressive streak. Still perfect as of ten minutes ago."

What? The General couldn't believe it. *Does everyone know about this but me?*

"You know about the bracket thing? Do they do that in South Korea, too?"

Noh answered, "I am very interested in discussing your selection method when we meet in person. I have learned enough about basketball to know that choosing winners with such precision requires insights into the complexities of the game that I am anxious to discover. As you can imagine, I am most curious about how such skills could translate to success in the City."

"Oh," the General exhaled, internally panicked. "I don't

know that I can, you know, explain—wait, in person? We're going to meet in person?"

"Yes, forgive me, I am ahead of myself. It happens that I will be flying out to the United States this weekend. I don't have to be on the eastern coast until later that night, so I set up a connection through Seattle so that I might stop in for a time at your KM Center. I had hoped that I could meet you and your tribal officers and witness your process in your own Tribal Room. I presume you will be there."

The General had to quickly suppress some shocked words. Instead, he said, "Oh, of course, absolutely. We're always here. Come by any time."

"I will be there at the Center at 11:50 AM, Seattle time. I look forward to it. For now, I have some things to attend to before I travel, so if you will excuse me…"

"Sure, yeah, I'll excuse—" and Noh shot straight up into the air like a comet and disappeared.

Perry stared silently into space for a while. He was replaying the scene in his head, and important details began to occur to him in reverse order. First, he realized that he had said, "I'll excuse you," which was moronic. Second, he wrapped his head around the idea that he had been noticed by the most powerful virtual environment designer on the planet for sports tournament guesses that weren't even meant to be real guesses. After two full minutes, the facts about Saturday's schedule clicked into place.

"Oh no," he whispered out loud to no one that could hear him. Noh's visit would change everything; all their plans for Saturday would need to be rethought. But the General didn't want to make an emotional decision. Good leaders didn't make emotional decisions. He was tempted to hold onto the news until he had a good plan, but he knew that he couldn't keep it to himself. He activated his comm link and summoned his officers back to reality.

When the General informed them that Noh was coming to visit. "Woah" was the least among a long series of exclamations from the group.

"So, I guess we're siding with the Ahtzon, then, right?" Killergremlin concluded.

"Why? I mean, not necessarily," said the General, slowly

coming back around mentally to his long-term ambitions.

"Stud, we can't go in with an illegal alliance, in public, with the freakin' Great Ahau literally looking over our necks. How would we do that?"

"Noh wouldn't stop us. I think he would let us do what we want. It's not like he's going to go report us to the Ahtzon."

"He wouldn't have to. Kaah Mukul is his city, and we still don't know anything about the Mascaab. We don't know if they're even in the city legally, and if they're not, then Noh could kick us all out without even thinking about it. He could ban us for life for no reason at all, and we wouldn't be able to do anything about it."

"Oh, please." The General was getting frustrated with his second-in-command's overreaction to the situation. "Look, I have it on good authority that Noh isn't going to interfere with the Mascaab situation. Besides—"

"Wait, what authority?" asked Killergremlin.

"A source," the General sneered. "He'll let us make our own decisions. And besides, he isn't coming because of what we're doing. He's coming because of my bracket."

"Huh?" said both of his officers.

"Typhoon150 said he had a line of contact to a deep Ahtzon source through these basketball brackets online. I told him what to write and he posted it under my name. Nothing happened with the code, and Typhoon is obviously MIA now, but the picks that were supposed to be part of the code turned out to guess all of the winning teams. It's all a big fluke, but Noh kind of thinks I'm a prediction genius now or something." He said the last part somewhat self-consciously, although he wondered if he shouldn't at least portray more pride. The officers seemed unimpressed.

"It doesn't matter," the General concluded. "For now, we have to focus on what to do about the Mascaab."

"Well," Killergremlin folded his arms, "I know you're the genius and all, but telling the Ahtzon is still the safer play. We get a reward, and we don't risk getting banned from Kaah Mukul."

Psychopedia nodded. "I agree. Going with the Ahtzon is better."

The General turned red, the corners of his mouth curving down as he exhaled through his nose. After some reflection, he had to agree that they were right: telling the Ahtzon was the safer play. But he didn't like doing the safe thing for safety's sake, and he really didn't like doing the safe thing under pressure. Nevertheless…

"OK," he said at last. "But we should wait to do it until just before the demonstration on Saturday."

"Why not just go now and save ourselves the time?" asked Killergremlin with an edge to his voice that the General didn't appreciate.

"Because," the General explained through gritted teeth, "we wouldn't get the reward unless it led to an arrest, and if the Ahtzon know about it too soon, they might move too quickly, the Mascaab might notice and cancel, and then we wouldn't have anything. We have to do it when we know that they can be caught, with them right in front of us." They all agreed. The discussion was over.

As Psychopedia began to categorically list all the questions that he had always wanted to ask Noh, the General's mind dwelt on how much he didn't like their situation. He continued thinking about tribes, alliances, dominance, and surprises for the rest of the meeting, on the way home, and while lying in bed. He finally drifted off to sleep having reached only two conclusions. First, he needed to exercise more authority within. Too many people were making decisions for him, and too many factors were forcing his hand. Killergremlin was getting out of line. He had to maintain control.

Second, he needed to do some research on college basketball.

[**West Division**: Elite Eight]
[Saturday, March 28]

Very early on Saturday morning, the General sat alone at the Tribal Room table, studying the dynamic table map. What they were planning to do, he now realized, was cowardly. It was the smart and logical move, but they were giving in to pressure when a bolder choice was on the table. It didn't sit right with him. Nevertheless, he had made his decision, and a good leader stuck to his decisions. Wasn't that right?

The chime from his e-mail box sounded. He glanced at his personal monitor. *Really?* he thought. After reading the message a few times, he slowly donned his mask and controls and descended into the northeast end of the city for an unexpected meeting.

On the outskirts of the walls of the Old City was an amateur Ullamaball court, a dusty, miniature street version of the big professional courts like the one in the Montezuma Arena. A few players were tossing the ball back and forth around the hoops, not very well, and they paid no attention either to him or the person he was meeting as they approached each other near a clump of palm trees just outside the tall, grey wall.

"Hey, Ohmen," the General greeted his old teammate cautiously. He stopped short when he noted that his former teammate was wearing red and white armor.

"You traitor! You joined the Scarmada?" He whipped out his gun to shoot Ohmen on the spot when four other Scarmada warriors surrounded him, gun barrels pointed at his head. The General kept his weapon up but didn't fire. He couldn't believe he had fallen into such a simple trap.

"Sorry for the ruse, Studblood," Ohmen said coldly. "I guessed that you wouldn't show up unless you thought I was still on your side. I have a message for you."

"OK," said the General, calculating the ways that he might be able to shoot, run, and survive.

"You aren't welcome in the Mascaab Alliance. We know you're interested, but don't bother. You can't join."

"Says who?" the General asked resentfully.

"Says the Scarmada. We're in, we're running it, and we've united enough tribes that we can be choosy about who else joins."

"I thought the Mascaab ran the Mascaab," said the General.

Ohmen scoffed. "The Mascaab leadership isn't interested in leading battles and coordinating alliances. They're in this for the money, not the power. The real leadership goes to whoever can actually unite the tribes in purpose. We're it. We've chosen who gets in, and we've chosen who stays out. You're out. You have no say in it."

The General stood there contemplating his former subordinate, desperately wanting to shoot him.

"I don't believe you."

"Of course not. You've never listened to me before. But the Scarmada wanted to warn you as a sign of respect to your seniority, so you wouldn't have to lose face later on. Someone of your experience could do well as one of the second-tier tribes in the city. You might even keep your DR in the top twenty."

The General opened his mouth to argue back, but stopped himself. This was a trick—a very obvious, uncreative trick—to keep him away from the Mascaab, but he wasn't exactly sure what was and was not true. Getting into a yelling match wouldn't do any good.

"So, why go through with this thing at the Montezuma if the tribes are already picked?"

"The introduction to the city is still necessary for establishing the superiority of our alliance and the inferiority of the rest of you. The whole city will be able to tell the difference by the end of the day."

"Then what's stopping us from going to the Ahtzon and telling them about you? You know they have a reward out."

Ohmen shrugged. "We know. Feel free to tell them what you want. We will allow you," he said, as aloof as a king granting a peasant's request. He turned away. "That's all. Have a good weekend, General."

The other four lowered their weapons and followed, leaving the General to think alone, bristling.

*   *   *   *

The Montezuma Arena was one of the must-see sites for first-time visitors to Kaah Mukul. The glistening exterior of the dome was stunning, but the best word that the General had for describing the interior was *seismic*.

The inside of the arena was much bigger than the outside—a little physics mischief by the game programmers—and entirely dazzling. The professional Ullamaball court itself was rectangular, surrounded by a high stone wall that slanted out at an angle on all sides, with two thick-rimmed, vertical hoops that jutted out towards the center court. At one end was a pair of doors from which the players entered for the game. At the other end was a single door, which opened into the tunnel that led up to the altar of the Central Temple. All of the big Ullamaball tournaments were single elimination. Many of the pro players had death tallies in the hundreds, which wasn't a big deal since that was the price they paid to be there. For the General and his tribe, the stakes of death were much higher, a fact which lingered in his mind.

The stands overlooking the court were formed by a long, single walkway that coiled along the elliptical interior, forming continuous tiers that were connected at regular intervals by long vertical stairways that sprouted from the center like spokes and ascended on all sides to the highest levels. Because no one ever needs to sit in a virtual world, there were no seats; the pathway allowed fans to move around the arena at will, or as much as the density of the crowds allowed. Fan bases established themselves in clumps of flags and team colors. Ahtzon officers wandered sporadically throughout the spectators. At this game, the crowds were unusually large, and the General noted a sizeable contingent of Ahtzon standing together in a section close to the floor, not far below where he stood. Halley was present in the platoon, just as the General had requested. At any time, the General could make his way down, report to Halley, and it would all be over. Maybe.

The General hadn't told anyone yet, but his meeting with Ohmen had prompted some internal debate about what had, just yesterday, been a final decision. He knew that he couldn't take Ohmen's threats at face value. The Scarmada were trying to play him, obviously. They didn't want him near the Mascaab. Why? Did they want him away from the arena altogether? Was it a power thing? Were they afraid he'd split the alliance, or worse, cut them out? He absolutely would, given the chance, and regardless of what happened in the arena that day, his second highest priority was making sure to put as many bullets as possible into as many Scarmada as possible. He was uneasy about not having the answers he wanted, but he was sure that he could outmaneuver anyone in the game. *No, not a game*, he corrected himself.

"Everybody in position?" the General called over his comm link, suddenly full of fire for things to get started. They had mustered every one of their tribesmen, all twenty-four of them, and had recruited a good deal more from across the arena for the hour. The possibility of fighting in a place like the Montezuma had made the request an easy sell, and he would see to it that they were all rewarded for their obedience. A good leader knew how to take care of those who fought for him.

"Everyone, we have less than sixteen…uh, fifteen minutes, so listen carefully," the General articulated dramatically. "Things will be happening quickly, and we need to strike fast and strike together when the time comes. Stay close to the officers at all times. Got that? You all ready to make this day go down in history?" He heard cheering through his headset, and then he felt a tap on his shoulder. His real shoulder. He jumped out of the city and removed his interface mask. The clerk was standing there.

"Stud, you have a visitor," the clerk announced. "Some Asian guy in a suit."

He's here. "Send him in!" The General cleared his throat and tapped on the shoulders of his counselors. It felt right, somehow, the creator of his whole world about to witness his greatest moment as a leader.

Myung-Ki Noh strode in with subdued ease, his hair looking slightly less wild than it appeared in his pictures, his body more compact and muscular than might be expected from a world-class software engineer. The General bowed slightly as Noh walked directly up to him and shook his hand. His officers handled the meeting with somewhat less poise. Noh graciously accepted all accolades, then addressed them smoothly and authoritatively.

"I don't want to interrupt you too much. Where are you now?" He took an empty chair while an imposing assistant placed a metal briefcase in front of him on the table.

"In the Montezuma," the General said, faltering a little at the nervous glances of his two officers. "We'd normally be, you know, patrolling our territory, but this is kind of a recon op."

"Excellent," Noh said, removing an interface that was more advanced than anything they had ever seen. "The tournament of Maak Suun is today. Who is playing now?"

The General drew a blank. Killergremlin spoke up just in time.

"Uh, the Dead Scourge just beat the Hobo Lobos. Really good game."

"That is unfortunate," replied Noh, "I had money placed on the Lobos." He donned his mask without another word, and the four descended back into the throbbing chaos of the virtual super-arena. Eight minutes until noon.

"Did you know our designers spent more time on Montezuma Arena than on any other aspect of the City?" Noh commented with some pride, his avatar standing beside the General and gazing out at the two teams that had just begun the next match. The General actually had known that. "It is designed to hold millions of people at a time, to host the largest worldwide gatherings in history. And this is just the beginning, what you see. I am proud of many things in Kaah Mukul, but I am most pleased that the arena has become a reality."

The General's mind raced back to Noh's interview and his own conversation with Killergremlin. "When you say that, do you mean like, it's a reality like how reality and Kaah Mukul interact? I heard the interview you gave in London. You were saying that about reality and art, right? Or about life and art? I was talking about that with Killergremlin, and we were trying to figure out if you were saying that stuff that happens in Kaah Mukul really happens in real life, like if this arena is a reality somewhere else?" By the time he had finished the sentence, he could tell that he sounded like an idiot, and he let his voice descend to an imperceptible mumble. Noh looked at him blankly for a solid ten seconds, then turned back to the Ullamaball game.

"I merely meant that I was pleased that we had executed the design for this arena. But I know what you are referring to. The real-world manifestations of what the Montezuma represents have yet to be seen, but they will appear—soon, I hope. In that interview, I was speculating about cases in Kaah Mukul that have interesting analogues with real life. You, for example." The General felt a sudden flush of self-consciousness. Fortunately, the faces of avatars didn't turn red. "You have been a tribal general for eighteen months, during which time you have won an impressive number of battles and earned a top five dominance ranking. I do not yet know if you carried that capacity with you into the city, or if you developed it because the city impelled you to develop it. More likely, the process is reciprocal. That is why I've taken such an interest in you, and why I believe that your remarkable basketball tournament picks are not entirely disconnected from your work in the Tribal Wars. There may be something special about you…" Noh's voice seemed to recede as the speech progressed deeper into his own thoughts, but he quickly reacquired his focus.

"Well, General Studblood, at the moment I have some things to do inside the arena for a project that I am planning. If I could leave you for a time, I will take care of my affairs and return to you later to finish our conversation. If you will excuse me…"

"Sure," said the General, flattered, confused, and relieved. He dwelt for a moment on the idea that the Great Ahau thought he was special, until he noticed the time. Three more minutes.

"Everyone set? It's almost time. Any minute now," the General broadcast to his officers.

"Where's Noh?" asked Killergremlin anxiously.

"He had to go do something. We're clear. Now we just have to find Tula. If you see her, get her to me."

Noon.

The General was approached from behind by a figure. He was surprised to see Tula dressed exactly as she had been at the Café. He gripped the holster of his gun and turned off his comm link to make sure no one else could hear what he was about to do.

"We are pleased that you are here for the demonstration, General Studblood. Have you and your tribe decided on membership with our organization?"

The General drew his weapon quickly and whispered harshly. "You have to answer one thing first. Did you promise leadership of the alliance to the Scarmada? Tell me now or I blow your head off."

Tula laughed, entirely undaunted. "Of course not. We have made no offers to anyone nor received any promises of allegiance prior to today." She stood close to him as he felt his real face go red. "Are you interested in leadership positions within the Mascaab? Opportunities exist, and we reward loyalty and effectiveness."

The General hesitated and felt himself sweating within his mask. Then he made a decision: a rash and potentially costly decision, but one that thrilled him. This was what great leaders did, he told himself. They decided.

"Yes, the Warriors of Tsepes will join the Mascaab alliance of tribes." The General remotely accessed the money from his personal account, drained it, and handed it over to Tula's outstretched hand.

Tula smiled. "Excellent. The rules are these. The Mascaab will begin an attack on all of the Ahtzon patrols in the arena simultaneously. You will be in position to attack the ones that are two tiers below. You will use this." From apparently nowhere, she produced a spear-like weapon, as long as a rifle, with a trigger button in the handle and an elaborate tip that looked like the open jaws of a beetle. "In one minute, go down to that patrol beneath us. We will have people watching you. If you attempt to betray us, or run away without fulfilling your duty, we will destroy your tribe. Understood?"

The General did not appreciate the threat but nodded that he understood. Tula nodded back before disappearing into the crowd. The General opened a channel to his officers and took a deep breath to fortify his resolve.

"Listen up, change of plans. I just made a deal to join us up to the Mascaab, and they gave us our first new weapon. Our assignment is to…"

"*What*?!" Killergremlin screamed into the headset. "Why? We decided *not* to do that, remember?"

"I changed my decision," said the General in as commanding a bellow as he could muster. His tolerance for insolence from Killergremlin was at an all-time low. "This is the best move. Now shut up and calm down." Without allowing for further argument, and there was definitely one coming, he opened a channel to the whole tribe.

"Listen up, everyone converge on my position right now. We're going to take out this entire squadron of Ahtzon on my mark." There was cheering and whooping from the warriors, and the General felt a surge of ambitious joy as he charged down to the Ahtzon contingent, his men behind him.

Some of the Ahtzon turned to look at him as he ran down, including Halley. He gave them no chance to pull out their weapons. With a wild yell, he raised the spear and activated it. Instantly, dozens of flaming blue darts shot out of the tip and sliced into the entire mass of Ahtzon like a swarm of steak knives, tracing curved, glowing paths in the air as they flew through and circled back in a frenzy. Everyone in the patrol was dead in a matter of seconds.

At that moment, the General knew he had been right. This weapon was for real, a treasure worth the price. He heard cries from the bewildered crowds as similar weapons were released on patrols throughout the arena. The game on the court stopped. The recruits of the Warriors of Tsepes let out a whoop and began to hunt down anyone that looked like a foe. Many in the stands began to flee while others cheered the unexpected spectacle of carnage.

The General felt an exhilaration he'd all but forgotten. He ran through the tiers, his spear burning in his hand as he sought single-mindedly for more Ahtzon to eliminate or Scarmada to punish. He relished every kill. There was no doubt that he had delivered, that this was his great moment. His mind raced through his ascension to the top of the alliance, a move that would dramatically change the balance of power between Atzon and Tribe forever. He thought of the look Ohmen would have on his face when he realized that his attempted threat had badly backfired. He thought of Myung-Ki Noh, wherever he was, who now had the assurance that the General was as unique as he had hoped. He thought of the morons at the clerk's office who would have been shocked to see him in his element, not the lazy, unproductive sloth—their words—that they had unfairly accused him of being. Maybe he would tell them.

A warning from Killergremlin snapped him out of his emotional high.

"The doors are closing! Everyone out of the building!" he

yelled. The General spun around and saw that the tunnel doors were indeed being sealed.

"Everybody out! Fall back!" ordered the General as he scrambled to the closest doors. But it was too late. The lighted symbol in his viewer made clear that everyone was marked; there could be no escape to reality. They had to stay and fight what was coming. "All Tsepsians, rally to me!" he called out. Raising his spear, he let loose his war cry. "No fear!"

The arena went silent. The lights and music stopped, the flash and pop of the Montezuma's special ambience disappeared. The Warriors of Tsepes rushed to consolidate themselves, using corpses to form makeshift trenches in the stands.

The sound of large, grinding machinery filled the arena. The hoops on the court retracted, the stone walls gave way, and the entire floor split in half. From underneath rose a platform the size of the court, covered with Ahtzon, more than the General had ever seen together. In the center of the army were four large artillery turrets, all pointed at the pockets of tribal warriors around them. The barrels of the turrets began to glow and seemed to release steady beams of light that joined in the center, becoming a blinding, ethereal pillar like some violent tear in the fabric of space. Standing transfixed, the General knew he had seen the light before. He couldn't remember where, but he felt intuitively that this light signaled something awful about to happen. He ordered himself to run, but found he was completely immobilized.

From below, the command came: "Fire!"

The turrets unleashed their barrage into the stands, four streams of instant death streaked with yellow flares. The legions of Ahtzon were unleashed into the stands under the cover of the guns and began to clear each tier. Those tribes that tried to wield their new spears against the onslaught were quickly mowed down.

The General found himself powerless. The Ahtzon were just one tier away, and there was no place to run. He called for a final attack, but no one answered. He crouched alone behind a stack of Ahtzon bodies, clutching the worthless spear. Things had gone so horribly wrong so quickly.

The Ahtzon came into view on his tier. He rallied himself for one final attack, raising the spear and knowing that as soon as he fired, he would be shot at. But there was nothing left to do. He ran at full speed toward the army. Then without warning, he was on the ground, shot from behind and above. His arms and legs no longer functioned. He lay still, alive but helpless as the squadron of Ahtzon passed behind him.

They were no sooner gone than someone came and turned his body over. Into his view came the face of a warrior wearing a Scarmada uniform. Ohmen. His voice sneered in glee.

"You made a choice. And it was bad. Now you have to pay for that."

As he spoke, two Ahtzon officers and the bearded face of the Scarmada leader also came into view. The General opened his mouth to yell, but the Ahtzon grabbed his body by the shoulders and dragged him away. From his earpiece, he could hear as the final shouts of Killergremlin and Psychopedia pronounced the end of the Warriors of Tsepes.

It was an act of utter, humiliating surrender for Perry to stay in his mask and watch as his broken body was solemnly dragged down to the floor of the court and through the tunnel that led to a columned walkway. From his compromised vantage point, the General could see the city of Kaah Mukul appearing between the columns, its metal, glass, and stone facades gleaming in the daylight. Then they were in an elevator, ascending to a platform high atop the Central Temple under an elaborately carved roof. Cameras were set up on either side to broadcast the proceedings to the viewing screens outside of the Montezuma, where people applauded the spectacular capture of those who had so vainly disturbed the tournament. The General's body was dropped onto a massive altar, facing up, and his chest armor was stripped off. A solemn, diabolical figure, an older man in a business suit, apron, and feathered headdress, approached the altar and looked down piteously. He spoke the name of General Studblood, accused him of sedition, pronounced him guilty, and plunged a shiny black dagger into his chest. The image around him began to lose clarity, and the last thing the General saw was his beating, disembodied heart held out for the entire city to see, and then his body being thrown off the altar and down the long, long steps of the temple to a pit under the sidewalk.

General Studblood was dead.

Perry removed the mask. He still felt immobilized, a passive observer to the destruction of what was, to him, his greatest achievement. Very slowly, he stood up from his chair and placed his gear in his duffel bag, beginning with the red and black bandana from his arm. Behind him, Killergremlin and Psychopedia pushed back from the table, both livid.

"Nice call, Stud. Really nice call. Why didn't you just do what we agreed to? We lost everything because of you. Now we have to start almost from scratch..." Perry ignored them and finished packing. Without a word, he walked out of the room with his head bent down and closed the door behind him.

He was passing the small Ullamaball amphitheater when he remembered Noh. He hadn't been in the room when Perry had left. He looked around for some sign of him, saw none, and ran out to the clerk.

"Went out that way fifteen seconds ago," the clerk said, not even looking up. Perry dropped his bag and ran out into the parking lot. Noh was getting into a sedan.

"Wait, wait. Wait," he puffed, jogging over to hold the door open. Mr. Noh seemed impatient.

"I'm sorry for your loss today, Mr. Lynwood," Mr. Noh responded. "But since there is nothing more to observe, I have to move on to other engagements."

"Wait, that's it? You come all the way over from Korea to watch me, and you take off after fifteen minutes without saying anything? You don't even want to ask me about basketball, like you were saying...?"

"Mr. Lynwood," Noh said abruptly, looking at him full in the face. "I came here because of curiosity and hope. I wanted to make sure that I did not exclude the possibility that you were the legitimate product of the city that I have been hoping for. But you are not. That was not entirely unexpected, but it was still disappointing. And now I must get to my plane."

"Wait, wait!" Perry was reeling so hard that he didn't know how to put his words together. "You're going to judge me on one bad call? That's not fair, Mr. Noh, totally not fair. You yourself said that I had potential. What about that speech you gave me a few minutes ago? I'm not dead, not in real life, and I'm still the same man I was before that happened. What about my bracket?"

"Is that really your bracket?" Noh asked, raising his eyebrows. Perry froze, then knew that he had waited too long to lie.

Noh sighed. "I thought not. I knew about that possibility when I came, but I had to be sure. Your record in the Tribal Wars, until today, had been impressive. You aspired to be a General, and to your credit, you became one. But from what I observed today, you are rather a pawn than a king."

"Now hold on," exclaimed Perry, his hands shaking. "I have been a great leader, you said so yourself, and you can't judge me based on one bad mistake. I still have a future."

Noh shrugged. "We are not guaranteed a future in life, Mr. Lynwood, we are just guaranteed a fate."

"How is that any different?"

"Fate is not in our hands. Time can be managed, inevitability cannot. My time is precious, your inevitability is…unfortunate. The city has shown us that."

"Come on, that art-in-life-in-whatever stuff doesn't apply to this. What just happened won't happen again. It's not like I'm going to get shot at the Montezuma a second time."

"Perhaps not," Noh shrugged. "I must go now. I wish you good luck with your bracket, Mr. Lynwood. You will need it, I suspect. I can think of no more visible hand of fate than a bracket, especially one that you didn't choose yourself." With that, Mr. Noh closed the door of the car and was driven off, leaving Perry in the parking lot alone.

*   *   *   *

That evening, after some driving, some drinking, and some taxi riding, Perry arrived home. He stood for a minute in the middle of the sparse and unkempt living room, then moved on to see the pile of dishes in his sink. He sat at his table and stared at a knife laden with a sticky skin of strawberry jam. Absently, he held the knife so that the tip was pointed into the table and let the handle swivel back and forth between his fingers. He thought about all the people and ideas he hated. He needed to go to sleep.

He retreated to his bedroom. His computer was still on. By force of habit and against the wishes of his exhausted body, he opened his e-mail and scanned his messages. He instantly wished he hadn't.

There, at the top of the list, was an invitation to an all-expenses-paid trip to Washington DC, to attend, by virtue of his miraculous bracket, a ball game in an arena.

[West Division: Final Four]
[Saturday, April 4]

Perry sat in his seat high up in the Verizon Center, wedged between the self-important CEO and the floppy-haired guy, and anxiously considered his situation.

He had not so much agreed to come as he felt compelled to come. In his darkest moments, he acknowledged that his life had imploded over the course of three weeks, and he had no reasonable explanation why. The border between fantasy and reality, it seemed to him, had become dangerously porous. It could be no coincidence that his final Kaah Mukul error had been to go to a sports arena and tempt fate, and in the same day, within mere hours, he was summoned to a sports arena to do the same thing in reality. He was sure that the resolution of his catastrophe would somehow occur over the course of this game. Why this was happening to him, he couldn't say. Noh's final words, like a curse on his soul, continuously echoed back to him. He realized how insane he would sound if he were to try and explain it. But a good leader...no, he was not a leader anymore. He wasn't anything anymore. All he had left was his name and, of course, his bracket.

In his hand, he held a printed copy of the cursed document. He had gone through it many times over the last week. At first, he was looking for the code that Typhoon150 had supposedly entered for him. After several days, he had personally confirmed that there was no code—not even the possibility of a code—embedded in the selections. It was no surprise that all of his e-mails to Typhoon's account went unanswered. He was sure that, like everything else that week, it had been a set-up, a trick to rob him. The Scarmada now dominated the Triabl Wars. Killergremlin was now the General of the depleted Warriors of Tsepes. Perry's former position at the clerk's office was filled by another. His house was at risk of foreclosure. The only thing he had left was the only thing he hadn't wanted, and it was going to end. And then what? There was no way to jump out of reality, no matter how surreal it was.

These were the thoughts that lingered in his mind like tar on his skin, difficult to shake even in his lighter, more lucid moments, when he laughed at himself for thinking that his fate was somehow tied to a fictional city in a computer or a piece of paper. There were no Ahtzon, no Scarmada, no temples or altars built for ripping out his heart. Surely, life's imitation of art had a limit. The worst-case scenario was that this would all be a waste of time. As for the bracket, he had done his homework. He knew that no one was giving Georgia much of a chance against a bigger, faster Nebraska team. He was probably bound to lose—*thanks for nothing, Typhoon150*—and he realized that he should embrace the inevitable, ease the anxiety about the unknowns in his life by accepting fate as it happened to him. But that thought didn't comfort him. Nothing truly comforted him.

The pregame introductions helped him understand that Nebraska was in white and Georgia was in red. He watched carefully, trying to remember what he had read about the players. There was an especially tall one who, he concluded, had to be the leader. He had always been good at picking out the leader.

The ball was tossed into the air, and the game began with a sense of instant acceleration. Both teams were nervous; balls clanked off rims more often than they went in. Perry tried to follow the patterns in the way each team defended or moved, but it went too fast. Each possession was different, although he noticed that Georgia often found ways to get the ball to the leader, who was always standing and pushing around opponents near the basket. That was smart, he thought. However, he also noticed that Nebraska seemed to make just as many baskets as Georgia, and the scoreboard confirmed it. By the end of the first half, the score was Nebraska 45, Georgia 46. He was winning.

A reporter came to them during half-time with questions. She addressed the tall, overly enthusiastic one first.

"Tucker, what do you expect out of your Nebraska team during this second half?"

"I'm happy with the way they're playing," he said, grinning so much that the two large red N's painted on both cheeks became illegible. "They've got no one who can guard my man 14, he's a beast, and Miller is playing out of his mind. I think they come back with some energy in this second half and finish it off." Then, with sudden, game-day-testosterone-fueled euphoria, he pointed both fingers in the air and yelled "Nebraska is Number One!" A host of Nebraska fans lower in the stands overheard and cheered their approval. The reporter high-fived Tucker, and the camera was turned onto Perry.

"Perry, Tucker seems pretty confident. What do you think about your Georgia going into the second?"

"Uh, well, they're up, right? I hope it stays that way." Some Georgia fans overheard and began a "Bull-dogs!" chant. Perry turned and gave them two half-hearted thumbs up, then put them down as if he wasn't sure that he'd done the right thing.

"You said it, Perry. It's anyone's game. We'll check in with you after the final buzzer." The camera went off, the reporter thanked them, and they left.

Perry checked his watch and excused himself to find the bathroom before the next half started.

The bathroom was crowded with rowdy basketball fans, but he found an empty stall and sat down to take some deep breaths. It was nice to finally have some relative quiet and solitude for a few minutes, regardless of how bad it smelled.

Alone with his own thoughts, he took stock of the game thus far. What he'd told the interviewer was true—they were up. Only by one point, one half of a basket, but winning was winning. And what the interviewer had said was also true—it was anyone's game. It could be his game. For the first time, it occurred to him that he might actually win. And with that thought, he began to feel a little silly for all the strange thoughts that he'd had leading up to the game. If he won, since he was the only one that had Georgia winning the championship, he would automatically take the Bracket Challenge if Georgia won in the Final Four. That meant a lot of money. He could move somewhere else. He could find a new city, a new game, a new team, he could start over. Not that there was anything like Kaah Mukul, but he could build his repertoire and reputation, maybe even attract some professional gaming endorsements. Things would work out.

He stood up, conscious that the bathroom had been getting progressively quieter over the past couple of minutes. As he did, his eyes met his blurred reflection in the metallic door of the stall. He could feel that his eyes were tired, over-stimulated. He rubbed them and reopened them. Suddenly, a glimmer of light appeared over the reflection of his forehead. It flashed and grew, completely silent, into a whitish-yellow pool of light that seemed to hypnotize him as he stared into it. He couldn't move. He fixated on it, as if there were nothing else in the world. The light grew brighter and brighter until it dominated his field of vision. And then it was gone.

He knew that light. The last time he'd seen it was in the Montezuma Arena, right before he died.

Movement came back into his limbs. He pushed the door, but it was still latched. His hands were too shaky to turn the lock, so he flung his shoulder into the door and lost his balance as he went through, slamming into the bathroom wall. A man washing his hands looked over and asked if he was alright. He raised his hand and mumbled that he was fine. But he wasn't. He was terrified and sweating. It smelled bad in there, like gasoline or drying blood. He looked above the stall to see if there was any kind of mirror or light source that could account for what he had seen, but he saw nothing.

Think, think, he told himself as he washed his hands and wiped his face. He looked pale in the mirror, and inside he felt haunted. *There must be an explanation.*

He walked outside and nearly crashed into a pedestrian. Everything looked normal, but not normal at the same time. Something was off. That light shouldn't have happened. That light only existed in Kaah Mukul. Reality was not Kaah Mukul. Life couldn't imitate *that* art. And he knew from experience that the light had a terrible meaning.

In the concourse, amidst the crowds, he looked around for some anchor on which to secure his sanity, some pure product of reality. He saw the concession stand. Food! Food could only be real. Hot dogs and pretzels and fats and oils; there was nothing so tangible. He got in the long line and searched for his wallet with shaking hands.

It will all be OK, he repeated in his mind, looking around.

There were carts with people selling t-shirts and merchandise. There was music and balloons and little kids holding plastic basketballs with Final Four logos on them. A small commotion started when a group with suits came up the elevator guarding someone in sunglasses. A few people began snapping pictures with their phones. Some celebrity. There was a non-descript door embedded in the concourse entryway that opened out onto the escalators. The door was opened as the celebrity approached. From between the bodies in the crowd, he made out a face, and a mane of spiked hair.

It was Myung-Ki Noh.

Perry jumped out of the line and ran towards the man. "Noh! Noh!" he called. The man he thought was Noh disappeared and the door shut behind him. Perry ran up but was stopped cold by a security guard. They wouldn't let him pass. Perry resisted, yelling Noh's name while the guards tried to calm him down. He tripped and fell on his back. When he looked up, he saw a large man with red hair standing over him.

"What's going on?" the man asked authoritatively.

Perry said nothing, just put up his hands, rolled onto his stomach, and stood up, slapping away any helping hands. He walked off mumbling apologies and returned to the bathroom. He entered the same stall that he'd used before and closed the door. The reflection in the stainless-steel door showed no ominous lights, merely his own pale, damp reflection.

His mind gyrated in seemingly endless loop. *Arena. Bracket. Noh. Ahtzon. Life. Art. Fate...Arena...Bracket...* He laid his head against the door, closed his eyes, and rested.

In what seemed a moment to him, he came to. He looked around to reorient himself. What time was it? He checked his watch. When he saw the time, gasped, then raced out of the bathroom and straight through the short tunnel into the arena. The clock on the Jumbotron confirmed that he had somehow missed most of the second half. Scrambling, he spun around until he remembered where his seats were. He scrambled over the knees of the irritated CEO and the floppy-haired guy and sat down, ignoring the questions about where he had been. There were five minutes left to play. The score was now Nebraska 72, Georgia 63.

He couldn't understand what was happening. The players were the same ones that had started the game. They weren't injured. They looked like they were doing the same things. But something unseen had changed, there was this imbalance now. As he watched, he became more and more frustrated by Tucker's persistent clapping and hooting on his right and Cole's more subdued cheers on his left. Couldn't they tell that something was wrong? Couldn't they see that his team was not playing normally? They should be nervous— everyone here should be nervous.

He looked around, squinting, at all the lights. It was too loud, too bright inside. His head hurt. Cheers rang out as a Nebraska player hit another three-pointer. He realized that they were really cheering against him. The imbalance was against him.

He looked around again. The people in the audience seemed to blur together; all he could see were the rows. The lines of seats became tiers that looked familiar, bigger. He looked down at the players on the court. It was hard to tell what was going on, but he could make out a ball and running. There were hoops, and as he watched, they rotated until they were vertical and thickened. He found himself trying to remember when he had returned to the Montezuma, and he thought how strange it was that Nebraska and Georgia had their own Ullamaball teams. Maybe Mr. Noh had done it.

By this time, the crowd was standing, cheering, and all Perry could think about was what would happen if he lost. The pattern would repeat, Noh had said. Fate. Noh knew.

He looked at the stairs by his seat and saw a woman in black running up past him. Why was Tula running? The game wasn't over yet. But he looked, and his team was losing. Maybe that was why. She had to get out before the Ahtzon came. Smart. Tula always seemed smart. It would be smart to leave right away too, he thought.

The Nebraska fans began to count down from ten. Something was wrong. He had lost, he knew that. He looked around the arena and could see the Ahtzon standing, poised to mow down the losers that tried to escape, waiting patiently for him at the exits. The floppy-haired kid was tapping him on the shoulder, asking him if he was OK, but he didn't answer. They had to get out before the doors closed, didn't they? A good leader knew when to run. The crowds were counting down.

3...2...1..!

Perry pushed out from the seats and shoved by the others as he ran up the stairs to the tunnel. He had to get out before they closed. Someone was calling his name and he heard heavy footsteps.

The Ahtzon were coming. He shouldered past exiting crowds and through the tunnel. He was out! But they were still chasing him, and when he yelled for Killergremlin to send back-up, he heard no response.

He saw some stairs, long and tall and moving. The way out! He made it to the top and looked down and around for his next move. The stairway below him was black and gleaming, and suddenly he realized that he wasn't out. He was at the top of the Central Temple. If he were caught, he would be sacrificed. Someone grabbed him from behind. He wheeled around and saw a big officer gripping him on the shoulder. No! He struggled and writhed, but he was too close to the edge and felt the rails sliding against his back like a snake. He spun wildly and felt his back flip over the edge as hands tried to clasp onto him, but gravity had him. His entire mass flipped over, and then, in a moment of horrifying clarity, he understood that he was falling very far.

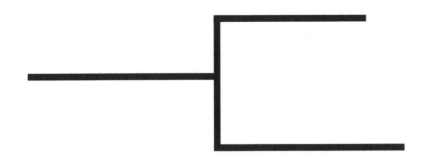

South Division

[South Division: Play-in Game]
[Wednesday, March 18]

Georgetown University's administration building stood grey and stark against the winter-white sky, an intellectually gloomy cathedral. The grassy area to the east, with its bare trees and a promise of shade in warmer months, hosted a small park bench. Sitting on the bench, eating handfuls of salted peanuts with gloved hands, was an unsmiling older man in a baseball cap. The man could have been a professor or administrator, and thus he attracted no notice from the huddled students moving between buildings. It was a skill that he had conscientiously nurtured: to be unimportant to a crowd but to command rapt attention from an individual. That day, the individual whose attention Mr. Graham wanted to command was named Carla.

Carla emerged from behind the grey building wrapped in a wool trench coat. She walked with her head erect while others were bent against the cold. She walked like someone who had been trained early to march under pressure. Graham waved discreetly to draw her attention.

"You're Graham, right?" she began without overture, removing something black from her pocket. "So, here it is. Like I said, it's a little scratched, but it still…"

Graham interrupted, his voice as even and quiet as a therapist. "Carla, I'm going to disappoint you right now and say that I don't want to buy your phone."

Carla paused, her hand instinctively going back to her pocket. "What?"

"I answered your ad so I could meet you here and offer you a job. Unless you think Langley is really paying you what you're worth."

Carla's eyes flashed with momentary consternation that few would have noticed behind the perfect poker face. "I think you have the wrong woman. I'm a freshman—"

"Just a note, for the future," Graham interrupted. "When you lie to someone who already knows the truth, it's a mutual waste of time. From what I hear about you, you aren't the kind of person that has much time to waste."

Carla looked at him cautiously. "And what have you heard about me, Mr. Graham?"

"That you're smarter than the above average Georgetown student, that your analysis of the Many Hands operation in Bangladesh turned out to be better than accurate, and that you're here taking college classes not because you actually need college, but because you work for a federal institution that pays you only what your diploma says you're worth. Or was all of that just gossip?"

Carla looked around again, checking individual faces as they passed. "If you're asking me to do something illegal…"

"I'm not asking anything. I'm offering. I'm offering you a chance to reach your potential. The organization I work for doesn't care about degrees, doesn't care about résumés, doesn't even care about money. It's a place where you can actually tell people what you think and it can go all the way to the top without the, ah, 'incessant trumpet of politics making everybody deaf and stupid.' Those are your words, right? Come work for us. You want to do analysis, fine. You want to be a spook, the kind they would never let you try to be, that can be arranged. There are no limits. And, if you agree right now, we'll reimburse you the cost of your tuition."

Carla studied her feet. "You know, the Agency is paying for this."

"I don't think I would need to mention that detail to our accountants."

Carla continued to scan nervously. "You don't just leave the CIA, especially not for mysterious reasons."

"Tell that to all the ex-CIA guys making six figures in the private sector. The Agency knows they can't compete with that. Just tell them you got a better offer with a private company. It will make them mad, but by the time you walk out the door, they'll be cursing the back-handed slap of capitalism instead of you. Just another big one that got away. We can make sure that we back it up with some legitimacy."

The recruit stared at him. "Are you offering me six figures?"

Graham raised an eyebrow. "Not to start, but you do a good job, you contribute, there's room for some upward mobility."

Carla shuffled again. "Twenty-four hours to think, and I want a full job description e-mailed to my account tonight."

Graham retrieved a mostly-blank business card and gave it to Carla. "When you decide, give me a call. Your first job is already waiting. You have your twenty-four hours, but don't use them all."

Carla began to walk away, slowly this time. She stopped after a few feet.

"So, why not just call and say that you wanted to meet with me? You know that even clandestine people like me can set up appointments."

"We wanted you to know how important we think you are to the long-term progress of our group." Graham glanced up at the gothic spires of Healy Hall. "It's a competitive world out there; the most successful recruiters are the ones that stand out. And as I've recently re-discovered, we are not the only ones recruiting."

Carla nodded, reached into her pocket for the phone, and lobbed it hard to Graham, who caught it reflexively. "You can add the twenty bucks to my signing bonus," Carla said, and walked away.

Graham also stepped away from the bench, the barest hint of a smile on his face, and began the long walk back to his car, dialing on his own phone as he went. It was time to give his superiors some good news. On the way out, he tossed Carla's phone into the chest of an oncoming student. Grabbing his coat around him, Mr. Graham walked away without looking back. It was starting to get windy.

[**South Division**: First Round]
[Friday, March 20]

The spacious lobby of the Corazon Resort on South Beach was sumptuously opulent. The board room, however, was bland, decorated only with an oversized watercolor of a coconut. Neeson Faulkner stood at the head of the table in the board room, a laser pointer in hand, mentally rehearsing the presentation that he was about to give. A projector beamed the slowly-moving image of a sailboat on the screen behind him. The boat oscillated up and down on the waves, noiselessly, the sail taut with a full, harnessed ocean breeze. Above the boat was an elegant corporate logo: *WindSkin*. The board room windows were open, and the sound of real ocean waves crashing just outside enhanced the projected image. Neeson practiced underlining the logo with his laser, going just slowly enough to permit vocal enunciation with all the necessary gravitas. He knew how important it was to hook them from the very beginning.

When the door to the board room opened and several individuals in expensive business attire entered, Neeson approached to give courteous and confident handshakes all around. The last to enter was Lance Reynolds, owner and CEO of the Corazon Resort, who was wide in the gut and the grin. He wore a string tie with the state flag of Texas on the collar piece. He shook Neeson's hand as if auditioning for an arm-wrestling match.

"Good to finally meet you in person, Dr. Faulkner," said Lance. "I look forward to your presentation. And who are you over there?"

Neeson turned to the younger man who had been standing quietly near the table's edge, looking uncomfortable in a tie but otherwise taciturn. "This is Dr. Jason Spade, WindSkin's chief engineer and the mastermind behind our proprietary software."

"How're doin'?" Lance asked, leaning over the table to shake.

"Just fine, sir." Spade responded.

"Where you from, Dr. Spade?"

"Star Valley, Wyoming."

"I thought I heard a kindred tongue. Not as strong as a good Texas accent, but still nice to hear. Good grip, too. That's a good sign." Lance made his way to his chair at the other end of the table. "OK then," he said as he sat down with a grunt. "Let's hear it!" Neeson took his preferred place to the right of the screen, gripped the laser pointer, and began.

"Energy independence," Neeson began, pacing himself with well-rehearsed poise, "has been the most sought-after commodity for big businesses for the past decade. Getting off the grid has a number of perks, not the least of which is financial. Most never get there because they don't know how, or they believe it to be impossible for any single business or hotel. But affordable, practical energy independence is attainable. It's here, at WindSkin." The red laser slid under the company name like a caress.

Neeson advanced to a slide showing a slick rendering of the massive Corazon Resort against the backdrop of the city and ocean. It was altered so that dark bands were interspersed vertically over the entire façade, like stripes.

"This," Neeson said with pride, "is your hotel with the most cutting-edge energy-generating structural overlay ever designed. Attractive and manageable, the overlay will also provide you with 95% energy independence forever. During the normal, sunny days in Miami, WindSkin is merely the most effective solar panel system on the market. But our product gets its name for what it does when the sun don't shine."

The slide switched to the recognizable space-eye-view of a hurricane swirling over the Florida peninsula.

"Hurricane season is usually a time to shut down, board everything up, and gas the back-up generators, just in case. But with WindSkin, every hurricane becomes your personal generator." The room was captivated. The hurricane picture always got them.

"You see, hurricanes are the most powerful storms on the planet. A single storm produces enough energy to power most of the country. Unfortunately, all of that energy is wasted on destroying palm trees and billboards. WindSkin will allow you to harness just a small part of that power. While most places are bracing, your hotel will be breathing."

The hurricane disappeared; in its place, a video of a single

WindSkin panel installed in a wind tunnel. As the panel opened, two digital meters in the corner showed wind speed and total amperage produced. A thin stream of white mist billowed up to show the trajectory of the powerful wind over the panel as the speed meter reached 152 mph. While everyone was focused on the video, Jason opened a briefcase and removed a small cross-section of the panel, the layer of photovoltaics on top and the array of cylindrical microturbines underneath. He handed it to Neeson, who stopped the video and called everyone's attention.

"This is WindSkin in the flesh, so to speak." He smiled with the group at the pun, as he always did.

A board member on the side muttered, "It looks so delicate."

Neeson heard. "I assure you, ma'am, these are tough machines. Each panel is individually capable of generating a current during wind speeds up to and including those produced by a Category 5 hurricane. The output of the panels in a hurricane is three times that of the panels in the sun. We will fit your resort with hundreds of these panels, all networked to our custom management software known as OPUS, which will analyze wind speed and solar output to identify the optimum state for each panel and maximize the electricity produced. One hour of sunny day with a typical ocean breeze will yield enough energy to operate your entire resort for the day. A half-hour of hurricane-force winds, you could store enough energy to operate for at least a week."

Neeson put down the cross-section and spoke as if making a personal plea. "What we are offering you is a technology that will eliminate your electric bill *forever*. You can do the math on how much money you'll be saving, but I guarantee you that whatever the number is, you can use 100% of it for the development of your hotel, or, even better, for the fund supplying your annual bonuses."

The board members laughed. Hurricanes plus real money equals sales.

"OK, very impressive," said Lance. "But seriously now, let's talk about aesthetics. Is this stuff going to block my windows? My clients aren't comin' down to Florida to look at the inside of a bunch of solar panels."

Neeson shook his head and returned to the picture of the hotel. "As you can see from our rendering, WindSkin doesn't cover the entire building. We can work with your engineers to design an ideal network that suits you and the tenants. We can even adjust the color within limits. Don't worry; your guests will still have that romantic sunrise."

Come on, I dare you to give me a hard question, Neeson gloated inside. He had them, he could tell. He wondered how he could have wasted so much time in business school when selling was so easy.

"Now," Lance said, leaning back in his chair, "my understanding is that this technology you're selling isn't totally up to code yet. What is your exact status?"

Neeson glanced inadvertently at Jason before answering. "Make no mistake, we have the technology. But to meet state and national regulatory requirements, we are actively measuring the performance of our panel networks at hurricane velocities back at our headquarters. It's more a formality than anything."

"Huh." Lance narrowed his eyes, unimpressed. "Pretty big gamble to come in selling a product that isn't market ready, ain't it?"

Neeson shook his head. "It's only a gamble if you don't know the outcome. I have full confidence that we can do what I say we can do. I'll be honest, it's a royal pain that the only thing standing between us and full-scale production of our product is a bureaucratic obstacle course. I'm sure you know what that's like."

"I do," Lance said, unconsciously rubbing over his ulcers. "So we have some time to consider things. We'll talk about it internally and get back to you should we decide to move forward." He stood, and most of the board stood with him. "I would like our architect to sit down with you and ask you the more technical questions. Y'all know Haj Hitok?"

"We know of him," Neeson said. "We would consider it a pleasure to work with someone of his reputation."

"Good. I'll set you up. In the mean time, you get all those hurdles jumped. If we decide to go forward, I want you guys up and running without worrying about tripping on red tape."

"I completely understand. I can personally guarantee our full compliance." Neeson beamed confidence as Lance nodded his appreciation, grinned his Texas grin, and left the room. His entourage of board members followed in a line, some pausing to shake hands. Neeson watched all of them carefully, trying to read their thoughts. In a minute, the two WindSkin executives were left alone.

"Whad'ya think?" Jason asked as he packed up the panel display.

"I think we've got a sale, if we can just convince Hitok."

"Yup," Jason said. He packed in silence for a while. "You know, I still don't know why you bring me to these things if you won't let me talk."

"If I had known that he'd consider your drawl a good omen, I would have given you the whole script to read. I told you before, having you here makes them comfortable, gives us that extra boost of technical credibility. That really is important."

"You have told me that," Jason sighed. "Now what?"

"Now," Neeson said, "we deliver."

*   *   *   *

A giant fan began to rotate with a low, throbbing hum. Slow at first, it picked up speed gradually until the individual blades merged in a blur of glinting grey. The wind barreled down the cement tunnel toward an angular tower of metal and glass as tall and wide as a van standing on its end. Bright pieces of yarn tied strategically around the top and sides of the tower lifted and vibrated erratically in the air, dancing with the deafening roar of strong wind and whirring machinery. Full-strength simulation #16 had begun.

From the opposite end of a thick viewing window, Neeson was watching. He stood straight and calm, refusing to give any attention to the technicians and the computer models. He had eyes for the tower alone.

"50," called one of the technicians. The tower was covered with WindSkin panels on every side, each one absorbing the powerful UV lamps shining down on them. As the wind began to pick up, individual panels to the left and right of the windward side began to crack open at acute angles. They were sampling the power of the air, tasting it, swallowing it down, sending the data back to the computers in the observation room.

"75," came the call again. The entire windward wall and two of the side walls now had panels open. It looked jagged, like a steel bird with ruffled feathers. Neeson didn't move. They weren't even close yet. This was barely a Category 1 hurricane.

A single green light turned on over the window. Energy generation was maximized and everything was working beautifully. He had once volunteered to stand in the wind tunnel at speeds approaching 90 miles per hour. It had knocked him flat onto his back on a safety mattress. The tower, though, was still standing strong.

"100." He could hear a faint creaking noise. Neeson widened his eyes a little but didn't look around to see if anyone else was worried. Someone would let him know if they were outside acceptable limits. This was where the test really began.

"125." The creaking became louder. All of the flaps on three sides, and some on the fourth, were open now. He began to mentally shout messages to the tower. *Hold on or close up!* The mechanical roar of the fans and the dull vibration of the tunnel itself became so loud that it was hard to hear anything else. The technicians were all yelling at each other just to be heard. *A little bit more…*

There was a sharp crack. One of the panels on the left wall blew straight back. It was broken on part of the hinge, and the thin hydraulic pistons were now rattling against the sides. The panel twisted and warped in the wind until the hinge broke off and the panel flew back and away.

"Where is the safety?" Neeson yelled, his gaze still unmoved. Only the shouted word "failure" was distinguishable above the din.

In a matter of seconds, it seemed that every panel on the windward side snapped back like cheap umbrellas. There was a sickening, squealing groan as the panels peeled away. The electrical guts of the tower were exposed and punished as its protective skin was torn apart by the impossible fury of the wind. A red light came on by the window, blinking in rhythm over the haphazard yelling of the technicians.

"Turn it off! Turn it off!" Neeson shouted without needing to. Too late, the brakes for the fan took hold and the wind subsided. In a few minutes, the hurricane was reduced to a mild breeze.

Neeson looked at his tower, now a twisted and mangled mess surrounded by a comet's tail of debris on the floor. He swallowed down his frustration with deep breaths.

"How far did we get?" he yelled.

"130 miles per hour," came the answer. Just twenty away from the target. Coming so close to victory was painful, much more than when they were completely failing during the prototype phases.

Neeson heard the clomp of boots on tile coming up behind him. Eyes still on the tower, he asked without turning, "What happened?"

"Workin' on it," said Jason. "Looks like the failsafe never did kick in." Neeson finally turned to throw a contemptuous look at the youngish, gangly engineer in the tucked-in plaid shirt. Among the engineer's many idiosyncrasies was his ingenious eloquence in stating obvious things.

"Why?" Neeson asked.

"I dunno. Software issue, probably."

"I doubt that," Neeson said immediately. "OPUS itself works fine. It has to be the local motor interface or the output portal. I need to know for sure by this afternoon. I can't go back to Corazon with a wind test that fails miserably at 125."

Jason cleared his throat. "You know, it could just be the panels really aren't up to this."

"They've done it before."

"One panel. Once. Now we got a hundred panels running multiple times? I'm just sayin'."

"I hear what you're 'just sayin,'" Neeson hissed. This was not the first time that they had had this argument, and Jason still hadn't learned to let it go. "These panels work. The software works. Something very simple is wrong. Can you fix it or not?"

Jason nodded slowly. "I'll head back up to the office and take a crack at it, unless you want to take a look at it yourself."

Neeson put up his hand. "This problem is yours to fix. And fast. I want another test on Saturday afternoon."

Jason scratched his forehead. "You want us to rebuild the test tower in less than two days, and you want them to come in on the weekend? That's asking a lot, Neeson."

"This is crunch time, Jason. We need good numbers now for this company to survive. We needed them last week. Tell them it's the price to pay for any future bonuses, not to mention salary. They'll understand."

"I doubt that, but I'll tell 'em." Jason walked away and went into the tunnel to break the news to the technicians who had just begun to autopsy the wreckage.

Neeson also walked away, turning his back on the gesticulating men and heading out of the control room, down the hallway, out the door, and into the humid Florida afternoon. He put his hands on his hips and lowered his head, feeling sweat accumulating along his hairline. He had heard that everything north of South Carolina was still really cold. That sounded good to him just then.

The wind tunnel facility had been built in the far corner of the booming business park known as Chlorophyll Valley, conveniently close to the WindSkin Corporation's headquarters. Dozens of green energy start-ups had set up camp there after state funding had made the undeveloped land a haven for alternative energy companies. The boom had been good timing for the WindSkin founders; it gave them access to connections and facilities that they wouldn't have had otherwise. Neeson looked over to his office on the second floor of a brick building atop a hill that was barely a hill. The WindSkin logo reflected brightly just above his window. Then he looked around at the other buildings within eyesight. They would all be part of the massive takeover he had planned for the next few years. If, of course, he could step over the one small, maddening, unidentifiable technical glitch blocking his way. His phone rang. He retrieved the headset from his pocket and placed it in his ear.

"Faulkner speaking," he said.

"How are things, Mr. Faulkner?" It was a familiar voice that always gave Neeson the mental image of a body being dragged across a frozen pond at nighttime.

"I'm fine, Mr. Graham. What can I do for you today?"

"I was wondering how your test went. Successful?"

Neeson cringed. "It was encouraging."

"I see," said Mr. Graham. "Hardware or software?"

"Hardware," he said without skipping a beat. "A weak panel at the 125 mark, probably affected some surrounding panels. Nothing that a good wrench wouldn't fix."

"Oh, well, then 'encouraging' is definitely the right word.

Are you running more tests?"

"As soon as we process the whole diagnostic," said Neeson. "We want to be thorough."

"Fine," Graham said, ending that topic. "I was pleased to see that your other demonstration is going well. Predicting the whole first round is very impressive."

"I'm glad you noticed."

"If this keeps working, then I see a very bright future for your company."

"Thank you, Mr. Graham." Neeson permitted himself a quick exhale of relief.

"That 'if' is important, remember."

"I'll deliver."

"Any sign that your partner knows what you've been doing?"

"Jason? No. He's a technical wizard and very creative, but I don't think there's an ounce of paranoia in him."

"Fine," Graham said. "Keep it that way. I'll catch up with you next week."

Neeson put the phone away and went back inside with a sigh to make sure the techs weren't whining about their weekends being taken over. It was up to him to keep control.

[**South Division**: Second Round]
[Saturday, March 21]

Neeson considered his reputation as a workaholic to be his greatest executive asset. He could demand hard work because everyone assumed he would work harder. His employees felt safe because the founder of their company was always vigilant. However, if they knew how little he thought about WindSkin when he came in at 5 AM, their opinion of him would be different. But being at the office that early, especially on a Saturday, ensured that no one ever found him out. As sunlight crept over the buildings and palm trees of Chlorophyll Valley, he sat alone: just himself, a cup of coffee, and OPUS.

By his reasoning, it was important to the company that he push OPUS to the limit of its capacity. What he was doing wasn't research *per se*; he had decided to call it an 'executive innovation initiative'. He had realized some time ago that OPUS could do more—much more—than control a panel grid. With a few custom algorithms, some innocent thievery of other programs, and some flashes of ingenuity in which he took genuine pride, OPUS had become a dream machine. Though his employees didn't know it, his initiative with OPUS had already saved the company once. With patience and discretion, he planned to propel the company far beyond the scope of green energy, into every facet of life. For Neeson, it had been a long time since his plans for the WindSkin Corporation had been limited to WindSkin.

At that moment in the morning, OPUS was all his. He opened his stock trader program on one monitor, his e-mail on the other, and leaned back in his chair. He deleted junk mail while the stock program made its complicated calculations. By doing e-mail, he could truthfully say that he had been working that morning. Not that anyone would call him on it. It was his company, after all. The very rules governing use of the OPUS servers had been dictated by him. To his thinking, access to OPUS was his right, though it was a right that should, for a time longer, be kept secret from the man who had created it.

The program was complete in ten minutes. Neeson's

investment portfolio was automatically updated based on the projections of OPUS, which confidently foresaw an increase in total value of 0.7% by the end of the day. Neeson smiled. For further gratification, he logged in to the ESPN site on his other screen and looked at his bracket, pristine after a complete first round of games.

These two programs represented his most elegant and successful experiments. When he'd realized that OPUS could be exploited outside of energy management, he tried and failed at a few forays that ranged from banal to dramatic. There were last year's mid-term elections, but everyone knew the outcome of those months in advance. He tried predicting box office numbers, but that didn't prove interesting. He tried to predict the movements of the seemingly random Wall Street arsonist, but there wasn't enough data to do anything practical. OPUS did best when given mountains of data.

It finally occurred to him that sports offered the greatest opportunity to show what OPUS could do, though it took some time for him to discover the ideal application. He found decades of highly detailed statistics for every sport he knew, all gathered by fanatics and professionals, all freely available online. Aggregated in the right way, the data was perfectly digestible for OPUS. But it wasn't enough for Neeson to just predict outcomes of individual games. Anyone could do that. He had to do something that had never been accomplished before. The idea of attempting to predict a March Madness bracket came to him at the end of November while he was watching a game at home. It was so obvious that it was thrilling to finally discover it. He had spent all that night, then all that next week and the weeks after, drafting the program and mining the data. He tested four years' worth of tournaments trying to get it right, feeding it all the stats that preceded Selection Sunday. Then he had sat back in nervous anticipation as OPUS worked for several solid hours before announcing victory. The accuracy of the output had been shocking. It had even called the 2011 Butler-Pittsburg game even though the outcome of the actual game had been thoroughly unpredictable. With some additional data sets and tweaks, the computer finally spit out the perfect brackets 90% of the time for any year of the past two decades. And, as he saw that morning, it had correctly predicted the entire first round of 2015.

Neeson sipped his coffee and spun away lazily from his monitors to look at the rising sun now in view through his window. WindSkin may have been his baby, but OPUS was his mistress. As for the stock market program, well, that was just a nice personal retirement plan. Nothing wrong with that. It wasn't something that Graham needed to know about.

By 6:45 AM, the sun was fully up and OPUS was off. Neeson had shut down his session on the server and moved on to the ordinary, tedious, anxiety-inducing tasks of running a start-up. At 7:00 AM, he received a phone call.

"Dr. Faulkner, this is Haj Hitok. I apologize for the early call. I believe Mr. Reynolds told you that I would be checking in."

"Yes, Haj, I was looking forward to hearing from you." Neeson's VIP voice was ready at hand no matter what time of the week it was. "We'd like to set up an appointment for you to come down and see…"

"Neeson, the reason I'm calling is that my schedule has had some changes, and it happens that I will be in the Miami area today only. Forgive me for the late notice, but I was wondering if I could visit your facility today?"

"Oh, well…" he scrambled to look over his calendar. "Well, I'm free any time before 1 PM. This afternoon we'll be down in the wind tunnel running tests, so…"

"Actually, that sounds ideal. I would like to see WindSkin in action. So it wouldn't be a problem if I came this afternoon?"

Neeson bit his lip and cursed himself for mentioning the wind test. "Absolutely. We'll look forward to seeing you then."

"Excellent. I will be at your office at 1:00. Thank you."

When the call ended, Neeson took a moment to breathe, check the clock, and strategize. Then he called Jason.

"It ain't even 8:00 in the morning yet," Jason answered groggily.

"Are you on your way?"

"I'm in the car, though I'd rather not be up at all. What's up?" Neeson explained Haj's call and heard Jason sigh over the phone. "Well," he said, "I kinda wish you hadn't of done that."

"Well I kind of wish I hadn't of either, but it's done," Neeson growled. "What's the status on the diagnostic?"

"Best I can tell," Jason diagnosed like a car mechanic, "OPUS either locked out the failsafe or just failed to initiate it. All the redundancies never activated either. Must be some kind of glitch in the load-sharing program. It was like they didn't actually want to deactivate. Like the panels got too greedy."

"You didn't program OPUS to be greedy," Neeson replied evenly.

"I programmed OPUS to be power hungry. That's pretty much the same as greedy."

"Jason," Neeson was losing his cool now. "It's a program. It does what we say. The fact that it isn't operating the basic safety protocols isn't a problem with the core of OPUS. That's a problem with the way the safety protocols were programmed. It can't be that hard. You need to get everybody rechecking the failsafe subroutines for the glitch right now."

"We've been on it," Jason replied after a silence in which Neeson could almost hear him rolling his eyes. "But the problem seems pretty well hidden in there. I can't guarantee that we can find it in time to be sure it will test well. And even if we fixed the problem, I can't guarantee that something else won't happen."

Neeson knew he was right. "OK," he declared, "we'll do this. We'll take the test only up to 110 and tell him that was the objective. If, for some reason, he wants to see us push the limits, we'll bring it up to 130. But I want you to install a manual failsafe, independent of OPUS, that will kick in at 115. WindSkin shuts down, all panels close automatically, everything powers down."

"Isn't that cheating?" Jason asked. Neeson cringed at his young engineer's completely naïve view of the world.

"Why? It's close to what WindSkin should be doing anyway. Going up to 110 will be a completely satisfactory test. And Haj is only here to inspect. A successful test will buy us time. It might even buy us a substantial sale with money up front, which will allow us to get it right. This is the way it has to be. Can you do it?" Neeson stood with his hands on his hips. He imagined that talking to Jason was like talking to a teenaged son.

"Yup." Jason hung up. Neeson ripped his headset off and began to pace the room.

*   *   *   *

At 1:02 PM, a car arrived at the front entrance of WindSkin. A sharply dressed man emerged from the back seat with a thin briefcase.

"Welcome," Neeson smiled widely, showing no sign that he had been waiting outside for ten minutes. He escorted Haj to the golf cart that would take them to the wind tunnel facility. On the way down, he pointed out the more interesting sites of Chlorophyll Valley while trying not to think about worst case scenarios. Haj made the task easy—as they drove up, he took special interest in the architecture of different testing facilities and quizzed Neeson on the bizarre specializations required by the surrounding energy research buildings. Neeson felt himself relaxing. Haj was already impressed with the corporate splendor. Everything would be fine.

Jason met them just inside the door and shook hands with the architect. As Haj entered the control room, Neeson glanced back at Jason with questioning eyes. Thumbs-up. *We're good.*

The techs were busy setting up and checking off protocols. None of them had a friendly look for the evil boss who was making them do panic work on Saturday. Neeson did nothing to placate them.

Haj entered the wind tunnel itself and circled around the tower with his hands clasped contemplatively behind him.

"Have you ever been in a wind tunnel before?" Neeson asked.

"Yes, I have used them to test models for some skyscrapers I designed in Indonesia. But those weren't as impressive as this." Haj looked around at the curved walls and the giant fan assemblies on either end. "You wouldn't allow me to be in the tunnel for the test, would you?" he asked, only half-joking.

"Sorry," Neeson smiled, "but this isn't our facility. We've been asked to keep people out of the tunnel for safety reasons. The room is designed to produce very high wind speeds that are consistent everywhere throughout the tunnel, so no matter where you stood, it would feel like a hurricane. It simply isn't safe. But you should come back here in August when we get the real thing outside."

Haj nodded his amused compliance. When all was ready, everyone left the floor, and the tunnel was sealed off. The tower of panels stood alone in perfect repose. Neeson took a deep breath as the fans began their turns. Full strength simulation #17. He looked over at Jason again for some redundant encouragement, but Jason just shrugged and crossed his fingers.

Panels began to open as the wind speed topped the 50 mph mark. Everything was progressing normally. Neeson noticed one or two panels that didn't seem to be opening quite right, but he didn't think that it was obvious enough to be noticed by someone seeing them from the first time. In fact, Haj seemed intrigued. As speeds topped 80, then 90, Haj stood closer to the window, peering intently in. Neeson began to get a good feeling. *We've got him*, he realized.

Suddenly, everything went dark. With the exception of blinking red indicators, every light inside the tunnel and control room turned off and left them in total darkness. A minute later, they were re-illuminated in the dull orange of emergency back-up lights.

"What happened?" Neeson yelled angrily, forgetting his VIP voice. No one had any idea. The computers were rebooting. No data was available.

"I'll go down to the basement," Jason said. "Call the facilities guy," he commanded over his shoulder to a technician. Neeson turned to Haj, who hadn't moved.

"I'm afraid we may have to wait a moment, Haj. I don't know what…"

"It's fine," Haj said, "I understand technical difficulties. You go find out what is wrong."

Neeson left the control room, making sure to close the door calmly behind him, then jogged furiously down to the basement as he flashed through possible people to blame. How much were they paying to lease this place? And the owners couldn't even ensure that the power supply could handle the specifications of their trials. Or the techs—had they taken short-cuts during the set-up because it was a Saturday morning and they were feeling sorry for themselves? Whatever the cause, what happened was unacceptable. Anything that didn't go according to plan was unacceptable.

The facilities manager, an old man with older tastes in professional fashion, was already talking with Jason by the time Neeson found them. Bouncing his flashlight beam over pipes and cable bundles, the manager guided them to the main power control center. The flashlight slowly made its way over the system until it settled on a breaker box. It was immediately obvious to Neeson why he'd stopped there. The bottom of the metal box was charred and partially broken, and as the manager carefully opened it up, they saw that the entire lower portion, including the wires protruding from it, was completely destroyed. The three men glanced at each other.

"What do you think? Some kind of overload?" asked the manager with a grim expression.

"Maybe," said Jason. "We were pretty lucky there wasn't a fire."

Neeson, who knew enough about electrical engineering to understand the seriousness of the damage, asked, "Is there any way to fix this today?"

The manager answered with a slow, pessimistic exhale. Jason didn't offer any hope either. Neeson looked up at the ceiling in frustration and considered his options.

"Look," he finally said, "you work on this for the next hour. I'm going to take Haj out to the town center for some lunch. Try and get things back running, but if not, we have to cancel the demonstration. It should go without saying that I would rather not do that." Once his meaning was clear, he went back upstairs, wondering if it were possible that Haj hadn't eaten lunch before 1:00.

*   *   *   *

In the center of Chlorophyll Valley, several enterprising real estate developers had constructed a cobblestone plaza surrounded by shops, restaurants, and entertainment facilities catering to the newly affluent, up-and-coming innovators and their clients and lackeys. Neeson escorted Haj to the patio seating of Club Kabob and placed his phone where he could see any updates as soon as they arrived.

"I'm sorry again for the disappointment," Neeson said, his VIP voice fully restored now. "The building isn't ours, and even though we gave them our load requirements upfront, it looks like their wiring just couldn't handle it. We were just getting to the exciting part, too."

"It is OK, Neeson. You do not have to keep apologizing. I have dealt with many testing glitches in my time, it's simply part of the process. At least I can report to Mr. Reynolds about the first part of the test." Neeson didn't want to pursue the subject of Lance

Reynolds just then, so the approaching waiter was a welcome distraction.

"The sampler plate, extra hummus on the side," Neeson ordered. Haj pointed at a building across the way.

"You have a KM Center here?"

Neeson nodded. "You know Kaah Mukul?"

"I helped them with some designs when Myung-Ki Noh was first starting it up several years ago. I've never been to one of the centers, however. If I'd been a smarter businessman," Haj gave a courteous nod toward Neeson, "I would have invested in the company early on. I thought his ideas were clever, but I did not see how profitable they would be and now I feel very foolish. Do you visit Kaah Mukul?"

"It's popular with a lot of the younger programmers around here. They'll go to play Ullamaball or something to blow off some steam during lunch or after work. Jason, who you met, takes his staff down there every so often as a group geek team-building exercise. That's how he justifies charging it to the corporate account, at least. Of course, it helps that there's a bar next door."

"But you don't play?"

"Oh, no," Neeson sipped his water. "I have an interest in it, but it's business related. Have you heard about their executive centers? They're only in the really big KM centers near corporate hubs like this. Anyone who has an interest in placing some marketing or design strategy in the Kaah Mukul world goes to these offices and can interface with Kaah Mukul business contacts directly using their private network. I was just there a few weeks ago to submit a proposal for installing a virtual WindSkin system on one of their skyscrapers."

"Really? What did they say?"

"Haven't heard back yet. If you know Mr. Noh, maybe you can put in a good word for us. It would sure help with our PR."

Haj shook his head. "I'm sorry, but I do not have a close connection with him. He is a very unusual and very distant man, and I only worked with him a short time. I cannot help you there."

Neeson shrugged it off. "Worth a shot." The waiter brought out their kabobs and pita on a platter, and Haj attacked his food with gusto. Neeson cast him a calculating look and put his own fork down.

"We are great admirers of your work over at WindSkin," Neeson said. "Corazon Resort is truly superb from an architectural standpoint—from all standpoints. It sets the new gold standard. I think I can say without exaggeration that Corazon Resort and WindSkin are the perfect match in terms of cutting-edge technology and leadership in their respective fields."

Neeson's phone vibrated with an update from Jason: *Need more time. Not pretty over here.* He put the phone aside as Haj continued to eat.

"Once we finish at the tunnel, I can take you back to our office and review our three-year plan, our budget and profit projections, and of course we can go over the grid schematics in more detail…"

Haj leaned back and laughed.

"You don't need to sell to me. The truth is that I am in your corner. I think what you have here is a very interesting innovation. I do have concerns about how well we could implement WindSkin over the whole façade of the hotel, as you have suggested. There are weight issues, aesthetic issues, issues of surface drag." Haj paused to sip his drink and waved his other hand in the air. "But these are all engineering issues, and engineering issues can be solved. I would very much like to sit down with you and your engineers to work through these issues once Lance gives the initial approval for exploratory design. And if all goes well, I may be able to think of some other properties internationally that would be even better suited for a WindSkin conversion."

"That would be greatly appreciated," said Neeson, his pulse quickening with both excitement and relief. He made sure to end the discussion about the Corazon on that note. "So tell me what you're working on now. Anything you can talk about?"

"I'm afraid that no, I cannot talk about it. Sorry." Haj was calm but cryptic. "I am interested in your work here. How did all of this start?"

Neeson responded easily, having told the story many times. "I was working as a project manager for a company that designed private, unmanned aerial drones up in North Carolina. Nothing you would have heard of; it tanked a few years after we left. While I was there, I went on vacation to the Outer Banks, not far from Kitty Hawk where the Wright brothers tested their plane. I happened to stop at this little old gas station with its own wind generator, and it just kind of hit me that larger buildings could have their own wind generators as well. I worked on the problem on my own time, came up with the basic concept of WindSkin, and decided to start my own company. At the same time, Jason was one of my engineers working on flight control systems, and he had some really interesting ideas about software design. I realized that his programming abilities would be valuable to the overall design of WindSkin. It took some time to persuade him, but he finally came on board as chief engineer. The energy tech boom was just heating up down here, so we relocated to Florida, worked up a prototype, and tested some panels in a small wind tunnel that we leased from the University of Florida. Then we applied for one of the Green Gov Grants and got one. That's brought us to this point. We have some venture capital interest going forward; they have already provided some supplemental funding and have a more substantial investment available upon completion of our testing. And that, combined with our profits, should propel us forward for the next decade. So, here's to Mr. Reynolds coming along at just the right time."

Neeson made a toasting motion with his glass. Haj reciprocated and drank.

"Which venture capital firm?" Haj asked.

Neeson swallowed hard. "Um, Graham Capital. I doubt you would have heard of them. It's small and new but they have a lot of money behind them." Neeson's phone vibrated again, and this time Haj noticed.

"Is that your engineer calling?"

"Yeah. It looks like they're still encountering some minor problems—what time does your flight leave?"

"Not until tonight, but I do have some other appointments to keep. I think I should probably move on if the test isn't immediately forthcoming."

"I understand. And I apologize again for how things ended. Maybe I can finish the demonstration over a teleconference?"

"That would be good, yes," Haj said, turning away slightly as Neeson paid the bill.

"And Neeson," he added as they began motoring back to the office park, "I think I need to urge you to get this issue fixed quickly. I understand these things, but Lance may not. He is not patient by nature, and he has many demands on his attention. I'm not saying it is fair, but he'll be pessimistic when he learns that your demonstration ended early. I will convey my positive impressions, but he will require very specific technical specifications, and he will need them soon. If you want this sale, I suggest you do everything you can to impress him within the week."

"We'll do our best." Neeson stopped the golf cart in front of Haj's car and turned with one last VIP smile. "Enjoy the rest of your stay and have a safe flight home." It wasn't until Haj's tail-lights were out of the parking lot that Neeson resumed his scowl and reread Jason's message. Something real messed up here. Manager wants to see you ASAP.

*   *   *   *

"A week?" Neeson bellowed. He leaned in to direct a disbelieving glare at the technician working on the fan. Intimidated by the unexpectedly intense encounter, the technician kept his eyes on his greasy hands.

"It's not just a matter of replacing the box, Mr. Faulkner. There was some damage from the overload in other circuits…"

"Hey, don't talk to me like I'm an idiot," Neeson menaced. "I could do all of this work myself if you gave me a wire cutter and some duct tape. Jason here could do it with just the tape." Jason shook his head a little and looked stone-faced. "There is no way this needs to take a full week to repair unless you're trying to drag this out. How much are they paying you per hour?"

The facilities manager stepped in to partially shield the red-faced technician. "Mr. Faulkner, I'm sure that once you let us give you a full review of the damage, you'll agree that with all the new parts that need to be ordered—"

Neeson licked his teeth and focused his ire on the manager. "I don't care what the extent of the damage is. Anything can be fixed if you have the skill. No offense." He gave a sideways glance at the technician, who took offense. "I need this place up and running in two days. We have an army of techs that I will gladly loan you if you can't handle it. Oh, and I expect a pro-rated refund on our lease for every day of testing we lose because of this."

"Mr. Faulkner, if you will just—"

"It's *Dr.* Faulkner."

"Fine, Dr. Faulkner, if I could speak with you privately for a moment, over here, I think we can get everything straightened out."

Neeson didn't want to talk privately; it felt more natural to yell in public. But he went with the manager off to the side of the room while Jason leaned down to speak to the tech. The manager looked over to make sure they were a safe distance from the others, then spoke softly.

"Dr. Faulkner, you need to know before the police get here."

"The police?" Neeson asked, off-guard.

"After looking at the damage, we think it's pretty clear that this was intentional. Someone broke in and…well, we're not totally sure yet, but it looks like there was some kind of charge set off. And there was a second one that went off at the same time that made sure the breakers didn't kick in. It caused three times as much damage as it would have otherwise. That's why it will take so long to fix."

Neeson was silent. *Sabotage?* He tried to think of other companies that would want to ruin his work, but there were no real competitors to WindSkin. At least none he knew of. Then again, it wasn't their facility. It could have been anyone. It could have been someone who had a grudge against the facilities manager. Maybe it *was* the facilities manager, trying some insurance scam at their expense. After a pause, he realized that he didn't care. His deadline was fixed. He looked back at the technician and reevaluated his position.

"OK, fine. We'll let the police do their thing, but then we fix the problem. I don't care who did it, as long as I'm back on schedule. I'll tell my people to get you whatever you need."

"That's good of you, Dr. Faulkner, but to be honest, I'd rather not have your people around. I hope you understand."

"I don't. What's wrong with my people?"

"I don't mean to sound rude, but we haven't ruled out the possibility that your group had something to do with it."

Neeson stared as if daring him to repeat his accusation. The manager didn't budge.

"Your team was here early, and you've been the only group

leasing the tunnel for the last two weeks. As you said, you have people who know their way around circuits. There's no reason to think that it wasn't you. I mean, your group."

Neeson paced irritably. "That's ridiculous. No one from my group would sabotage our own test."

"It's still a possibility. The police will think so, too."

Neeson knew that the manager was right. His people did have the most access to the facility. Corporate espionage was not unheard of, especially in cutting-edge technology industries. His mind jumped to the mysterious problem with the failsafe that his genius software designer couldn't seem to fix. He glanced at Jason and wondered for a moment if... but no, Jason had as much to lose from failure as Neeson did. And besides, Jason wasn't exactly the ruthless type. If he did have a saboteur in his company, it had to be one of the technicians. He suddenly regretted not caring more about their morale that morning.

"Fine," Neeson leaned in, his voice both soothing and contemptuous. "You have your people work as fast as they can. I can't tell you how important it is to me to get this done fast. When it's ready to go, don't call the office, call me directly. For the record, I don't think anyone in my group would do something like this. It wouldn't make sense. But at this point, I want to avoid all risks."

The manager nodded that he understood. Neeson and Jason stepped out, but not before Neeson gave one final look of death to the facility technician, who returned a different gesture when his back was turned. Neeson instructed Jason quietly as they walked.

"Listen, we're going to let them do their thing, for now. I don't like it, and I think we could do it better, but it would be best not to interfere right now. The manager is suspicious of us, and I can't entirely blame him. We may have some cops coming over to ask us questions. I want you to tell everyone to cooperate fully. But if anyone has any leads, if anyone saw *anything*, I want them coming to me personally first, got it?"

Jason looked back at the door. "You think that one of our people did this?"

"No, no. I think we were just in the wrong place at the wrong time. But I don't want to give that manager any reason to be more suspicious of us than he already is. Let's just stay out of his way."

Jason looked at his boss with raised eyebrows. "You seem to be taking this well. I mean, better than you were."

"It's the hand that we were dealt. We just have to play it through and hope that we get dealt something better soon. I'll try to buy us some time with our clients. You get that failsafe fixed."

"Yup, on it." One more beat of silence, and then, "What about that investor of yours? Are you going to have to tell him about this?"

"I have a meeting with him next week. It will probably come up, he always finds out about this stuff somehow."

"Anything I can do?"

"No," Neeson shook his head. "That's on me."

[**South Division**: Sweet Sixteen]
[Friday, March 27]

The baseball diamond at Dulles Elementary was surrounded by lawn chairs, blankets, and people in sunglasses. It was Friday afternoon, and the sky was grey and cloudy: perfect for game watching. A team of eight-year-old boys and girls in bright yellow tee-shirts were fielding against a batter uniformed in dark maroon. The coaches on both sides were shouting instructions and trying to drown out the parents, who were also shouting instructions. No one paid much attention when a balding man in a dress shirt came walking onto the grass near left field, mumbling into his cell phone. Just another dad who couldn't quite leave work at the office.

Neeson pocketed his phone and approached a figure reclined on a lawn chair beneath a tree. The man was wearing a loud shirt and a Tampa Bay Rays cap and eating a bag of candy by the handful. He barely turned when Neeson forced himself down onto a patch of clover beside him.

"Who's winning?" Neeson asked, truly uninterested.

"Gator Mart is up by two, 5th inning, no outs. They're making a good showing, but I think Hardy Hardware has a stronger bullpen. The kid with the nose-scratching addiction has a mean streak."

"Do you have a favorite, Mr. Graham?"

"I don't believe in having favorites," said Mr. Graham, scratching under his cap. "I find it easier to root for the one who wins. It helps me to avoid disappointment."

They watched an at-bat in silence.

"Bracket's looking good," said Graham, after the pitcher walked a skinny kid whose head was too small for the helmet. "Good call on North Dakota beating Kentucky."

"This time next week I can have it laminated for you to take home."

"Everything else OK?"

"Fine."

"How is your mole hunt going?"

"There is no mole hunt," Neeson began, as if he had anticipated the question and resented it preemptively. "There is no proof that anyone in my group had anything to do with the incident at the tunnel. I'm not entirely convinced there was an 'incident' at all—I think the wiring was done poorly. But it doesn't matter. Assuming everything goes well, the wind tunnel will be ready this afternoon, and I'm going to personally run a test tomorrow. Then I'll have a video to show to all future clientele, and we can finally start closing some deals. If someone in the company has mixed allegiances, which is unlikely, I'll find out soon enough. In the mean time we will have a momentum that will be very hard to slow down."

"Glad to hear it," Graham said, without conviction. "So you aren't at all concerned about something else going wrong in the company."

"Not at all. Our security has been upgraded. I personally paid for the installation of new hidden cameras throughout the wind tunnel building. All the door codes and locks have been changed. We are secure."

"Yeah?"

"Yeah."

"And you aren't at all concerned that OPUS may not be secure?"

That drew a quick head turn from Neeson. "OPUS is under my lock and key. If there was a hint it wasn't secure, I would know about it." Then, after a minute of silence which Graham didn't fill, "Why do you ask?"

Graham cleared his throat, like a lawyer beginning a line of questioning. "Your demonstration of OPUS using the basketball bracket was supposed to be unique, something no one else could replicate. That's what you told me."

"That's right."

"Have you seen the ESPN bracket standings lately?"

"Not since…are you saying that there's someone else with a perfect bracket?"

"No," said Graham, "I'm saying that there are *three* others with perfect brackets. Not only that, all three of them have brackets identical to yours all the way to the Final Four. That's a pretty improbable thing to happen, don't you think?"

This was disturbing news for Neeson. His greatest fear to that point was that OPUS wouldn't perform. Now he realized that he should have been worried that other systems might perform also. Unless his own system had been...Neeson suddenly realized where the conversation was going.

"Do you know who they are? The bracket holders?" Neeson asked.

"Of the two in the ESPN set, one is a college kid at Nebraska, the other's a middle-aged clerk in Seattle. A third one just popped up: a 22-year-old receptionist in Connecticut. Even made the morning news. Sound like anyone you know?"

Neeson sighed. "I don't think so."

"I didn't think so, either."

"OK." Neeson nodded, digesting the information. "OK. I'll find out what I can and double check the use log for the software. In the mean time, will you let me know if you discover anything about these other guys? If my company was compromised, I want to know."

Graham turned to look at Neeson directly for the first time, speaking with a reptilian whisper. "Do you remember when our paths crossed, and you were so desperate for venture capital that you told me about this secret software that you were developing? Out of the absolute goodness of my heart, I got the loan for you on the condition that you prove that you had what you said you had. Remember that? Now you owe us a significant return on our investment. The people I work for, they don't care if the company lives or dies; they barely care if you live or die. These people with the other brackets, we aren't watching them because we want to protect your assets. We're watching them to find out if they have a system like yours, and if their system happens to be better. If your system is the best, then we're more than happy to do business. But if not, we go bargain shopping, and you'll need to find your next safety net elsewhere."

"But," Neeson stammered, trying not to betray his alarm, "We made a deal. We *have* a deal."

"Try to prove that in court, I dare you." Graham smiled thinly. "In fact, try to prove that I exist at all. No one else has seen me. I've signed nothing. You've accepted our anonymity as the price to pay for our help. And, as part of our verbal agreement, you promised to develop OPUS and to keep it secret, safe, and locked away from any other interested parties. Right now, we have little confidence that you've upheld your end. The people I work for are not nervous by nature. They are opportunists. I suggest that you don't give them any reason to cash out early."

Graham held his gaze to make his point, and Neeson forced his selling smile. "Graham, I can promise you, *guarantee* you, that OPUS can beat any other system out there. And I can promise…"

"Thank you, Neeson, your confidence is noted. I'm going to watch the game now."

Neeson bit his lip and cast his unfocused gaze out on the field. This was how meetings with Graham always ended. He hated feeling like a fish on a hook. Just once, he wanted to end things on his own terms. But he couldn't; not while he owed Graham three million dollars.

He pulled out his phone to check his messages. After a minute, he smiled faintly. "So we'll meet again after the championship?" he asked, his phone back in his pocket.

"I'll let you know," Graham replied without looking.

"Fine." Neeson stood up and brushed off his slacks. "If you want some good news sooner than that, I might have some."

"Yeah?"

"I just got a message from ChangZhang's corporate advertising division. They want to meet. WindSkin is about to go digital."

Graham snickered to himself. "Congratulations. Let me know if your fake panels for fake wind are as successful as the real thing."

Neeson was about to defend himself, but opted against it and began to walk away.

"Hold on," Graham called. "This thing. You're doing this in Kaah Mukul?"

"Yeah."

"Are you doing it through a KM Center?"

"Yes. Why?"

Graham paused to throw peanuts into his mouth, as if literally chewing on his thoughts. "Forget it," he said finally. Then he cupped his hands and yelled, "Come on, buddy, eye on the ball. You got it." Neeson walked back over the grass, away from his oppressive financier who, he was sure, had never been a father in his life.

*   *   *   *

The executive floor of Chlorophyll Valley's KM Center was far removed from the gaming action. In place of the gaudy Mayan paraphernalia was a business-casual setting that looked much more like the lounge of an airport. Light duets of classical guitar and pan flute masked what little of the yelling came up from the lower floors. Neeson had been sitting and tapping impatiently on his phone for the last six minutes, waiting for the coordinator to let him into one of the private video conference rooms.

"Dr. Faulkner?" an aide poked her head through a door. "In here please. Sorry for the delay; there has been a slight change."

The door closed behind him in the small conference room, and the screen before him came to life.

"Good afternoon," said the image of an Asian woman in ChangZhang Corp attire, apparently aware of his local time.

"Uh, yes, is everything in order for my meeting with Mr. Huang?"

"Dr. Faulkner, your meeting is not with Mr. Huang today," said the woman. "You are being transferred now."

In a moment, Neeson saw the screen filling with grey streaks. Unusual. When an image clarified, Neeson noticed immediately that he was not seeing the real world. Instead, he was looking into a great glass office with walls that slanted down and out. Reddish-orange sunlight was shining in on one side. In the center of the room was a desk, and standing in front of the desk was a digital image that he recognized from the cover of Forbes.

"Dr. Faulkner, I am Myung-Ki Noh," said the man.

"Mr. Noh, it's an honor," Neeson felt himself scrambling mentally. "I wasn't told that I would be speaking with you today."

"Yes, I told Mr. Huang that I would handle your case. I have some things to discuss with you."

"Absolutely. I'll be happy to answer all of your questions."

The digital image of Noh nodded. "I was wondering if you

could tell me about your basketball tournament bracket."

Neeson maintained his professional comportment, but just barely. "You surprise me again, Mr. Noh. I wouldn't think that you would follow such things."

"You would normally be right. But in this case, I have a special interest in it. I take it from your response that the bracket named 'WindSkin1' is truly yours."

"Yes, it is."

"Good. I was also wondering if you could claim ownership over one or both of the other two brackets. You can answer me truthfully."

Neeson shifted in his seat. "I'm sorry?"

"It is no use being evasive. I am the best detective in my city and it was not a difficult puzzle. A member of my staff brought the perfect brackets to my attention because one of the bracket holders is a Tribal Wars general named Studblood—in reality, Perry Lynwood. I have a great interest in what happens in the Tribal Wars. I asked my staff to learn more, and I was surprised to find that another bracket holder—you—had recently petitioned us to install a product on a Kaah Mukul building. It would be an unusual coincidence, if there were ever coincidences in Kaah Mukul."

Noh paused, but Neeson kept his face impassive.

"I inquired into Studblood's background and the records of his tribe, and I found that one of his most recent recruits, Typhoon150, joined Studblood's tribe one week before the brackets were to be submitted. Typhoon150 hasn't returned to the city at all for the past week. I found that Typhoon150's membership is based in the KM Center of Chlorophyll Valley, Florida, where you sit now. The name on the membership is not yours, but given your efforts to be covert, that is not surprising. I have an advertisement from your company that came with your petition, and it boasts of your product withstanding hurricane force winds, potentially up to 150 miles per hour. Typhoon, 150. Now tell me, Dr. Faulkner, if my detective skills have failed me."

Neeson sat in his chair with his palms on his legs, lost in contemplation. After a second, he blinked and said, "What would you really like to know?"

Noh leaned forward. "You have gone to great lengths, and

very clever lengths, to get my attention. I can only conclude that you must have a method, some algorithm for identifying winners that exceeds everything else that has ever been tried, and you want it known to the ChangZhang corporation that it is available, supposing rightly that the company would be interested. Your plan obviously worked. But now that you have my attention, I want to know if what you have is really worth my time. You should know that I will be visiting Mr. Lynwood to evaluate him personally—tomorrow, in fact—and I have already been looking into the young man in Nebraska. Naturally, I will be looking into your own history more carefully."

"That seems like a lot of extra work, Mr. Noh."

"Yes. But I have my reasons. You may save me some trouble now, however. Is there anything else that I should know?"

Neeson cleared his throat. "Actually, yes. I believe you will find that there is one more perfect bracket that you are not aware of yet. In Connecticut. There should be four all together."

Noh smiled, surprisingly communicative for an avatar. "Very good, Dr. Faulkner. I will make sure to remain in contact with your office."

"Thank you," said Neeson. "Uh, I did want to ask if you were moving forward with placing WindSkin in Kaah Mukul."

"I believe that, should your system prove its potential, our company would be most pleased to include WindSkin on a building somewhere in the Olmec district, as a way of strengthening our working relationship. Have a good afternoon, Dr. Faulkner."

The image on the screen vanished behind a ChangZhang logo against a white background. Neeson remained in his chair, unmoving, silent, until a knock on the door informed him that his time was up.

When he left the KM Center, he found it cold and close to raining outside. The winds from the north had finally arrived. Dark clouds had gathered in from the ocean, turning the twilight sky into a churned expanse of black and grey. He looked at his golf cart and thought unenthusiastically about driving back to the office in the rain. Then he looked at the bar next door and made an easy choice. He texted his secretary to hold all messages and calls until he got back, and he went in.

Rain was now pelting the roof of the bar, but it was barely audible over the chatter and music. Neeson sat in a booth, alone, rolling a shot of bourbon between his fingers. He had to *think*. Things had gotten too strange, too out of hand. He felt as if he were in a dream and had become suddenly aware that it didn't make any sense.

Slowly, methodically, he pieced together the events of the last few weeks. OPUS, a powerful software with unprecedented capacities, had a mysterious, perpetual flaw that caused problems during simple wind tunnel tests, problems that hadn't shown up in the preliminary trials. Before an important demonstration, someone with technical prowess had deliberately wrecked the electrical system of the fan. A video game player with the very telling name of Typhoon150, based in the KM Center just a half mile from his building, was associated with at least one perfect bracket. There were three other perfect brackets in the world; four total, when there were normally zero. While his own bracket had been made to impress Mr. Graham, the others had drawn the attention of the world's most influential technology magnate. And all Neeson wanted and needed was to sell his company's product. *What was going on?*

He finished his drink and refilled. Conclusions based on the facts came relentlessly. There was, without question, someone within his company that wanted to destroy, delay, or exploit WindSkin or OPUS. Or both. This person was technically skilled. This person knew Kaah Mukul. This person knew OPUS, had access to OPUS, and was possibly advertising OPUS using Neeson's own program. The list of candidates who fit that description was short, depressing, and infuriating. Once he was sure about who it was, he would have to confront a traitor in his organization. Afterward, he would have to deal with a demoralized staff while keeping everything a secret from potential clients. Every thought sucked him into an ever deeper morass of anger.

A basketball game was on the TV somewhere over his head. Marquette vs. North Dakota—a match-up that had been particularly improbable for almost everyone. Marquette had come all the way back from a slow start to dominate in the second half. During a time-out, one of the commentators began to talk about what it took to make a come-back. "Toughness down the stretch," he said. "Bend but not break! This team has proven once again why you play the whole game!" Neeson smiled a little grimly. He liked those lines. Maybe he could use them on his employees as he saved them from the brink of financial ruin. Maybe he would quote them in some future magazine interview for a piece about his rocky road to success. There would be a hurricane pun in the title, he was sure. "Bend But Not Break" sounded really good. That was WindSkin; that was him.

With one more drink he summoned enough will, albeit slightly inebriated will, to return to the office. He would purge the treasonous elements from among his personnel; he would regain control of his company for good. But when he approached his office, he found his secretary standing anxiously by his door.

"I'm sorry," she said, somewhat frazzled, "you have a lot of messages. The Corazon Resort just called two minutes ago."

Neeson stepped into his office, closed the door, and returned the call. The person he spoke to was Lance Reynolds' assistant. She regretted to call him that night, but she had to inform him that "we have decided not to pursue the purchase of WindSkin."

Neeson reeled back into his chair, rolling it a full two feet from the desk. "But I was told I would have a week to demonstrate WindSkin to your specifications. My people are preparing the demo as we speak."

The woman was very sorry, but it was Lance's final decision. She wished him a good evening and hung up. He looked at the phone in disbelief, his thoughts spinning. The next number he dialed was for Haj Hittock.

"Haj, this is Neeson Faulkner. I'm sorry to disturb you this evening, but this is urgent."

Haj was silent for a moment, then responded regretfully. "They told you that they decided against the sale. I'm very sorry about that. I would have warned you, but I found out just this afternoon."

"What happened? Can I still get them back?" Neeson heard himself sounding desperate but couldn't stop. "I'm running the simulation tomorrow. I could have a full video prepared by noon. Whatever it takes."

"Neeson, it's more than just the test. They were OK with waiting, but they began to hear rumors. I didn't hear them myself. They said there was doubt that you even had functioning panels, that your panels worked up to 100 miles per hour and then crashed, that your software wasn't working with the overall design. Apparently they heard this from several different sources. Lance began to consider WindSkin a gamble, and he doesn't like to gamble, so they shut it down. Do you know where these rumors could be coming from? Are they true?"

"No, they aren't true," Neeson snapped back. *But I know where they are coming from.*

His mouth and throat dry, Neeson said more contritely, "Thank you for everything, Haj. I won't forget your support." He hung up and logged into his neglected email. Of the fifty-three unread messages, seventeen were from potential clients, all sending their regrets. The rumors had spread far and fast, like an air-borne plague. No one gave reasons, but the wording between them was remarkably similar.

The saboteur had crippled WindSkin. *His* company.

Neeson laid his head back in his chair, restraining the impulse to smash everything in his office. Someone had done these things to him.

He sprang into an investigation with zeal, starting with the access log in his computer. There it was, starting in January: evidence of unauthorized access. He traced the breach back through the corporate network until he found the source. It was not a surprise.

Then, in an inspired stroke, he called the KM Center. He claimed to be an IT security worker who had stopped a hacker named Typhoon150 and had later connected the handle to a KM account of the same name. He wanted to confirm the connection and get the contact info for a pending lawsuit. The inexperienced desk clerk readily gave him the name.

Neeson hung up the phone slowly and sat in silence at his desk, his heart pounding, his lips grimacing until they trembled. He looked up on his wall and studied the pair of mounted antlers that hung over his bookshelf.

And he broke.

[South Division: Elite Eight]
[Saturday, March 28]

Early on Saturday morning, a phone call.

"Jason, this is Neeson."

"Mornin', Neeson."

"I hate to bother you, but I need you to come in for a half-hour and help me run a test at the wind tunnel. Could you come in at 11:00?"

"This can't wait until Monday?"

"I'm afraid not, no. It's important."

Jason gave a low hum while he thought. "OK, but I have to leave at lunch."

"Thank you."

*   *   *   *

Neeson sat alone in the control room of the wind tunnel. The computers were on, the simple red logo of OPUS blinking at him from the corner of the software's home screen. Neeson's face was rigid, as if he had died in his sleep. But his mind was active, his thoughts not so much burning as they were churning. His intentions were singular and simple, a state ideal for an engineer.

At the distinctive clomp of Jason's boots, Neeson swiveled around in his chair, unsmiling.

"OK, I'm here. What's so important?" Jason asked.

"Our clients," Neeson enunciated, "have given us an ultimatum. They need footage of a successful test this weekend. It's very important that we deliver. I thought we could manage it together if you helped me out at the beginning."

"Uh-huh," Jason grunted, looking around. "You didn't tell me that the repairs were all done. This looks like it took a lot of work to set up. You did all this yourself?"

"That's right. But I know you're a busy man, I won't keep you too long. There is one thing I want to do first." Neeson turned around to face the wind tunnel window. "There's an indicator here that some of the panels on the lower left wall aren't secured. Can you run in and do a manual check while I see if the indicator light goes off?"

Jason shrugged and stepped down through the doorway and into the wind tunnel. The clomp of his boots echoed clamorously off the solid cement walls, filling the chamber with sound until he stopped at the tower platform. As he bent down to look at the panels, he heard a heavy metallic click and a loud buzz overhead. Red lights began blinking on all four walls. The room was sealed. Jason whirled around and saw Neeson looking at him, statuesque, still unsmiling, from behind the Plexiglas window.

"Hey, what…?" A mechanical whining started up from either end of the room. The fans had begun to spin.

Jason ran over to the door and pulled on the handle. It wouldn't open. The fans sped up, creating a breeze. He found the emergency shut-down button by the door and slammed it with his palm. But it didn't work. It had been inactivated. The screws that held the button panel in place had been stripped so that it would be impossible to open. Jason pounded on the glass.

"Neeson, what are you doing? Open the dang door!"

Neeson put his mouth up to the thin microphone attached to the control desk. His voice came over the speakers in the tunnel, loud enough to be heard even over the wind that was making Jason's shirt snap sharply around him.

"Typhoon150."

Jason looked through the window into Neeson's eyes, which were hard and nearly lifeless.

"I have to admit that I never saw you coming," Neeson mused sadly as he sat down heavily in his chair. "I had always considered you the safest bet in the world: smart but unambitious, independent but loyal. If it hadn't been for the Kaah Mukul thing, I never would have believed it was you, much less been able to prove it. But now I know."

The wind blew harder. The indicator in the tunnel read 50. Jason pressed himself against the door, trying to find shelter in the shallow depression. Muffled, he yelled, "I don't know what you're talking about! Stop the fan and open this door *now*!"

"It worked, by the way. Your plan killed the company. I lied about the clients wanting video. We have no clients, thanks to you. Maybe you knew that already? You saw to it that tests failed when we most needed them, that everyone who ever expressed any interest in WindSkin was lied to from multiple angles. We didn't have a chance."

Jason raised his arm to keep the wind from pelting his face. Panels on the tower were fully opened.

"I spent all night in here thinking about why you did it, but I figured that out, too. When did you figure out what I was doing with OPUS? Months ago? Was it after I started running the subroutines? You must have gotten curious, hacked into my system, saw my bracket program, saw how valuable OPUS could be. You wanted to kill the company so that you could take OPUS with you, all to yourself. I really never did see it coming. Do you already have your own clients, Jason?"

Jason was leaning into the wind now, barely keeping his balance. It was hard for him to keep his eyes open. The indicator read 100. Neeson sat back, observing remorselessly as the wind meter ticked up steadily. A panel that hadn't been secured well broke off and flew just a few yards from Jason's head. Jason did what he could to pound the window again and yell as the wind hit 110.

Suddenly, Jason fell backwards and disappeared under the window. Neeson stood up and walked over to the glass. As he approached and scanned the floor, he failed to notice that all the panels were suddenly, simultaneously, closing. A few seconds later, the power to the fans stopped and the brakes came on. Neeson whipped back to the control panel to see what was happening. The screen had a warning: **Failsafe: Direct Override**. It was Jason's program, created for Haj's benefit and never tested because the electrical systems had failed too soon. Neeson had forgotten. He typed swiftly, trying to override the override, but it was too late. The full power down was mandatory. Turning back to the window, he saw a haggard and angry Jason, hair askew, standing inches away from the glass, rubbing the back of his head.

"You are completely out of your mind!" Jason yelled.

"Calm down, Jason, you aren't hurt." Neeson considered holding this conversation through the thick safety glass, but wearily decided against it. There was no point. He pushed the button to unlock the door, and Jason barreled through, panting and livid.

"I should sue your hide. How high would you have let that

fan go if I hadn't installed the failsafe, huh?"

"First tell me this," Neeson demanded, wondering if Jason would punch him and preparing to punch back. "How, after everything we did to build this thing, after all the work that everyone did, how could you decide to work so hard to destroy this company?"

Jason was still breathless, but he had enough to sound threatening. "Neeson, you are the dumbest, blindest... Which one of us created that bracket program? Or the stock market program? Which of us decided to try using *my* system to make money on the side instead of fixing the real problems of WindSkin?"

"I was trying to make sure this company had a future! I was trying to make sure *our company's* system reached its full potential! If you hadn't ruined everything, if you had just fixed the problems instead of deciding to hit and run—"

"If I had fixed the problems? You were so busy playing with your side projects that you didn't notice that WindSkin is a complete failure. The whole thing's a flop, OPUS or not. You think we never got a sale because we couldn't get the specs we wanted? We couldn't get a sale because WindSkin is a bad product. The panels are too expensive, too bulky in a group, too delicate individually, and too unreliable in a network. Even if we had made a sale, there is no way that we could have installed it successfully. I kept trying to tell you early on, but you kept sayin', 'Oh, we'll deal with it, it's fine,' until eventually I just gave up trying to tell you anything. I stayed on as long as I did because I thought you'd eventually leader up and do something to turn us around. Then I find out that the whole time you didn't really care. This company was a dead horse limping along only because you needed it to live long enough so that you could sell us out. I did everyone in this company a favor by putting it out of its misery."

Neeson folded his arms, relaxed somehow now that he had been proven right. "You have one hour to pack up and leave your office. I've already told the security guard that you would be returning to clear things out, and that you aren't allowed to even touch your computer. Your passwords and clearances have all been removed."

Jason didn't move. "You think I'm just gonna forget what

you did to me just now?"

"No," Neeson said, "but I don't think you're going to tell anyone about it. You see the camera over there?" He nodded to his left, where a video camera was looking down on them. "It just recorded this whole conversation. You say anything, and it will come out that you sabotaged the company and caused massive electrical damage to private property. You can remember today all you like, but if you take me down, I take you down."

Jason stared at him with a colder, more disgusted look than Neeson had ever seen on his face.

"I guess we both better shut up and move on then."

"I guess so."

One more glare, then Jason turned his back on the control room and walked away, his boots punctuating the vitriol in his eyes. Just before he reached the door, Jason turned back.

"Just so you know, I didn't have to do much to keep OPUS down. It really was turning off the failsafes on its own. It's a problem with the system itself. I wasn't kidding when I said it was power hungry. It overreaches when it has too much successful reinforcement. Sound familiar? If I were you, I wouldn't put too much faith in those side projects of yours. They'll let you down eventually." And Jason left.

Neeson was alone. Exhausted, he leaned his head forward and covered his eyes. He had been right about Jason, but now that the confrontation was over, he realized that his rashness may have kept him from thinking everything through. Slowly, he went about packing away and turning off what he could. The tower of panels was left alone, tall and opaque, as Neeson turned off the lights and left.

The air was cool, humid, and pleasant as Neeson walked to his car. But when he turned the key, he found himself without anywhere to go. He didn't want to go back to the office, not while Jason might still be there. He just wanted to get away. He left Chlorophyll Valley and kept going, mile after mile, until he arrived at the shore. There was a small public beach that Neeson preferred. Hardly anyone was there this time of year. He got out of the car and stood looking over the hazy ocean, hands on hips, his sleeves rolled up, his tie loose. The wind blew hard, shifting around him and making his shirt billow against his chest, but he liked it. It felt good to breathe new air.

As he replayed the events of the last hour, it occurred to him that he may have sent Jason packing too hastily. There were questions that he had neglected to ask. Had Jason actually pitched OPUS to anyone? Was there a sale in the offing, and was the brackets demonstration his calling card? He knew that Jason was responsible for the perfect Seattle bracket, but he could only guess about the other two. Were they all plotting this together, or were they just hapless hoops fans, easily manipulated by an engineer who was anything but the guileless cowboy Neeson had thought him to be? Neeson mulled over the possibility of three other people—four, counting Jason—profiteering off of the success of OPUS. His OPUS.

An even more disturbing thought crept into his consciousness. Jason had said that OPUS was glitchy, destined to fail in time. But no, it was probably a bitter lie. Neeson himself had performed the trials that demonstrated his program's reliability. He could trust the system.

His head hurt. He was tired from staying up all night, and the adrenaline rush of his rash plan's execution was wearing off quickly. He rubbed his eyes, now heavy from the glare of the sunlight off the ocean and the wind pelting his face.

The phone beeped. He looked at the number. Graham. Neeson let it ring, then for the first time since he'd started taking Graham's money, he silenced and pocketed his phone. He would talk to Graham when his plan was clear, foolproof.

After a few fortifying breaths of sea air, he drove back to Chlorophyll Valley. There were things to do. He would e-mail the staff and inform them of Jason's departure. He would finish the paperwork with HR. But most importantly, he needed a recovery plan. His side projects with OPUS, no matter how important they were to Graham, had to be considered a lower priority at the moment. The more he drove, the longer his immediate to-do list became.

As Neeson drove into the nearly empty parking lot, he noticed a man he didn't recognize coming out of the building. The man was older, upright, and assured despite a stress-lined face. He inspected Neeson with alert, penetrating eyes as Neeson walked up. The man extended his hand.

"Are you Neeson Faulkner?" asked the man.

"Yes?"

"I thought you might be. Your secretary indicated yesterday that you are often here over the weekend. My name is Bryan Casing. I have something that I would like to discuss with you."

"Are you interested in purchasing WindSkin?" Neeson queried hopefully.

Casing gave a thin smile. "I'm afraid not. I have a more unique offer to make."

"I see," Neeson said, summoning his professional demeanor. The world had caved in around him, and this guy wanted to chat. "I'm sorry, but I have a lot to do today, Mr. Casing. Why don't you call my office and have them set up an appointment for later in the week…"

"I'm afraid that I'm only in town today," said Casing. "I only need a few minutes of your time, and I think that you'll be interested in my proposal. Do you have an office where we can talk privately?" Neeson narrowed his eyes suspiciously. A messenger from Graham, perhaps? But it could also be something useful for the company. In spite of his misgivings, he brought Casing up to his office with the determination to kick the man out in three minutes if he proved a waste of time.

They entered his office together. Neeson took his place behind his desk, turned on his monitors, and offered Casing a chair. But Casing had paused in front of the antlers that hung over Neeson's shelf.

"Are you a hunter, Neeson?"

"I used to be. I've been too busy to get out in the last few years. Why don't you sit down and we can discuss why you're here."

But Casing didn't sit. He continued to stare at the antlers. "May I ask you something, Neeson? Do you like to hunt by yourself or in a group? Or, are they called parties? Hunting parties?"

An odd question, and Neeson's patience was nearly exhausted. "Are you here to ask me about my antlers or my business? Because, frankly, I…"

"I just thought it was interesting that you chose to decorate your office with a hunting trophy, in an environmentally friendly energy company, no less. But to answer your question, I am here to ask about your business, yes." Casing unhurriedly turned away from the antlers and sat. "I'm here on the recommendation of Haj Hitok. You remember him? He told me that you met last week."

"Of course," said Neeson, now listening.

"He spoke very highly of your product and your company, said that coming up with WindSkin showed unusual creativity and ingenuity. Those are signs of the kind of people that I'm interested in."

"Interested in for what?"

"I would like to tell you about a special project that I'm working on at a new facility in Kentucky, one in which we could use people with your…"

"Wait, wait, wait," Neeson interrupted brusquely, furious at the realization that this was a job interview. "Did Haj send you down here to offer me a job? Look… it's Bryan, right? Thanks for the offer, but WindSkin is just getting off the ground, and, despite what you may have heard, I don't plan on abandoning my company any time soon. Tell Haj that I appreciate the gesture, and I'm sorry you wasted your time, but if you'll excuse me, I have a company to run." Neeson stood, opened the door, and suggested that Casing leave.

But Casing stayed in his chair, observing him like an ornithologist contemplating a dodo. Then, to Neeson's amazement, the older man resumed his pacing around the room.

"I'm sorry to hear that, but I understand," said Casing as he looked out of the window. "It really is a wonderful project. Perhaps you have others in your company that might be interested. We have been contemplating a three-year rotation schedule for corporate workers…"

"Bryan, we are not interested in loaning out our supply of talent for…what is it? Never mind, we aren't interested. Now, please…"

Casing wasn't listening anymore. He was looking intently out of the window with a concerned expression, the aloofness gone. Neeson walked up behind him to see what was so interesting.

Down on the sidewalk in front of the building, two men were shaking hands. One wore cowboy boots and was holding a box full of desk ornaments. The other wore a baseball cap.

"Do you know them?" Casing asked.

Neeson didn't answer because he was already out the door, sprinting down the stairs to the exit. Graham was talking to Jason. There was no possible way for that to be a good thing. Neeson ran out of the door and tore around the building to where the two had been talking. But he was too late. Graham was gone, and Jason's car was just leaving the parking lot. Neeson yelled for Jason to stop, then ran through the parking lot and behind the building, looking for any sign of Graham. He found none. It was possible that he and Jason were in the same car.

Neeson stood near the entrance with his hands on his hips, somewhat out of breath.

"Missed them, huh?" Casing said, coming up behind him. "I suppose I was too late as well. Recruitment is a much more stressful job than I thought going into it. You lost a worker, didn't you? Probably your best one. But don't blame yourself. He can be convincing." Casing sighed, then offered his hand to Neeson. "Thank you for meeting with me. I wish you and your company all the best. It's just as well that you didn't hear me out. I knew right away that you weren't a good fit for us. It's quite obvious—though you never answered my question—that you hunt alone."

Casing nodded good-bye and stepped away without looking back, leaving Neeson seething on the sidewalk. Contempt burned in his veins; contempt for Jason, contempt for Graham, contempt for everything and everyone. But he forced himself to bottle those feelings. He had work to do, a company to control, and a betrayal to overcome.

And yes, he did hunt alone.

[**South Division**: Final Four]
[Saturday, April 4]

In the aftermath of Perry Lynwood's accident at the end of the first Final Four game, Neeson was asked to give one brief statement to arena security and several statements to reporters. Like the other two bracket holders, he had very little to say. No, he hadn't known Perry from before. Yes, he'd seemed quiet and depressed and a little odd. No, he didn't know why he ran out. Yes, it was tragic and strange. And then the inevitable question:

"So, how do you feel going into your game?"

Neeson smirked. "I can guarantee you that I will be winning this game," he said every time.

"How can you be so sure?" he was asked. He would smile and shrug and walk away, ignoring all other questions. It would be excellent footage to play before his victory interview at the end of the day.

There was enough time between games that he could take a break. He left the arena and went down the street toward the center of Chinatown. He found a trendy sandwich place and settled into a booth with a really good roast beef on wheat to get caught up on his messages.

Confidence. That was his plan. He would convey confidence so that when he won—and what alternative was there?—the mystique surrounding him and his company would rise above any anonymous slander or rumor. Who wouldn't want to buy from the man with the golden touch, who seemed to know things that no one else did? There was no better image for a CEO.

Change is in the wind, he repeated to himself as he finished his sandwich. That was the line that he somehow needed to work into his interviews. It had taken him a week to realize the truth in that statement. He had come to accept that losing Jason was the best thing to ever happen to his company. Sure, Jason was a good engineer, perhaps more talented than the rest of his staff put together. But he was also the main force holding it back. After he'd left, Neeson himself had been able to find the bug that Jason had put into the failsafe protocol. They had recorded a test with the panels closing at 135 mph and enduring while closed up to 152. He had promptly sent the video around to all of his former potential clients with a message decrying the outrageous campaign of misinformation launched at his company, undoubtedly from some rival. Granted, he hadn't heard from anyone yet, but that would change over the weekend. His clients would be foolish not to capitalize on his newly enhanced profile, especially after he won the deal with ChangZhang.

He hoped that Jason was watching from whatever hole he was hiding in. He hoped that Jason had seen the pitiful victim of his "Typhoon150" prank lose his mind. Jason's horse was out of the race, and Neeson was in for the win. As for the other two, he had no reason to fear them. The frat kid was merely riding his school's wave of success. There were probably thousands of people projecting Nebraska to get that far; someone was bound to get lucky. The other one, the secretary, he just looked like he wanted to go home. He clearly had no real stakes in the game; they clearly weren't plants of Jason's. Both Cole and Tucker had chosen UCLA to win the next game, but BC had the best player by far in the Williams kid, and they'd had a more dominant tournament run. With the win, Neeson was guaranteed the million dollars, half of which would be a nice little floater for the company. In a few weeks, after business picked up, he might even pay off Graham and finally cut that awful chain from his neck. His company, including OPUS, would finally be his alone.

He hadn't heard from Graham that whole week. He didn't care.

His inbox cleared, he checked the time. He would have to be getting back to the arena soon. He wanted to be on time for his big game.

Neeson finished his sandwich, left a nice tip in the jar on the counter, and walked back toward the arena entrance in no hurry. All kinds of people, tourists and street vendors and homeless people, bustled around him on the sidewalk. No one seemed to recognize him, but that would change, he knew. Two more games.

Just outside of the entrance, Neeson saw someone that he recognized. Someone wearing a UCLA baseball cap.

"Nice hat, Mr. Graham," Neeson smirked, "but I think that you're cheering against the home team."

"Maybe," said Graham, eating a fist full of something from one of the vendors. "You think OPUS is going to prove itself tonight?"

"I think it's proven itself well enough for the past three weeks. Why are you here?"

"You didn't think I would miss your moment of glory, did you?" Graham asked as he sidestepped some pedestrians.

Neeson waited for a real answer. When it didn't come, he asked, "How's Jason doing?"

"He sends his regards."

"You saw that his puppet bracketeer took a nasty fall a while ago? That's why you don't buy the knock-off version, Mr. Graham, you buy the real thing."

"You seem awfully confident for someone who still has a game to watch."

"I am. And when I win, I will declare this proof of principle a success, and I will expect you to hold up your end. My company is on the verge of a boom, and your continued investment will be just what we need to push us over into a sustainable profit margin."

"What makes you think that we even need OPUS anymore when we just bought the designer?"

Neeson's smile faded. "You don't need him to reinvent something that I've already perfected."

"Jason seems to think that your success isn't as guaranteed as you're making it out to be."

"Jason is a liar," Neeson barked, drawing a few startled stares from people walking by. Neeson noticed the attention and walked Graham around the corner where they were less visible. "Jason is a traitor and a back-stabber. He can't be trusted."

"We're not in the business of trusting, Neeson. We're in the business of acquiring. We acquired Jason because he has a skill set that we need. Who knows, perhaps someday we'll acquire you as well."

"I'm not for sale, Graham. And we had a deal."

"Calm down," Graham ordered. "Our deal still stands. You just might be an investment that could pay off." Graham took a step forward and leaned uncomfortably close to Neeson's right ear. "But I want to remind you of something you seem to have forgotten. You are still in our debt. You still haven't finished your end, and you still have no buyers for your highly risky product. In other words, you are still sitting squarely under my shoe. And if you find yourself on loser's row at the end of the day, then my foot comes down hard. I will own you."

Graham took a step back and brought another handful of food to his mouth. "Enjoy the game," Neeson sneered at him, then walked away.

Neeson quickly entered the arena, his good mood totally spoiled. The game was about to start. He was going to win this game just as he had won the previous sixty-one. Graham would have to make him an offer, and Neeson would tell him to shove it. No, no actually he would take the money.

When he sat down, he was excited and determined. He barely acknowledged Cole or Tucker or the pretty girl that to whom Tucker had generously offered Perry's seat. Neeson clapped loudly and vigorously as the game started. He remembered that he actually liked basketball.

He ended up applauding for most of the first half. Boston College came out strong and held a solid lead. Tucker leaned forward to see Neeson and yelled, "Man, Good Williams is killing it for you." On cue, Good Williams banked in a jumper with no time on the shot clock to put BC up by ten. The crowd roared as Tucker began to explain to Cole the difference between Good Williams and Other Williams. Other Williams, sitting at the end of the bench, jumped up and waved his towel to hype up the spectators behind him.

Neeson was so happy that he stood up to give an ovation. He looked around the arena and saw laid out before his eyes all of the variables at play in winning and losing—all of the variables he had harnessed and quantified in OPUS. The BC coach with his 40 years of experience and his previous NCAA championships, both as a player and as a coach. The BC team with its seniority and high assist-to-turnover ratio. Even the BC fans, who had sold out every game in Boston and had come out in much stronger force than the west coast UCLA fans.

He was having fun. He thought about setting up an arena in Chlorophyll Valley—nothing too big, mostly for regional events.

WindSkin Arena. That sounded good. He looked over at the younger man, Cole Kaman, whose face was a mask of tension.

"Come on Cole, you should be enjoying this more," he nudged. Cole looked back at him acidly.

"Whatever."

Neeson backed off without pressing. After all, he didn't want to give Cole any unwarranted confidence. Cole was riding on pure luck; it couldn't be a comfortable feeling. Good Williams stole the ball and passed it up for an easy lay-up. Boston College was up by 12 at the half, and Neeson felt good enough to buy himself a beer. On the way up, he was stopped by a reporter.

"What do you see going into the second half?" the reporter asked.

Neeson smiled. "I think Boston College is showing what I thought they would. They're poised, they're confident, they look like they want it more. My kind of people. I think, by the end of the night, we will each be a win away from one big celebration on Monday evening." The reporter thanked him and left.

Coming up behind him, Tucker overheard their conversation. "I don't think you should be so sure yet, man. There's still a lot of time in this half. A twelve-point lead is nothing."

Neeson laughed it off. "Come on, BC is destroying this team. Williams almost has a double-double already. Do you really see those guys making some miracle comeback?"

"All I'm saying is that you may be jinxing yourself by claiming victory this early."

"I'm not Perry. I don't do jinxes. Winning, on the other hand… " He left Tucker and went to buy himself a beer.

The second half began much like the first. BC continued to dominate, but UCLA didn't completely go away. With five minutes left in the game, BC was up by eight—enough for Neeson to begin strategizing what he was going to do for the final few minutes. The cameras would be on him eventually, if they weren't already, so he had to make a good showing. Applause during the final two minutes, then standing applause for the final minute. And he had to be smiling—not like an idiot, but satisfied, assured, vindicated. He thought it would be good to find some BC fans somewhere close by so that he could hand out high-fives and clap victoriously. He saw a clump of them two rows back and estimated how long it would take him to run up conspicuously.

He snapped back into focus when the crowd around him gasped and stiffened. Looking down, he saw a BC player on the floor, crumpled on the ground and holding his knee.

"Whoa," Tucker exclaimed, "did Williams just go down?"

"Wait, which Williams?" demanded Neeson. But he didn't need to ask.

"He's not getting up," Tucker said, with hints of both remorse and sinister glee at the sudden loss of color in Neeson's face. "I think you're in trouble, man."

A sudden panic gripped Neeson by the throat. His mind began ticking back through his data he had fed to OPUS. Had he included injuries in the massive data sweeps that had created the brackets program? Of course he had—he couldn't have left off something like that. BC had a very low injury rate. Good Williams hadn't been out with injuries during the regular season. Could this possibly have been taken into account? With a swift mental kick, Neeson brought himself back to the game. He couldn't lose it now. Yes, there was an accident—but that didn't affect any of the other myriad factors still at play, still accounted for, still under control. The coach was the same. The other players were the same. Just under four minutes left—what could happen in that space of time? Good Williams probably would have been benched for the last minute anyway since they were so far ahead. Neeson focused on deep breaths as two teammates walked Good Williams off the floor.

But as soon as play resumed, the feeling of the game began to change. UCLA got a quick steal out of a timeout and scored an easy lay-up. BC took a bad shot that clanged off the rim and directly into the hands of the UCLA point guard, who sprinted back up the floor and shot a quick three-pointer. Thirty game seconds after Good Williams was out, BC's lead was cut in half. Neeson watched all of this without speaking. Tucker, on the other hand, spoke quite a bit.

"I told you! I told you!" he crowed. "You don't call it till it's over, that's why you play the game. There is change in the wind, my man." The last remark made Neeson go rigid.

UCLA made another strong drive and got fouled. Neeson breathed easier when they missed both free throws. Everything was okay; this would play out correctly. Thousands of data points and hundreds of hours of intense computation could be depended on. Four minutes left.

Both teams traded baskets for the next minute and a half. Neeson found himself cheering anxiously every time BC did something even remotely good. "Come on, come on!" he yelled. To his horror, BC responded by making a bad pass that led to another UCLA shot. Three-point game.

Tucker leaned over and started quipping. "You sure BC stands for 'Boston College' and not 'Big Chokers?'" Cole laughed until he saw Neeson's glower, which remained stubbornly focused on the court.

With 1:42 left to play, UCLA rebounded another BC shot and launched it up court to a guard, who went in to make a lay-up and was fouled in the process. "Ooooh!" Tucker stood, "And one! And one! Tie it up, baby!" UCLA made the shot. Tie game.

This is impossible, Neeson thought. He couldn't have come this far only to lose because of a freak injury. OPUS couldn't have missed the possibility that the team would completely collapse without one player. BC called a time out. With the crowd on its feet, Neeson leaned in to Cole.

"So, Cole, you said at the press conference that you didn't have a system for picking the teams, right? Just between you and me, you have one, right? Or someone gave you suggestions?"

Cole raised his eyebrows and glanced at the engineer sideways. "Really, I didn't even think about it. I was just doing it for a girl. Why, you have one?"

The teams were back on the court, and Neeson left Cole's question unanswered. Just a minute and a half to go. Anything could happen.

BC got the ball out of the time out and made a jump shot. Back on top. UCLA brought the ball down, taking their time and passing a lot at the top of the three-point line. With five seconds left on the shot clock, the guard forced up a three-pointer that was contested. The shooter fell backwards on the floor with his hand in the air as the ball barely missed the fingers of the blocker, arched, and went in. The shooter jumped up and pumped his fists as his team tried to refocus him. BC came back fast and took advantage of the momentary lapse to drive up court. The ball went to Other Williams, who crashed straight into the chest of the UCLA center as he rolled the ball high off his fingers. The ball dropped into the hoop as the referees whistled a foul.

Foul! Foul! Good! Neeson thought, but his joy was short lived. The refs waived off the basket and called an offensive foul on Other Williams. UCLA was still up by one with fifty seconds left.

"What? You've got to be kidding me! That was no offensive foul? Whose pocket is he in, huh?" Neeson yelled, slamming his beer cup to the ground. Cole had his hands in the air, whooping in surprise. Neeson wanted to tell him to shut up, that it wasn't like it was his bracket anyway. He knew what Jason had done. UCLA made a jumper to bring their lead to three. Forty seconds left.

Neeson felt his phone vibrate. It was a text message from Mr. Graham. "Consider yourself acquired." He almost flung the phone up the stands to where he imagined Mr. Graham was looking on with the calculation of a stalking spider, but he restrained himself. He wasn't going to lose control. He simply had to analyze the variables at play and come to a rational conclusion. Good Williams had been injured. By whom? He didn't know; he hadn't seen. Other Williams had been penalized. Why? No good reason. Boston College should be winning this game by a landslide—by an 83% probability margin, to be precise. But they weren't. Therefore, the only rational conclusion was that they were being sabotaged. This had happened before; OPUS had been sabotaged before. Was it possible that Graham himself had been in on this all along? Had it been Graham and Jason from the beginning, out to exploit and humiliate him? And Cole and Tucker, too. They were all connected, weren't they?

BC tried an ill-advised three that missed wildly. Then they fouled the UCLA players after the in-bounds pass, forcing them to shoot free throws. Neeson's heart sank as one, then the other, went through. Five point game, thirty seconds left.

"Cole," Neeson had to shout over the crowd just to be heard, "Listen, I know about the bracket. I know it's not yours. It's OK, I won't say anything, but I just need to know how Jason did it. How did he recruit you? Did he know you from before?"

Cole just stared back. "Jason who? What are you talking about?"

Neeson pulled back, furious. *Liar!* his mind accused. He knew! He stood in mute shock as BC took another bad shot and UCLA got the rebound. Foul shots. There wasn't any time or energy left for the Boston players. With fifteen seconds left, everyone knew that UCLA had won. Tucker pulled Cole to his feet and started the crowd of UCLA fans singing: *Nah Nah Nah Nah, Hey Hey Hey, Goood-byyyyyye!*

Neeson erupted. Shaking with rage, he grabbed Cole with both hands at the shirt collar and screamed into his face. "That game was mine, you cheater!" Cole tried to push him off, and Tucker grabbed Neeson by the arm to separate them. Neeson threw Cole down over the seats and aimed a punch directly at Tucker's jaw. Tucker ducked, the punch glancing over his scalp, and pushed into the engineer's abdomen. Feet slippery with spilled beer, Neeson jammed down onto the seats, struggling against the crowd closing in. Two security guards shoved into him, and when he kicked back, one used pepper spray. The engineer cried out with incoherent rage and pain as he was muscled up the stairs and out the tunnel. Through his tearful, squinting eyes, he got one last look at the arena, but he could see only what he had lost.

Midwest Division

[**Midwest Division**: Play-in Game]
[Tuesday, March 18]

The rolling hills of the Kentucky countryside were covered with morning frost. The sky was white and getting lighter as the weak winter sun rose up gradually from behind a bank of eastern fog. It was light enough to see the gigantic hole in the ground, with all the steel and cement that formed the first foundational walls of a massive structure. Construction workers huddled together, taking quick, practiced sips of near-scalding black coffee as they waited for their heavy tractors to warm up. The grunt of diesel engines interrupted what would otherwise have been a completely quiet Tuesday morning in the countryside.

The architect Haj Hitok surveyed the site from beneath a hard hat pulled down to his eyebrows, keeping his hands in the pockets of his thick coat. To his left was a companion, also bundled warmly.

"You know, I am going to be in Miami this weekend. It's supposed to be 24 degrees down there," Haj said to his companion.

"I hope you mean Celsius."

"Of course."

Haj's companion was a much older man. Thin strands of grey hair strayed out from underneath his hat, and his keen eyes were heavily framed with wrinkles and the effects of history, his head tending to bow forward just a little.

They stood together in silence for a while. "You have a big hole to fill here, Haj," the older man said absently.

"That is easy. All we have to do is put a building in it. But then, you will have to fill the building. Frankly, I believe our job is easier than yours."

"You might be right. It is a competitive market out there. But with this, we will have a competitive advantage. If you're going to recruit, it's good to have something either very old or very new. I'm very old, this is very new. Together we should be hard to turn down."

"But you are not old, Bryan."

Bryan Casing smiled to himself. "I've aged more than my

fair share. I'm hoping that this place will help me pay back the balance."

The two walked back toward the foreman's trailer, their boots crackling over frozen mud embedded with marks from large tire treads. Haj had to leave soon.

"I am curious about something," Haj asked. "How will you know whom to target? There are many people who work for me who are smart and talented, but when I try to consider if I would recommend them for this, I just don't know."

Casing folded his arms and leaned his shoulder against the door of the trailer, smiling faintly in reverie. "I had this physics professor in college, Dr. Seldon, who had a saying: 'The talent factor is a strange attractor, but skill is the rarity that yields singularity.' He had a lot of sayings like that and I've pilfered most of them. The metaphors aren't very good, but what he was trying to say was that talent doesn't merely stand out. It has a gravitational pull that attracts people and opportunities. Highly talented people—as you well know— always seem to end up at the right place at the right time. And the more focused and refined the talent is, or the more that talent has been transformed into true skill, the stronger the pull is. The candidates who are right for us are rare, but I expect it to be relatively easy to identify them because ours is exactly the kind of organization that they would attract. Call it social physics. By the way," he mentioned as an aside, "if you do come across anyone that we might be interested in, let us know. I know the kind of circles you run around in; we would take your recommendations seriously."

Haj prepared to leave. "I will. Unfortunately I still have some of my best stranded in a small apartment in Bangkok, waiting to see if things will change enough to get back on schedule."

"How long will you keep them there?"

Haj shrugged. "Who knows? Things as they are…what do you think? Can they recover without a war?"

"Beats me," Casing conceded. "It's a political crisis complicated by crop failure complicated by an unstable economy complicated by sectarianism complicated by China complicated by a popular uprising, complicated by, complicated by. If I were you, I'd bring them home and set them on a different project."

"I'm sure they agree with you." Haj shook Casing's hand. "I

will see you in a few months. Contact me if you need me, but I think everything will be fine in my absence for the time being."

"Thanks again, Haj. Take care," said Casing, and he watched his architect walk out to the waiting car and drive away. Then he sought shelter in the warm trailer to do some planning. It was funny, he thought, that the conflict in Southeast Asia had just come up in casual conversation. They had been looking at it so intensely over the past few weeks. He thought of checking in on how the Thai project was progressing but decided against it. He trusted his people.

Casing checked his watch. His internal clock was skewed by several layers of jet lag, which had a greater effect on him than he let on. Recruiting was a young person's game, and, therefore, he had young people to do it. He thought it best to take a nap before driving up to Louisville. His meeting at the KM Center there was going to be very late, and he needed to be at his best.

[**Midwest Division**: First Round]
[Thursday, March 19]

Tucker Barnes looked up at the ticking clock mounted above a portrait of Henry Kissinger. 11:19 AM in Lincoln, Nebraska. The first game of the tournament had already begun. But instead of sitting on his couch, wolfing down mountains of his patented Skyline Platter chip and dip with his friends, he was sitting on a folding chair in an office. He had a tie on. And, like an idiot, he had forgotten to charge his phone, so he couldn't even check the scores. Opening Day was ruined.

He stood up as the door next to his chair opened. An 18-year-old girl in a long brown skirt emerged, bidding an effusively grateful farewell to her host, an old man with a smile that stretched the width of his wrinkled face. Wol Pot, the Ambassador Extraordinary and Plenipotentiary of the Kingdom of Thailand, kindly sent her on her way, and then, still smiling, looked past his security guard to Tucker.

"Who is next?" he asked.

Tucker double-checked his clipboard, although he knew very well who was next.

"Sir, you have a few minutes to rest. Then you meet with Lena James, who is an editor for our school newspaper. She's also the head of the largest social action club on campus." Wol Pot nodded happily and turned back into the department chair's office, where he'd been receiving student visitors for the past two hours. The point man for Wol Pot's entourage, a younger man named Mongkut Thaifun, leaned in to whisper something to the Ambassador, then approached the door with a water pitcher in his hands.

"Would you be kind enough to refill this for the Ambassador?" he asked in impeccably refined English. "Also, you mentioned that he will be meeting with the editor of the school paper. Could you provide us with a copy of today's issue?"

In the break room next door, Tucker filled the pitcher and scanned the headlines of a wrinkled copy of the *Daily Nebraskan.* "Huskers to Crush Mt. Saint Mary's"; "RHA Expands Student Guest Meal Plan"; "Student WebCams Expose Humanitarian Atrocities."

Tucker could guess which headline Lena wrote; in fact, he knew who had FedExed the webcams.

When he returned, Tucker found Mongkut waiting outside the door. "Mr. Barnes, one more thing." Mongkut was almost whispering, and Tucker had to lean forward to hear. "It would be very nice if he were to have more of these breaks in his schedule. If he had his way, he would talk to the students all day, but he needs his rest. He doesn't always—doesn't ever—like to take the advice of his physician," Mongkut smiled ruefully, "so it would be kind of you to put an unexpected break in his schedule now and then."

Tucker nodded. "Are you his doctor?" he asked, handing over the water pitcher. "I thought you were, like…"

"The butler?" Mongkut finished the sentence wryly, saving Tucker from making a tactless error. "No, though sometimes I fill that role. In fact, I attended medical school at Duke University."

"Wow. That's cool. Good basketball school. I mean, not this year, but usually. But I'm sure the medical school is really good, too." Tucker sought for a quick change of subject. "How did you get to work for Wol Pot?"

Mongkut smiled thinly. "Some other time. We're ready for the next student, please." Tucker nodded and went to retrieve Lena James from a crowded classroom down the hall.

Ambassador Wol Pot and his delegation were in the city of Lincoln for a summit of Southeast Asian countries hosted by the Secretary of State, a native Nebraskan. Wol Pot also happened to be a friend of the political science department chair, Dr. Theodore Tonkin. Dr. Tonkin had prevailed on Wol Pot to come early and speak at the university. The ambassador had agreed, on the condition that he could have an additional full day to talk exclusively to students. It was a wonderful arrangement for everyone, except Tucker. Tonkin had placed his best undergraduate research assistant in charge of organizing the student interviews, and Tucker had agreed. Only later had he realized the awful timing of the event. During his favorite time of the year, he had to spend the first day as an usher.

When he opened the door to the classroom, his eyes quickly found Lena's. She gathered a notepad and a digital recorder and threaded her way through the remaining students waiting for their ten-minute slot with Wol Pot. As she passed Tucker, she squeezed him affectionately around the waist. Tucker closed the door behind them.

"How's he doing with all these meetings?" Lena whispered, slipping her hand into his.

"He's good for an 80-year-old guy," Tucker whispered back, leaning down a bit to compensate for the full foot of height difference between them. "Everyone loves him. I think he could do this all day."

"That's good," said Lena, "because I don't know how I'm going to fit everything I've got for him into twenty minutes."

"Lena, you have ten minutes," Tucker warned, "and you're just supposed to interview him."

"What else do you think I would do?" Lena asked defensively.

"I'm telling you, you need to take it easy on him. His doctor was telling me that the man needs to rest. Don't try and get him to fight the Man or anything. Just get your interview and let him do his thing."

"If he were really doing his thing, if his leaders were doing *anything*, we wouldn't be getting streaming video of starving children from his country every day. You expect me to just act nice when—"

"Yes," he scolded like someone with authority to scold. This drew, as it always did, a particular ire from Lena's eyes. "You can't let this turn into another thing like it did with the mayor."

They arrived at Tonkin's office, the door now closed. Lena maintained a steady, accusing stare as she patted his crooked tie. "By the way, your roommate called me and told me to bring you this." She opened her purse and pulled out a tablet computer. Tucker kissed first the tablet, then her cheek.

"Babe, you saved my life." He reached for the computer but she pulled it back, holding it aloft.

"Uh-uh. For this, I get an extra ten minutes."

Tucker looked at Lena, the computer, and the clock. "Five," he said at last.

"Seven."

"Fine."

She handed over the computer and patted his backside as she opened the door herself.

"Sa-Wadt-Dee Kah," she said sweetly. The ambassador responded in Thai, and she approached the table to shake his hand. Tucker closed the door, hoping that he wouldn't have to pull her out of the room to avoid an international incident. Such a thing wouldn't be unprecedented. The mayor would agree with him.

A member of the diplomat's security detail motioned for Tucker.

"There are some reporters outside that say they have an interview scheduled."

Tucker shook his head. "He's not doing any reporters today."

"That's what I told them, but they asked if they could talk to you about it."

"They asked for me?" Mildly surprised, Tucker put his ear to the door to ensure there weren't any raised voices, then walked with the guard down the empty hall and out of the building's side entrance. In the bone-biting chill of the afternoon, a man and woman huddled close together next to the bike rack. The woman put out her gloved hand to Tucker.

"You're Tucker Barnes? I'm Abigail Razzione, and this is Richard O'Shea. We're reporters for *The Chronicle Star*." The man waved, and then retreated his hand back under his armpits.

"I'm sorry," said Tucker, who wasn't sure if he had ever heard of *The Chronicle Star*, "but the Ambassador isn't talking to any reporters today."

"We know, but we didn't get a chance to interview him yesterday. Our plane was late, and our editor really wants the story. He's doing students now, right? We could pass for students." Abigail glanced at her companion. "We only need ten minutes. Just say we're with the school newspaper."

"Someone with the school newspaper is talking to him right now," Tucker said impatiently, "and his schedule is already full. If you want to talk to him some other time, then talk to the department secretary. I'm just a research assistant for Dr. Tonkin, and I'm just in charge of the interviews for today."

"Oh, that's great!" said Abigail enthusiastically. "Could we meet with him at least? He's the one who invited the Ambassador, right?"

"You mean Tonkin? No. I mean, yes that's correct, but no, I won't take you to see him. You'll have to contact the department secretary to set that up."

"Now just a minute!" Abigail said with sudden indignation. "I don't think that you fully appreciate the full implications of what you're doing by stone-walling us. Might I remind you of the First Amendment's declaration of freedom of the press? Don't you understand the vital role of journalism in the pursuit of truth and the preservation of our national—"

"Hold it, Abby, hold it." Richard O'Shea nudged Abby without uncovering his hands.

"But I had it memorized!" she murmured.

"I know. That was good, but we should probably speed this up. We're all going into hyperthermia." Then he turned to Tucker. "Sorry, we've been working on this whole routine where she… never mind. You say that you can't get us in to see Ambassador Pot or Dr. Tonkin. How about letting us meet with a member of Pot's staff. A lawyer? A secretary? A traveling barber?"

"Not happening." Tucker folded his arms.

"Okay then, maybe you can answer some questions for us. You're around, you're in the rooms, you can probably give us a little behind-the-scenes action, right? C'mon."

Tucker shrugged uncomfortably. "Maybe. But, like I said, I'm just an undergrad. I really only write memos and things for Dr. Tonkin. I'm not actually in the rooms where everything is going on. Just so you know."

"Excellent. So how are Pot and his staff holding up under the strain of so many problems at home and so much international attention? Happy? Healthy?"

"Yeah, he seems like a pretty happy dude. I mean, he knows that things are serious. His lecture yesterday was pretty harsh against the United States and China, but he's really nice in person."

"So he sides with Many Hands, then?" Abby spoke up quickly.

"No. He's in favor of an international aid package and didn't consider Many Hands legitimate, at least not as a way for the country to recover. The whole speech is on YouTube, by the way."

"What about his staff? Are they all backing him? Is there a voice that stands out stronger than others among his group?" Tucker thought briefly about Mongkut. He always seemed to be in Wol Pot's ear. But Tucker was irritated by the questions and decided against answering any more.

"I don't know, they don't talk when I'm around. Honestly, I've only gotten them water and told them where the bathrooms are." Tucker looked at the pair, hoping that they were done with the conversation.

"There must be some kind of insight you can give us," Rick prodded.

Tucker shook his head. "Not about this stuff. If you asked me about good take-out places or Nebraska basketball or something like that, I'd have more to say."

Abby narrowed her eyes and examined him from behind her scarf, then sighed in resignation. "That's fine. You can go back in; we're going to go thaw. Thank you for your time."

"OK," said Tucker, shaking the hand Abby offered. "Sorry about the mix-up. Just call the department secretary and she can set you up for next week if there's a spot open for Wol Pot or Dr. Tonkin."

"Thanks," said Abby, turning toward the parking lot. But Rick lingered.

"Just out of curiosity, do you agree with him?"

"Who?"

"Wol Pot, about his stance against Many Hands and being for international aid."

Tucker opened his mouth to say something, but shrugged instead. He'd already said too much. "What he thinks is his business."

"I see," Rick said thoughtfully under his scarf. Then, as Abby pulled at his elbow, "So, how far is Nebraska going in the tournament?"

Tucker smiled in spite of himself. "All the way."

The two reporters jogged briskly around the building, and Tucker turned to the door to swipe his student ID as quickly as his numb hands would permit him.

That was weird, he thought, walking back down the hallway

to resume his post next to the office door. He powered up the tablet and listened at the door again, just in case. He couldn't hear anything, but before he could straighten up and pull his head away, the door swung open and he was ear-to-chest with Mongkut. He raised his head slowly to look at the doctor and smiled, embarrassed at the impression of eavesdropping. Mongkut was expressionless.

"The ambassador would like five more minutes with the young lady, please," he said with the slightest hint of annoyance.

"No problem," said Tucker, giving a little wave to the door that was closing behind the doctor. His eyes flicked down to his watch to see that Lena had already been in there for twenty minutes. Just like she'd asked. *Well*, he thought, pulling up the CBS site on his computer, *Lena gets her way and I get to watch some basketball*. The day was starting to feel normal.

[**Midwest Division**: Second Round]
[Saturday, March 21]

Saturday morning was no excuse to stay in bed late; that was the rule of the Barnes household. Therefore, it was 6:13 AM when Tucker sat down on the steps of his childhood home, double-knotted his shoelaces, cued up his running music, and jogged into a March morning still wrapped up in pre-dawn mist. The white ghost of his warm breath in cold air emerged in rhythmic puffs that quickened as he reached his stride. The road before him was straight until forever, cutting right down the middle of field after frosted field. It was a route he had run thousands of times; it was the one place on the planet where his head was the clearest.

Tucker had begun to feel a little sheepish about coming home every weekend. He knew that at some point he would live too far away for the escapism of sleeping in his own room, letting his mom do his laundry, eating his dad's cooking, pretending that independent adulthood wasn't imminent. He also knew that his parents would never stand for an able-bodied Barnes boy regressing into dependency. And they had no cause to fear on Tucker's account; despite the concerns occasionally voiced by Lena, he did have life plans beyond just coming home and watching basketball. But it was nice to still have time before all of that.

The road ended at a fence encompassing an empty, icy field. For a minute, Tucker stretched and watched the jagged edge of shadow retreat as weak sunlight moved over the stubbled ground. He liked the inevitability of daybreak. He waited until the sun had reached a certain furrow, then, with a deep breath, he turned around and jogged steadily back the three miles to the squat, baby-blue house with the meager oak tree in the front. His usual finish-line sprint ended at the mailbox. Picking up the newspaper, he read the headlines as he stretched out in the warm living room.

In the kitchen, his father was cooking breakfast while his mom was doing her morning check on the seedlings growing inside windowsills throughout the house.

"Set the table, son," Henry greeted him from the stove. "I'm coming for that sports section when I'm finished here."

The kitchen was modest and only had room for a small table in the corner. Most of it was covered with remnants of a coupon-clipping project and a month-old issue of *The Economist*, both belonging to his mother. Tucker shoved it all aside, covered it with the comics section, and set down a stack of plates and silverware.

"Here you go," Henry said as he set a dish of toast with gravy on the table. Then, with a ceremonial cough, he laid down a curved, pewter object with an engraved thatched pattern next to Tucker's plate.

"You giving up so soon?" Tucker asked, mouth already full.

"Hard to mess with perfection. I lost Notre Dame and Xavier already. I still have Nebraska, of course, but compared to yours, the rest just can't compete. I figure I should concede early and gracefully. You still have to beat the rest of the family, though. No one else wanted to give up yet. Your mother thinks your good luck will tank by Sunday."

"That's right!" Regina called from the hallway.

The metal piece belonged to a souvenir statue of the Eiffel Tower that Henry had collected during his time in the Peace Corps. The statue broke down into five pieces: the four individual legs, and the central tower. Every year, on the week before Selection Sunday, the statue was divided up between his parents, his two older brothers, and himself. After the tournament, the bracket winner got to display the Tower prominently in the place of his or her choosing. For many of the past ten years, that place was on the kitchen counter, on top of Tucker's old Transformers lunchbox. His mother grumbled about losing counter space to a trophy display, but Tucker insisted on his rights as bracket champion. The glory of beating his older brothers and parents had not diminished with time. Tucker flipped his dad's piece in his hand with a satisfied smirk and set it next to his plate.

"So, what are the headlines this morning?" his mother asked, taking a seat next to him and filling a plate.

"Huskers dominate!"

"I know that one, honey, anything else?"

"Let's see... gridlock in Congress, arson on Wall Street, death, death, death, and... crop failure in Thailand. Those are the main ones."

"News is about as cheerful as today's weather," Regina remarked on her way to a sip of coffee. "So what are the headlines going to be next week?"

It was an old game that Regina played exclusively with Tucker. She had made sure that all of her boys knew what was going on in the world and had quizzed them regularly when they were young. But Tucker retained current events so easily that he got bored, so Regina changed the game: she began to make him guess what would show up in the next week's paper and offered a dollar every time he got something right. She had to stop handing out money when he got to high school—he was cleaning her out—but it remained a tradition between herself and her youngest son. Tucker didn't mind.

"Next week?" Tucker hesitated only long enough to finish his bite. "Next week Tucker Barnes watches eight more hours of basketball and blacks out after a Skyline Platter overdose."

"Speaking of that, you get enough sleep last night? TV was on pretty late." Henry joined them at the table and began rifling through the paper.

"Hey, I got more games in last night than I got in the whole first two days. This summit thing is taking up all my time."

"You aren't still making up schedules for that Dr. Tonkin, are you? Doesn't he have people for that?"

\ "Yeah, but he's been asking me to do a lot of background research for him, just little things that he doesn't want to give the grad students, looking up stuff he can't remember, that kind of thing. Like, he wants me to write a page on why the South Koreans decided to be neutral in the whole famine aid debate. I don't think it will come up at the big State dinner tonight since none of the Koreans will be there, but he still wants to know. It won't take long to write, but when he asks me to do a bunch of these things, it starts to add up."

"But he's paying you, right?" Henry asked.

"Yeah, he's paying me."

"And you're gonna get free food at this dinner?" It was an article of faith among the Barnes men that free food was nearly sacred.

"It's supposed to be barbecue. It might be good, if it isn't fake barbecue."

Henry raised an eyebrow over the edge of the newspaper. "It's the Secretary of State, I'm sure he knows how to put on a good spread."

"Not that he's the one doing the cooking," added Regina. "So, why *is* South Korea staying out of this?"

"Because they're worried about the barbecue, too." Tucker said slyly, Regina whacked him lovingly with the spoon. "I don't know, I don't think there's a lot of public support in their country to get involved, and the president has his own problems. Tonkin says the U.S. wants them involved, and I think it might help if they were, but, you know, that's how it is. Tonkin doesn't think they're committed enough to be helpful, anyway."

"Then why is he having you write the paper?"

"Probably to prove that he's right."

"I see," said Regina, who always took pride when her little boy said something smart. "When do you have to leave, honey?"

"Now," Tucker said, swiping the last bite from his mother's plate and narrowly avoiding her retaliatory swat. "Five minutes ago. Lena wants to meet this morning so she can try to get me in on her latest project."

"So things are going well with you two, then?" His mom had finally come to her favorite subject.

"We had our 'Drama-free February'. That was our deal. We'll see how it is after March. This was when she dumped me last year. I wasn't paying enough attention to her with all the games. She won't like it this year, either."

Tucker glanced over at his dad, expecting the typical wisecrack about how basketball was more important than girlfriends anyway. But Henry was absorbed in a pile of papers that showed crinkles and bends from being handled by worried hands. Looking back to his mom, Tucker saw her shake her head slightly.

"Okay, Dad, gotta go now." Tucker's voice sounded cheerier than necessary.

"OK, son, OK," Henry lifted a hand without raising his head.

"You do good tonight," Regina said, hugging him. "Don't embarrass us in front of all those diplomats. We don't want them going back to their countries talking smack about those darn Barnes."

"Mom, they won't even know I'm there."

"That's my boy," she smiled. "I love you, sweetie."

Tucker ran upstairs for his laundry and returned outside to find his car already running.

"Have to let these things warm up," Henry said, stepping out of the driver's side. "It pays to take care of them, especially in the winter."

"Yeah, Dad, I know."

"Well, I left some gas money for you in the cup holder. Remember to use premium."

"Dad, you don't have to give me money. Really, I don't need it. You and mom—"

"Your mother and I are doing just fine," Henry interrupted him. For a moment, the two men stared at each other silently. "You go focus on school and such and let us old folks take care of ourselves."

There was no more room for argument. Tucker opened the car door and slid in as his dad stepped back.

"Oh, and don't forget." Henry, smiling a little, pointed to the side seat where he had placed his piece of the Eiffel Tower. Tucker hopped in behind the wheel. Then, waving good-bye to his dad, he drove off down the cold, straight road, his dad becoming smaller and smaller in his rear-view mirror.

*   *   *   *

The barn on Secretary Maxwell's ranch was anything but a barn. It was shaped like one and painted like one, but the wide red doors opened to row after row of round tables, each spread with fine linen tablecloths and set with wine glasses, candlesticks, and centerpieces made of small hay bales and corn husks. In the serving area, engraved silver chafers piled with food sat steaming on red-checked tablecloths, while a line of caterers stood in white shirts and ties to make sure the barbeque was served correctly. Tucker had actually grown up with a barn, and to him the room had the feel of an amusement park attraction. But it wasn't his barn or his party, so he didn't care.

Representatives from all over the Pacific coast of Asia began to gather at 6:30. Most were prompt, some tardy. The dinner was to mark the beginning of a four-day summit on Southeast Asian politics, so it was full of all the niceties and ceremonial good expressions that always prevailed before a tense, high-stakes political scrum. Delegates, aides, business leaders, and other guests were assigned seats that assured maximum diversity, and State Department staffers circulated tensely between tables making introductions and encouraging everyone to try the hors d'oeuvres. After all, it was a conference on bringing nations together, on unity, on the kind of diplomacy that would prevent a severe multinational military conflict. For Secretary Maxwell, the best way to begin achieving those goals was through well-orchestrated mingling over roasted corn on the cob.

Tucker had opted out of sitting next to the diplomats, much to his boss's disappointment. Tonkin was always trying to get him more interested in international affairs as a career, but Tucker steadfastly resisted. It was a great job by undergraduate standards, but not what he wanted to do with his life. So, for the night, he found an empty seat at an empty table that was far enough away that he could watch the games on his phone—fully charged this time—and not bother anybody. And he would still get the free food.

As he leaned back, watching a tiny Syracuse player shoot a three-pointer in transition over a hapless Arizona defender, he felt someone walk up behind him. A hand patted his shoulder. He looked up to see a man not much older than him with a friendly, slightly familiar face and a plate of kabobs stacked haphazardly. A woman was close behind him. He couldn't quite place them until the man spoke.

"Tucker!" Richard O'Shea greeted, sitting down across from him. "You look much warmer."

Despite Rick's full plate, they looked like they had just entered in a hurry. They were slightly out of breath, and Abby's hair was still staticky from a hat recently pulled off. But in that moment, they showed no hurry. They both settled into their seats, and Abby began to inventory her purse while Richard took a kabob in each hand and slid several pieces of meat into his mouth.

"Uh, are you guys supposed to be here? I thought it was no press tonight." Tucker actually cared less about getting them in trouble than having to share his table. Now it would be harder to follow the games.

"Oh, we're not press tonight," Rick said offhandedly.

"What, so you used to be reporters and now you're not?"

"Well, it comes and goes." There was no sign that he wasn't serious.

"Um… so what are you now?"

Rick glanced at Abby, who looked up from her purse to answer. "Attachés," she said. "We're representing a guest that wasn't able to attend."

Tucker didn't know how to respond. They clearly weren't attachés or reporters. He wondered if he should warn security, but nothing about them seemed dangerous. They were more like wedding crashers than spies, and they didn't seem to warrant starting a commotion. But if they became more annoying…

"Don't worry, Tucker, Maxwell knows we're here. See? Look at all this food he gave us!" Rick brandished an ear of barbequed corn and grinned. "So enough about us. Who's winning?"

"What?"

"The game—dude, I can see it on your screen. Is Arizona winning?"

Tucker took a deep breath and contemplated ignoring the man. But it was an irresistible part of his nature to talk about basketball.

"Arizona's down 12 to with three minutes left."

"Ha!" Abby was suddenly in the conversation, pointing her finger at an unsmiling Richard. A few people at the closest table turned to investigate. "Ha!"

"We have a little bracket bet between us," Richard explained. "Arizona was in my Final Four."

"That was stupid. What did you bet?" Tucker asked in spite of himself.

"The loser has to buy a freezer-full of Ben and Jerry's ice cream," Abby said gleefully. "And I've almost finished my winnings from last year."

"Wait a second," said Richard. "Why was that stupid? How could anybody see Syracuse over Arizona when Arizona went 10-0 to end the season and Syracuse is a 12-seed?"

"Because," Tucker responded, "they have no perimeter 'D'. They won games because they could run and block shots, but when teams shoot from outside, they panic, start to overplay men on the perimeter, and open themselves up. And Syracuse is all about the outside shot, so that's what's happening. You need to watch more SportsCenter, man."

Rick sat back and picked up another kabob thoughtfully.

"So you knew Arizona would lose, huh?"

"Uh, yeah."

"Huh." Rick chewed and swallowed. "Just out of curiosity, how many games did you guess right in the first round?"

Tucker shrugged and smiled slightly. Rick was about to press more, but Secretary Maxwell stood up at the podium just then, looking authentically clichéd in his suit, string tie, and cowboy hat, holding up his hands for silence.

"Welcome, honored delegates and guests. On behalf of the United States of America and the great state of Nebraska, I want to express my deep and sincere appreciation that you have all gathered in a spirit of cooperation and goodwill to address the delicate and devastating circumstances facing the nations of Southeast Asia..."

Rick leaned over to Tucker as the Secretary droned on, whispering loudly, "Why are you smiling? Seriously, how many did you get right?"

"Shhh," Abby hushed. "Rick, that's rude."

"Sorry," whispered Rick. The Secretary continued.

"Tonight we will have the distinct honor of hearing from several individuals with tremendous knowledge and compassionate insight into the plight of the people living in this region. First, we will hear from Mr. Wol Pot, the honored ambassador from the Nation of Thailand. Mr. Wol Pot has demonstrated political courage and integrity in speaking out against the national and international gridlock that has prevented humanitarian aid from being delivered to starving citizens in his ..."

Tucker's phone vibrated, interrupting the silent streaming feed from the game. It was a text from Lena: Is Wol Pot speaking yet?

Tucker bent over his phone in the dim light, laboring over the smudged touch screen. Almost.

Another text. How soon?

He wrote back hastily. What u care?

Just tell me when, Lena sent back.

The Secretary was wrapping up his introduction at that moment: "…he has been tireless in petitioning foreign governments for aid and in speaking up for the suffering among his people. We would like to thank Mr. Pot for his presence here and welcome him now to the podium."

Tucker noticed that the applause for Wol Pot was wild among some tables and non-existent at others. This would be a tough crowd to negotiate, and the old man looked somehow older and frailer as he stood to speak than he had just the day before.

"My esteemed—colleagues, my brothers and sisters in the world," he began. "We are here to do good. But how does one do good? How can one do good when each path is dark and unknown? How can one do good when there are so many to lift and carry and so few to help?" Wol Pot's voice trailed off, contemplative, and in that moment, Tucker remembered that Lena was waiting for his text. He pulled out his phone and pecked "now" as Wol Pot started speaking again. He would ask her why she wanted to know later.

"I understand that there is a great sports tournament underway in this country. I have a young friend with an interest in American sports. He has told me about something called a 'Hail Mary'. It is my understanding that this is something done at the end, in desperation, something done with a prayer and a fool's wish. After ten months of impasse and thousands of my countrymen on the brink of dying, I believe that it is time for a 'Hail Mary'."

Tucker looked around the room. Everyone, including the couple at his table, had their eyes riveted on the old ambassador.

"I find myself here," continued the ambassador, "in a city named for the great Abraham Lincoln. I am here surrounded by a generous abundance of food in this hall. I am in one of the largest food-producing states in the richest country in the world. How does one do good in such a place?"

Bodies began to shift in chairs. Tucker noticed Rick put a half-eaten kabob down on the pile of empty skewers on his plate.

"At this very moment in which we are finishing an evening

meal, hundreds of my people are dying of starvation. At this very moment in which we are enjoying cordial conversation, the world's most powerful nations refuse to formally sit down together and agree upon a course of action. At this very moment when college basketball teams are facing each other in games, protesters are battling with the police in the beautiful streets of Bangkok. I ask you, my friends, how does one do good at such a time?"

Wol Pot's voice had regained its strength, and he no longer looked frail. If anything, he looked resolute. Tucker glanced up at the Secretary of State, sitting behind Wol Pot. He had his hand slightly raised, about to signal an aide, apprehension on his face. Something very unexpected was happening.

"I would like to announce, at this time and in this place, I begin a hunger strike. Here, in this land, I will not eat until the mighty countries of China, Thailand, and the United States of America agree to come together for the poor of my country…"

The rest of his words were drowned out by a cacophony of scraping chairs and urgent chatter. Secretary Maxwell was issuing rapid-fire instructions to a tight circle of aides, and one of them had already pulled out a phone to take video footage of Wol Pot standing serenely at the podium, surrounded by a chaotic crowd. The next moment, Mongkut Thaifun rose to the ambassador's side, whispered something, then pulled him back to sit down at the head table where, Tucker noticed for the first time, Wol Pot's plate was completely empty.

"There go the Burmese," Rick commented, watching a group of six men in collarless white shirts and longyis stalk out through the side door.

Abby stood up. "We should be going too," she said to Rick.

"You're leaving now?" asked Tucker.

"Nothing to see anymore," Rick said, "and we didn't get much sleep. Tell your boss to have fun!" They stood to go, but then Rick turned around again. "Seriously, how many…"

"None," Tucker snapped. "I didn't miss any. Now stop bothering me, I think I'm about to have stuff to do." He stood, pocketed his phone as soon as there was a foul called, and walked over to Tonkin, who looked like the ceiling had crashed on his head.

*   *   *   *

To Tucker's relief, Tonkin didn't need him anymore that night. The Secretary of State had called an impromptu meeting with the US and Thai delegations, and Tonkin had been asked to stay as a mediator for Wol Pot. Tucker had been allowed to go home, but his boss had made it clear that he would need a lot of help the next day. There was no point in Tucker mentioning that the next day was Sunday.

As he drove west on Route 6 toward downtown Lincoln, Tucker wondered about the old ambassador's motives. The hunger strike was a gutsy move, no doubt, but it was hard to see how it would be an effective one. One drastic move usually led to another, and there were some big players in the conflict. The headlines next week could be pretty intense. He let the scenarios play out in his head until his thoughts drifted inevitably from international politics and into reflections on the shot selection and NBA readiness of certain college hoops players. If he hurried, he might make it home before the last game.

Lena. He suddenly remembered that he'd planned to call her and find out why she wanted to know when Wol Pot's speech was starting. The speech wasn't broadcast—she only knew about it because Tucker had mentioned it. He had mentioned it, right? She was probably lighting a candle for him or something. She did things like that. He voice-dialed her number and held his phone aloft in his hand.

As it rang, a police car came up fast, its lights flashing. He tossed the phone on the seat so he wouldn't get pulled over for texting. But the police weren't after him. The car sped off the next exit and appeared at the parking lot of a large grocery store to the left of the road. It joined three other squad cars already there, blue and red strobes whirling away. Tucker squinted at the scene as he passed by—was somebody getting thrown onto the hood of a car? But then it was behind him. Lena's phone went to voice mail.

"Hey babe, crazy stuff happening, call me back," Tucker said after the beep.

Tucker arrived at his apartment a few minutes later and sprinted in expecting to see his roommates watching the last two minutes of a game. But they weren't. To his amazement, they were watching the news.

"Did you see it out there?" one of them asked, not looking away from the screen.

"See what?" Tucker leaned toward the image of a reporter in front of glass doors. "Wait, is that the thing at the grocery store?"

"At *three* grocery stores. They're calling it a 'flash famine'. Bunch of people were at the stores, and about thirty minutes ago, they all just turned and grabbed as much food as they could and ran out of the store. Seriously messed up, there were like eighty people and they took all the food. Like, empty shelves. Two old ladies got trampled. The ones they caught say they're going to be shipping the food to some country in Asia. And I just ate my last Hot Pocket for dinner. You got some I can have?"

But Tucker was watching the TV where grainy surveillance footage was playing on a loop. There it was—all of the aisles crowded with people shopping like normal, filling up carts. Then all at once, they turned, grabbed as much food as they could throw into their carts, and rushed out in a body, knocking over several cashiers and bystanders. It was a shocking display of sudden group movement, like they'd all had simultaneous panic attacks. Squinting his eyes, Tucker could see very clearly that some of the people who rushed out had something taped to their shirts: a distinct banded pattern of red, white, and blue. The flag of Thailand.

Tucker felt sick and more than a little angry. He now knew why Lena had spoken to Wol Pot for so long. And he now knew why Lena needed to know the exact moment that Wol Pot announced his hunger strike.

He yanked his phone out of his pocket and dialed, eyes still on the TV. As he dialed, he said to his roommates, "I'm surprised you're watching this instead of the game."

"Oh, we're not. They were in a time-out." And they flipped the channel back.

Lena's phone went to voice-mail again. Tucker stepped into his bedroom and closed the door. After the beep, he whispered harshly, jabbing the air with his finger to make his point. "Babe, I know what's happening and we got to talk about this. If they trace this thing back to you, and then they trace it from you back to me, then we're both screwed. We gotta talk. I can't believe…" He waited a few seconds and hung up. Tossing the phone on his desk, he lay down to think. He didn't expect her to call back tonight—she was obviously busy. But tomorrow...

And that's when it occurred to him. *I was going to go grocery shopping tomorrow. I'm out of Hot Pockets, too.*

[**Midwest Division**: Sweet Sixteen]
[Thursday, April 26]

"Tucker, come in."

Dr. Tonkin welcomed his young undergraduate assistant into his office from behind a moderately disheveled desk. Three people were already occupying one corner of the office, each holding notepads and looking like they were ready to be told what to do. Tonkin himself looked tired.

"I'd like you to meet the new additions to our staff," he said with some irony. His previous "staff" had been made up of Tucker, four graduate students, and the department secretary. But the sudden, unexpected increase in Tonkin's workload went far beyond the limits of the group's normal capacity. The Wol Pot hunger strike was now in its fifth day and had become a State Department fiasco, pulling Tonkin into a whirlpool of meetings, press conferences, and the minutiae of international communication. Tonkin was the liaison with Wol Pot who was trusted by both the Thai and the US, so he was stuck in an overwhelming situation. But if the work overwhelmed Tonkin, then it also overwhelmed Tucker. The department had secured some flexibility from Tucker's teachers, giving him extra time to work, by Tonkin's request. Everyone that worked for him was asked to focus on the situation. But even with that, they still needed help.

"You might know John from some of your classes," Tonkin said, pointing to the bearded student closest to him. "He has offered to help out with odd things: answer calls, take minutes, and such. And Tanya here is my new volunteer website updater and online person. And here we have Carla, who has offered to help me with some translations. She's new this semester, just transferred from Georgetown, right?"

Tucker gave benign nods to the recruits.

"Tucker," Tonkin introduced, "has been working with me for the past year. He knows everything about how I work and how my office is set up. Anything you need supply-wise, ask him. He's been answering some e-mails and doing some media monitoring, so Carla, I may have you take over some of that if it keeps up at this pace. I need Tucker to focus on doing write-ups for me. By the way, Tucker, I have a press conference tomorrow, so I may have you look over my statement tonight." Tonkin paused for a moment as he lost his train of thought. "For now, I need Tanya to stay and talk over some things with me. Tucker, find chairs for John and Carla, they should have computers by this afternoon. I'll let you decide where they should be set. Can everybody meet here again at noon?" Tucker looked at the other three and wondered when or if he'd be having lunch.

John and Carla followed Tucker down the hall to the graduate student offices, a big room full of desks with dividers between them, most crammed with textbooks on foreign policy, journals, and empty cellophane wrappers.

"John, take this one," Tucker said, gesturing to the first empty space he saw. "It has a phone hook-up. Sorry it's so cramped. Carla, you can have this desk."

"Do you have any coffee around here?" Carla asked, putting her purse down. Tucker led her through the labyrinth of chairs to the coffee machine in the far corner of the room. She stood straight and moved with confidence, like someone who naturally expected to be in charge. She would have been intimidating to Tucker if he hadn't been a foot taller.

"So, you can translate?" Tucker asked. "What do you speak?"

"I went to high school in Laos, so I'm fluent in Laotian. I speak a little bit of Thai and Mandarin, too, but not as much."

"Your parents were in the military?"

"My dad is a military contractor. He sets up communication equipment and trains soldiers on how to use it. What about your parents?"

"My parents met in the Peace Corp, but we moved back here when I was little. Now my dad teaches history at the middle school in Ashland and coaches basketball, and my mom teaches French. And they both run the family farm. We stayed pretty busy growing up." Tucker realized that he was explaining more than he needed to. "Your folks still over there, with all that's going on?"

"No," Carla said, "but I still have friends there. Hey, listen." She tossed her hair back and lowered her voice. "About Dr. Tonkin.

He seems kind of stressed with this whole thing. Is this… I don't know how to ask this. Is this typical of him? Everyone talks about him like he's this foreign policy genius, but in the office today he seemed like he was in over his head."

Tucker shrugged. "I mean, this isn't exactly what he had in mind for this week. The Secretary and him thought this would be four days of talking and hammering out a joint statement about unity and good will. But now it's been a week of press conferences and tough questions and a deadline for getting everyone into formal negotiations before an old Thai man keels over from starvation in front of the world. So, yeah, he's in over his head, but he is smart. He wouldn't be in on all these meetings if the big guys up there didn't trust him. Or if Pot didn't trust him."

"Sounds like you've been doing a lot, too," she said, smiling. He smiled back, a little dazzled.

"Um, yeah," he said. "I mean, I help out, do some research for him sometimes when there's something he doesn't have time to look up. Not that he always reads them. I did a thing on South Korea last week and he hasn't said anything about it. But with everything going on, I don't really care."

"South Korea?" Carla looked confused. "Aren't they neutral?"

"Well, yeah, but—it doesn't matter. The memos are the small stuff. Checking his speeches and press statements takes a lot longer. He needs more done tonight, which sucks. I have a lot of people coming over to watch the game tonight."

"Wait, he has *you* check his press statements?"

"Yeah, why?"

Carla surveyed him with meditating eyes. "Why don't you let me do it?" she finally asked. "You deserve a night off, and he said he was going to have me do some of the writing anyway, if things get too busy. Why don't you just forward me whatever he sends you, and I can take a look at it and get back to you. He won't even have to know it's from me; I'll send it back to you when I'm done."

Tucker felt a sudden surge of gratitude. Here was a woman who understood the importance of basketball. "Are you serious? You'd really do that? But it's gonna be two or three pages, and you'll have to fact check everything, review the most recent statements from everyone that's involved, think up possible follow-up questions. You sure you got that?"

Carla shrugged. "That's what I'm here for," she said. "Actually, if you have some other revisions that you've done for him, I can read over those to get a sense of how you've been doing it."

"Sure, I can e-mail you like fifty of them. I've been doing this stuff for a year. Listen, if you finish in time—and you probably won't, but still—you should come over to my place. There will be plenty to drink all night."

"Maybe," she said. Then she looked at the time. "Hey, I need to make a call before noon. I'll be looking for your e-mails then, huh?" She spun on a dime and stepped crisply away. Tucker caught himself watching her leave. He flinched slightly, instinctively, as if anticipating that Lena would slap him up the back of his head at any second.

*   *   *   *

The sun was just setting that evening as Tucker drove west to the Mollifly Motel, a few miles outside the city. In the passenger seat was a peace offering sealed in Tupperware.

He had to park his car three blocks away and walk up. What had formerly been a dive completely unknown to anyone but the desperate or cheap had become a permanent campground for international reporters and activists. Wol Pot and his delegation had moved there from a high-profile downtown hotel the day after the hunger strike began, as it wasn't exactly effective to protest poverty and hunger in an elegant four-room suite. The small motel was feeling the pressure of image, too. It had been forced to take down the sign touting its great continental breakfast after a wave of snarky comments on the cable news channels.

The motel itself was now inaccessible; police had cordoned it off and security details were posted at every entrance. The public could gather, but only on the opposite side of the street. A reverent congregation of forty or fifty supporters, each holding a lit candle, stood in vigil. Tucker recognized several from NSAC, the Nebraska Social Action Coalition, of which Lena was the ringleader. Some in the vigil were praying, some were chanting, some in English, some in Thai. Tucker made his way to the front of the crowd, using the streetlamps and candlelight to find the back of the head of the person he had come to see.

It had been five days since he'd seen Lena, two days since they had spoken on the phone, and six hours since he'd received the e-mail strongly suggesting that he show up to the vigil. He hadn't written back; she didn't know that he wasn't planning to stay.

"Wazzup, girl," he said, tapping Lena on the shoulder.

"Finally, you're here," she said, turning and shushing him. "You can get a candle over there."

"I can't stay. I've got everybody at my place to watch the game. You should come too, babe."

She heaved an angry sigh meant to be understood by everyone nearby, though Tucker ignored it.

"Look, I even brought you some Skyline Platter so you'll know what you're missing." He lifted the lid from the Tupperware container and revealed a crooked stack of chips, homemade peach salsa, and melted cheese that was the nucleus of his locally-famous party dish. A man next to him turned at the smell and looked at the food with some longing.

"What is wrong with you?" Lena scolded. "This is a vigil for people who are fasting!" She snatched the container out of his hands and closed the lid tight. Then she grabbed his arm hard and pulled him out of the crowd to a safe distance.

"Tucker, if you didn't come to support us, what are you doing here?"

"I came here for you," Tucker said defensively. "It's freezing out here! You're starving. You've barely eaten more than Wol Pot."

Lena just folded her arms and raised her eyebrows with the disapproving look Tucker had seen countless times.

"Lena, you all are wasting your time holding candles out here in the cold when you could be back at my place getting warm, is what I'm trying to tell you."

"I'm sorry, wasting my time? You came here to tell me that I am wasting my time by showing my support for a man that you and I both know and respect? You're telling me that it would be a better use of my time to come down to your place with all your drunk roommates and watch a stupid game?"

Tucker bit his lip to keep from reacting to the blasphemy of "stupid game."

"Okay, that didn't come out right. But babe, listen to me. I know what you all are trying to do. I get it. And you're right. I like the man, too. But I'm saying that it doesn't matter how many people you get out here and how many news programs show you all on prime-time TV, it isn't going to change the reality that…"

"That is *not* what we're trying to do, Tucker. We are *not* trying to manipulate anyone here! There are people dying of starvation right now, and we have it in our power to let them know that however long it takes, we will work to get them the help that no one else is giving them. The only way a hunger strike works long-term is if there's continuous support and attention, and that is *my* responsibility. *Our* responsibility."

Tucker looked down at his impassioned girlfriend, always most beautiful when she was fighting for a cause, and shook his head.

"Lena, he's almost done. If he survives long enough to be extradited, he either won't last long as a leader, or Many Hands will assassinate him, or…"

"Many Hands wouldn't do that," Lena butted in.

"Oh no?" Tucker had to stop himself. He hadn't come to debate politics. "Lena, all you're doing is keeping him up with a bunch of candles and creepy chanting. Meanwhile, the best basketball team in your school's history will be playing Gonzaga in one of their most important games ever. And it's all happening when your boyfriend has a *per-fect* bracket for two rounds straight. This will never happen again!"

Lena snorted disgustedly. "How can you think that witnessing the heroic effort of someone who's right here is less important than watching some college boys play basketball a thousand miles away?"

Tucker couldn't help himself. "You're the one who planned this whole thing for the same night. The whole school, except for you and these people, will be watching this game at the same time, indoors, with heat, and with surround sound. And I can tell you that you do not want to be listening to that man's stomach growling in surround sound, 'cause—"

"Tucker!" She smacked him hard on the shoulder. "That man is doing something real, and you know it. The only reason you came out here is because you feel guilty that *I'm* doing what *you* should be doing."

"Oh, I'm the one that should feel guilty, huh? I'm not the one that secretly convinced a bunch of kids—including all of your NSAC friends—to go rob grocery stores to make a statement. You know how many people got arrested because of what you did? And you did it so that *he* looks like the one who organized the whole thing," said Tucker, gesturing to the motel.

"I told you," Lena snarled, holding her breath. "I wasn't there."

"Don't talk to me like I don't know you. I know who called that play. And by the way, it was a really bad idea, and I would have told you that if you had talked to me about it before."

By this time, the argument had become so loud that much of the crowd had turned to see what was happening. Lena realized that they were drawing attention and tugged Tucker down the street another hundred feet. But they had nothing more to say. They stood in silence, staring past each other's heads.

At last, Tucker said, "I'm going back. Come if you want. And for the record, I didn't come out here because of guilt. I came out here because I haven't seen you in five days, and I wanted to give you the chance to come be with me."

"Well then why don't you stay, and you can be with me?" Lena challenged, speaking through a whole spectrum of emotions.

For a moment Tucker didn't say anything. But then, "I have to get back. They're throwing this party for me. Call me when you're done."

He walked away from Lena, away from the murmuring crowd, away from the side-lined cameramen and reporters, and went back up the street to his car. As he walked, he pulled open the Tupperware container, picked up the entire stack of chips and cheese, and crunched down hard through the middle.

*　　*　　*　　*

It wasn't until the second half of the second half that Tucker noticed Carla, coat still on, standing near the door. It was hard to notice anyone; his apartment was jam-packed with roommates, neighbors, friends, people Tucker didn't even know. Thanks to his roommates, word had gotten out that the man with the perfect bracket was having a party. By half-time, there were so many people crowding around their relatively ancient TV that Tucker's roommates begged their neighbor to let them use his nice 54-inch flat screen. The neighbor agreed after they handed over a hefty deposit. Now, with five minutes left in the game and Nebraska riding a barrage of three-pointers to victory, it was getting hard to see even that massive screen. Everyone was standing, jumping, cheering with every big play. There was a couple in the middle of the couch that made out every time Nebraska made a shot. After one particularly fast run of Nebraska field goals, Tucker couldn't take the affectionate display anymore and got up to go to the kitchen. That's when he noticed Carla, wedged in between some of the latecomers. She gave him a small, uncomfortable wave when he noticed her. Tucker was surprised—Carla seemed like the outgoing type in person, but she looked out of place among the partying fans.

Tucker squeezed through the press to get over to her, but once there, he still had to yell to be heard. "What do you think?"

"Fun," she yelled back.

"Yeah?" The conversation stalled out before it really had begun.

"So I finished reviewing that press statement." Carla started pulling something out of her purse, but Tucker held up his hands.

"Whoa, whoa, whoa—this is game time. That's sacred time. When we're watching a game, we are here," he pointed down with one hand, "and work is waaaaaay over there." He pointed out the window toward campus. "Let me get you that beer I promised, and we can look at it in…" Tucker peered over the heads of the crowd to see the screen, "…two minutes of playing time."

He waded into the kitchen, wondering how he might be able to get the all-business girl to loosen up a bit.

His roommate poked his head in. "Dude, somebody at the door for you."

Tucker stared blankly. "Tell him to come in."

"They said they wanted to talk privately."

"They? Wait…a guy and girl?" His roommate nodded. Tucker rolled his eyes.

"Okay, do me a favor—give this to the blonde girl in the back and tell her I'll be there in a few minutes."

Tucker approached the door hoping to end the conversation very quickly.

"Tucker! You are the man!" Rick yelled with both arms up in the air as soon as Tucker appeared. Abby stood behind Rick, applauding. "You could have told us you had another perfect round in your bracket! Why don't you *ever* call?"

"Uh, how did you know…"

Abby had put her arm around Rick and patted him on the shoulder. "We saw an article about you in the school paper, and Rick had to go look you up on ESPN to make sure. That's really amazingly impressive, Tucker."

Tucker shook his head. "What are you doing here? How did you two even find me?"

"Yeah, like it's really hard to find an address for a college student. You know about the internet, right?" Rick snarked.

"I asked you what you were doing here," Tucker asked, now very impatient.

"The bracket par-tay, of course." Rick looked over Tucker's shoulders at the game, now in its final thirty seconds.

"And…" prompted Abby, "there's something that we want to talk to you about. Privately."

"Right," said Rick. "That, too."

Tucker shook his head. "Look, I still don't know who you are. I have no idea why you keep bothering me. But whatever it is, I don't want to be involved. So if you wouldn't mind just leaving and letting me get back…"

"We understand," said Rick, semi-serious now. "You don't want to talk with us at all, you want nothing to do with us, you just want to watch some games. We get that, you've actually made that very clear from the beginning. So, let's do this. Thirty seconds, we pitch our idea, then we leave. If you don't like it, you never have to see us again."

Tucker hesitated. Rick looked at him steadily while Abby stood holding Rick's arm, her eyes a little graver. An explosion of applause in the living room indicated that the game was over. People started to get up and move around. Tucker sighed.

"It's going to be a madhouse here until everyone leaves. We can go to my room. For thirty seconds."

Turning to lead the way, Tucker stepped right into Carla.

"Oh, sorry—everything okay?"

Carla looked around him at Rick and Abby.

"Weren't we going to talk after the game?" she asked.

"Oh, yeah, um…this is going to take thirty seconds, I swear. Grab whatever you want, and I'll be right out." They passed quickly into the hallway.

"So, was that the girlfriend?" Rick asked, following Tucker into his room.

"Uh, no, Carla is from work, Lena is the girlfriend…why do you need to know all this?"

"That one's not hard on the eyes, all I'm saying."

"Rick!" Abby warned. "Sorry, Tucker, sometimes he steps out of bounds." She shot Rick a look as she handed Tucker a folded piece of paper. It looked familiar when he smoothed it out.

…peaceful end to the crisis in Southeast Asia to be accomplished through mediation, given the reluctance of western countries to become too involved and the reluctance of the smaller ASEAN countries to trust Chinese intervention, which stems not just from China's open antagonism towards Many Hands, but also from their long history of seeking to take geopolitical advantage of the smaller nations. Without a local nation like South Korea mediating the conflict, or until one side gives up or wins, Many Hands and the Chinese/Western coalition will be locked in an extended conflict with potentially dangerous consequences. However, the South Korean government currently lacks the political will and social backing that would be required…

Rick and Abby looked on while he read. "Recognize it?" Abby asked. "You misspelled 'government', by the way."

"Thanks," said Tucker sarcastically. "How did you get this?"

Rick jumped in. "We found it in your boss's recycling bin. We wanted to ask—"

"Wait, you went through Dr. Tonkin's trash? I seriously need to call the police on you people."

"No, Tucker," Abby paused to glare at Rick. "We didn't break into your boss's office. We went there this afternoon to see if he could get us a visit with Wol Pot, but he got called out to talk with somebody. While we were waiting, Rick started messing around, doing some shooting practice with paper in the recycling bin. That's how we found this—Rick couldn't make the stupid basket into the trash can and he finally uncrumpled the paper claiming that there was something wrong with it."

"Which there was," Rick inserted loudly. "Staple in the corner totally threw off the center of balance."

"Anyway, when we figured out that you wrote it, we realized that you were the one we needed to talk to. You see, the world has changed a little since you wrote this, but your idea is still good. The South Korean higher-ups might be willing to go along with some of the suggestions that you give here."

"How do you know that?" Tucker asked.

"Because," said Rick, "we've been talking to the South Koreans. That's why we're here."

Tucker surveyed the two, Abby looking earnest and worried, Rick also looking uncharacteristically serious. The more he learned about these people, the less he understood them.

"Here's the situation," Abby continued. "Wol Pot will probably end the hunger strike soon. We think he will actually leave over the weekend. That gives us a small window of opportunity to send them a message…"

"Whoa, whoa," said Tucker, backing up, "I'm not going to do anything, like…"

"No, no," Rick corrected, "she means we want to literally give them a written message."

"Oh."

"Right. Sorry, bad choice of words," Abby apologized. "Anyway, Wol Pot may have won over a lot of Americans, but he still has to report back to the Thai government, and they aren't very happy about what he's done. If he goes back and all he has is the plan that our State Department has put on the table, he won't last a week in any kind of position of power. If that happens, the Thais go the way of Myanmar and become a Many Hands state. But, if we can get Wol Pot this message before he leaves, that the South Koreans can step in to ensure a balance in the negotiations, then he goes back with some leveraging power and he can help them turn things around for good."

Tucker processed what he was being told and shrugged. "So go tell him. Or go tell Tonkin. He's the one in those meetings. Why are you talking to me?"

"Tonkin's under pressure to push Maxwell's plan. Maybe he would have considered it if he were under less pressure, but at this point he's just repeating what he's being told; he isn't seriously considering other options, even from you."

"He said that?"

"Uh, no. We inferred it. Your memo was in the recycling bin, right? As for Wol Pot himself, he's not taking any more official visitors or calls. He's basically hunkering down with his aides to make his final decision. So we need *someone* to get this message to him just to let him know that there's another way."

"Then tell the South Koreans to figure out how to tell him."

"Tucker, you aren't listening. Our being here right now *is* South Korea trying to tell him. We kind of are South Korea. Anyonghaseyo." Abby bowed slightly.

Tucker folded his arms and thought. "You think I can get in to deliver this message?"

"We think you can, yes." Abby extended an envelope to Tucker.

Tucker put his head down and listened to the party breaking up in the living room, reminding him of the parts of his life that used to be normal. His roommates would be eating the last of the Skyline Platter, analyzing the play-by-play on the couch. His neighbor would be moving his TV back, freaking out about scratching it. Lena might be stopping by to check in—and Carla would still be there. Tucker's head snapped back up.

"Your thirty seconds are up."

"So will you do it?"

Tucker looked at the envelope and rejected all courses that would make his life more complicated. "No," he said at last. "I don't want to get involved. This isn't my responsibility. You can find some maid to slip this under his door or something, but I'm not in."

"Tucker, you know what will happen if he doesn't get this

message. We know you know. You have to think beyond yourself here."

Abby sounded so much like Lena in that moment that Tucker immediately stopped listening. Stone-faced, he shook his head.

"Fine," said Abby, a little critically. She handed him a card. "Here is our number. You call us when you change your mind."

"I thought you said I wouldn't ever see you again," Tucker said with a spark of irritation.

Rick grinned. "We said that you wouldn't *have* to see us again. But if you decide to help us out, you may *get* to see us again."

Tucker didn't say anything. He just nodded towards the exit, and Rick and Abby filed past him, down the hall, around a few remaining partiers, and out the door.

"Who were they?" Carla asked, coming up to him as he closed the front door behind the departing couple.

"Oh," Tucker shrugged, wondering how exactly to answer that question. "Just some people that have been trying to get interviews with Dr. Tonkin. I keep telling them that it has to wait until next week, but they keep coming back to bother me about it."

"They want to talk with Tonkin?" she repeated slowly.

"Yeah," Tucker said, wondering why she suddenly looked so alarmed. He didn't think long.

"Come here a minute," she said, grabbing Tucker's arm and pulling him back into the hallway. Tucker was so surprised that he didn't think to resist. Carla put him against the wall and pulled up close.

"Uh, you should know that I have a girl—"

"Shut up, I have to tell you something," she ordered quietly. He shut up. "I think I know who those people are." She brushed her hair from her forehead as if thinking things through too late.

"OK." Tucker wanted the answer.

"I…am not exactly a student here," she began. Tucker rolled his eyes.

"Does everybody have a secret identity this week?"

"I said shut up," she ordered again. "I was sent down here as a recruiter to check out a potential hire."

"You came to give me a job?"

"No," she snapped, "Tonkin. I came to see if he was really as brilliant as everybody thought he was. But my boss said there might be other people that were also interested in him. That has to be who they are."

Tucker was dubious. "That's stupid," he said. "If someone wants to hire Tonkin, why not just interview him like normal people?"

"This *is* the interview. Watching him during this Thailand mess is the best way to see how he operates; it's telling us everything we need to know. Besides, my firm isn't exactly normal. Not many people know who we are and my boss wants to keep it that way."

"OK," Tucker muddled. "So what am I supposed to do about this?"

"Keep them away from Tonkin," Carla responded immediately. "Just for another week. You would be doing him a favor. Can you do that for me?"

Tucker looked down at the girl and heaved a deep, weary sigh. "Whatever. So I guess this means you didn't fact-check Tonkin's statement, huh?"

Carla looked briefly confused.

"Of course I did. It's right here." She pulled out a USB key. "It's all fine."

"Hey, if you want to keep doing my job so I can get in some game time, I'll do whatever you say." Tucker reached out for the USB key.

It was right then, just as his hand was touching Carla's and she was still within inches of his face, that Tucker heard a gasp from the living room. He turned around. Lena was standing there, staring as if she'd just been slapped in the face.

"What's she doing here?" she asked, focusing on Carla.

Tucker quickly moved toward her, his arms in the air like a man at gunpoint.

"Babe, relax, she was just telling me about office stuff. It wasn't anything," he said. But Lena wasn't listening to Tucker. She was still staring at Carla.

Carla cleared her throat. "I was just leaving," she said as she made her way carefully around Lena. Tucker noticed the two exchange some look of unspoken, private communication. Carla turned away and left. Others in the room pretended not to notice.

"You two know each other?" Tucker asked.

"We've met. She didn't tell you?"

"No," Tucker said. "I just met her this morning. When did you meet her?"

Lena looked down at the ground and wrung her fingers. At last, clearly unresolved in her internal conflict, she said, "We should talk about it later. I just…I just came by to tell you that Wol Pot just announced that he's ending the hunger strike. It's all over. I thought you might want to know." Then she turned around and nearly ran out of the front door.

Tucker just stood there. When he finally looked around, he noticed his roommates staring.

"I got no idea what just happened," he told them, and went back to his room to think.

*   *   *   *

Late that night in his room, lying on his bed, he fingered the card with a phone number written in careful penmanship that he guessed was Abby's. He flipped it through his fingers for a few minutes, then opened the envelope with the message in it and read the details. Thailand would denounce Many Hands and accept a Chinese offer to provide assistance to the hard-hit regions in the north, including a free two-year power infrastructure project using electricity produced in southern China. South Korea would provide funding and a small force of neutral inspectors who would report directly to Thai authorities to ensure against long-term Chinese encroachment. It didn't say what the South Koreans would get, but there must have been something. It could work.

Tucker read through it a few times and lay back on his bed to think some more. He looked at the clock. Typically, he would have called his dad by now to deconstruct the game. But it wasn't a typical night. And if he did what he thought about doing, he might not have a typical night for a while.

A few minutes later, he picked up the phone and dialed the number.

The phone rang once.

Rick answered. "Hello?"

"It's Tucker."

"Hey! You're still awake?"

"Yeah, sorry, I didn't think about the time. I've been…did I wake you up?"

"No. Abby's asleep, but I just found *Jurassic Park* while I was flipping channels. I love this movie. What's up?"

Tucker rubbed his head. "Let me ask you something. Let's say I sent your message. How would I do it?"

Rick shuffled with something in the background. "You know Wol Pot's doctor, Mongkut Thaifun?"

"Yeah?"

"I hear he likes basketball."

[**Midwest Division**: Elite Eight]
[Saturday, March 28]

Tucker arrived at the campus rec center holding his good sneakers in his left hand. While he had been dubious when Rick and Abby told him to show up at the gym at 6:30 AM on a cold Saturday, it somehow didn't surprise him to see Abby behind the admissions counter, giving him a thumbs up and waving him through. Two of the four friends that he had miraculously convinced to wake up that early on a weekend were already there.

The court had been newly refurbished and the floor, still smelling slightly of varnish, reflected a polished golden yellow. Tucker stood dribbling a ball at the free-throw line, filling the spacious rectangular interior with a reverberating clamor. To him, it was a beautiful sound, loud and lonely, matched only by the quick *schwoop* of the ball going through the net. There was a pure and distinct rhythm to it: bounce, squeak, breath, clang, *schwoop*, bounce, over and over. The simple rhythm of sports.

The basketball game was the only part of Rick and Abby's plan that he liked. He had been going over it in his mind, internally reciting the lines that they had given him. He glanced at the bag with the unusual gift inside. It all seemed way too complicated. No, they had explained, he couldn't just meet Mongkut somewhere and hand him a note. There were too many ways for a meeting with anyone from the Thai delegation to get leaked. If Tucker were seen with Mongkut in some back alley, their meeting would be immediately viewed as suspicious. But if they had a good reason for meeting, if they did things in broad daylight, there was no chance that their meeting would raise any eyebrows. If anything, their story would make for a heart-warming human interest piece.

"And we should know," Rick had explained. "We were journalists."

Tucker's other two friends arrived, making five all together. The guest of honor was the last to come. Dr. Mongkut Thaifun strolled in, dressed more casually than Tucker had ever seen him, and looking slightly unsure that he was in the right place. Tucker jogged over to him.

"Dr. Thaifun," he said, reaching out to shake hands, "good to see you again. I'm glad you could make it."

"I am also," said the doctor, pulling off his heavy jacket. "Please call me Mongkut."

Tucker made quick introductions and wasted no time as he took Mongkut and another friend on his own team. They checked the ball at midcourt and began.

Mongkut ran fast, too fast for a half-court game. He could play, but he tried too hard, shot too quickly, and turned the ball over a few times. Tucker wanted to tell him just to calm down and pass the ball, but he couldn't bring himself to. He knew that this man had just spent the last week locked in a motel room in a foreign country trying to attend to a man who was deliberately starving himself. It probably felt good to be out and doing anything. But Tucker's friend, who did not know Mongkut's story, had no reservations.

"Hey man, chill. Move the ball around," he said. The doctor nodded quickly and calmed down obligingly. Tucker made sure to get him the ball when he could.

After a few games, Tucker followed Mongkut to a water fountain just outside the door. Mongkut took a long drink, then stood up with a smile.

"I thank you for the invitation," said the doctor. "This has been very good for me. It has been a long week, and there is still much to come."

"I know. I figured it would be nice for you to do something that wasn't diplomacy."

"Indeed," said Mongkut, "though basketball can be diplomacy, too. Did you know that the relationship between China and South Korea was greatly enhanced in the 1980's by a visit from the Chinese youth basketball team? It's true. Sports can be a wonderful tool for bringing people together."

Tucker thought of continuing the conversation with the line, "Speaking of South Korea…," but Mongkut went on with little pause.

"What do you think of our situation? How did we do here?" the doctor asked seriously. Tucker had to be frank.

"Honestly, I don't know if the hunger strike helped. I mean, did anything really change? Did anything get resolved?"

Mongkut laughed humorlessly. "No, nothing is resolved. China insists that the Prime Minister publically condemn the Many Hands organization and revoke all of their rights and drive them out at gunpoint. But they do not understand that Many Hands is the only means of support that many in the highlands have. And they are doing more than just bringing food. They are rebuilding roads and providing healthcare. The villages in the Thanon Thong Chai range depend almost entirely upon Many Hands functionaries for the resources that the government should be providing."

"So you side with Many Hands?" Tucker couldn't keep the tone of incredulity from his voice, and Mongkut heard it.

"No, no, not at all. It is my opinion that they are a very dangerous organization, and certainly not to be trusted. They did not come through the front door, to use your American expression. They are a threat to our political system, but the prime minister is a politically expedient man." Now it was Mongkut who couldn't conceal a tone of disgust. "He understands that it will not be the Chinese who will re-elect him, so he is reluctant to alienate the many people who depend upon Many Hands. He has not been pleased with the ambassador's decision to attract the world's attention in this way."

"So is Wol Pot going to lose his job?" Tucker wondered for the first time what Wol Pot's decisions might mean for his many staff members. Mongkut smiled and squared his shoulders.

"Perhaps. But not before doing all he can. He is a very crafty politician, despite appearances. He will work hard to keep as many doors open as possible, until it becomes clear which door is the right one. "

Tucker swallowed hard. This was his best opening. "I think I might be able to help with one of those doors," he said softly, feeling a little light-headed now that the moment had arrived. "I actually have something for the ambassador, if you would be willing to give it to him. It's from me and a couple of friends that really want the best for your country. It's one of the reasons I invited you here."

Tucker unzipped his bag and removed some bubble-wrap from around a wooden frame. Inside the frame was a copy of Tucker's perfect bracket, all of the winners highlighted through the Sweet Sixteen. In his sloppy cursive, he had signed it, "To

Ambassador Wol Pot: Champions Endure." Mongkut smiled widely.

"March Madness!" he said, holding the frame closer so he could read the teams. "My class at medical school would have a brackets contest every year. I was very bad."

"Most people are."

"This is amazing. Did you really get them all right?"

Tucker felt suddenly embarrassed, getting praise for tournament picks from a man whose leader had just finished a daring international gambit. "So far. We'll see how I do after the Elite Eight."

"I am certain you will be successful, after so many intelligent guesses." Mongkut carefully folded the bubble wrap back around the frame. "The Ambassador will be pleased. It is a rare and unusual gift."

"Yeah," Tucker said, remembering his task at hand. "It was really the idea of some new friends of mine. If the ambassador doesn't like the frame, he should feel free to change it." He pronounced the last words slowly, deliberately. Mongkut looked up into his face quickly and read his meaning.

"I see," he said, inspecting the frame. "I think you should give this to him yourself," he said.

"Uhhhh…" Tucker uttered. He hadn't expected that. "No, thank you, I'm sure he's still tired from everything this week, and I know you all gotta pack. You can go ahead and deliver that for me."

"Please," said Mongkut earnestly. "I believe he would be greatly honored by your visit." Tucker paused indecisively, but the doctor seemed insistent.

"Fine," Tucker surrendered.

"Very good," said Mongkut, looking back through the door at the players waiting for them restlessly on the court. "But first, one more game."

*   *   *   *

They drove up to the Mollifly Motel in a non-descript car with tinted windows, driven by a member of the ambassador's security team. Tucker sat in the back with Mongkut, and even though he'd showered just ten minutes earlier, he was sweating.

When they reached the police barricade, the car slowed down

and rolled past the place that had been crowded with Lena's fellow vigil-keepers just a few days before. The area was empty now, save for some litter, some congealed wax, and a few leftover signs drawn in crude magic marker. A news truck was parked just down the street, but it was closed and locked. Tucker was glad. He didn't know if he'd most fear being seen by Lena, Tonkin, or Carla; any footage of him going into Wol Pot's locked motel room would make his life much more complicated than it had already become.

Wol Pot and his delegation occupied just one small room on a floor that smelled strongly of cigarette smoke and Indian take-out. There were five people crammed inside but very little activity. The ambassador was lying on his bed calmly, dressed lightly in spite of the chill outside. Wol Pot looked visibly thinner, weaker, his characteristic glimmer diminished. But he still smiled when Tucker came in. The old man recognized the student, and he reached out a hand for Tucker to shake.

"I give you my thanks for removing my physician from the room for a few hours. He has been making me eat and drink things and they have not agreed with me well."

Tucker laughed obligingly, but Mongkut moved forward quickly and put the framed bracket in Wol Pot's hands.

"Tucker and his friends wanted to send a gift to you with their compliments to Thailand," he said, glancing back at Tucker.

"I read of this," said Wol Pot as he examined the gift. "The Perfect Bracket of Mr. Tucker Barnes. I was given your school newspaper and saw the article on the sports page. It helped me to forget about eating for several hours." The ambassador looked at the gift thoughtfully and quietly repeated the phrase 'Champions Endure'.

Tucker tried not to look self-conscious as Mongkut leaned down to speak quietly in the ambassador's ear, then removed the back of the frame. Wol Pot lifted the bracket out and saw the small note card taped to the back. The room was completely, attentively, stiflingly silent as the old man considered the message. Finally, the ambassador closed the frame, looked knowingly at his physician, and leaned his head against the wall.

"In your tournament," the ambassador addressed Tucker, "there is a phrase, ah, for a team that is small but achieves beyond their expectations. A Cinderella team, correct? As in the story?"

Tucker nodded.

"Do you think there will be a Cinderella team in this tournament?"

"There already is: Georgia. They're good, but people have kind of ignored them." Tucker answered too eagerly, and his words died quickly in the solemn room. Wol Pot studied the bracket again.

"And yet you have predicted them losing."

Tucker cleared his throat and mumbled "Yes."

"Hmm," the ambassador pondered as he looked again at the contents of the note card. "I trust this message comes from a trustworthy authority?"

Tucker said yes again, but less eagerly. He still had little evidence that Rick and Abby were anything legitimate.

"Do you know, Mr. Barnes, that Thailand is a wonderful country with wonderful people and a wonderful culture? I don't suppose you have ever been there, but you should try to go in your lifetime. Perhaps by then we will have achieved the destiny that we would choose, the destiny that our people deserve." The ambassador's face became reflective, and he seemed to lose his train of thought for a moment. "But Cinderella is a fairy tale," he sighed. Then, abruptly gathering himself and smiling, he said, "Thank you for your visit, Mr. Barnes. Thank you for this extraordinary gift. We have been pleased to know you and to visit your university. And please thank your friends as well."

Tucker let out a relieved "You're welcome," and found himself being shepherded to the door. Looking back one more time, he nodded to Mongkut and retreated to the car.

A few minutes later and several blocks away from the motel, Tucker received a text. He had another meeting that afternoon. A much more stressful meeting.

*   *   *   *

The "Corn On Blue," located downtown, held a special significance for Tucker and Lena. There was a table against the wall, beneath an abstract painting of Charlie Parker, where they had broken up two of the three times in their relationship. It was also where they had gotten back together once. Whenever one of them invited the other to the C.O.B., it meant something important had to be said. For this reason, Tucker walked through the doors with the pace and resolve of a man at peace with condemnation. Lena was already at the table, swirling a half-empty glass of water with a lemon slice on the rim. Happy hour was still thirty minutes away, so the crowd was light.

Tucker sat across from her but didn't look up immediately. When he did, Lena was scrutinizing him with tired eyes.

"Did you remember that we have that quiz in West African History on Monday? I know you haven't studied."

"I'll study in the morning," Tucker groaned. "I have a lot to catch up on before that."

"You should at least look over the…"

"Tomorrow," he said more forcefully, "if that's fine with you."

"It doesn't matter if it's fine with me. It shouldn't be fine with you." She brushed the napkin under her glass, flattening it out. "You should come over tonight and we can make dinner and review. Or talk. We haven't had a night together in a long time."

Tucker sighed and looked over at the bar counter. "I can't. There's a big game tonight."

"I thought you said the big game was Thursday night!"

"This is a bigger game."

Lena rubbed her temple and nodded to herself. "That's right. There's always a bigger game. I don't know why I keep forgetting that this will never end."

"What are you talking about?" Tucker protested. "It ends next Saturday. I mean, Monday. There's a whole week between games. I promise you, I will take you out on Monday night. We can go get sushi or something."

"I don't want a man who buys me sushi after weeks of ignoring me because of basketball," Lena snapped. "I want a man who actually does something useful with his time, who's actually going somewhere."

Tucker thought about all the basketball he hadn't watched in the last two weeks. "Fine with me," he said, standing up. "I'll go somewhere."

Lena grabbed his arm and pulled him back down. "Tucker,

don't be like that. I'm just having a really, really hard time figuring you out."

"That shouldn't be so hard by now."

"But it is. Do you know what people say to me about you? 'Oh, he's such a nice guy, so fun, so genuine, everything right there on the surface.' I don't know what to say to that, because you and I both know that there's a lot more under the surface that people never see because you never show them. And sometimes that makes you seem like two different people. You say you don't want to go into politics after law school, but you do so much work for Tonkin that it puts you way behind in schoolwork. You say you respect Wol Pot, but you won't stand up for him, even with me. Sometimes you act like you want me around, but sometimes it seems like…like you don't. You tell me that you know life isn't a game, but all you ever seem to think about are games. I'm getting tired of trying to make sense of what you do."

Tucker stared at Lena's exasperated face. "I have no idea where all this is coming from, but I'm going to change the subject to what we should really be talking about. What is all this with Carla?"

Lena pursed her lips and looked carefully at Tucker.

"We should talk about that, you're right. But before we do, I want to ask you how you're doing. I mean, how you're really doing."

"What?" Tucker raised his hands in complete disbelief. Only Lena could dodge a question about her suspicious connections with the spy in his boss's office by delving into the details of his emotional well-being.

"I'm just… I'm worried about you. I'm worried that all of this stuff that's been happening has made you revert to the place you were the last time we broke up. You seem to be doing the same things, wasting a lot of time watching basketball, just losing direction generally, getting obsessed with that bracket thing—"

"I am not obsessed—"

"—I don't even know how you're spending your time anymore. I don't even know what you did this morning. You didn't go to your parents' house like you usually—"

"How did you know that?" Tucker asked, startled.

"I drove out to your house this morning. I was going to

surprise you by going jogging with you, but you never came. You didn't answer your phone. Not even your parents knew what was going on." Lena looked into Tucker's eyes. "Where were you?"

Tucker leaned back in the booth, irrationally relieved that Lena hadn't followed him that morning. "I don't have to tell you about everything that I do. Just because I don't live up to your expectations for me—which is impossible, by the way, unless I'm like running for president or stopping wars all by myself—it doesn't mean that I'm not doing things with my life. I told you a long time ago what my plans are, and they haven't changed. I don't care if you, or my parents, or Tonkin, or Rick and Abby, or anybody wants me to do something else."

"Who are Rick and Abby?"

"Who is Carla?" Tucker spat out. He took a deep breath. "Look, we have already had this exact same fight in this exact same booth, and I don't need to have it again. So unless we're going to talk about what we really need to talk about, I'm going back to my apartment. I have some dip to make."

Lena watched him stand up to leave. "Wait," she said softly. "We'll talk."

Tucker sat down and folded his arms, waiting for a good explanation.

"I met Carla a few days ago. She found me. She offered me a job, and I took it. I won't be around much longer. In fact, I'll be gone by tomorrow, they have a project for me this week."

Tucker raised an eyebrow. "You want to leave before the end of the semester, a year before graduation?"

"It's an opportunity, Tucker, a once-in-a-lifetime thing. Real leadership, real activism, real resources. I can do what I've always wanted to do, follow a path that college really can't give me."

Tucker stared ahead in disbelief. The place inside that always compelled him to return to Lena started to ache.

"You trust Carla? You know she was in Tonkin's office too, trying to get him into whatever weird organization she's recruiting for."

"I know," Lena said. "And they're not a weird organization. They're an amazing group of people working for social justice all over the world. I asked them if they would offer you a job, too. They said no. I was hoping that maybe they had changed their minds when I saw Carla at your house last night, but they hadn't. But Tucker listen," Lena reached out across the table to hold Tucker's hand, and he felt himself melting a little, as he always did when she touched him. "We can still ask. Now that you know about them, if we both pitch the idea that we can work together—"

"Hold up, hold up," Tucker pulled his hand back, his head reeling. "First of all, who are 'they', and second, what makes you think that I'm going anywhere? I have school to finish, I've got law school to do, I've got things to do back in Ashland, I can't just go with whoever these people are—"

"You would be with me!" Lena pleaded. "If you stay here, you may meet your goals but you won't reach your potential, I mean your real potential. I feel like I'm the only person really pushing you to succeed, and if I go—"

"Wait," said Tucker, "that's what you're worried about? You think as soon as you leave, I'll drop out of school and start smoking weed or something? Are you my girlfriend or my life coach?"

"I'm both, sometimes, and you know it. Would you even be where you are without me? Unless I'm on you all the time, you miss opportunities, you waste whole mornings like today—"

"Oh really? You want to ask Wol Pot if I wasted my morning?" As soon as he said it, he knew that he had slipped up. "I mean, Tonkin had me…"

"Woah, what?" Lena sat up with interest. "Did you see Wol Pot this morning? I thought he was locking everyone out. How did you get in? How did he look?"

"No," he stammered, "I mean, yeah, I saw him, but we didn't, I just gave him a present. I can't really talk about it. It was really nothing."

"But did he say anything?" Lena pressed. "Do you know what he's going to do? Is he finally going to endorse Many Hands?"

Tucker shook his head. He could feel himself starting to sweat. "I don't, um, forget it. I want to talk about what you said about…"

"No, no, no, you don't change the subject now. I need to know this, and you know you can't lie to me. What is he going to do? You know if he caves to international pressure, if he lets China come in and take over and stop Many Hands, it means starvation and panic and probably war. So you have to tell me, what is he going to do?"

She stared into his face, her eyes wide, trying to read everything that he was trying to hide. He turned away and mumbled, "I can't talk about it."

"Of course you can't." Lena shook her head in disgust and swore under her breath as she stood.

"Where are you going?" Tucker asked.

"To finish packing." She gathered her bag and made a motion to leave, but turned around.

"Do you want to know why they didn't offer you a job, Tucker? I asked Carla about it. I explained what I knew about you, and she even said that she knew what I was talking about. But they still didn't want you. You know why?" She paused a second to let him think. "She said that you weren't the kind of person who would succeed in their work. They said that you didn't care enough. And the worst part was that I couldn't disagree with her."

She stopped herself, pausing as if wanting to say good-bye, then pursed her lips tighter and stepped out of the restaurant. Tucker watched her through the window as she took out her phone and dialed. She crossed the street, and only after crossing did she look back, hesitate, then turn and disappear.

[**Midwest Division**: Final Four]
[Saturday, April 4]

Tucker sat wedged between a messy desk and a water cooler in the Verizon Center security office, nursing his sore knuckles with a bag of ice. He'd been sitting there for nearly twenty minutes—long enough to calm down from the brawl with Neeson, long enough to start a couple of dead-end conversations with the moody Cole Kaman, long enough to look at everything around him three times over. There was an autographed picture of Michael Jordan in a Wizards uniform holding a ball aloft over some poor rookie. There was another picture of the 2003 George Mason Men's basketball team, exultant after their win against top-seeded UConn. Among the papers on the desk, Tucker noticed a police sketch of a big man in a grey hoodie with a goatee and glasses, and he thought about asking Cole if that was really what the Wall Street arsonist looked like. But seeing Cole slumped forward in his chair, hands covering his face, Tucker thought better of it.

There was a commotion outside the door, and after a minute, the arena's chief of security, a gruff, balding red-head, shoved in two staggering teenage boys.

"Do not move from these chairs," the security chief barked. "We'll call your parents shortly." The door slammed shut and one of the teenagers, alcohol heavy on his breath, leaned forward toward Tucker.

"Hey! You're the Bracketeers, right? You're that guy that punched that guy! Awesome." Tucker smiled briefly. That was the substance of fifteen out of the eighteen text messages he'd received in the past half-hour: "Dude, nice hit!" The other three were from his mom, who was not happy with what she'd seen. It was Regina who had, after a long conversation with her son about the way his life was going, strongly suggested that he go to be alone as a kind of retreat to help clear his head. It would be good for him, she said, to have some time just to himself away from everything. Now she felt guilty about her advice and openly wondered in fragments of digital text if he would be better off with his father or brothers or some friend next to him. Henry, for his part, sent a congratulatory message praising his right hook.

One of the teenagers slurred, "So like, how did it start? Was it a money thing?" Tucker shook his head.

"Nah, he was just mad that he lost."

"That's not cool," said the boy with a righteous sigh. "They aren't throwing you out, are they? I mean, for fighting?"

Tucker shrugged. He had been wondering that same thing since they'd arrived at the office. The other boy shook his head in sympathy.

"Oh dude, they're gonna throw you out. I have a buddy that got into a fight during a hockey game last year and he was banned from the arena for a month. For fighting at a hockey game! Where they fight, like, right there! Isn't that the craziest?"

"So what was the final score?" Tucker asked the boy.

"At the hockey game?"

His friend punched him in the arm. "No, you idiot, at the basketball game just now."

"Oh yeah, you didn't really see the end. It was sweet—UCLA made one more three-pointer at the buzzer and that put them up 78-73. Other Williams had a towel over his head for like ten minutes and wouldn't move until somebody made him. He was totally crying, we could tell. It was awesome."

The security chief came in, and Tucker was relieved when he spoke to the teenagers first. They each got fines and phone calls to their parents. Then, amongst many loud complaints against the injustice of it all, they were gone. The chief turned to Tucker and Cole.

"You boys are giving me ulcers," he groused. "Here's the deal. We've reviewed the tapes we have, and we spoke with the eyewitnesses around the scene. They all back up your claim that Mr. Faulkner initiated the incident without being provoked, and that you, Mr. Barnes, stepped in to help. In most cases we would dismiss any party that was involved in a fight in the stands and ban them for the remainder of the season. But it seems that, under the circumstances, there is some interest in making sure you come back for the Championship. I'm not very happy about it, personally, but you will get to come back on Monday—"

"Thank you," Tucker exhaled.

"—under certain conditions," the chief continued, glaring at Tucker. "During the game on Monday, you two will be sitting on opposite sides of the court. We will be watching both sections carefully to make sure that we don't have a repeat of what happened today."

He looked at both of them and shook his head like a disappointed parent. "I don't know what's wrong with you people, but if you two don't control yourselves on Monday, if you step out of line even a little, we won't just kick you out, there will be significant legal action. You understand me?" They both nodded.

"So can we go?" Cole asked, his voice exhausted.

The man sighed. "No, there's one more thing. I've been kept apprised of the search for your stalker, Ichabod, in case he was to try something in the arena. I got word tonight that they've found his apartment in Connecticut. He wasn't there, but, based on some evidence they found, it looks like he may be headed south. So he might be around. I don't think I have to tell you that you should inform the police if either of you sees or hears anything." The chief waved to the door. "Now, please get out of here."

They happily complied.

Outside, they had to pass through a cadre of reporters and cameras who wanted the inside story on this most bizarre side plot to the tournament. Tucker was so caught up in getting through that he didn't notice who was driving their car until they were underway. The man in the driver's seat turned and said in an awful New York accent, "Where to, Mac?"

"Are you kidding me?" Tucker yelled.

"We kid you not!" beamed Rick O'Shea beneath a chauffer's cap. "Nice hit, by the way. We're going to remember you in case we ever need to sneak a secret message to an amateur boxer."

"Ummmm…?" asked Cole.

"We haven't met yet," said Abby, extending her hand. "We're old friends of Tucker's. I'm Abby, this is Rick. We're happy to finally meet you." Cole shook her hand and immediately sat back as far as he could in the seat.

"Unbelievable. Is there a job that you guys don't have?" Tucker asked.

"Ah, the real question is, is there a job that you don't have,"

Rick replied. "We say yes. But that can be fixed. We'll wait till we get back to the hotel to talk about it more. Cole, we don't really know about you yet. I think we can arrange a more formal meeting for Monday."

"What for?" Tucker asked.

"We're going to keep that a secret for now."

Cole rubbed his temples with his palms. "Well, sorry to disappoint you before I even know what's going on, but I'm going home. I'm done here."

The announcement silenced the car, and Tucker turned to him, almost hurt.

"Wait, you can't do that! You can't get this far and then just leave before the last game." Tucker looked at Cole's stony face and realized that he really knew nothing about this person. "You would seriously leave before the championship game? That's just not right, man."

"Oh, that's not right?" Cole retorted angrily. "My entire life hasn't been right since I filled out that stupid bracket. I've been stalked by a giant psychopath with a sling who wants to kill me because he thinks God told him that my bracket will make the world end. Today I had to explain to reporters how some guy I didn't even meet until this afternoon went completely crazy and jumped off an escalator, and then two hours later a middle-aged businessman tried to beat me up on national TV. And that's not even the stuff that matters, y'know? My girlfriend's mother has cancer, and I haven't heard from her in…" Cole stopped, swallowed his thoughts, and proceeded much more slowly. "If she ever was my girlfriend. I don't know why I said that. But listen, I'm tired. I'm going back home, back to my apartment, I'm going to take like five sick days in a row, and I am never touching a bracket again. Ever. So, it was nice meeting all of you, but I am done and gone."

Tucker didn't know what to say. If it were one of his friends back home, he would tell him that quitting was wrong, that he needed somebody to play against in the final game, that Cole had to hang in. But Cole wasn't his friend, and Tucker couldn't dispute that the guy had had a rough few weeks. Tucker was still stewing about it when they arrived at the front entrance of the hotel. Cole jumped out immediately. His hand was on the door when he leaned down for a final word to Tucker.

"Thanks for helping me out back there, by the way. I don't think I said that yet." Then he closed the door, hard.

"I don't believe him," Tucker said, shaking his head and about to leave the car himself. "After everything, he's just going to walk away."

"Nah. He'll be back," said Rick.

"You think so?" asked Tucker.

"Give him a night to sleep it off; he'll have a new perspective. And he'll remember the million dollars. In the mean time, hold on a second, stay in your seat." Rick pulled out. "We have to talk to you about something while we go on a lovely tour of the D.C. night life."

Tucker shook his head, irritated that he wasn't going to bed yet. "I'm not doing any more spy missions for you people."

"We won't ask you to. Would you like to know who we really are?"

Tucker leaned back in the seat. "Um, are you recruiters for a big company interested in smart political people?"

The couple looked at each other. "That's actually quite close," said Abby. "How did you know we were recruiting?"

"You aren't the only ones," said Tucker. "Another recruiter told me that you guys were in Lincoln to try and get Tonkin. That same person ended up giving my ex-girlfriend a job."

The couple looked at each other again, even more surprised. Tucker took a second of pride at finally having the upper hand in a conversation.

"That's interesting," Rick pondered, "and we want to ask you more about our competition later, for sure. But for now, you're only half right. We weren't there to recruit Tonkin."

"Me?" asked Tucker, bewildered.

"Nope. We came for Dr. Thaifun."

"Oh." Tucker stopped to reprocess everything that had happened in the last few weeks. It had made sense when he thought that the couple was after his boss. But now it didn't. "So how come you kept bothering me about Tonkin?" he asked.

Abby explained. "Well, at first we were just trying to get on the good side of anyone who had access to the Thai delegation. Tonkin was our best shot, and we thought you were just a lackey who might be able to get us into the room with him."

"Which you didn't," interrupted Rick. "Thanks for nothing."

Abby continued. "We wanted to see if the rumors about Mongkut were true. He has apparently been the architect behind Pot's international outreach since the disaster started a year ago."

"In that way," Rick interrupted again, "he's kind of the Thai Tucker. Not to be confused with someone who tucks in his ties."

"Huh?"

Abby gave Rick an annoyed sideways glance and went on. "So that's why we were in Lincoln in the first place, to see if it was worth trying to lure Dr. Thaifun away. But that kind of changed after we met you."

Rick started to loudly hum the tune "Till there was yooooouu." Abby promptly whacked him, and he stopped.

"After we met you, we looked into you a little bit. The more we looked into you, the more interesting you became. I don't think you realize how rare it is for someone as young as you are to take such a prominent position in the office of such a high-profile figure as Dr. Tonkin. Has anyone ever mentioned that to you?"

"A few grad students have," Tucker said quietly. "My mom seemed to think so, too."

"You were, by far, the youngest and least prominent person at that State dinner. You were writing memos and press releases for Tonkin—you probably didn't even know this—that were making it into some pretty high-level circles under Tonkin's name. Tonkin, by the way, has everything you've ever written in a file that—"

"He showed you my file?"

"Uh, no," Abby confessed sheepishly.

Tucker was still processing. "Are you saying that you hacked—"

"More like electronically perused," said Rick. "It's kind of my forte, not to brag. The story we told you about getting your memo from the recycling bin was a lie. Sorry. But now we have the complete works of Tucker Barnes in a collectible volume. Very interesting reads. We compared some of your recent work to the stuff that Tonkin had sent up to the 'powers that be' in the State

Department and elsewhere—"

"So you hacked into the State Department files, too?"

"No, no, get over the hacking thing. We got all this off of Tonkin's computer. It seems that he's been borrowing your ideas word for word for at least six months, maybe longer. He should be paying you a lot more than he's paying you. "

Tucker was surprised by the accusation, but it made sense. As he looked out at the brilliant lights of the Kennedy Center, he realized that he wasn't even upset by Tonkin using his ideas. Tucker was writing them so that they could be used. What he found more disturbing was the increasing number of people around him that seemed to have secrets he was the last to know about.

"What about the message to Wol Pot?" Tucker asked. "Did you lie about that, too?"

"Well, yes and no," Abby said. "The South Koreans really did need to get that message through. We don't really know all the details of how it happened, but somehow there was a high-up Korean who found out that our boss had people—us—in Lincoln. They asked him to have us get that message to Wol Pot. I honestly can't tell you why the Koreans couldn't do this themselves, but we were happy to do them the favor. Anyway, we were going to just do it ourselves, but by this time we were really interested in you, so we decided to test you a little bit, see what you would do if we took you off the sidelines and threw you into the game. And you were brilliant."

Tucker raised his eyebrows. "How did you know I would go through with it?"

"Ah," Abby explained as they came to a traffic light. "We knew that you knew that getting the Koreans involved was a good idea. And you didn't just know it. You could *see* it, couldn't you? You see, we think you have this talent. You seem to be able to take in a lot of information about complex social systems, and then you can make really accurate predictions about outcomes."

"It's the reason your brackets are so good," Rick cut in excitedly. "It's because you have a sixth sense about teams."

"And it's the reason that you can intuit what will happen between conflicting countries when you're given a lot of information. You are a prodigy at group behavior prediction."

"I didn't know you could be a prodigy at that," Tucker said, dubious.

"Of course you can," Rick opined confidently. "There are prodigies for everything. If projectile spitting were an Olympic game, at some time there would be a five-time gold medalist."

They drove within view of the Washington Monument, lit up like a torch against the night sky. Tucker shook his head again. "I still have no idea where you're going with all this."

Rick handed back a piece of paper. "Where we're going with all this is to a very nice skybox at the Verizon Center. It's brand new. You're invited up during half-time at the game on Monday. Abby wrote down the name of the thing so you won't forget. Our boss will be there. He wants to meet you to discuss an opportunity with you."

"You mean a job?"

"No. I mean an opportunity."

Tucker took the paper and flicked it in his hands. "OK then. Are we done?"

Rick looked at Abby to make sure. "Yup. No! We got you another seat for the championship game. For Cole, too."

"Really? I thought ESPN took away the ticket when I said—"

"It's taken care of. You've got one extra. Fill it well."

"Oh. OK then. Thank you, that's really cool." The car had pulled back up to the valet stand in front of the hotel. Tucker opened the door. "I guess I'll see you Monday," he said, swinging himself out. But Rick and Abby were jumping out as well, handing the keys to the valet.

"What are you doing?"

"Oh," said Rick. "We're working here at the hotel all weekend. Thought it best to hang around. We're doing the late shift tonight as bell-hops. Is that what they still call us?"

Abby nodded. Tucker rolled his eyes, escaped to his hotel room, and fell asleep very quickly.

*   *   *   *

In spite of everything, Tucker still awoke at 6 AM the following morning. He left his room in a maroon University of Nebraska sweatshirt, stretched a little outside the hotel, and began to jog west toward the Lincoln Memorial. Running felt good, even after only five hours of sleep. Just the day before, he had met three strangers who were bizarrely linked to him through their freak brackets, and now, not even twenty-four hours later, one was unconscious in a hospital, one was in jail, and one was so scared about a stalker that he was going home. The blunt-force trauma of the events had dulled with sleep but not dissipated. He was glad to have a day before the championship to just do normal things. He would call his dad that morning and try to convince him to come out for the game. They could go see Washington—neither he nor his dad had been to the city in a long time. And he would definitely not think about international politics, mysterious recruiters, disrupted basketball games, or ex-girlfriends.

As he jogged toward the Lincoln Memorial, he passed the long black marble scar of the Vietnam Veteran's Memorial. He stopped when he saw it and paused to glance at the endless list of names. He had taken a seminar the semester before about warfare in the 20th century. The memories of all the dates and maps he had studied gave way to lingering impressions from a veteran guest speaker. The man had talked about chaos, about the brutal nature of war that mercilessly determined which young soldiers lived and which died. He had talked about the missteps that had brought the war about before people really understood what was happening. As he stood there in the chilly morning, Tucker reached out on an impulse and touched the names. Decisions and consequences. He glanced over his shoulder, remembering that the Korean War Memorial was close by somewhere. Then he reminded himself that jogging was supposed to make him forget about all of this.

Turning abruptly away from the wall, Tucker resumed his paced run back toward his hotel. When he was within eyesight of the top of the hotel building, he noticed a man coming out from a doorway on the opposite side of the street, about thirty yards away. The man wore an old grey sweatshirt with the hood over his head, and early morning sunlight glinted off of his glasses as he began to jog in Tucker's direction. The man crossed the street deliberately and seemed to be coming straight at him as he jogged closer and closer. Tucker suddenly felt very uneasy and wondered if he should alter his course. *No, it's light out, other people are around, there's no reason to be paranoid,* he told himself. *Just ignore him.*

But Tucker couldn't ignore him. The man stopped in the sidewalk, blocking Tucker's way. He hadn't realized how large the man was, but Tucker, who was tall himself, had to look up to see the man's bearded face. His unkempt goatee reminded Tucker of the sketch he had seen in the security office.

"Uh, can I help you with something?" Tucker asked, suppressing a shudder. The man did not smile, did not move, didn't even seem out of breath from his run. He just looked at Tucker with his hands deep in the pockets of his sweatshirt. The right hand bulged in the pocket. It was holding something.

"You got a problem?" Tucker couldn't keep the note of belligerence out of his voice, even with this behemoth. He made a motion to find a way around.

"You're one of the two," said the man, more an accusation than a comment. "The last two."

"I'm one of the last two guys with the bracket, right. Is that what you're talking about?"

"Are you going to win?" asked the man, his face frozen, unsmiling.

Tucker normally couldn't resist that kind of a verbal challenge, but under the circumstances, he tempered his response.

"I hope so."

"I see," said the man. "It must be exciting for you. The future."

"Uh-huh."

The man lingered. "Have you seen the future?"

"Not really," said Tucker. "Look, you're kind of blocking the sidewalk. Can I get back to my running?"

The man scratched his chin, then stepped aside. Tucker began to move forward, making sure to give the man a wide berth. After he passed, the man yelled, "I'll see you later, Tucker Barnes. Tell Cole Kaman that I missed him, but I won't again."

Tucker ran, not jogged, the rest of the way to the hotel. At the revolving doors, he looked behind him and saw no one. The man had not followed him. Tucker bent over, breathing hard, and contemplated the sickening realization that he had just come face to face with Ichabod.

Still sweaty, he ran up and knocked softly on Cole's door. It was only a few minutes after seven, and Tucker was actually surprised when he heard active movement from inside. He was even more surprised when the door opened on a girl with dark hair and sleepy eyes.

"Oh, I'm so sorry, I thought this was someone else's room," Tucker said.

"Are you looking for Cole? He's here, he's just still asleep."

Tucker must have looked as dumbfounded as he felt, because the girl laughed and said, "Sorry, I should have introduced myself. I'm Nera. I'm Cole's girlfriend."

"Oh, yeah, Cole talked about you. I thought you weren't coming."

"I wasn't planning on it. But he texted me yesterday morning and I just felt like this was a big deal and I should be with him. I wanted to surprise him before the BC game, but I got caught in traffic on the New Jersey turnpike and didn't end up getting here till really late."

"Uh, that's great! I mean, that sucks that you missed the game, but it was actually kind of a disaster anyway, so…"

"Cole told me about the fight. He said that you really saved him."

"Nah, I just…" Tucker's voice trailed off. "So Cole is staying for the championship now? For sure?"

"Yes, Cole is staying. I talked him into it last night, which wasn't easy, given everything that's already happened to him in public. But I got him to stop worrying so much and come to peaceful terms with the universe for the weekend. As long as nothing crazy happens between now and the game tomorrow, I think he's actually kind of excited now."

"Uh-huh, OK," Tucker said. He cleared his throat. "So he isn't concerned about Ichabod showing up?"

"Oh, he is, and I am, too. I don't know if you heard, but we were both in that building that he burned down. But I realized during this past week that you can't live by fear. We don't know what will happen, but we won't choose to *not* do things just because we're afraid of the possibility that something bad *will* happen, you know?"

Tucker nodded at the wisdom of her statement even as he

wrestled internally with the wisdom of keeping his meeting with Ichabod a secret. He shuffled his feet on the hall carpet and patted a rhythm on the door.

"That's good, that's all good," Tucker said, looking down the hallway. "Listen, I've gotta go shower and stuff. So I guess I'll see you two around."

"Definitely. I'll tell Cole that you stopped by. Was there anything you wanted to tell him?"

Tucker thought with momentary panic. "Nope. No, just checking up on him. I'm good. See yah." Nera closed the door as Tucker treaded slowly down the hall.

In his mind, he could hear the voice of his mom asking him if he had really thought things through. He heard the voice of Lena chastising him for placing a basketball game before the safety of another human being. He heard the voices of Rick and Abby and quickly shut them off. The ding of the nearby elevator snapped him back to reality. He was on his own, and he was making the decision that he wanted to make. There would be plenty of time to tell security about the threat from Ichabod after Monday's game. Nera was right about not doing anything out of fear.

And as he went back into his room and saw the complete statue of the Eiffel Tower he had placed on the hotel dresser, he imagined one more voice: his dad, reminding him about the free buffet breakfast.

*   *   *   *

In her hotel room back in Lincoln, Carla assembled some papers on the desk and prepared to check out. She just had to wait for a phone call. It was starting to snow outside, and Carla wondered if this would mean sleeping in the airport tonight. She hoped not; she could use a good night's sleep before her next assignment.

Her cell phone rang. She put it on speakerphone. "Graham?" she asked.

"You done there?"

"I'm done. My flight leaves in two hours. Everything's closed out."

"And the girl?"

"Energized. Lena's plan is already in effect. She's en route."

"A very good first job. Well done," Graham said with no warmth.

"Thank you," she said, then paused. "Are you sure we didn't make a mistake by not making an offer to Tucker? Everything I've found points to him being the genius behind Dr. Tonkin's recent success, and Lena raves about his abilities."

"I decided based on your assessment, Carla. Are you saying that you were wrong?"

"No, no," she backpedaled, "I still think that splitting Lena and Tucker up was important for Lena to do what you want her to do. And Tucker is probably unrecruitable. For all his abilities, he has zero ambition. Did I tell you that his life's dream is to be a small-town lawyer for farmers? Hard to tempt somebody like that."

"But?"

"But talent is talent. Maybe we shouldn't have let him get away completely."

"He hasn't gotten away," said Graham cryptically. "It's time for you to move on. I'm sending you a file now. Are you ready for a bigger assignment?"

"You mean I get to recruit bigger fish than Nebraskan co-eds?" asked Carla, still curious about where she would be flying to in the morning.

"We do more than just recruit," said Graham.

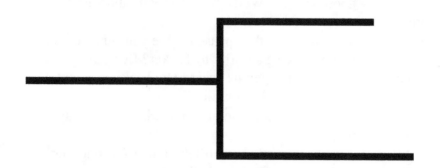

Championship Game

[Championship Game: First Half]
[Monday, April 6th]

The small ICU room at George Washington Hospital was completely dark except for the dim light that made it from the hallway under the closed door. A machine near the bed was running with the low hum of a pump, and the still body of Perry Lynwood was face up, eyes closed, and breathing in slow intervals. The chart hanging next to the door indicated a nurse check-in at four PM and a neurology consultation at five. It was four-thirty. No one else was in the room to see the intruder.

He had entered with a compact rolling suitcase which he put next to the bed. Then a small camera was attached above the television. It was placed to get a clear view of Perry while remaining concealed from anyone who wasn't looking for it. The intruder checked his phone to make sure the video feed was sending out a signal. Lastly, he set a bouquet of daisies still in its cellophane on the bedside table and placed next to it a get-well card with a picture of a disassembled C-3PO and the line "It could have been worse." The intruder slipped through the door and glanced both ways down the hallway. No one was watching. He left, removing the pilfered latex gloves he was wearing and tossing them in the nearest trash can. The entire operation took four minutes.

*   *   *   *

"We're going to be late."

Nera checked the clock on her phone and looked out the window at the painfully inert D.C. traffic. Cole was next to her, rubbing his knee compulsively. Across from them was Tucker, also anxiously monitoring the time. The only one enjoying the limousine ride was Henry Barnes.

"Relax," Rick O'Shea called from the front passenger's seat. "We're closer than you think, and Abby's the fastest driver I know. As soon as we get off 14th Street, we'll go sixty all the way to the back door. You'll have plenty of time to hit the red carpet and get some poses in before game time."

"There's a red carpet?" Cole asked.

"He's kidding," Nera nudged him with her shoulder.

"There's just a really long line through a metal detector."

Henry leaned forward.

"How do you know my son again?" he called up to Rick.

"I told you," Tucker said with a little irritation. "They work for a friend of Dr. Tonkin's. They're, um, consultants."

"Consultants," Henry repeated. He looked back up at Rick, who was craning his head to see the group. "And what exactly do you want from my son?"

"Dad, come on. Not everyone is trying to play us. Don't worry about Rick and Abby, they're for real," Tucker urged.

"Don't be so sure," Rick shot back. "Clearly we're taking him for a ride." Everyone groaned at the pun except for Rick, who thought it was hilarious.

"Mr. Barnes," Abby spoke up when Rick had calmed himself down, "you're right to be cautious about the people that might try to exploit Tucker and Cole. A lot of people see them as celebrities, or think they have a system for choosing winners or something. I don't expect you to just take it on trust that we're legitimate."

"Okay," Henry said. "So what should I take it on?"

"You'll see in a minute."

They had finally reached the Verizon Center and were half a block away from the entrance to the underground parking lot. From where they sat, it became clear why the traffic was so bad. A large group of protesters had gathered on the other side of the street and were yelling at another limousine just about to turn in. Police were struggling to keep them behind barriers.

"Who would protest a basketball game?" asked Cole.

"I'll give you a hint. The flag sticking up from that limousine is the South Korean flag," said Rick.

"South Korea is protesting the game?" asked Cole.

"No," Tucker interjected restively, "Americans are protesting South Korea. The Koreans were trying to mediate a secret deal between China and Thailand, and they got it done, but the deal was leaked over the weekend. And now, all the pro-Many Hands people are mad at South Korea for interfering. My ex-girlfriend is a big Many Hands fan; she's probably furious. This is the kind of thing she would be at, too." Tucker glanced out the window as the thought occurred to him.

Cole was still confused. "So... who's in the limo? The President of South Korea?"

"It's the foreign minister and his posse," Rick spoke up. "They were in town already and had been planning to come to the game for weeks. No one cared until this weekend. Somebody got the word out about their travel plans at *just* the right time. Good ol' leaks."

Abby nosed through the traffic, driving close to the line of screaming protestors on the sidewalk. Tucker found himself looking for Lena's face, but he didn't expect to see her. There was a reason she had never gotten caught for anything. If she were there, she would be in the back, with a cell phone and an alibi.

"Wait, " Henry said to the couple in the front seats. "How does the protest prove that you're legitimate?"

"Well, it proves that the foreign minister of South Korea is legitimate, doesn't it?" Abby replied. "Two hundred screaming activists can't be wrong."

"So?"

"It's the Koreans' skybox that you four will be visiting during halftime. We'll be there all game."

Tucker looked up in surprise. "You didn't tell me that," he said.

"You never asked," said Rick.

The car reached the valet stand and stopped. As the four in the back exited, Rick and Abby rolled down their windows. "We'll see you kids during half-time," Abby said cheerfully. "We can't wait to see you square off in that first half stunt, that's going to be fun. May the best bracket win!"

Tucker bent down to Abby's open window. "Now listen. I didn't come here for any more political stuff, OK? I don't want to talk to any ministers or delegates or anything. I just want to watch the game. You got me?"

"You have been got," Rick nodded. "We just want you to meet our boss. We know that even back-room international power-brokers like yourself have to unwind a little." Tucker stood back up, completely unconvinced that they weren't hiding another secret.

Cole, Nera, Tucker, and Henry walked in through the arena's VIP entrance, flashing their ESPN credentials. In a few minutes, they were surrounded by the chaos of the main concourse. The time had come for Tucker and Cole to split and go to their seats on opposite ends of the court. They looked at each other awkwardly for a moment.

"Hey listen," Tucker said, extending his hand. "Don't try and kill yourself or anything when you lose. The security guy is already mad at us."

Cole grinned, a small flash of excitement lighting his face for the first time. "Same to you, man," he said, and the two pairs separated.

*   *   *   *

Tucker and his father paused for a moment when they stepped out of the concourse and into the arena. Both men had been watching games for years, cheering at games for years, playing in games for years. They had been steeped in the atmosphere of excitement unique to college ball: fanatical, joyous, anxious, and pulsing with school pride. But something was different in this game. They both felt it as soon as they saw the 20,000 seats filled with a kaleidoscope of red and white and blue and yellow. It was a shiver, a recognition that the national championship was different than just another big game. There was a grandness to it, rightfully earned from being the pinnacle of the longest and most chaotic tournament in all of American sport. For the two men, the bigness was sensed, but neither one was a poet.

"Huh," said Henry.

"I know," said Tucker.

Tucker led the way to their seats. They were to sit in the middle of a host of University of Nebraska fans behind one of the baskets. Most of the students were already on their feet, laughing and cheering and practicing their stratagems for getting on national television. They recognized Tucker and applauded him and his father all the way to their seats, Henry waving to everybody in sight, the binoculars around his neck swaying between the two sides of his unzipped jacket. Tucker hadn't seen his dad so energized in years.

"This really is something," said Henry again as he stared up at the Jumbotron, then down at the dancers and cameramen moving around on the floor. He placed a small tray of nachos on Tucker's lap—a tray he had insisted on buying for his son—and settled in with satisfaction.

Tucker looked across the court at the UCLA fans sitting

opposite. "Hey Dad, can I see your binoculars a sec?" Henry handed them over and took back the nachos. After a minute of scanning, Tucker found Cole sitting in a seat surrounded by a group of shirtless fans whose bodies were completely painted blue and yellow. Nera was holding Cole's hand and pointing animatedly down at the court.

"You see Cole over there?" Henry asked. "How does he look?"

"About the same as he looked on Saturday. Like he's expecting a bomb to explode under his seat. Nera looks like she's having fun, though."

"Well, this will be good for him," Henry pontificated comfortably. "That boy seems like he could get out in the world more."

Tucker turned the binoculars up and to his right, pointing them at the row of private skyboxes that lined the upper ridge of the first level of stands. He counted over until he found the one that he thought contained Rick, Abby, and their South Korean hosts. It was difficult to make out anything behind the glass. There was a lot that he still didn't know about Rick and Abby and their mysterious power-broker boss, and he certainly didn't want to get dragged into a political conversation with the South Korean foreign minister. The possibilities of half-time made him nervous. But then he heard the music demanding that everyone get up off their feet, and as he saw his Nebraska Huskers come on the court and start dunking one after the other in a line, he realized that he didn't want to think about halftime. It was time to get in the game.

*   *   *   *

Across the court, Nera was explaining Cole's psychic powers to a group of attentive undergrads. "Oh yeah, I'd say we knew that there was something special about Cole as soon as he was hired," she lied. "We started calling him 'The OraCole' because he just seemed so in tune with the world."

"Woah," said a skinny blue student who had the body of a twelve-year-old. "So do you, like, guess the stock market and stuff?"

"Uh, no, it's just, you know, basketball and real estate things." Cole leaned closer to Nera. "You shouldn't talk me up so much. You know I'm probably going to lose this thing."

Nera put her finger over his mouth. "You predicted every single winner of every game in the tournament, Cole. I think you can start to enjoy that a little." Cole shook his head.

"Luck does not hold out this long."

"If luck had an expiration date, it wouldn't really be luck. Come on, embrace this. We are winning this thing!" She turned around to the crowd and raised her voice. "Am I right? We are *winning* this championship!" Fans around them started cheering "U-C-L-A!" and Cole looked on, impressed all over again with this woman who had all the social talents he lacked. He could even ignore, for a moment, his escalating feelings of discomfort at how much attention she was drawing to him.

The main lights dimmed as flashbulbs began to sizzle around the arena. On the Jumbotron, a loud, explosive homage to the journey of both teams climaxed with a spotlight on each team's bench. The players lined up for the announcement of each team's starting five. Nera squeezed Cole's hand, her whole face joyful, and Cole smiled. *Fun*, he thought. *This is fun. This is a couple of hours of fun in a very safe place, and then life goes back to normal. Better than normal.*

The pregame spectacle exploded and the pyrotechnics boomed. When the lights returned and the court was made ready for tip-off, the crowd stayed on its feet and kept the noise level high. There was no way for Cole to notice a cheap plastic basketball, the size of a grapefruit, bouncing erratically down the stairs past his row. It was finally picked up by someone with a fake yellow afro several rows down.

"Cole Kaman?" the man called. Other fans pointed up in his direction. "Cole Kaman?" He came closer, and Cole heard. The painted man tossed him the ball. "You drop this?"

Surprised, Cole caught the ball and looked at it. His name was written out very clearly with permanent marker, the "K" oddly warped over a long cut which ran along half of the rubber seam. Something rattled inside the ball. He slipped his fingernail into the seam and opened it like an Easter Egg. There was a piece of paper inside, folded into a tight square, clearly torn from the program booklet that was being given away at the arena entrances. He looked around above the crowd, scanning for a set of glasses and a goatee, but saw no one recognizable as his stalker. He looked over at Nera, who was distracted by a conversation with the person sitting on her other side. Cole shoved the ball and note in his pocket.

"Hey, I'll be right back," he said to Nera, making sure not to meet her eyes.

"Where are you going? The game is starting right now!" she called to his back.

"Bathroom," he said. "Just stay here and don't move till I get back."

"Well, hurry up!"

Cole half-nodded and ran up the steps to the tunnel entrance. He looked around to make sure that nobody was watching him, but all eyes were on the court. Hands shaking, he pulled the note from his pocket and unfolded it. The words were scratched out in black marker.

> *Just like this ball,*
> *False prophets will fall.*
> *I am here, and I will call.*

For just a moment, Cole wanted to throw up. He crumpled the note and stuffed it back in his pocket, then let himself lean his head against the cool tunnel wall. In the stadium, the crowd erupted—someone had made the game's first basket. *Now what?* Cole mulled. He wanted to just ignore the note. It wasn't signed by Ichabod; he hadn't actually seen him. But who else could it be? No, Ichabod was somewhere in the arena, watching them, moving at will around their section. The security guards—they must have seen him. He stood up from the wall to go ask.

"Excuse me, are you Cole Kaman?" asked an official-sounding, gravelly voice. Cole turned to see a man in a blue jacket with a tag on it. The man's eyes observed him sternly from beneath the rim of a baseball cap.

"Yes?"

The man pulled out a badge from his pocket and flashed it quickly at Cole. "I'm Deputy Federal Marshall Bell. I was just coming down to find you. We have received a tip that Ichabod is in the arena."

"Did you see him?" Cole tried to keep his voice low, but his nervousness betrayed him. The security guard at the tunnel's entrance glanced at them but did nothing.

Marshall Bell shook his head. "No, this is a tip we got from one of the scalpers outside. He said a big man with a goatee and glasses bought a ticket off of him just before the game was about to start. The scalper said that the man made some comment about 'a reckoning' that sounded like possible terrorism, so he told a cop. When the cop showed him the sketch of Ichabod, it was a positive ID. The seat number that the scalper gave us is empty, so we're doing a search throughout the arena as we speak. Based on Ichabod's description, he should be relatively easy to spot, though he's proven evasive in the past."

Cole dug out the basketball and note and handed them over. "Actually, I was just on my way to tell somebody about this. This ball rolled down the steps just a minute ago. The note looks like what Ichabod sent me last time."

Marshall Bell took in the note with one quick glance, then looked closer at the writing on the ball. "This is him," he confirmed.

"So…what's going to happen? Do we all have to leave? I mean, evacuate?" Cole asked nervously. "I mean, he may try something again, right? What if he sets the building on fire with all these people inside?"

The Marshall shook his head and pointed to Ichabod's note. "I don't think so. See this line right here? *False prophets will fall.* That's prophets, plural. He's not out for arson tonight. Our thinking right now is that he's specifically here for you and Mr. Barnes."

"Tucker?"

"Yes. Ichabod's M.O. is going after people or groups that he thinks are forces of evil. The working theory right now is that his initial arson attempts were meant to draw out that evil from the world, smoke 'em out. In his head, your perfect bracket is evidence that you are the evil one he's been looking for. If that's true, then it stands to reason that he will come after Tucker also."

"What about the people with us? Is he going to target them, too?"

The man scratched his beard.

"There's no way to know. What we need to do now is have you keep a low profile. And we need you and Mr. Barnes on board with us. Can you get in touch with him? Do you have his phone number?"

"Actually, we're supposed to do a stunt during a time-out in a few minutes. We're supposed to meet out at half-court. Should we not do it?"

"No, this is good. Tell Mr. Barnes to meet us at the Greene Turtle Restaurant on the east end of the building immediately after you do your thing. We'll make a plan. But for now, just remain calm. Our guess is that Ichabod probably won't make a move until the end of the game, when he knows which bracket is perfect."

"You mean, he's going to attack the winner?"

"Mr. Kaman, relax. We'll find him before the end of the game. Don't worry."

Cole nodded and took a deep breath. For a moment, he looked over the Marshall's shoulder at the escalators going down to the exits. "Hey, what if I just left?" Cole said in a rush, his heart pounding. "Could I just leave and make him follow me? Wouldn't that keep everyone safer?"

The Marshall took a step forward, forcing Cole to back away from the concourse. "I wouldn't recommend that, Mr. Kaman. If you leave, we don't know what he'll do. He might go after you, but he might panic and do something drastic in the arena. No. You stay and wait until this all plays out. Understand?"

Cole nodded again, waited for an uncomfortable moment, and returned to his seat meekly.

The Marshall watched him go all the way back down to his seat, then checked the time and took out his phone. As he walked briskly down the concourse, phone to ear, he swerved toward the closest trash can and tossed in the basketball and torn piece of paper. One hand now free, he took out a handful of peanuts from his pocket and shoved them in his mouth.

*   *   *   *

With ten minutes to go in the first half, Tucker left his dad and made his way down to the closest corner entrance to the court, showing his credentials at several points. A floor coordinator with a walkie-talkie and a pencil behind his ear was waiting for him.

"Good," said the coordinator when Tucker approached. "Okay, the other one is already waiting on the opposite side, so we'll just stay here until the next full time-out. You remember what you'll be doing?"

Tucker nodded.

"Good. Big night tonight. How about you? Been enjoying the game? Nice looking cheerleaders you've got out there."

Tucker smiled in agreement, but stopped smiling a couple of minutes later when he noticed that the man was still staring at the cheerleaders. A courtside view of the biggest game in college basketball was totally wasted on this guy.

The time-out was called with six minutes to go in the half. As soon as the players hustled to their benches, Tucker jogged out to the middle of the court, waving to everybody in the stands. He was flanked by a producer with a microphone and a cameraman. Walking in quickly from the opposite side was Cole.

"Ladies and gentleman," the announcer boomed as the two men met at half court and shook hands. "Out of ten million brackets entered in the Tournament Challenge this year, only two have made it to the big game. Please welcome Cole Kaman and Tucker Barnes!"

Tucker thrust both fists up in the air, turning around to take in the cheers coming from every side. Cole put a hand up and waved. He was enjoying it more than he would admit.

The announcer continued. "Their predictions have been impressive, but now, they are going head to head in the ultimate psychological game of prediction: paper, rock, scissors!"

The crowd laughed and cheered appreciatively, and the producer positioned Tucker and Cole to face each other at center court. The cameraman zoomed in on their hands and sent the image of their extended fists to the Jumbotron.

"Are you ready?" the producer roared like a revving engine. Both men nodded.

"Remember, best two out of three. And...1....2....3...shoot!" Cole flashed paper, and Tucker, with scissors, yelled in triumph and snipped Cole's fingers victoriously.

"That's one for Tucker Barnes. Here we go with round two...1...2...3...shoot!" Tucker nearly flinched, but showed rock. Cole flashed paper again.

"And one for Cole Kaman!" The crowd cheered and called out suggestions in an incoherent roar. Tucker leaned in to focus. *There's no way he puts out paper three times...*

"And round three for the win! Ready...1...2...3...shoot!" Tucker produced rock. To his instant humiliation, he saw Cole's long, flat hand. Paper.

"Paper beats rock, and Cole Kaman wins!" The UCLA fans began a chant of Cole's name while the Nebraska fans booed. Tucker threw back his head in frustration, only partly for the Jumbotron shot. He knew it didn't matter. But still.

Cole gave another polite wave, allowing himself to enjoy the victory a bit, then stepped forward to shake Tucker's hand. As the announcer gave a testimonial about the insurance company that had sponsored that event, Cole leaned in, smiling, and startled Tucker by saying, "Hey, we have a big problem. Meet me by the Greene Turtle restaurant right now. It's about Ichabod."

Tucker's stomach tightened, but he nodded that he understood and jogged off while the players made themselves ready to get back on the court. As Tucker approached his seat, Henry was shaking his head in mock shame.

"Son, what in the world were you thinking? Rock two times in a row?"

Tucker didn't slow down and barely made eye contact with his dad as he passed by. "Hey Dad, I gotta go talk to a friend real quick. I'll be back before the half."

"Okay, but we're not through with this conversation, young man. We need to have a serious talk about what they're teaching you at school."

"You got me, Dad, I've been skipping out on the paper-rock-scissors lecture," Tucker called back. Pausing at the top of the tier to take one long look at the resumed game action, Tucker sighed in frustration and went out into the concourse. He found the entrance to the Greene Turtle and saw Cole standing next to a man with a blue jacket.

"Tucker Barnes? I'm Deputy Federal Marshall Bell. Have a seat." Tucker sat. The Marshall explained the situation.

Tucker was incredulous. "How'd he get in? How'd he get past security? Isn't the guy like a giant? How is it that no one has seen him?"

Bell's retort was ice cold. "There are fifty thousand people here. We are doing our best."

"Could you show him the basketball?" Cole suggested, trying to ease the tension.

Bell didn't flinch. "No, I already gave that to Forensics."

"So what are we supposed to do if we see him?" Tucker asked more amenably. He wanted to get this conversation over with and get back to his seat as quickly as possible.

"Don't make a scene, just move away quietly. I'll have people watching both of you, and if something looks wrong, they'll move in. Do you have any other friends in the stands? Someone you could run to if the need arose?"

"We know people in the Potomac Skybox," said Tucker. "We were going up there at halftime."

Marshall Bell's eyes registered brief surprise. "The Potomac? Where the South Korean delegation is?" He didn't so much ask as state.

"Yeah. That should be safe, right? They have security."

Bell paused, as if calculating. "Sure. That could work. But listen, I want you to do this. Go for halftime, but then stay for an extra ten minutes if they'll let you. We can only assume that Ichabod will be watching your seats, and if you don't show, he might make a move that gets him noticed. It's a risk, as I explained to Mr. Kaman, but it might be the thing we need to try if we still haven't found him."

The two young men nodded their compliance.

"Okay, let's get you back to the game. You have cell phones?" Two more nods. "Give me your numbers so I can text you any updates. We're going to find this guy and shut him down, so just stay where you are and try to enjoy the game."

"Don't have to tell me," Tucker stated with finality. "I've missed too much of this game already."

Bell fixed him with another appraising stare, and the two bracket holders were waved out of the restaurant.

"He's pleasant," Tucker muttered.

"He's just trying to keep everyone safe," Cole returned. "Ichabod is a dangerous dude."

Tucker glanced at Cole with a pang of guilt.

"Hey, I should tell you something." Tucker licked his lips. "I, uh, I think I saw Ichabod yesterday morning. While I was out jogging."

"What?"

"He came up to me in the street and was really weird. Kept asking me if I thought I would win and if I liked seeing into the future. He didn't say his name or anything, but I figured it was him after—" Tucker tripped over his words and paused for a moment. "After he mentioned you by name."

Cole exhaled slowly and ran his fingers through his hair.

"Sorry, man, I actually went up to tell you, but you were asleep and Nera answered the door and... I just thought that things would be safe and it would be a bigger problem if you left."

Cole looked around and shrugged. "It doesn't matter now, we all know he's here. I didn't say anything the first time I saw him either. But he's seriously crazy, so next time, tell someone. A lot of people ended up getting hurt because I kept what I knew to myself."

"Absolutely. You're right." Tucker turned as he heard heightened cheering from the stadium. "So is Nera okay with everything?" he asked.

Cole cleared his throat. "Um, I should get back. See you at half time."

Both men settled back into their seats for the final three minutes. The score at the half: Nebraska 23, UCLA 24.

[Championship Game: Halftime]

The entrance to the Presidential luxury suites was down a short flight of stairs off of the second-floor concourse. It was a much-touted feature of the recent Verizon Center renovations, and it was specifically designed to give visiting dignitaries maximum security and maximum amenities at a maximum price. The isolated skybox entryway had a guard in front of it. A second guard was stationed in front of the Potomac Skybox, ready to stop any stranger who might try to disrupt the peace of the South Korean delegation.

A minute apart from each other, Tucker and Henry, then Cole and Nera, made their way to the entrance and were admitted past the guards. From a safe, unseen distance, the blue-jacketed Marshall Bell observed their entrance while he talked on the phone.

Further away still, another pair of eyes noticed the Marshall's peculiar, clandestine behavior. The Marshall was agitated but trying to hide it. Whenever he tried to speak, he only got two words out before halting. Whenever he was interrupted, he would roll his eyes or wipe the sweat from beneath the baseball cap on his balding head. The conversation wasn't going well. The Marshall finally said "yeah," hung up, and immediately dove into his pocket and pulled out a handful of chocolate-covered peanuts. To the careful eyes watching, this was clearly no lawman.

But the time to act had not yet come. Patience.

*   *   *   *

"Tucker! Seriously, rock twice?"

It took Tucker a moment to orient himself to the voice yelling gregariously at him from across the ritzy skybox. Twenty plush seats were lined up in the center of the room like a small movie theater, but most of the people were milling about the sides or back, circulating around the large spread of food and the minibar. The front of the room was dominated by the most dynamic, provocative virtual display that any of the four had ever seen, embedded somehow into the large viewing windows. They could clearly see the hip-hop dance troop performing in the half-time show, but the view was impossibly close and crisp. The illusion of being *right there* was almost too good, like a dream that felt too real.

The four were so mesmerized by it that Rick O'Shea was able to walk right up behind Tucker and slap him on the shoulder completely unanticipated.

"You know what's interesting about you, Tucker," Rick philosophized glibly, "and I was thinking about it even before you choked down there. You are a genius with these complex, dynamic groups, but I think you have some trouble one-on-one. Individuals don't cancel each other out, so they're harder to predict moment by moment. That may be your kryptonite."

"Wait, wait, Tucker's a genius? And Superman?" Cole asked.

Henry shrugged. "It's news to me, too, and I raised him."

"But it doesn't surprise you, does it?" Rick said with a wink.

"No, sir. Like I said: *I* raised him."

Their focus went back to the display. "Amazing, isn't it?" Rick said. "It's new ChangZhang technology. The company bought the booth so they can test these new displays. They want to capture that Kaah Mukul magic and translate it into a massive crowd experience without having to wear those awful headsets. And what you're seeing isn't even the full effect. They turned it way down for halftime. You should stay up here when the game starts so you can see the full display and feel the rumble of the surround sound. Of course," he added without missing a beat, "nothing beats having the pages of a good book in your hand. Am I right?"

Rick led them up to the food table which they attacked without hesitation, Henry first in line. They were soon joined by Abby, accompanied by an older man who caught their collective attention without saying a word. His graying hair and genial step conveyed the assertive aura of one who had long ago become accustomed to being the most important man in the room.

"Cole Kaman, Nera Pedrad, Henry and Tucker Barnes, I'd like you to meet Dr. Bryan Casing, our beloved boss."

Casing shook everyone's hands cordially. "I've been looking forward to meeting all of you. Have you been enjoying the game?" They all had. "Good. We've been following the unexpected twists and turns with you four, so let's hope that all that begins well, ends well." He turned to Cole. "I'd made a point of watching the Boston College game, and I was quite concerned when Dr. Faulkner provoked that fight with you at the end. Did you ever find out what made him do it?"

Cole shrugged. "He thought I'd cheated on my bracket, like someone had told me what to put down or something. I think he just had issues with losing."

Casing was quiet for a moment. "It's tragic when someone invests so much in winning that they can't deal with failure. Nothing is worse than an inability to cope with the inevitable."

"I guess," said Cole, who was unprepared for deep conversation.

"So very true," Rick mused as he put an arm around Abby. "I remember when I first met Abby and I knew immediately that we'd be together. She was miserable for months trying to ignore my existence. It was fortunate that, when my ways finally prompted the inevitable to occur, it was only her fiancé that lost his marbles."

Abby clasped Rick's hand and nodded soberly. "Poor Raúl."

"Well," said Casing, turning back toward Tucker and Cole, "I'm certain that whoever wins and whoever loses will make gracious exits tonight. What you have both done is astounding. Even so, it can be hard to be as accepting of the end of a lucky break as you are to accept the beginning."

Rick raised his cup. "It's like Bryan always says: 'Control is the goal, eat rolls in a bowl, patrol all the shoals, and extol all the Coles'. Or something like that."

"Yes, something like that," Casing nodded with a wry, somewhat forced smile. "Tucker, I can't imagine what it must have been like to have such close and continual contact with Rick and Abby these past few weeks."

"We can," Nera said under her breath.

"I know that you don't have a lot of time, but I wanted you all to go meet our host, Mr. Myung-Ki Noh. He's upstairs, and he insisted that he get the chance to meet you two." Casing pointed to Cole and Tucker.

"I've heard of Myung-Ki Noh," Cole said. "Doesn't he have something to do with Kaah Mukul?"

"He invented Kaah Mukul," replied Casing, amused.

"Oh. Wow."

"All of this technology you see, those screens up front and everything else, it's all a beta test and some of the people in the room are potential investors, including us. So eat up, he's excited to show you some of his latest toys." Casing turned to Tucker and his dad. "Although, I was hoping to borrow Tucker here for a few minutes before you go up, if you don't mind, Henry."

"Take him," said Henry, who had returned to the buffet.

Casing motioned for Tucker to sit down on one of the chairs overlooking the arena.

"I wanted to thank you for helping out Rick and Abby with the Wol Pot situation," Casing said as he sat across from Tucker.

"It didn't help much," said Tucker. "Now that everyone knows about the deal, it's going to get real hard for them over there."

"Yes, the leak was unfortunate. Many Hands is not a group that balks at playing countries off of each other."

"You think Many Hands leaked it?"

"It sounds like something they would do, don't you think? In fact, it's my understanding that those protestors outside have significant financial backing from some suspicious Southeast Asian sources. You can ask the foreign minister about it later, if you get the chance. He's quite worked up about it." Casing waved his hand to change the subject. "But I didn't pull you over to talk about politics. I have an offer for you."

"You're finally going to tell me who you people are?"

Casing nodded. "I will, soon, but since we don't have a lot of time right now, I just wanted to introduce you to an idea and we can discuss the details later. My group is building a research facility in Kentucky which we are looking to fill. Rick and Abby have suggested that you would be a good fit, and I'm inclined to trust their judgment. The facility itself won't be ready until next year, but there is plenty to prepare for until then. You could begin working with us by the first of May, after the end of the semester."

Tucker found himself feeling simultaneously confused and honored. "Dr. Casing, that all sounds cool and all, but I'm not interested in research."

"What are you interested in, Tucker?" Casing asked.

"I mean, I'm going to law school. Where I come from, there are a lot of people that need legal help. They get screwed over by big companies and banks all the time. I want to go back and help and be the kind of lawyer who fights for them, you know, works for the people there."

Casing nodded thoughtfully. "That's a worthy goal, Tucker. Your intentions are good, and if that's what you decide to do, you will have my full respect. But I want to open your mind to another possibility." Casing leaned forward, a glint of youth lighting up his eyes. "Tucker, you have rare talents. They're relatively raw, and, it seems to me, not ideally utilized. What we want to do at our facility, it won't be like any other place in the world. If you come work for us, I promise you, you'll be able to reach a measure of your potential that no other endeavor could help you achieve."

"Doing what?" Tucker asked. He still knew next to nothing about what Casing was offering.

Casing smiled. "Our research groups will have a unique organizational structure, and they'll be competing to—" Casing paused, searching for the words. "The thing you need to know right now, Tucker, the reason you'll be so good at this is because you'll be organized into *teams*."

Abby stepped up behind them. Casing noticed and reached over to pat Tucker's shoulder. "Go ahead. Don't keep Noh waiting. I want to stay in his good graces."

"This way," Abby called, gathering Tucker, Cole, and Nera. Henry had elected to stay close to the cookie platter and talk to Rick. As they went to a small door in the corner of the room, Tucker looked back at Casing, who nodded back. At that moment, Tucker realized with some astonishment that for the first time in years, he felt like his own future wasn't entirely set in stone.

Abby ushered her group through the door and up a wide staircase that led to a smaller room on top of the skybox. As they walked up, Cole whispered to Nera, "You know what's weird? Just before the Final Four while he was telling me about his brackets paranoia, Perry asked if I had ever been to Kaah Mukul. Now we're going to meet the man who made it. Weird, right?"

Nera whispered back, "You know what's weirder? If you write 'Kaah Mukul' backwards and translate it from ancient Mayan, it literally means 'city of the gullible'. Could there be a connection?" Cole laughed and raced Nera up the last few steps. Nera won.

The room into which they emerged was as cluttered and uncomfortable as the skybox beneath them was opulent. Black cables snaked around haphazardly between network servers and monitors. In the center of the room was a black swivel chair facing a recessed window that jutted over the arena. A shock of spiky hair poked out above the chair and hands holding controllers moved about rapidly on either side. Abby tapped the man's shoulder. He put up one finger to ask them to wait a moment, and then, with a few twists of his wrists, he emerged from where he had been, removed his mask, and joined them in the real world.

"I'm pleased to meet you," said Mr. Noh matter-of-factly, looking out the window to the clock counting down on the Jumbotron. "We haven't much time." He stood, somewhat shakily, and pulled out several face masks from an open box on the floor. "You may put these on. Here's one for the girl also. You see how you can adjust it?" Cole didn't, but Mr. Noh left little time for questions as he set up the three young people with folding chairs and controllers.

"Like this," Tucker whispered, and Nera reached over to help Cole fasten the face wrap.

"All set? Good. Let's go down," said Mr. Noh. Instantly, Cole's visual field was clouded over in a gray mist, and he had the sensation of jumping off a high dive into a warm pool. When it cleared up a moment later, they were inside a room similar to their skybox, but larger and completely glassed in, almost crystalline in appearance. It overlooked a regulation-sized basketball court, devoid of players, fans, or life of any kind. Cole looked down and saw himself, rippling with muscles beneath armored blue leather. He tried to make himself turn around so he could find Nera, but he couldn't stop running into the walls.

"Need some help?" At Nera's voice in his earpiece, Cole's muscular avatar turned too quickly and smacked into her.

"Uh, sorry," he said. "These hand control thingies must not be working right."

"Didn't you ever have a game console growing up?" Tucker came over, another huge figure moving with the grace of virtual gravity.

"Well yeah, but this is a little different than Halo. Just give me a minute, I'll figure it out."

Cole got himself out of his sticky corner and turned to find Myung-Ki Noh coming toward them.

"Welcome to the Montezuma Arena," he said, arms opening to the arena's grandeur. "Normally this space is reserved for Ullamaball, but the arena is closed for the day so I can work on integrating the basketball game into the staging system. Please go to the window and watch."

The three went over to the seamless windows and looked down. In an instant, the court was filled with virtual basketball players from Nebraska and UCLA, and the mammoth stands filled with screaming fans. The sounds came to their ears, and they felt transported back to the real game.

"Whoa," Nera said softly. Mr. Noh seemed to like her reaction.

"Aside from myself, you are the first in the world to see this," Noh explained. "Soon, every major sporting event in the world will be available in the Montezuma, viewable from any KM Center—for an admission price, of course, and a significant fee for the league involved. A deal with the Premier League is already in place. Soon, Ullamaball will no longer be a popular virtual sport among the host of real ones. It will be *the* most popular sport, because all sports will be virtual."

The three just stared for a moment. "So, those are all the real players, right? Are all the people around them real, too, and you just kind of…beamed them in there?" Nera asked,

"Yes and no," said Mr. Noh. "We have small holographic cameras placed around the court to capture everything. For now, the people in the stands, are from the first tier only, and each captured individual has been cloned several times to fill the arena. This is superior to simply populating the area with generated avatars because the live footage gives a sense of the spontaneity of the crowd movements."

Nera became curious. "So, were we in here?"

"Perhaps. Where were you seated?" Nera indicated their seats. Noh turned to a virtual control panel beside the window, and all at once the players and crowds were moving very rapidly in reverse.

"We are here now at the last play of the first half," Noh said, stopping the footage. "You may be in luck since you are seated so close to the court. It becomes a little less certain as you get higher. And…" Noh zoomed and modified dexterously and finally homed in on two people, Cole and Nera, hunched forward as the final seconds ticked off. "There you are." Noh clicked one last time, and the images of Cole and Nera were suddenly in six different locations in the arena, as if part of a large kaleidoscope.

"Cool," said Nera, waving to one of her selves.

"Uhhh," Tucker looked on incredulously, "so, you want everyone to come to these virtual games instead of going to games in person? Isn't the game always going to be better live?"

Mr. Noh stuck out his chin. "Not for much longer," he enunciated confidently. "You saw those experimental displays down below? That is another phase of the same project. For years, people tried to use virtual worlds to either replicate the real world or to create worlds that are completely fantastical. What no one understood until Kaah Mukul was that this technology could be used to merge reality and virtual reality to enhance all sensory experience. In ten years, no one will be able to tolerate an unmodified sporting event. They simply won't offer enough stimulation."

None of them spoke as they looked at each other with a shared sense of skepticism. Nera said, "Mr. Noh, this is very impressive. But why are you showing it to us?"

"Because I wanted to have you here, in the city, to explore a mystery with me," Noh said, shifting into a more contemplative tone. "You see, this whole phenomenon with your brackets seems to be intricately tied to Kaah Mukul for reasons which are still unclear to me. Consider these improbabilities. First, I made contact with Dr. Casing, who wants to use my technology for some custom applications. Then, my staff drew my attention to the success of the bracket of Mr. Lynwood, formerly one of our most successful but deeply flawed Tribal War generals. Further investigation cross-checking KM accounts with registered bracket names led us to find a link with a potential client, Dr. Faulkner, who confirmed to me that he was using his bracket to subtly showcase a complex outcome prediction system, which I may still buy. Mr. Lynwood's bracket, it turned out, was actually set by Dr. Faulkner's system without his knowledge."

Cole and Tucker looked at each other. Some of the events of the Final Four now made some sense.

"But the connections did not stop there," Noh continued, "Mr Lynwood was also unwittingly involved in a city-wide simulation of a political scenario that the Chinese government wanted to test. That simulation eventually led to my involvement with negotiations between the Chinese and my own government. Those negotiations prompted us to find a way to discreetly make contact with the ambassador of Thailand, who was indisposed in the United States. Through a chance conversation with Dr. Casing, I discovered that he had a potentially useful contact already established in the city of Lincoln. And who was that contact? Why, it was Mr. Barnes, a third perfect bracket holder. By this time last week, I felt there was some strong connection between these bracket holders and Kaah Mukul that I had yet to fathom. You might imagine that I was unsurprised when I discovered that the bracket holders would all be coming to Washington on the very same weekend that I had long been planning to visit. After Saturday's events, I knew that I had to bring you here to offer any further insights into the deeper meanings of our connection. Which brings me to you, Cole Kaman."

Cole, who's mind had wandered during Noh's lengthy explanation, looked up. "Me?"

"Yes, you are the one that may be the key to this mystery. You have never been to Kaah Mukul, obviously. You seem to have no connection with any of our operations or with any of the other bracket holders. You have never crossed my path until now. I can only conclude that you have some connection that I have failed to discover, or that your connection is fated to be established in the future. What do you think? Can you enlighten me?"

"Uh…I don't know. I have no clue. I just filled out a bracket." Cole uttered, looking at Nera and Tucker for help.

Noh stepped away and looked out the window at the basketball court. Tucker cleared his throat. "Well, Mr. Noh, this has been really, really cool and interesting, but I think the game is about to start, so we should probably be headed back now, if you're finished with us." Noh acted as though he didn't hear for a minute, while the others stared awkwardly.

Then he said, "Yes, of course. I was just signaling Ms. Razzione to retrieve you. But to answer your question, Mr. Barnes, I am not finished with you. I will expect both you and Cole back in the city at some point in the near future. I have given you free premier access to any KM center in the world. And if there is anything else I can do for you, do not hesitate to contact me."

The three said good-bye and Tucker jumped out, eager to get back. But Cole hesitated, and Nera waited for him.

"Mr. Noh?" Cole asked. "I was just wondering, if all these connections with Kaah Mukul really mean something, then what do you think that means for me not being connected?"

Noh paused. "You are not connected yet," he corrected. "You are the truly random variable in the events leading up to today, which means that I cannot foresee your role. I hope that you and the city will be able to help each other, but, as we saw with Mr. Lynwood, a relationship with Kaah Mukul does not always end well. We will see." Noh's words drifted off in meditation.

Cole nodded, mumbled "Thanks," and jumped back into reality, where Tucker and Abby were waiting for them.

"What was that about?" Tucker asked. Mr. Noh sat silently in his chair, deaf to their conversation.

"Cole's existence makes it impossible for Mr. Noh to foresee the future," Nera answered dryly.

"Whatever," Tucker said as he looked out the window. Then he swore. "The game's already started." He was down the stairs in a flash, Nera right behind him. Cole and Abby followed at a more leisurely pace.

"What did you think?" Abby asked as they descended.

"Cool. Uncomfortable. Confusing," Cole listed.

"That sounds like him. Have you ever been in one of those virtual set-ups before? Be careful with those masks. Bryan told me that they can cause epilepsy in some people after a lot of use."

They entered the skybox again. Cole found Nera waving him over to a seat. Tucker was pulling his dad away from a lively conversation with Rick about sustainable wheat farming. Everyone else was watching the game. Cole sat beside Nera with a heavy sigh. Nera waited a moment, then leaned over to whisper in his ear.

"So when are you going to tell me why you had to leave so many times in the first half?" she asked calmly.

Cole hesitated. He would rather have forgotten about all of that, but he knew that Nera deserved to know what had happened. He leaned over and began to quietly tell her everything about Marshall Bell and the sighting of Ichabod.

They were interrupted by a yell from Rick. "Hey, focus on

winning this thing, Cole! I've got triple or nothing on your team with Abby. Don't let me down!"

Cole waved sarcastically at Rick, and turned back to Nera, but when he saw the look on her face, he realized it would be better to wait until she talked to him.

[**Championship Game**: Second Half]

Tucker didn't know what to think.

The full brunt of the ChangZhang reality enhancement system was turned on two minutes into the second half. The screen displays went from captivating to overwhelming: every player's movements were highlighted by fiery auras of transitory color; the ball itself seemed wreathed in many colors of flame. The sound system amplified every ball bounce, every rim hit, every grunt, every whistle. The depth and dazzle of the system quickly overwhelmed the four visitors, who weren't used to such an invasion of their visceral sensibilities.

So this is what an acid trip is like, Tucker thought. He kind of liked it.

Henry nudged Tucker irritably. "Can we go back to our seats now?"

Tucker held him off. "In a minute. I think Noh is watching, and Dr. Casing doesn't want to offend him. A little longer."

"In one more minute all the veins in my head are going to pop," said Henry, shifting uncomfortably in his seat and looking away.

Tucker noticed that Cole was also uncomfortable. He had walked up to the window on the far end of the room where he could see the game unimpeded and was bouncing nervously on the balls of his feet.

"Hey Cole, are you OK?" Rick called. "It does take some time to get used to."

"Yeah, I'm good, but I think I like the normal view bet—"

A splattering of something red rocketed up from the seats immediately below the skybox and collided with the glass directly in front of Cole's face. It splashed a sticky mess and oozed down in streams. For a moment, the conversation in the room ceased as everyone turned to see what was going on. The next second, their view was plastered with colors of every kind as food and soda were thrown in an instant attack. The enhancement system amplified some screams and what sounded like a chant.

Tucker ran to where Cole was standing and looked out

through the filth coating the window. They could see a small group of people yelling angrily down below, fists pumping toward their skybox. Then *BAM! S*omething heavy slammed into the glass. They were throwing shoes.

The enhancement system was shut down and the room became relatively silent. The sounds of the commotion outside filtered through only faintly, and there was so much on the windows that it was hard to tell what was going on. Inside, the body guards for the South Korean diplomats grabbed their protectees and began to escort them to the door. But before it was opened even a crack, they slammed it shut and began looking for ways to brace it. There was yelling in the hallway, closer than the crowd in the arena. Something banged on the door, then they heard the grating sound of punches hitting bone, the screams of pain from the effects of pepper spray and tazers, calls for help, and calls for justice.

The occupants of the skybox ran to the back corner away from the windows and doors while bodyguards yelled into their phones. The word came that arena security was already on its way.

Tucker pushed his way back over to the window and tried to see individual people, just in case there was anyone that he knew.

"Is there something we can do?" asked Henry, who looked like he was actually itching for a fight.

"No, Dad, let the security guys do their jobs."

From what Tucker could tell, the situation was being brought under control. Down in the stands, the security guards, along with ordinary civilians furious that these people were interfering with the game, were fighting with the core of protestors and tackling them to the floor. The game itself had stopped. In the hallway, guards were removing the combative demonstrators one by one until all was quiet once more. When they thought it was safe, the bodyguards opened the door and began to survey the situation.

Tucker found Nera looking worried and Cole with his head down, his fingers dug deep into his hair.

"You OK, Cole?"

"This thing is spreading," Cole mumbled without raising his head. "First it was Ichabod, then it was Perry and Neeson. And now, people in the stands are going crazy. This is like a zombie movie."

Tucker raised his eyebrows at Nera.

"No one's losing their minds, Cole," Nera consoled. "Not

because of the game, anyway. These were just opportunists looking for a big stage."

Tucker tried to lighten the mood. "If people are turning into zombies, we'll have to fight them from here. I'll get the vegetable tray to use as a shield. You grab the cheese knife." Cole didn't laugh. "Look, it's OK. Believe it or not, but this isn't the first time that I've seen something like this. It happened at our city hall last year. It's not crazy. It's stupid, but it's not crazy."

The door burst open. A small legion of security guards, headed off by the big red-headed chief, walked in and surveyed the room. They were all sweating.

"Is everyone OK?" he asked the group. "My sincerest apologies to all of you. It seems that this was a flash mob organized by a few angry individuals. I know that it seemed out of control, but it's unlikely that you were in any real danger..."

He paused as he noticed some familiar faces in Cole and Tucker. "Wait, *you two* are here?" he exclaimed. "Of course, of course you're here." The man would have said more, but the foreign minister approached angrily and began to berate him. In the commotion, Casing approached the four visitors and ushered them over to Rick and Abby.

"They'll be clearing out this box," Casing said, leaning close to talk over the escalating voices by the door. "The dignitaries will leave soon, but Mr. Noh will remain in his control room to ensure that the interface windows are still operating properly. Do you feel comfortable returning to your seats?"

Tucker and Henry nodded. Cole looked pale and shook his head slightly, but Nera put her arm around his waist. "Yeah, we'll go back," she said.

"Good. I'll be joining some colleagues in another box, and Rick and Abby plan to..."

"We plan to try and get courtside," Rick said cheerfully.

"OK. Let's stay in touch. And let's hope that nothing else eventful happens off the court."

He turned toward the door, flanked by Rick and Abby, and Tucker called out after them, "Go Huskers!"

"Triple or nothing, Tucker!" Abby called back. "Don't choke on me!"

Tucker and Cole exchanged a look. "You good?" Tucker

asked.

Cole looked at Nera. "I'm good. But Ichabod is still out there."

"Look man, the way I see it, these protestors did us a favor. If security was tight before, they're going to be twice as alert now. Nobody will be able to make a move without drawing attention."

"Maybe," said Cole. "But I keep thinking about what Noh said, how I was the reason that he couldn't predict what would happen to us, that I was making everything random."

Tucker looked at him blankly. "What does that even mean?"

"I don't really know. But all this seems pretty random, doesn't it? And we're not even halfway through the game. Do you think…" Cole's voice trailed off. "Never mind. I'm just being dumb. Let's go get this over with."

Cole moved toward the door, and the four walked down the hallway, now littered with scattered remnants of the skirmish. As they went out into the concourse, they passed by a small group of people kneeling on the floor with their hands on their heads, some red-faced and bruised, surrounded by guards and policemen. Some wore t-shirts with multicolored hand prints all over.

"Thanks for nothing, morons," Tucker called. One of the protestors began to yell back, but shut up when Henry started toward him to deliver a piece of his mind. Tucker pulled his father back to avoid an incident.

They reached Cole and Nera's tunnel, and Tucker took a final look at Cole's still-pale face. "You good to go?" Tucker asked. Cole nodded, and they all went in to witness the end of the game.

*   *   *   *

When game play resumed, the teams on the court seemed simultaneously rejuvenated and thrown off by the odd distraction. The sense of unity among the people in the stands as the protestors were jeered and then removed vanished once everyone remembered what was at stake. The players were fast and sloppy and made some mistakes, but in a few minutes both teams were back in rhythm. UCLA scored, Nebraska answered. The score ticked up steadily: 40-43, 46-45, 48-48, 52-54… No one could break away, no matter what happened. Neither team could shake the other from its heels. Tucker was standing on every possession, yelling instructions to the players and outright curses to the refs. Across the court, Cole was bent over with his arms folded, repeating "Come on, come on, come on," under his breath. Every so often, Cole looked around to see if Ichabod was hovering in some corner. He never was.

Seven minutes into the second half, Cole looked up to the top of the staircase where Ichabod must have stood earlier. Something had clicked in his mind.

"Do you think Noh is still up there in his booth?" Cole asked Nera.

"Probably. That's what Mr. Casing said. Why?" Cole didn't answer immediately. He drummed his fingers rapidly on his knees and looked back up to the top of the stairs.

"You know that thing that Noh showed us, how he has cameras on us that he uses to make the crowds in that virtual reality stadium? What if the cameras picked up the image of Ichabod when he dropped that ball down? If he could pull up a picture, we could tell security exactly what he's wearing and what he looks like. And we'll know, too, in case he comes around."

Nera looked back at the game and sighed heavily. She clearly did not want to go.

"You don't have to come," Cole said. "I just have to go check this out."

Nera looked painfully torn. "No, you shouldn't go anywhere by yourself. Couldn't someone else go up? What about Rick and Abby?"

Cole pointed down to the floor where Rick and Abby had taken positions as sweat-moppers beneath the hoop. They weren't in a position to help.

"No," said Cole decisively, "I know what to look for. I'll be faster than anybody else. Besides, I can't even concentrate on the game knowing that he's out there. If I have a chance to help catch him, I should do it."

Nera considered the proposal. "Fine, I'll come with you. But let's run."

*   *   *   *

The tumult from the protest now gone, a single security guard had resumed the post at the entrance to the luxury boxes, a bandage over a red patch on his cheek bone where he had sustained a hit by the flash mob. The other guards were overseeing the hand-off of protestors to the police, and the rest were patrolling the interior of the arena. The lone guard, suffering from a post-adrenaline crash, was hesitant to let Cole and Nera through until they reminded him who they were. "Just lock the door after you, OK? I'm the only one here for now."

Inside, the skybox was dark and surreally quiet. Light coming in from the window cast bizarre shadows as it filtered through the thick coats of sticky-colored liquid and chunky food residue. Cole and Nera made their way up the stairs and found Mr. Noh exactly as they had left him. They tapped his shoulder, startling him. In a minute he was out.

Cole explained his plan. and Noh grinned. "Interesting," he said, turning to a standard computer display to search for the 2D rendering they needed. He found Cole and Nera's seats and began to search forward through time.

"Okay, this should be about it," Cole noted. Noh slowed down the footage and Cole leaned in close, a finger hovering over the screen. The ball bounced down, and the fan below them came up. They backed up a few seconds.

"There, can you make that bigger?"

Noh clicked and zoomed with practiced speed. "Is that your monster? He looks smaller than what I've heard."

But Cole wasn't listening. The man discreetly dropping the ball down the stairs and walking away wasn't Ichabod. It was, indisputably, the man he knew as Marshall Bell.

"What the…" Cole began. "Is there a way to save this image?"

"I could upload it to your phone," Noh suggested. "Will this help you track down your stalker?"

Cole didn't know. Nothing made any sense anymore.

While Noh uploaded the image, Cole called Tucker.

"What?" Tucker answered, straining to hear over the excitement of the crowd.

"Tucker! I'm in the skybox with Mr. Noh. We just found out that Marshall Bell was the one that dropped that ball down to me. Ichabod's message is fake; Bell is lying to us."

"What?" Tucker asked loudly. "What do you mean? How do you know that?"

"Noh found it on his video equipment. I'm looking at the picture right now. It's definitely Bell."

A pause. "So what do you want to do?"

"I don't know. What do you think?"

"Just go tell a security guy to... wait, I just got a text from him right now." Cole heard a ping on his own phone. He had gotten the same text.

Urgent- U need to get back to G. Turtle booth right now. Ichabod news. -Bell

"What now?" asked Tucker. "What's our move?"

Cole looked around at the room. "Can you get up here in the next minute? I have an idea, I'm going to text him to come up here instead."

"Oh man, you're killing me. There's like six minutes left in the game! Do you really need me to be there?" Cole didn't even have a chance to respond before Tucker answered himself, "Never mind, I'm coming. If I'm getting played, I want to know why." And then, "I hate this so much."

Cole pocketed his phone and turned to Noh. "Can you do me a favor? Is there a way to put this image on the screen downstairs? I mean, is there a way for me to signal you to put it up?"

Noh nodded. "I have cameras in that room. Just wave."

"Really? OK, good. Nera, um, you need to stay here with Noh and get ready to call security if it looks like things are going bad."

Nera frowned at Cole. She was not used to this new, energized persona he had suddenly taken on. "What are you doing? Let's just get him arrested."

"No, no," said Cole. "For the first time in three weeks, I have a chance to get some answers. I want answers."

"Me, too," Noh chimed in.

Cole texted Bell to come to the Potomac Skybox. Bell, after a moment, agreed. Cole ran out quickly to tell the security guard to let Tucker and Bell in, his mind racing as he considered the conversation that he wanted to have.

Tucker entered a few minutes later, and Marshall Bell thirty seconds after that. The Marshall looked grim, none too pleased about the unexpected change.

"Why are you up here?" asked Bell.

"Better view. Why did you want us?"

The Marshall paused, realizing that something was amiss, but continued. "I'm sorry to interrupt you again so close to the end of the game, but we've been contacted by Ichabod and we know what he wants."

"Before you go on," Cole interrupted, speaking over his sudden nervousness, "you should know that we know you're lying. We know that the message from Ichabod wasn't real."

"Excuse me?" Bell responded evenly. Cole waved to the camera and pointed to the interface window. The five-second clip of Bell dropping the ball filled the screen and repeated on a loop.

"With one signal, security is going to come in here and we're going to report that there is a man impersonating a Federal Marshall and an arsonist at the same time. But before we do, we want to know who you are and why you're doing what you're doing."

The man looked up at the footage, then back at the surprising pair of young interrogators. He froze for only a moment before sniffing and shrugging.

"Well, this makes things easier for me," he said. He slowly reached into his jacket and pulled out a tablet computer. Motioning Cole and Tucker over, he brought up a screen split between two video feeds. One showed the dark image of a man sitting before a computer monitor. His face couldn't be seen, but he was wearing glasses and a grey hood. The other image was of a hospital room, with someone asleep in the bed.

"I came up here with a very elaborate story about Ichabod's endgame to make you give me what I needed, but now that you geniuses have seen through it, I can be more direct. The video on the right is Perry Lynwood's room at George Washington Hospital, not far from here. If you look closely, you'll notice a small suitcase underneath the table by his bed. That suitcase contains a bomb. Now, I need you to tell your friend up in the booth not to call security or I trigger the bomb right now."

They froze. This was, to say the least, an unexpected response to their inquisition.

"Why should we believe you?" Tucker retorted.

"You don't have to, but you should," said Bell as he removed something skinny with his other hand. He held his thumb over a device with a red button.

Cole looked at the device in total shock. He quickly turned to the camera and waved Nera off, mouthing "Do … not… call… security."

"Now," Bell continued, "I need to know just one thing from each of you, and then I will be on my way and nothing else will happen. I need to know if you, or someone you know, or maybe someone you never met, had a special system for picking your brackets. This is very important. A yes or no will do."

"This is about the *brackets*?" Cole nearly screamed. "Are you out of your mind?"

"Maybe. Yes or no?" Bell shook his wrist with grim playfulness.

Tucker and Cole looked at each other.

"No," they both said.

Bell studied their faces very carefully, his finger still over the red button. "I'll ask again. Is it at all possible that your bracket picks were not made by you, but by some method or program or other person? Answer fast, lives are in the balance."

"No!" Tucker said loudly, his arms open wide. "They were just normal picks. I do this every year. Now please put that trigger away and we'll forget all about this."

Bell continued to examine their faces. He sniffed again. "I believe you," he said, putting the trigger back in his pocket. "But the person you see in the other video feed does not. You see, he thinks the plan is that he will pretend to be Ichabod, and you will reveal your system as a way of convincing him not to blow up your friend. You'll notice that he has the same trigger that I do, over by his right hand. He has instructions to detonate if he thinks he is being fooled."

"So, tell him that it's over and he doesn't need to!" Cole urged.

"No," said Bell. "I'm going to leave right now, alone and unimpeded. I won't let him know that it's over until I'm safely away. As long as you don't call security on me in the next ten minutes, all you have to do is convince that man that you have a secret brackets system and everything will be fine. You'll be heroes, really. Perry is lucky to have friends like you." Bell reached over and pushed a button on the tablet to activate the video chat option, then handed it to Tucker. "Better make it good."

The two looked at the tablet in shock. The man known as

Bell stepped away and casually walked out the door, wolfing down a handful of M&M's.

A ping from the tablet drew Tucker and Cole's attention. The hooded figure had begun to type, and a message popped up in a chat box.

Tell me your secret. Now.

Cole looked frantically at Tucker. "You have to think of something."

"Why me? I don't know what to say!"

"You're the one in college. Maybe you learned something in a math class you can use. I don't know this stuff."

"I'm pre-law! How much math do you think I know?"

"Do you know any stats?"

"Maybe a little, stuff from research, but not much. Go get Noh."

"But he needs something now! Just think of anything."

A message popped up.

Well?

The figure reached out to grab the trigger by his hand. Tucker typed.

No, we're here. We're going to explain our secret system now. Please don't use bomb.

The figure took his hand back and typed.

Tell me.

Tucker hesitated above the screen, his mind completely blank. He looked out at the window and heard the crowd roar at something. He thought of all the technical terms he knew that might sound realistic. Then the words popped into his head, and he smiled.

Bracket predictions made using a non-linear Skyline Plotter.

*   *   *   *

Just outside the Potomac Booth, Mr. Graham deposited his Marshall Bell blazer in the trash can, satisfied that he had covered all his bases. What Jason Spade had told him was true. OPUS hadn't leaked, and there was no other system out there to compete. He could now safely report that to his superiors. All that remained was to tie up the last loose ends of the day. He needed to meet the girl Lena at her hotel near Dulles. She had proven herself in planning the flash protest, and she would be very useful in her next assignment in Thailand. He had not been entirely happy with the order to let her wreak havoc during the game, but in the end things had worked out better than he had planned. There was, of course, the matter of Neeson. He would take care of that tonight. The only lingering concern was the presence of his rival recruiter, but it wasn't a significant problem. He had gotten what he wanted, as he always did.

Graham exited the hallway, his eyes on his phone, when he stepped on something. A hand. The guard that had been posted at the hall entrance was on the floor, face coated with blood and radio still in his belt. Graham didn't even have time to pocket his phone before someone jumped at him from the side. A huge hulk of a man overwhelmed his field of vision.

No, no, no! thought Graham. *It's the real one!*

He felt something smash into the side of his jaw, and everything went dark.

*   *   *   *

Tucker had only typed a few lines before he knew he was in way over his head. The fake Ichabod would write things meant to make him sound insane, but he'd immediately follow up with technical questions about algorithms and data sets.

"We've got to get Noh to help us out," Tucker said after making something up about two-way ANOVAS. "I can't keep this up. Tell Nera to unlock the door and get Noh to come down here. Wait, but you have to tell me the score first."

"Seriously?" Cole exclaimed.

"Just do it!" Tucker commanded.

Cole squinted at the Jumbotron through the stained window.

"2:50 to go, 64-62, UCLA." He turned to signal the camera, but then stopped short when the door of the skybox opened abruptly. The doorway was filled with a menacing hulk.

Cole had forgotten just how big Ichabod was, wide in the shoulders and erect as a redwood. The goatee and shaggy appearance were gone, but the glare off the glasses was still there. He was wearing a souvenir t-shirt and a ridiculous blue-and-yellow wig which he threw down as he stepped into the room.

Tucker, still engrossed in the tablet, didn't register Cole's voiceless attempts to get his attention. In an instantaneous burst of fury, Ichabod leapt over to Tucker and ripped the tablet away, flinging it across the room. With a backward sweep of his hand, he slammed Tucker across the chin and sent him sprawling.

Cole made a desperate break for the open door. He had gone only a few feet when Ichabod caught him by the back collar and jerked him over the row of seats. A paralyzing pain burned through his back; he suddenly found his voice and yelled in agony.

The camera! Tucker spun around to signal a frantic call for help to Noh and Nera, scrambling over chairs to put a safe distance between himself and Ichabod. But Ichabod wasn't going for him. Seeing the camera mounted on the wall, the juggernaut snapped it from its base and threw it at Tucker's head. Then with both men cornered, Ichabod reached into his pocket.

At the sudden silence in the room, Cole gingerly pulled himself up from between the seats. Ichabod had pulled something out of his pocket and was swinging it back and forth like a hypnotist.

"Two of the four. Half the horsemen," he said quietly. His deep voice was strained with agitation. "I knew who you were years ago. It goes down from two to one to oblivion. It says so. Pestilence and Death. It doesn't matter which is which, but I know. The fire made me see it, it cleared my eyes. Four to two to one to nothing, complete obliteration. This will happen now."

Ichabod began to twirl the object with his wrist, slowly at first but quickly picking up speed, slicing through the air in rhythm with his relentless footsteps. *What was that thing?* Cole could see two strings pulled taut by something weighted down between them. Something heavy that was now spinning faster and faster. A sling. Goliath had a sling.

"You four," the madman continued, twirling a little faster

now. "You were going to do it by making *predictions*, witchcraft in the form of prophecy in the form of sheep's clothes. You wanted glory." The insane arsonist fixated on Cole and walked an unhurried pace toward him. His movements sparked a random memory in Cole's panic-sick mind. He saw an image of a nature show about great white sharks and remembered how they swam steadily, methodically, because they knew nothing in the ocean could ever stop them. Ichabod seemed to Cole to move like a shark. *What a stupid thing to think about right before you die,* he scolded himself, his hand instinctively shoving back through his floppy hair. Still trapped between the rows of seats, he fought spasms of pain as he stumbled away from the oncoming giant.

"Pride was the downfall of the son of the morning. His bracket lost, you know who I'm talking about. There is always a downfall. The tower fell. The columns fell, the ceiling fell. The stones do it. The fire does it." Ichabod's voice swelled like a preacher's, his sling whirling in tight, fast rotations by his side. "Which will fall first now?"

Ichabod reared back, his hand raising above his shoulder to launch the stone. Tucker sprang up in a crash of chairs and launched himself onto Ichabod's back. For a moment, Tucker was on top, but with a primal roar, Ichabod threw him headfirst to the floor and grabbed for something to bring down on the unmoving body. Without a single thought, Cole vaulted the seats awkwardly and lunged at Ichabod. But the giant madman caught him in the chest with a massive forearm, hammering him to the ground and knocking the wind out of him. Snapping his sling back into a lethal spin, Ichabod pinned Cole to the floor with a heavy foot on his chest.

"Where is your glory now!" he bellowed, his face horribly contorted in triumph.

Suddenly, the room was filled with an ear-splitting siren. Disoriented, Ichabod released the sling haphazardly, missing Cole entirely, and covered his ears with a furious scream. The screens came to life and strobed unbearable, piercing light intermixed with the deep red image of a bloody human heart. Ichabod whipped out another rock and launched it at the screens, fracturing the images but not stopping the sensory onslaught. Finding himself free, Cole gulped air and struggled to crawl away in the confusion. But the distraction didn't last; Ichabod threw down the sling, slammed his foot onto Cole's throat, and raised his arm to bring Cole's life to a final, crushing end.

The blow never came. Ichabod was tackled from behind by a gang of security guards, the shock of tasers crackling as he lurched and convulsed in blind fury. Among the mass of men trying desperately to subdue the giant was Henry, landing blows as often as he could.

Cole felt someone grab him from behind and flinched in pain. "Relax, relax, it's me," Nera said, enfolding Cole in her arms. "You're safe, it's over."

Suddenly noticing Tucker inert on the floor, Henry jumped off Ichabod and sprinted to his son. "Tucker? Son!" he called. To his relief, Tucker rolled over with a groan and rubbed a lump that was forming on his head.

"Hey, Dad," Tucker said, dazed.

"Hey, son." Henry checked his son over, then stood up. "You don't look so bad."

Tucker chuckled and groaned. "Wow," he said, "I can't remember anything after…" His eyes fell on the tablet computer, face down on the floor.

"The bomb!" he said loudly.

Tucker scrambled to stand but collapsed back, pointing to the tablet. Henry retrieved it, and Nera helped Cole over to see what was happening. The foursome looked at the screen. The feed was still running.

"Look at that," Tucker said, pointing. The feed from Perry's room hadn't changed, but the feed from the fake Ichabod's room showed the figure in the sweatshirt pacing, a phone held nervously to his ear. The trigger had been left alone on the desk.

Cole studied the image and looked over at Tucker.

"Am I crazy, or does that look like…?"

Tucker nodded. "I think it is."

Cole typed:

Neeson?

The man looked at his computer screen, dropped the phone, and quickly hit a button on the keyboard. The feed cut to static.

"What is going on here?" The livid chief of security, his face as red as his hair, had just marched in. He passed by the now-subdued behemoth beneath the squadron of guards, and then looked at Tucker and Cole with absolute disgust.

Tucker put up his hands and tried to explain. "Listen. There was a federal marshal, Marshall Bell, but that wasn't his real name. He showed us this video of Perry Lynwood's room and said there was a suitcase that had a bomb in it. He said that—"

Cole urgently called Tucker's attention to the screen again. The security chief looked over their shoulders. The video feed from Perry's room showed a visitor walking in. He was young and skinny, with a scraggly face that was too big for his body and ears that made him look like an elf. On the bedside table, he placed a box of chocolates, then sat down to stare sadly at Perry's unconscious bulk. He pulled up a chair by the bedside and sat, mouthing words they couldn't hear. The visitor's feet nudged the suitcase. Curious, he nudged it again, then flipped it up on the chair next to him. Cole shut his eyes hard and almost yelled out loud when the man started opening the zipper.

Nothing happened. There was nothing inside. The visitor seemed confused and put the suitcase back exactly where it had been.

No bomb.

Cole exhaled deeply and put the tablet down. The security chief gave them a harassed look. "Please. Please. Go. Away." Cole and Tucker were more than willing to obey.

Observing everything from the open door that led to the loft, Noh raised his hand in farewell as the two bracket-holders limped toward the hallway. Cole wobbled over stiffly to shake his hand.

"Thank you, Mr. Noh. That thing you did with the screen saved our lives."

"I told you," Noh said, smiling broadly. "Kaah Mukul would help you. It was fate."

"I guess so," Cole said. "How did you do that thing with the lights and sirens?"

"I programmed that for a customer." Cole and Nera looked at him quizzically. Noh shrugged. "Wealthy people often have strange requests."

"Wait, the game!" Tucker yelled, stopping abruptly in the doorway. "Is it over?"

Henry nodded. "Yes son, it's over."

"Who won?"

* * * *

Two blocks away, in a quiet side street away from the crowds exiting the arena, Mr. Graham walked alone. He held his baseball cap, now heavily stained with blood, flat against a wound on the side of his head. His car was close enough, in a parking garage just around the corner, but he limped heavily and his breath billowed out through the unseasonably cold night air.

A limousine pulled up beside him, and one of the windows rolled down.

"Need a lift?" asked a voice. It was a voice that Graham knew. It was Bryan Casing.

"It's been a long time, Alex," said Casing, talking slowly. "What happened to your head?"

"Walked into a wall," Graham said with irritation, starting to walk again. The limo kept pace with him.

"It looks bad," said Casing. "Do you want me to look at it?"

"I'm fine," said Graham. "And, as I recall, you don't have a medical license anymore."

"You might need stitches. GW hospital is just down the road a ways."

"No, I just need to get to my car. I'll live."

The limo stopped and Casing stepped out. Graham picked up his pace, but Casing kept up easily.

"How is work these days?" Casing asked.

"Brutal," said Graham, wincing.

"Well, I'm sure they consider you a skilled and welcome set of hands. One of many, am I right?" Graham stopped in front of the parking garage and turned to face his old rival full-on.

"Goodbye, Bryan," he said, and he turned away.

"Alex," called Casing, "are you sure you don't need any help now? It could be dangerous to drive with a head injury, and that looks nasty."

"I live dangerously."

"You? 'Graham, the man with the plan in a can?' You used to be more careful."

"Well, you know what they say about mice and men."

"Was that a mouse or a man that did that to you?"

Graham stopped. "Good-bye, Bryan. I'll be fine."

Casing heard the tone of finality in his voice and shrugged. "Suit yourself." He waved for the limo and got back in. "See you around," he said, and closed the door.

Behind them, Graham watched until the limo turned the corner before walking into the parking garage and straight to his car. Reaching into his pocket for his keys, he brought out a bag of peanuts by force of habit. The bag crinkled. It was empty. Fuming, he opened the car door, paused, and slammed down on the roof with all his might.

Post-Game Analysis

[Thursday, April 10th]

The lights were off in the video vault of the Boston College athletics department. On the large television monitor looped a silent recording of the last five minutes in BC's recent Final Four loss to UCLA. The back-up point guard known callously, and now nationally, as "Other Williams" was sitting alone, leaning back, watching it all unfold again and again. He had been there a long time.

There was a knock at the door. Williams sighed, but didn't move. Only at the second knock did he stand and open the door. It took a moment for his eyes to adjust to the hallway lights, but he quickly recognized the man standing there.

"Uncle Bryan?" he asked, surprised.

Bryan Casing smiled but offered no hug or contact. He stood still and straight as ever in a grey suit and blue tie that made him look, to Williams, much like a basketball coach.

"Good to see you, John. May I come in?" asked Casing.

Williams turned on the lights and stood aside. Casing paused before the monitor and watched the plays unfold. "Self-teaching or self-punishment?"

"Maybe both," said Williams. "Why are you here?"

"Partly to check in. Your mother tells me that you've been a little depressed lately."

"I've been better." Williams looked away.

"Anything I can do?"

"Like what?"

"I don't know. I never do, but I always want to ask." Casing sat down and Williams did too. "You shouldn't feel bad. You and your team fought hard with your best player down. You lost to the team that would eventually win the tournament, so at least you have a lot of company."

"I messed up," said Williams. "I had my opportunity, it was my time to step up, and I lost it. We had that game before I came in."

"It could have gone better, yes, but it was hardly a catastrophe. You've improved dramatically just in the last few games. Everybody thinks so. You were confident. You didn't back down. Tyson Williams will be in the NBA next year, which probably means that you will be the starting guard. Lots of opportunity to prove yourself again."

"You think I'll ever shake the 'Other Williams' thing?"

"You put in the work, get some good breaks, and maybe you'll get back that great nickname you had in high school. It will be nice to see The Original Score running again."

Williams half-laughed, the closest he had come to smiling in a while.

Casing shifted his mood. "You know your father is getting out in a few months. Do you have any plans?"

Williams shook his head.

"I've offered him a job," Casing went on. "It isn't much, just some janitorial work. It won't kick in until my new building is completed, so he'll try to find something local for the next year. You should have some time in the summer to catch up, if you want."

"I don't know if I want that," said Williams.

Casing nodded sympathetically, then leaned back in his chair.

"You heard that they captured the Wall Street arsonist, Ichabod, during the Championship game? A lot has come out about him since then. His real name is Eli. Apparently, he has a lot in common with you. He was a college athlete, did you know that? He played baseball at Syracuse. Pitcher. Grew up without his dad in a run-down neighborhood. He had a lot of talent, just like you; he's even as tall as you are. Of course, he's different from you in that he has a severe mental illness and he dropped out after his freshman year to burn buildings and launch rocks at people. But the other similarities are interesting, aren't they?"

Williams stared blankly. "I don't think I see your point, man."

Casing smiled. "Just saying that your life could be a lot worse, given what you've been through. And you still have a good future, if you want it."

He stood up and put his hands in his pocket. "I have something for you," he said as he retrieved a folded piece of paper and handed it over. Williams unfolded an NCAA bracket from that year, filled out with all the winners. Every team was marked with a yellow highlighter.

"That's the perfect bracket that belonged to Cole Kaman,"

said Casing. "I met him and asked for a signed copy, but he gave me the original. He said he didn't want to keep it. I thought it would be nice for you to have. He signed it at the bottom."

Williams looked down in the lower left-hand corner and saw a sloppy *C__ K___* and the simple words "Good Luck!" written in black pen. Williams held it up to Casing.

"Why would I want something that predicts us losing?"

Casing focused a penetrating gaze on Williams.

"Motivation."

Then he put his hand in his other pocket and retrieved another piece of paper. Williams unfolded it to find a blank bracket, formatted for the year 2016.

"This," said Casing, "is for you to fill out now. It's up to you, but I suggest that you put BC going all the way." Williams looked at both pieces of paper, one in each hand, then looked back up.

"I have to go," Casing said. "I'll be back up soon after your father gets out. It'll be nice to see him outside." The older man moved toward the door.

"You know," Williams said, standing, "I still don't really know anything about you. I keep waiting for you to tell me."

Casing laughed to himself. "It's funny, I have a new hire that keeps reminding me of the same thing. You college kids and your curiosity." He hesitated as he considered the opportunity, but finally shook his head. "I'm really a story for another time. I'll tell you as a graduation present, how about that? In the meantime, you have a season to prepare for."

Casing patted Williams on the shoulder and left the room. A young couple was waiting for him outside, and Williams saw the man give him a quick wave before the door closed shut.

Williams sat there for a while, considering his Uncle Bryan's words. He looked back up at the screen just in time to see the last painful five seconds of the game tick down and then automatically restart at the five-minute mark. With decisive movement, he turned the machine off and the screen went black. Then he looked around for a pen, found one, and began to fill out his bracket.

About the Author

Dr. David Sloan is a novelist, former neuroscientist and a consultant in the health care industry living in Baltimore, Maryland.

He has never had a perfect bracket. Not even close.

Follow David Sloan on Twitter: @DrDavidMSloan
Visit: vergencevalley.wordpress.com